"What aren't you telling me?"

Westley's question jerked Felicity's gaze to meet his intense stare. She felt her heart pound as her instincts warred with Ian's directive.

"Felicity, I can't protect you if I don't know what is going on."

True. Westley was the only one standing between her and a potential killer.

Two killers, in fact.

And if Westley didn't know there was more than one threat out there, then how effective could he be?

She inhaled, blew out the breath and said, "My father's death wasn't an accident."

D0052788

Terri Reed
and
USA TODAY Bestselling Author
Valerie Hansen

Hearts of Courage

Previously published as *Mission to Protect* and *Bound by Duty*

LOVE INSPIRED
INSPIRATIONAL ROMANCE

If you purchased this book without a cover you should be aware that this book is stolen property. It was reported as "unsold and destroyed" to the publisher, and neither the author nor the publisher has received any payment for this "stripped book."

LOVE INSPIRED®

INSPIRATIONAL ROMANCE

Recycling programs for this product may not exist in your area.

ISBN-13: 978-1-335-53297-8

Hearts of Courage

Copyright © 2020 by Harlequin Books S.A.

Mission to Protect
First published in 2018. This edition published in 2020.
Copyright © 2018 by Harlequin Books S.A.

Bound by Duty
First published in 2018. This edition published in 2020.
Copyright © 2018 by Harlequin Books S.A.

Special thanks and acknowledgment are given to Terri Reed and Valerie Hansen for their contributions to the Military K-9 Unit miniseries.

All rights reserved. No part of this book may be used or reproduced in any manner whatsoever without written permission except in the case of brief quotations embodied in critical articles and reviews.

This is a work of fiction. Names, characters, places and incidents are either the product of the author's imagination or are used fictitiously. Any resemblance to actual persons, living or dead, businesses, companies, events or locales is entirely coincidental.

This edition published by arrangement with Harlequin Books S.A.

For questions and comments about the quality of this book, please contact us at CustomerService@Harlequin.com.

Love Inspired
22 Adelaide St. West, 40th Floor
Toronto, Ontario M5H 4E3, Canada
www.Harlequin.com

Printed in U.S.A.

CONTENTS

Terri Reed's romance and romantic suspense novels have appeared on the *Publishers Weekly* top twenty-five and Nielsen BookScan top one hundred lists, and have been featured in *USA TODAY*, *Christian Fiction* magazine and *RT Book Reviews*. Her books have been finalists for the Romance Writers of America RITA® Award and the National Readers' Choice Award, and finalists three times for the American Christian Fiction Writers Carol Award. Contact Terri at terrireed.com or PO Box 19555, Portland, OR 97224.

MISSION TO PROTECT

Terri Reed

Search me, O God, and know my heart:
try me, and know my thoughts:
And see if there be any wicked way in me,
and lead me in the way everlasting.
—*Psalms* 139:23–24

This book is dedicated to the military working dogs
and the service women and men
who defend our country.

Thank you to my editors,
Tina James and Emily Rodmell, for including me in
this series and for your support and patience. Thank
you to the other authors who gave me so much
encouragement during a difficult time. Thank you
to Leah Vale for your never-ending friendship. And
thank you to my family for your unconditional love.

ONE

The back door of Canyon Air Force Base's military working-dog training facility stood open. It should have been closed and locked tight.

Alarm slithered through lead trainer Master Sergeant Westley James like the venomous red, yellow and black coral snake inhabiting this part of Texas.

Something was wrong.

As he entered the building an eerie chill went down his neck that had nothing to do with the April early-morning air. The stillness echoed through the center as loud as a jet taking off. His pulse spiked. He rushed to the kennel room and drew up short.

The kennels were empty. All of them.

Lying on the floor in a pool of blood were the two night-shift dog trainers, Airman Tamara Peterson and Airman Landon Martelli. Each had been shot in the chest.

Grief clutched at Westley's heart. Careful not to disturb the scene, he checked for pulses. None.

They had both been murdered.

Under the left arms of Tamara and Landon were a

red rose and a folded white note, the calling card of a notorious serial killer.

Horror slammed into him. The news report he'd heard this morning on his way to work had become reality.

Boyd Sullivan, aka the Red Rose Killer, had escaped prison and was back on base.

Staff Sergeant Felicity Monroe jerked awake to the fading sound of her own scream echoing in her head. Sweat drenched her nightshirt. The pounding of her heart hurt in her chest, making bile rise to burn her throat. Darkness surrounded her.

Where was she? Fear locked on to her like a guided missile and wouldn't let go. Panic fluttered at the edge of her mind.

Memories flooded her system.

Her father!

A sob tore from her throat.

The familiar scent of jasmine from the bouquet of flowers on her bedside table grounded her. She was in her bedroom of the house on Canyon Air Force Base in southwest Texas. The home she'd shared with her father before his accidental death a month ago.

Her breathing slowed. She wiped at the wet tears on her cheeks and shook away the fear and panic.

Just a nightmare. One in a long string of them.

According to Dr. Flintman, the base therapist, she suffered mild post-traumatic stress disorder from finding her father after his fall from a ladder he had climbed to clean the gutters on the house. Knowing why her brain was doing this didn't make the images seared in her mind any less upsetting.

She filled her lungs with several deep breaths and sought the clock across the room on the dresser.

The clock's red glow was blocked by the silhouette of a person looming at the end of her bed.

Was her mind playing a trick on her again? Or was she still stuck in her nightmare? She blinked rapidly to clear the sleep from her eyes.

Her breath caught and held.

No trick.

Someone was in her room.

Full-fledged panic jackknifed through her, jolting her system into action. Self-preservation kicked in. She rolled to the side of the bed and landed soundlessly on the floor. With one hand, she reached for the switch of the bedside-table lamp, while her other hand searched for the baseball bat she kept under the bed.

Holding the bat up with her right hand, she flicked on the light. A warm glow dispelled the shadows and revealed she was alone. Or was she?

With bat in hand, she went through the house, turning on every light. No one was there.

She frowned and worked to calm her racing pulse.

This wasn't the first time she'd thought someone had been in the house.

But this time had seemed so real.

Back in her bedroom, she looked again at the clock. Wait a minute. It was turned to face the wall. A shiver of unease wracked her body. The red numbers had been facing the bed when she'd retired last night. She was convinced of it.

And her dresser drawers were slightly open. She peeked inside. Her clothes were mussed, as if someone had rummaged through them. She wasn't a neat freak or anything, but her military training and her air force father had taught her to keep her things in proper order.

What was going on?

Was the stress and grief of her father's passing messing with her brain, as her therapist suggested? Was she losing her mind?

Wouldn't that just be the icing on the cake? Her mother already thought she was nuts for choosing to join the United States Air Force and train military dogs for service rather than follow in her footsteps and pursue a high-powered career in corporate law.

Felicity set aside the baseball bat.

Maybe someone was pulling a joke on her.

She dismissed the idea quickly. She didn't know anyone that cruel.

She turned the clock to see the time. Five after five in the morning. Perfect. The one day she could sleep in, and her psyche wouldn't let her. She wasn't expected at the training center until tonight. She usually had Sundays off and worked the Saturday-night shift, but had traded with Airman Tamara Peterson, who was taking a few days of leave to visit her parents and wanted to head out Sunday morning.

Felicity glanced at the clock again. Maybe she could nap for an hour or so more, then go to church.

Noises outside the bedroom window startled her. It was too early for most people to be up on a Sunday morning. She pushed aside the room-darkening curtain. The first faint rays of sunlight marched over the Texas horizon with hues of gold, orange and pink.

They provided enough light for Felicity to see a parade of dogs running loose along Base Boulevard. It could only be the dogs from the K-9 training center.

Stunned, her stomach clenched.

Someone had literally let the dogs out. Most of them, by the looks of it. At least a hundred or more canines filled the street and were quickly leaving the area.

Felicity's chest constricted. Had Tamara or Landon, the other trainer on last night's shift, forgotten to lock the gate? That didn't seem likely. Both were experienced trainers. Uneasy dread gripped her by the throat.

A dog barked, reminding her that the canines needed to be rounded up and returned to their kennels. She didn't want any of them to get hurt. Some of the dogs suffered PTSD from their service, while others were being trained to serve. Many were finished with their training and ready to be partnered, but set loose like this...

Galvanized into action, she hastily dressed in her battle-ready uniform.

On the way out the door, she grabbed her cell phone, intending to call her boss, Master Sergeant Westley James. Before she could dial, her phone pinged with an incoming alert text from the training center.

Urgent. Dogs' kennels tampered with. Red Rose Killer escaped prison and believed to be on base. Use caution. Report in ASAP.

Felicity stopped in her tracks. Her heart fell to her feet then bounced back into her throat as fear struck hard through her core.

The Red Rose Killer.

Boyd Sullivan. Cold eyes, merciless.

She shuddered.

Two years ago, after being dishonorably discharged

from the air force during basic training, Boyd had returned to his hometown of Dill, Texas, and killed five people whom he'd believed had wronged him in some way.

The media had dubbed him the Red Rose Killer because he would leave a red rose and a note for his intended victims, taunting them with the warning—*I'm coming for you*. Then he made good on his threat, and each victim was found with an additional red rose and a new note tucked under their arm, with the words *Got you*.

A Dill sheriff's deputy and her K-9 partner had been the ones to bring down Sullivan. He'd been captured, convicted and sent to prison.

And now he'd escaped and was on base.

Why would he release the dogs? She remembered he always liked the furry creatures.

She dialed Westley's cell.

He answered on the first ring. "Felicity. Did you hear the news?"

"Yes. There are dogs everywhere in base housing," she told him.

"They are everywhere on base period." His voice sounded extra grim. "We need to bring them in."

"I'll retrieve as many as I can here and bring them over to the kennels."

"Good. I'll send others over to help." There was a pause then he said, "I should tell you there have been two murders."

She stilled. Fear whispered down her spine. Her pulse spiked. "Murders?" She swayed. *Please, Lord, no.* "Tamara? Landon?"

"Yes."

Her heart sank. Tears flooded her eyes. That explained why the dogs were loose. She knew neither trainer would be so careless. "Did Boyd Sullivan kill them?

"That's the assumption. Each was found with a red rose tucked under their arm and a note that read, 'Got you.'"

"Boyd used that same tactic in Dill. But why would he go after Tamara and Landon?"

"I don't know," Westley replied. "But right now the dogs need us."

Westley's no-nonsense tone made her pull herself together. The last thing she wanted was for him to consider her weak. He was stingy enough with his praise, especially for her. He was always watching and waiting for her to mess up, but just because she was the newest member, and the youngest on his team, didn't mean she didn't belong.

Strangely, though, she didn't feel the familiar prickling at the back of her neck that his words normally brought.

Her usual irritation with her handsome boss was muffled by grief and the need to act. This time he was correct. The dogs needed her.

She wiped at the tears falling down her cheeks and took a shuddering breath. "Of course. I'm going to find our dogs."

"Be careful. Boyd is still out there."

His husky tone sent little shivers over her skin. She frowned, annoyed by her reaction. Though his words expressed concern for her, she knew his real concern was for the dogs. She could only imagine his upset. The dogs were his life.

Had Westley been the one to find Tamara Peterson and Landon Martelli? How had they been killed? Who would tell their families? Had they suffered? A million questions ran through her head, but she forced herself to stay focused. To be strong. Her mother would be proud of her. Maybe. "I'll be careful," she assured him and hung up.

After pocketing her phone, she dug through her satchel for a small canister of pepper spray and slipped it into her front pocket. In case she met Boyd along the way.

Master Sergeant Westley James paced by the back wall of the large auditorium-style conference room.

Shortly after discovering the bodies of his trainers and alerting the base's USAF Security Forces, Westley had received a call from the base commander to report here. His stomach twisted with grief and shock as he glanced around the room, noting an eclectic mix of high-ranking officers and civilian personnel. With over seven thousand people on base, keeping Canyon Air Force Base running took a large staff.

He couldn't sit, though most everyone else had taken a seat. His heart still beat too fast. This wasn't where he should be. He needed to be out searching for the dogs. He struggled to stay in the moment.

The base commander's executive assistant, a civilian, Brenda Blakenship, had come in a few moments ago to say the debriefing would begin when the base commander and the basic-training commander arrived. Then she'd left again. Conversations in hushed tones were a reflection of the somber mood.

As the lead trainer of the military working dogs

training center, Westley oversaw the welfare of the two hundred and fifty dogs currently being trained in multiple disciplines from explosives and electronic detection to patrol. He was also responsible for the trainers and the various handlers from different branches of the military. It was a challenging post. He loved it.

And now the lives of two of his trainers had been senselessly taken, and the dogs were wandering the base, putting them in jeopardy. He itched to be out there looking for the dogs. Many of them were traumatized from combat service, which would make retrieving them that much harder. If the dogs were approached by someone they didn't know and trust... He feared for the safety of both dogs and humans.

Could this day get any worse?

His phone buzzed with an incoming text. He glanced at the message from Master Sergeant Caleb Streeter, another trainer, and was gratified to read the number of dogs brought safely in by the training staff. But there were still many left to recover.

The door to the auditorium opened. Westley put away his phone as Brenda entered with a folder in her hand and a grim expression on her face. Behind her, the base commander, Lieutenant General Hall, strode into the conference room, his face ashen.

"I've just received word that Chief Master Sergeant Clint Lockwood was found dead in his home of a gunshot wound to the heart," Lieutenant General Hall stated flatly. "A red rose and note were also found."

Shock rippled through the room.

Westley placed a hand on the wall to steady himself. The horror of finding the two trainers' bodies was still etched in Westley's brain. And now to hear that Lock-wood was gone as well…

Lord, why would You allow this?

Westley didn't hold his breath waiting on God to give him an answer. Westley was used to God's silence. As a scared kid hiding from the constant chaos of his parents' fighting, he'd often asked God to make them stop. But the fighting never did. Not until his dad was incarcerated, which threw Westley into a different sort of chaos.

Questions came at the base commander with lightning speed from those seated around the room.

"Has the weapon been found?" the air force recruitment commander asked from his seat at the front of the room.

"Have we locked down the base?" the chief master sergeant of the 12th flying training wing called out.

"Have the FBI, OSI and the local police been notified?" the cyberspace operations commander asked.

"How did Boyd Sullivan escape prison?" the vice commander of the medical wing demanded to know.

Lieutenant General Hall raised a hand to silence the group. "Please, I will answer your questions as best I can. The weapon has not been found. The base is on lockdown. The feds and the local law enforcement will work closely with both Security Forces and the Office of Special Investigations." A fierce light entered the Lieutenant General's gaze. "Our problem is not how Boyd Sullivan escaped prison, but how he got on base."

"Is he targeting those who were in his basic military training?" Security Forces Captain Justin Blackwood asked.

"He must have had help," the commander of the airlift wing pointed out.

Lieutenant General Hall once again raised his hand and the room quieted. "If he holds true to form, he will most likely go after anyone he deems has wronged him. No doubt Sullivan blamed Chief Master Sergeant Lockwood for the dishonorable discharge."

Westley's fingers curled into fists at his sides. Boyd would pay dearly for his evil deeds. Westley prayed no other lives would be taken by Boyd's hand.

"We must consider Sullivan will go after those in his basic military training." Lieutenant General Hall nodded at Brenda.

She opened the file folder in her hand. "I've compiled a list of the personnel currently on base who were in the same training class as Boyd Sullivan."

"Our first order of business is to secure these individuals and anyone else who had prior interaction with Boyd," Lieutenant General Hall interjected. "Then we will root out the person who has helped this predator get on base."

As Brenda read the names, Westley tried to remember if Tamara or Landon had been in Sullivan's BMT group, or even been on base at the time. He didn't think so.

"Staff Sergeant Felicity Monroe."

Hearing his trainer's name jerked Westley's thoughts back to the conference room. Felicity. His stomach dropped as his pulse spiked. She was supposed to have been on duty last night, but had changed shifts.

Had she been Sullivan's intended target?

Fear streaked through his system like a fighter jet heading to battle. He couldn't let another person for whom he was responsible die. Not on his watch. He had to protect her.

Without asking permission, Westley raced out of the auditorium. He had to find Felicity.

Felicity's search for the dogs wasn't going very well. With the base alive and on alert, the dogs sensed the anxiety rippling through the air and were skittish. She moved with a slow, easy gait so as not to spook two dogs in her sights, a three-year-old German shepherd named Tiger and a two-year-old Belgian Malinois named Riff. Both were sniffing around the commissary.

As she approached, both dogs lifted their heads to eye her, their tails swishing.

"Come," she commanded while holding a treat in her hand against her thigh, which would bring the dogs in close enough to grab by the collar.

Tiger abandoned his sniffing to comply. As he took the treat from her, she hooked her fingers beneath his collar and swiftly attached a leash to the ring. Now to get the Malinois.

"Riff," she said. "Here, boy."

The dog's ears twitched but he made no move to obey. She and Tiger stepped closer. Riff moved away, nose back to the ground. Frustration beat at her temples. "Come on, Riff."

The dog had done well inside the confines of the center, but out in the open, not so much. Now she understood why Westley had said the dog wasn't ready to be paired with a human. She'd disagreed at the time and had even accused him, albeit silently, of holding back Riff because he didn't like her. Now she knew her boss had been right.

Riff had a long way to go in his training. She didn't relish admitting that to Westley. He'd give her that tight-lipped nod that irritated her nerves and made her feel as if she didn't measure up to his standards. Her commanding officer certainly knew how to push her buttons...unfortunately.

Tiger spun around and barked, his tail rigid and his ears up.

Seconds later she heard the sound of pounding feet and her adrenaline spiked. She reached for her pepper spray with her free hand and whirled with the can up and her finger hovering over the trigger, ready to protect herself from an assault.

Westley held his hands up, palms facing out, as he skidded to a halt. "Whoa. It's me."

Not Boyd, as she dreaded. Heart racing, she lowered the canister, thankful she hadn't let loose a stream of stinging spray.

Tiger relaxed and moved closer to Westley.

Felicity took in a deep breath. Exasperation made her voice sharp when she said, "You scared me." Her gaze jumped to Riff as the dog ran away. "Riff!"

The dog disappeared around the corner of the building.

"You were right," she conceded. "We need to work on his recall."

"We will," Westley assured her as he took Tiger's lead from her hand. "Right now, my only concern is you."

The grim set of his jaw alerted her heightened senses. Had she done something wrong? Made a mistake? Her defenses rose, making her straighten. "Me? I'm doing my best to bring the dogs in."

For a moment, confusion entered his gaze then cleared. "Lieutenant General Hall believes Boyd Sullivan is targeting those who were in his basic-military-training class," he replied, his voice harsh.

She took a step back. The same alarm that had flooded her this morning, when she'd thought someone was standing at the foot of her bed, seeped through her now. Had it been Boyd? A shudder of revulsion worked over her flesh.

"But that doesn't make any sense," she said. At Westley's arched eyebrow, she added, "Neither Tamara nor Landon were in our group."

"Exactly," he said. "I think you were his intended target last night."

She sucked in a breath. Her lungs burned as his words sank in. She swallowed convulsively as her mouth dried from the terror that was already pumping in her blood. She shook her head. "You can't know that for sure."

Was she responsible for her friends' deaths?

A spasm of guilt and pain twisted her insides. She wanted to fall to her knees and ask God why, but with Westley standing there, she remained upright and silently sent up the question. *Why, Lord?*

"He also killed Chief Master Sergeant Lockwood."

The air swooshed out of her lungs. The basic military training commander. The one who'd kicked Boyd out of the air force. Felicity was friends with Maisy Lockwood, the chief master sergeant's daughter and a civilian preschool teacher.

Agitation revved through Felicity's system. She trembled with the restless urge to move. "I need to see Maisy. She must be devastated."

Westley nodded. "Seeing her will have to wait. We

need to take Tiger, here, to the training center then go find more dogs."

"We can put him in my backyard. I'll set out water on the back deck. He'll be fine there while we search."

He seemed to contemplate her suggestion. She gritted her teeth, expecting him to argue with her. He always thought his way was best, and because he was in charge that left little room for discussion. She prepared to defend her suggestion but he nodded, which surprised her. "That works."

Unsure what to make of Westley, she led the way down Base Boulevard to her house. Her gaze snagged on the black curbside mailbox. The drop-down door was propped half-open.

What was going on? It hadn't been open when she'd left the house earlier. Her steps faltered. Was her sanity really slipping?

Just this morning she'd imagined someone standing at the foot of her bed and now this? She didn't want to think about the other times when she'd had the feeling someone had been inside her home.

Maybe she needed to take up Dr. Flintman on his offer of medication to suppress her mild PTSD. She would have before except she didn't want to be medicated and give Westley any reason to wash her out of the training center. And she worried that would be a big one, given that he already had it in for her. From the day she stepped into the center, she'd had the feeling he wanted her gone.

"What's wrong?" The concern coating Westley's words shimmied down her spine.

For all his fault-finding with her, he was being a

supportive boss today. Unusual but appreciated. She needed to take a deep breath and gather herself together.

"Nothing, I hope." But she couldn't tear her gaze away from the mailbox. She stepped closer and she pushed the door, intending to close it, but something blocked it from shutting.

Aggravated, she yanked the door all the way open. A red rose popped out to lie flat on the open metal flap. She gasped and jerked her hand back as if the flower was a copperhead snake.

Then her eyes focused on a folded white sheet of paper.

Her knees threatened to give out. Boyd had been here.

One thing was clear—she hadn't been imagining things. Yet, her mind tapped with the niggling knowledge that strange things had been happening long before today. Her body went numb as fear drenched her in a cold sweat.

"We need to call Security Forces."

Westley's deep, gravelly voice rumbled in her chest. She could only nod. Her tongue stuck to the roof of her mouth.

After he made the call, he turned her to face him. "Look at me," he instructed.

She stared at him. Morning sunlight reflected in his light blue eyes and gleamed in his dark hair. She couldn't deny he was handsome, and at this moment, he, of all people, anchored her. If she wasn't so freaked out, she'd find that odd. She wasn't sure the man even liked her. But there was concern in his eyes now. Concern for her. Crazy, really. But then again, it had been that kind of morning.

She took a breath and then swallowed. "I think he may have been in my house."

"What?"

"When I woke up this morning someone stood at the foot of my bed. But when I turned on the light, no one was there." She didn't mention the other times she'd had the sensation that someone had been in her home or was watching her. Today was bad enough.

"Are you kidding me?" he sputtered. "Why didn't you report it?"

She bristled at the censure in his tone. "I thought I was imagining things." Her heart beat painfully in her chest. She yanked her gaze from him and stared at the house. "But why leave a note and the rose when he could have killed me in my sleep?"

Westley studied her face, making her want to squirm. "Could it have been a nightmare?"

The sympathy and understanding in his tone sent another rush of anxiety through her. Did he suspect her PTSD? Had Dr. Flintman talked to her boss? The thought horrified her.

"Maybe," she admitted, not willing to fully commit to the diagnosis and what that might mean for her future with the K-9 unit.

"You've suffered a tragic loss recently," he reminded her more gently than she would have thought him capable, making her wonder if he'd suffered the loss of someone close to him as well.

Losing her father to a senseless accident was a scar she'd carry with her forever. And it may be the cause of her imaginings, yet... "It doesn't make sense," she said again.

"What doesn't?"

Would Westley think she was going nuts? She was loath to give him any more reasons to view her in a bad light. He'd already made it clear he thought she needed to improve her training skills because he constantly corrected her whenever he observed her with the dogs.

Still, she had to confide in someone. And he was here. "Weird things have been happening lately. Long before Boyd escaped prison."

His dark eyebrows drew together. "Like what?"

She took another bracing breath. Was she really going to share this with him? Did she have a choice?

"Little things," she said. "Like objects moved and doors and cabinets left open when I know they were shut." Like her clock being turned toward the wall this morning.

Had Boyd been standing at the foot of her bed? She shivered. Could there be someone else on base who had it in for her? Or was she imagining it all?

But the rose and note were real.

"Maybe whoever helped Sullivan onto base is trying to scare you," Westley said. "But why would Boyd and his accomplice want to terrorize you?"

Distaste boiled up and twisted her lips. "The only reason I can think of is because I refused a second date with Boyd during BMT."

Westley sucked in a noisy breath. "Just like a couple of the victims in Dill."

"Yes." She hated that she'd even gone on the one date, but she'd been lonely and he'd been interested. "He'd seemed charming and nice at first."

Her words gave her pause. Didn't they say that about most serial killers? Neighbors and colleagues were often shocked to learn they'd been living or working closely with someone capable of such horrendous acts.

"Then he'd made it abundantly clear he wasn't a believer. A must for me."

Was Westley a believer, she wondered. In the six months she'd been in his command, she'd never had a deep or personal conversation with him. He was too guarded, too critical. She wondered what made him tick beyond his perfectionism.

"Did he hurt you?"

The anger lacing Westley's words sent a funny little ribbon of warmth winding through her. But, of course, Westley would feel anger. In spite of his questioning if she belonged in the unit, he was a man of integrity and honor.

"No. I fended him off when he got handsy at the end of the night."

"You can take care of yourself," he said, with a good dose of pride lacing his voice, which confused her.

His words might have been a compliment, but she crossed her arms in front of her, squeezing her rib cage as tight as she could to keep from splitting into a million pieces. "There are times when I wished I didn't have to." She hated that her voice broke.

Westley dropped the lead he held and stepped on it to keep Tiger from running off, then he slipped his arms around her and drew her to his chest. He felt solid and strong. The spicy scent of his aftershave teased her senses, making the shock of his actions even more startling.

"I won't let anything happen to you," he vowed.

She believed him. Despite how infuriating she found him at times, she respected his work ethic and his diligence in making sure the dogs were well trained before being assigned a handler. He never said something he didn't mean. And he always followed through on his word.

But the last thing she needed was Westley thinking she was needy. Besides, the United States Air Force had strict rules about fraternization. She wouldn't risk her career for a hug of comfort.

She disengaged from him and stepped back seconds before a black SUV roared down the street and stopped at the curb, followed by a Security Forces vehicle.

Westley picked up Tiger's lead and had the dog heel at his side as they waited.

Tech Sergeant Linc Colson climbed out of the vehicle with his canine, a female Rottweiler named Star, but the pair hung back as Special Agent Ian Steffen from the Office of Special Investigations stepped out of the black SUV. Felicity knew the fortyish officer through her father, who'd also been a special agent with the OSI.

Ian's speculative gaze bounced between Westley and Felicity. Felicity's stomach clenched. Had Ian witnessed the hug?

"Master Sergeant James," Ian said, acknowledging Westley's salute.

Felicity raised her hand to touch her temple in respect of the man's rank.

"At ease. Are you okay, Staff Sergeant Monroe?" Ian asked.

"I am, sir." She gestured to the mailbox. "But there's that."

Ian slipped on a pair of latex gloves and removed the rose from the mailbox, placing it inside an evidence bag. He then unfolded the note and read it aloud. "'I'm coming for you.'"

The ominous words reverberated through Felicity, burning an acidic trail along her veins. There was no doubt who wrote the note. Boyd Sullivan. The Red Rose Killer.

"The crime-scene unit will dust the mailbox for prints," Ian told her as he placed the note in a separate evidence bag. "But doubtful Sullivan was dumb enough to leave any behind."

Boyd may have been a hothead and full of himself, but he'd been smart. The first time he'd gone on a rampage he'd evaded capture longer than anyone thought he would. A tremor of anxiety worked its way over her skin.

Once Ian had the rose and note stowed away, he said to her, "How are you holding up? Your father was a good man and my friend."

Tears burned her eyes. She blinked them back, along with the sharp pang of grief. "I'm managing."

He nodded, compassion softening the lines in his face. "This doesn't help. You are to come to base command with me."

"But the dogs?" Her priority—her job—was finding the canines and returning them to their kennels safely.

"I'm sure Master Sergeant James and Tech Sergeant Colson can handle the dogs," Ian stated firmly. "Lieutenant General Hall wants anyone with a connection to Boyd brought to base command."

She glanced at Westley. He gave her a slight nod.

Linc stepped up. "Actually, sir, Lieutenant General Hall would like Master Sergeant James to return to base command, as well. But we'll take the dog to the center first."

Felicity climbed in the passenger side of Ian's SUV as Westley and Tiger followed Linc and Star to the other vehicle. They drove away while Ian and Felicity waited until the crime-scene-unit techs arrived and took possession of the rose and note.

As Ian drove them to the northwest end of base, he asked, "Do you know what your father was working on prior to his death?"

Startled by the question, she shook her head. "He never divulged his cases to me."

Ian remained silent for a moment. "Do you believe his death was an accident?"

She stared at his profile. "He fell off a ladder cleaning the gutters of the house."

Yet even as the words left her mouth, the nagging thought she'd had since the moment she'd seen her father lying on the ground roared to the surface.

Graham Monroe had been an extremely cautious man. He would never have gone on the sloped roof without either someone holding the ladder, or without hooking a safety harness to the metal rung he'd attached to the roof. So why hadn't he tied off to protect himself from falling that fateful day?

Dread filled her. "Are you telling me my father's death wasn't an accident?"

Had her father been murdered?

TWO

"Dude, what were you thinking?"

Linc's pointed question stabbed at Westley. They were friends so Westley didn't take exception to the tone or the probing. Taking Felicity into his arms was a huge slip in judgment. He knew the rules. Fraternization with a subordinate could get him and her bounced out of the air force.

A stupid move.

But in that moment, she'd looked so vulnerable he couldn't stop himself from comforting her. The fact that she'd felt so right snuggled against his chest burned a hole through his heart.

She fit him…they fit together—just as he'd imagined.

For the past six months, ever since she'd walked into the training center as a newly promoted staff sergeant, her blue-green eyes sparkling and her infectious grin shining like a ray of sunshine on a cloudy day, he'd been struggling with his attraction for the rookie K-9 trainer.

It had to stop.

Hadn't he been telling himself that every day he

worked with Felicity? Yes. And every night when she would slip into his dreams.

He didn't understand it.

Not liking her should have been easy.

She was so annoyingly optimistic and bubbly. Her rookie mistakes sent his blood pressure skyrocketing and her ability to calm the dogs, though surprising and admirable, grated. Which made no sense at all.

The dogs trusted her from the get-go. And that fact told him about the type of person she was. The dogs sensed her kindness, trustworthiness and gentleness. But letting himself show any emotion regarding the rookie trainer was out of the question.

He'd even been harder on her than anyone else so no one would think he liked her. But that had only upset her, and in return made him angry at himself. He couldn't win.

All those things made his lapse in judgment minutes ago that much worse. And he had no reasonable explanation for taking her into his arms.

He had no room in his life for her. Period. He wasn't interested in forming any type of emotional bonds. He learned not to growing up, because ties only break and when they do they hurt.

He cast his eyes down, not knowing how to answer. Before he could, the tech sergeant spoke again. "Leaving the debriefing without permission wasn't cool, man," he said.

Oh. That. Yeah, the base commander, Lieutenant General Hall, and Captain Justin Blackwood, Westley's supervisor, would no doubt chew him up and spit him out with a reprimand. Westley sent Linc a sidelong glance. Did that mean Linc hadn't witnessed the embrace between Westley and Felicity?

He blew out a breath of relief.

If Felicity hadn't stepped back when she had, they'd both be in deep hot water.

"I wasn't thinking," he admitted to his friend. He ran a hand through his hair. "When I heard Felicity's name called off that list of Boyd Sullivan's potential targets, all I could think of was getting to her."

He couldn't let another person he was responsible for be hurt. Not after losing two last night.

"Excuse me?" Linc shook his head. "I don't think I want to have heard you right."

"She was supposed to be on duty last night, but she and Tamara swapped shifts."

Linc's eyes widened with understanding. "I see. Make sure you tell Lieutenant General Hall."

Westley barked out a humorless laugh. "Yeah. I will."

And he'd also have to find a way to protect Felicity and, in doing so, keep them both out of trouble.

As Ian brought the SUV to a halt in a parking spot in front of the base-command offices, Felicity stared at him. Her heart pounded in her chest as the implications bounced around her mind. "You didn't answer my question. Do you think my father's death wasn't an accident?"

"There's no evidence to suggest foul play. But the timing seemed odd," Ian admitted as he turned to face her. His eyes were troubled. "Your dad was working on a case that was highly sensitive, but we can't find his case notes or his laptop."

Anxiety slammed against her ribs. "His office was

packed up and brought to the house, but I didn't see any files or his computer."

She thought back to the box that had held pictures of her, chronicling her life from a young, gap-toothed kid to her official BMT graduation photo in her dress blues. There were the many photographs she'd taken over the years with her beloved professional-grade camera and gifted to her father to decorate his office. And, of course, all of his framed awards and certificates, a custom-made penholder and other paraphernalia that wasn't worth much beyond sentimentality.

"What about his home office?" Ian asked.

She shrugged but couldn't shake the dread crawling up her spine. "I can look. But Dad was as well-ordered and uncluttered as they come. I sorted through his desk and file cabinet searching for his will, which was filed under *W*. I didn't see any folders or files that looked official or had anything to do with his work."

She'd also found her parents' divorce papers, which had added to her sadness in the days following her father's death. Calling her mother in San Francisco with the news had been hard. Hearing her mother, usually so in control, sobbing on the other line had pierced Felicity's heart.

Her parents had still loved each other even though they'd chosen to go their separate ways. Neither had remarried. As a teen, she'd secretly hoped they'd reunite, but that had never happened.

"Are you investigating my dad's death?" she asked.

For a moment, Ian was silent, but her heart beat so loud in her ears, she was sure he heard it as well.

"Not officially," he finally replied in a measured tone. "I am looking into your father's last case. But

I'm having to start over. Now with the Red Rose Killer on base, everything else will have to be pushed to the back burner."

Her chest tightened with a wave of grief. "What was my father working on?"

Ian hesitated. "A hit-and-run off base. A witness reported seeing a Canyon Air Force Base decal on a motorcycle. Your father was trying to identify the bike and its owner."

"That's not much to go on," she said. "Many airman and officers ride motorbikes."

"True. But the last message I had from your father suggested he had a lead."

"And that person might have killed him and made it look like an accident." Sourness roiled in her stomach.

"Possibly. But keep this under wraps, okay?"

"Of course."

Digesting what Ian had told her, Felicity slowly climbed out of the SUV. Her mind spun with possibilities. Was her father's death not what it seemed?

She tripped slightly over her own feet. Everything she'd heard, everything that had happened today, was all so overwhelming.

"Steady there." She recognized the deep voice, and felt a firm hand gripping her arm.

Surprised, Felicity looked up to find Westley waiting on the walkway with Linc, Star at his heels.

Westley's touch was gentle but she shrugged off his hand, hating that he'd glimpsed her clumsiness. "I'm good."

"We dropped Tiger off at the training center," Westley told her as he fell into step with her. Linc, Star and Ian walked behind them.

They headed inside the base-command building. The four-story structure housed the administration staff as well as the photo lab and the OSI offices. Stepping into the elevator, Felicity felt dwarfed by the three men.

Even the dog made her feel tiny.

Ian, on her right, was several inches taller than her five-foot-six-inch frame, while Westley stood at least six feet tall. Behind her, Linc towered above her and Star's breath created a hot spot on the back of her leg.

Silly. She hadn't suddenly shrunk, but she stood straighter, as if an extra inch would matter. But once again, her world had been shaken and being average height wasn't enough. She wanted to be taller and stronger to better protect herself, her coworkers and the dogs.

The elevator doors swooshed open. All three men and the dog waited for her to exit before falling into step behind her. It was like leading a procession of three giant trees as they approached the base commander's office.

His assistant met them in the reception area and led them to a conference room.

"Staff Sergeant Monroe," Brenda said with a soft smile directed at Felicity, "I'm glad to see you safe and sound."

Felicity kept her expression neutral, but inside she cringed. She was trained by the best in the air force, but so were Tamara, Landon and Chief Master Sergeant Lockwood, who'd all died last night. "Thank you, ma'am," she replied politely.

"Lieutenant General Hall will see you now." She opened the door to the conference room and announced them.

"Come in." Lieutenant General Hall rose from where

he sat at the end of the long oval conference table. Tall and imposing, with his back ramrod-straight, the base commander was a force to be reckoned with. Felicity's dad had thought highly of the officer. They were on the same bowling team. Lieutenant General Hall had given the eulogy at her father's funeral. The reminder had her swallowing several times to ease the ominous tightening in her throat.

After Lieutenant General Hall returned their salute, he said, "At ease."

Felicity dropped her salute and took a position with her hands tucked at her back. Her gaze landed on another man, who had risen from his seat at the table. He was dressed in a grey business suit, but something about him led her to believe this wasn't a man to trifle with. His green eyes regarded her with curiosity and speculation.

Lieutenant General Hall resumed sitting, as did the stranger. The lieutenant general's intense grey eyes landed on Westley for a moment then moved to Felicity. "Do you know why I asked to see you?"

Refocusing on Lieutenant General Hall, she said, "Sir, I assume because of the Red Rose Killer."

"Yes. It seems Boyd Sullivan is back." There was no mistaking the hard edge of anger in his tone. "He's killed three people so far."

Another wave of grief hit her. "Yes, sir. I'd heard that."

She needed to see Maisy and offer her what comfort she could. Though having just lost her own father, Felicity knew there wasn't much comfort to be had. Losing a parent was devastating.

Lieutenant General Hall tented his fingers. "We just

received word that more people have received a rose and note like the one found in your mailbox."

Felicity sucked in a sharp breath. "Who, sir?"

"We'll get to that," he said. "First, I'd like to introduce you to Special Agent Oliver Davison of the FBI."

Oliver rose and nodded. "Since this is a federal case, I will be working with OSI and base security."

Ian stepped forward and shook Oliver's hand. "Glad to have the backup."

Felicity exchanged a confused glance with Westley. Why were she and her boss included in this meeting?

A knock sounded. Brenda opened the conference-room door. "Captain Blackwood and Lieutenant Webb have arrived, sir."

The two men, along with their canine partners, walked in. Brenda retreated and closed the door behind her.

The dogs sat at attention while the men saluted.

Lieutenant General Hall returned the salute and instructed them to relax.

As the only female soldier in a room full of handsome and higher-ranking men, Felicity's shoulder muscles tensed. But she would not allow herself to be intimidated. This wasn't the first time she'd been surrounded by men, nor would it be the last.

It's a man's world. You'll never fit in. Her mother's words when she'd learned that Felicity had enlisted echoed through her mind, but Felicity refused to accept her mother's pronouncement. Sure, Felicity had experienced some sexism over her four years of service, but it only made her more determined to prove herself worthy.

Westley stepped closer to her side. The overwhelming sense of camaraderie his nearness generated surprised her. He may be miserly with his praise and exacting in his teaching style, but her boss had her back. Which was confusing, distracting and, she had to admit, comforting.

"All of you take a seat," Lieutenant General Hall instructed.

When Westley moved to pull out a chair for her, she gave him a pointed look. He retreated but nonetheless sat in the chair beside her. The last thing she needed was him showing her deferential treatment because she was in danger.

Or was it because she was a woman? Did he see her that way?

She narrowed her eyes at him. No, that couldn't be. He was too hard on her at work for her gender to be an issue.

He raised a questioning eyebrow.

She refused to be coddled by anyone, especially Westley. She looked away.

The other men took seats, with the dogs settling behind their chairs. Ian remained standing.

"We're waiting for a few more people," General Hall said. "Would anyone like some water? Coffee?"

Everyone declined the offer.

A few moments later, Brenda escorted in three women.

When Maisy Lockwood walked in, Felicity's heart jumped. The preschool teacher's pretty eyes were red-rimmed and her countenance, usually so cheerful, was somber. Felicity gripped her chair's arms and fought for the self-control not to rush to her friend's side.

Behind Maisy came First Lieutenant Vanessa Gomez in her green nursing scrubs. Her dark hair was caught up in a clip at the back of her head and her brown eyes glowed with worry. Last to file in was Airman Yvette Crenville, the base nutritionist. The willowy blonde stopped and, with one look at those gathered in the room, seemed ready to bolt. There was no mistaking the pinch of fear in her pretty face.

After the formal greetings, the three women took seats at the table.

Lieutenant General Hall's gaze filled with sympathy. "Miss Lockwood, we are all grieving over the loss of your father."

Maisy sniffed and nodded. "Thank you, sir."

Lieutenant General Hall's gaze moved to Vanessa and Yvette. "Thank you also for coming in. You both, along with Staff Sergeant Monroe, received a red rose and threatening note from Boyd Sullivan, aka the Red Rose Killer."

Stunned, Felicity turned her gaze to the other women. After Felicity's date with Boyd, he'd moved on to Yvette, who'd also been in their BMT. The pair had dated until his discharge, when she'd publicly broken up with him. But as far as Felicity knew Vanessa, a critical care nurse, had no connection to Boyd. She'd been in officer training at the time.

"Base security will be on high alert, especially at the preschool, hospital and base housing," Lieutenant General Hall said.

"You think Boyd will come after me?" Maisy's voice rose.

"Your father was my friend," Lieutenant General Hall stated, his voice tinged in sadness. "I won't take any chances with your safety."

"I don't understand, sir," Vanessa said. "Why would Boyd target me?"

"That is an excellent question, Lieutenant," Lieutenant General Hall stated. "One I will leave to Captain Blackwood and his team to uncover. Until then your safety is our priority."

"Thank you, sir," Yvette said, her voice wobbly. "This is so scary."

"Not to worry, Airman Crenville," Lieutenant General Hall replied in a soothing tone. "Boyd will be captured quickly."

Yvette shivered. "I hope so."

Sweeping his gaze over the female personnel, Lieutenant General Hall said, "The four of you are dismissed."

Felicity rose with the others but paused as Westley stood and touched her arm.

"Wait for me in the hall," he said in a low voice.

She blinked at the request. She wanted to ask him why, but her desire to talk to Maisy overrode her curiosity. She nodded and hurried after Maisy. She snagged her friend by the elbow once they were in the hall. "Oh, honey, I was so sorry to hear about your dad."

Maisy's eyes filled with tears. "It was horrible."

Felicity drew Maisy to a bench along the wall as Vanessa and Yvette walked away. "Here…sit."

Maisy sat and wiped at her eyes. "I don't understand how this could happen."

Neither could Felicity. The whole thing seemed surreal. Boyd Sullivan escaping prison, getting on base in the dark of night and killing three people and terrorizing three more. She prayed God would bring Boyd to justice quickly.

"He took my dad's cross necklace," Maisy said, drawing Felicity's attention.

That was odd. Boyd hadn't collected souvenirs from his past victims. At least not that Felicity recalled. What did it mean when a serial killer changed his MO?

She shuddered with anxiety, afraid they were going to find out before all was said and done.

When the door closed behind the women, Westley had to fight to remain in place and not follow Felicity out. He didn't like not having eyes on her. If anything happened to her…

"Have a seat," Lieutenant General Hall told the men who had stood as the ladies left the room.

The men resettled themselves in their seats around the conference table, all attention focused on the base commander.

Lieutenant General Hall pinned Westley to his chair with an intense stare. "Master Sergeant James, care to explain why you left the meeting earlier without permission?"

Westley sat up straighter, glad Felicity was in the hall and not witness to his dressing down. He gave the lieutenant general his reason, hoping he didn't reveal more than concern for his employee.

"It appears you were right to be alarmed for her welfare," Lieutenant General Hall said. "I'll overlook your lack of protocol this one time."

Easing out a relieved breath, Westley inclined his head. "Thank you, sir."

"Now, how do we ferret out the person who helped Sullivan get on base?" Lieutenant General Hall's gaze traveled over the men at the table and settled on Oliver Davison. "What can you tell us about the prison break?"

"We've confirmed Sullivan bribed two guards into letting him out of his cell and into the docking bay, where he crawled into the back of a laundry truck and escaped," Oliver said.

Westley's phone buzzed with another incoming text from the training center. He glanced at it and was glad to read the growing total of dogs recovered.

Lieutenant General Hall focused on Captain Justin Blackwood. "How did he get on base?"

"Sir, we're still working on that," Justin replied. He sat at the table with his hands braced on his knees. "All personnel are being asked to report their whereabouts for the past twenty-four hours. It will take us time to verify every alibi."

"And what of Sullivan's half-sister?" Oliver asked. He consulted his notebook. "Staff Sergeant Zoe Sullivan."

"We are looking into her, sir." Line spoke up for the first time. He'd taken a position leaning against the wall rather than sitting at the table. "She's a flight instructor and is currently in the air. But when she lands, we'll be questioning her."

"Keep me informed of your progress," Lieutenant General Hall said. He trained his gaze on Justin. "You also received a rose and note, did you not?"

Justin nodded. "Yes, sir."

Surprise washed through Westley.

Oliver asked Justin, "What has Sullivan got against you?"

"I was one of his basic instructors, sir," Justin replied. "I called him on the carpet on multiple occasions for slacking off and harassing the female recruits."

"Stay vigilant, Captain," Lieutenant General Hall instructed.

"I will, sir."

To Westley, Lieutenant General Hall said, "How are you progressing on recovering the dogs?"

"We have half recovered so far, sir." Not nearly enough. There were still so many dogs missing. Westley hated to think about what could happen to the dogs if they made their way off base or deep into the woods or onto the runway. "Everyone on base is helping to bring the dogs in safely."

"Excellent." Lieutenant General Hall turned to First Lieutenant Ethan Webb. "What I'm about to tell you doesn't leave this room."

"Yes, sir," Westley murmured in agreement along with the others.

"It seems Sullivan has been busy," Lieutenant General Hall said. "Either before coming here or shortly after, he visited Baylor marine base and left a rose and note for Lieutenant Jillian Masters."

Westley's gaze shot to Ethan, who sat across the table. Jillian was Ethan's ex-wife, though she'd retaken her maiden name. "Why would she be a target?"

Ethan's jaw firmed. "Jillian had a run-in with Boyd shortly before his discharge. She'd been on base observing a K-9 seminar I was conducting. This was back when we were married. Boyd tried flirting with her, and it didn't go over well. Jillian can be…cutting when she wants."

Westley had only met the woman once. She'd definitely had an edge to her.

"But we don't know when Sullivan was at Baylor?" Linc said. "He may not be on base now."

"We can't assume anything," the OSI agent, Ian Steffen, stated. "We have five known targets. We need to be vigilant and catch him, if and when, he makes a move."

Acid churned in Westley's gut at the thought of Felicity in danger. Granted, she was in the law-enforcement track and trained to take care of herself, but so were Sullivan's other victims, and yet the fiend had killed three well-trained airmen.

At least with her at the training center, he'd be able to keep an eye on her during the day. He'd ask for permission to send home a German shepherd named Glory to protect her at night. Glory was a fierce dog with great protective instincts.

Hall slammed a palm on the table. "I will not have this maniac running rampant on my base."

"If I may suggest," Ian said, "you reassign Staff Sergeant Monroe to a more visible base position, where she will draw Boyd out in the open. Sullivan has to know security will be beefed up at the training center now, especially with two homicides on site."

Westley's heart pounded as the agent's words echoed through the room. "You want to make her a sacrificial lamb?" The thought of deliberately putting her in harm's way made his blood run cold.

"You don't think she's up to the task?" Ian asked, his tone soft but intense.

Westley didn't doubt Felicity's abilities. He just didn't like tempting danger. Not when that danger was in the form of Boyd Sullivan, a man who had already killed eight people. "No. I mean, she'll be safer at the training center."

Ian arched an eyebrow. "Duly noted. However, of the three female targets, she's the only one in the law-enforcement track."

Lieutenant General Hall sat back and rubbed his chin. "The base photographer is being transferred to another assignment. Does Staff Sergeant Monroe know her way around a camera?"

"I can answer that, sir," Ian said. "I know for a fact that she does. Her father's office was covered with photos she'd taken."

Westley had seen her with a nice camera on numerous occasions, taking pictures of the dogs. And he'd seen the images. Though she'd claimed photography was a hobby, as far as he was concerned, her work was professional-grade.

But Westley couldn't protect Felicity if she wasn't at the training center. Responsibility weighed heavy on his shoulders. Knowing he was going out on a very thin and fragile limb, Westley met the OSI agent's gaze. "I want to be detailed to her protection."

Ian studied him with speculation in his eyes. "I see no issue with that."

Surprised at the lack of argument from the agent, Westley went even farther out on the limb and addressed the lieutenant general. "And I want a dog to be with her at all times. Even at night." Asking for something that traditionally wasn't allowed was risky. Every military working dog was a valuable asset and when not deployed was kept in the kennels at the training center.

Lieutenant General Hall studied him for a moment. "Okay. I will allow it. Use the dogs as needed during this situation." He sat back. "Then it's settled. Staff Sergeant Monroe will be transferred to the photo lab under my command." Lieutenant General Hall zeroed his gaze on Westley. "And you will be detailed to her protection along with a canine." Lieutenant General Hall turned to Justin. "You good?"

Justin nodded. "Yes, sir."

Westley sucked in a quick breath of triumph and nervousness. That meant he was going to be Felicity's shadow 24/7. Keeping an emotional distance when they'd be so close would be harder.

But if he failed to protect her, she could be the next victim. He couldn't allow that to happen. Wouldn't allow it to happen. If anything happened to Felicity, he'd crumble beneath the weight of guilt.

He'd walk on coals if need be. Anything to protect her.

"She will be your responsibility to keep safe, Master Sergeant James." Lieutenant General Hall's gaze narrowed. "Are you up to the task?"

Pulse spiking, Westley nodded. "Yes, sir."

Game on.

THREE

The door to the conference room opened, drawing Felicity's attention away from Maisy. Westley stepped into the hall and beckoned Felicity back inside.

"Just a second," she called to him. Turning to Maisy, she said, "Did you drive over?"

Maisy nodded. "Yes." She rose and hitched her purse higher on her shoulder. "I have to get to church to teach my Sunday school class."

"Are you sure you're up for that?"

"Yes. I need to be with the kids." Maisy hugged Felicity. "Be careful."

"You, too." Felicity stepped back. "I'll call you later."

Maisy smiled and hurried out of base command.

Squaring her shoulders, Felicity met Westley at the door. The hard light in his eyes didn't bode well and a hundred thoughts—none of them good —raced through her mind.

"Is everything okay?" she whispered.

He didn't reply. Instead he stepped aside so she could reenter the conference room. She held her salute until the base commander told her to relax.

Lieutenant General Hall regarded her steadily. "I understand you know how to work a camera."

Surprise washed through her. "Yes, sir."

"Excellent. You are being reassigned to the photo lab effective immediately."

"Excuse me?" Felicity stared at the lieutenant general then her gaze darted to Westley. His inscrutable expression irked her. Had he signed off on this transfer? She didn't want to leave the training center. She wanted to work with the dogs. Was this photo-lab assignment some sort of punishment? Had Westley used the situation as an opportunity to have her removed from the training center?

Lieutenant General Hall held up a hand. "Now, hear us out." He nodded at the OSI agent.

Ian tipped his chin at her. "Of the potential victims, you're the only one trained to handle the likes of Boyd Sullivan."

His words sounded like a compliment. Still, confusion pounded at her temples. She glanced around the room at the men seated at the conference room table. When Westley had requested she rejoin them a few minutes ago, she'd had no idea what to expect. Certainly not this. "What do you want from me?"

"You take on the role of base photographer," Ian said. "This allows you to be visible, to roam the base at will taking many, many photos."

"You'll then upload the images to our database," the FBI agent said. "We'll run the pictures through our facial-recognition software. If Boyd is on base and you can capture his image then we'll have a better chance of finding him before he hurts anyone else."

She turned this over in her head. Her gaze strayed

to Westley again. The muscle in his jaw ticked, as if he was clenching his teeth. Was he upset or happy to be rid of her? She didn't know. He was so hard to read.

Her gaze swept over the other men staring at her and waiting for a response. How did one reply to being asked to act as bait for a serial killer?

But Ian was correct. No way could Yvette or Vanessa take on the role, despite the training all air-force personnel went through. Felicity imagined her father would want her to take on the challenge. Her mother, on the other hand, would flip out when she learned about this. Not that Felicity had any intention of telling her mother until after the fact. Or ever.

Straightening her shoulders and standing tall, she turned her attention to Lieutenant General Hall. "I will do whatever is needed, sir."

Approval shone in his eyes. "Well done. Then I will let you and Agent Steffen work out the details. You'll report for duty in the photo lab tomorrow morning."

"Yes, sir."

Lieutenant General Hall looked to Ian. "I'll let you take it from here."

"Take a seat," Ian told her as he pinned her with his gaze. "I'm not going to lie to you. This could be dangerous. We don't know what Boyd will do. We do know he is ruthless and cunning."

Swallowing back the trepidation clawing up her throat, she nodded. "I understand, sir."

"Despite his objections to your new assignment, Master Sergeant James has volunteered to be detailed to your protection."

Felicity absorbed the information like a blow to the gut. Why had Westley objected? She didn't want to jump to conclusions, but she was…disappointed. "I don't need Master Sergeant James's protection."

Ian raised his eyebrows. "It's not up for debate, Staff Sergeant Monroe."

She slanted a glance at Westley. He stared at her with a hooded gaze that made her fingers curl in her lap. "Who will run the training center?"

"I'll check in often with the center, but Master Sergeant Streeter will take over until Boyd is caught and put back in prison," Westley stated in a tight voice.

Caleb Streeter was a seasoned trainer and more than capable of handling the center. But he wasn't a master level trainer like Westley. She didn't understand how he could give up control. He ran the center like his own personal company. His way or the highway.

She wanted to ask Westley why he'd volunteered and why he disapproved of her taking the photography position, but with so many people staring at her, she decided her questions would have to wait.

She returned her attention back to Ian, who regarded her closely. No doubt he was waiting to see if she was going to continue to argue. No way. She wouldn't be that person. She was up for taking down the Red Rose Killer. She nodded her head in acquiescence.

"Now that that's settled," Ian said. "We are forming a task force to include all of you. We will add to it, as we need. But for now, all information is to be kept confidential. We don't want the base or the general public to be aware of what we are doing to bring Boyd to justice. A traitor on this base is helping Boyd. We don't know who it is." He turned his gaze to Justin. "We need to find this traitor, Captain."

"We're doing our best, sir," Justin said. "We will interview everyone on base."

"Who were Boyd's friends on base?" Oliver asked.

Felicity noticed the look exchanged between Justin and Linc before Justin spoke again. "Boyd was buddies with Airman Jim Ahern, who works in aircraft maintenance."

"We will be questioning him," Linc said.

"Good," Oliver said. "I want to be there when you do."

"Yes, sir," Linc and Justin both said.

"I want you all to report back here tomorrow at sixteen hundred with updates." Lieutenant General Hall rose. Everyone in the room snapped to attention.

"You all have your orders," Lieutenant General Hall said. "I have arrangements to make with Miss Lockwood for her father's service." He walked out.

As Felicity and Westley headed for the door, Ian said, "Staff Sergeant Monroe, if you'd wait a moment. I'd like to speak to you privately."

The scowl spreading over Westley's features made Felicity tense.

Finally, he directed his gaze on her. "I'll wait in the hall."

She nodded and sat down.

Westley walked out, followed by the others. When she and Ian were alone, Ian said, "I want you to search your house for anything that might be related to your father's last case. Tell no one. We don't know who to trust."

She swallowed the burn of wariness. "Yes, sir."

Whoever had been in her house might also be looking for her father's case notes. A shiver ran over her.

And that would mean her father hadn't died by an accidental fall…

She fought to catch her breath.

He *had* been murdered.

Numbed by the realization, she left the conference room.

True to his word, she found Westley waiting for her in the hallway. She wanted to tell him about her conversation with the OSI agent, about the case her father was working on and the fact that maybe she wasn't going crazy. But Ian's words reverberated through her head.

We don't know who to trust.

"What did Agent Steffen want?"

From the paleness of Felicity's face, Westley guessed something significant. And the way she stared at him, with wariness in her blue-green eyes, sent a fissure of alarm sliding down his spine.

She shook her head. "Nothing that I want to talk about."

So there was something, but she didn't trust him enough to share. Hurt spread through his chest. How could he protect her if she distrusted him? And why did she distrust him? Hadn't he always treated her professionally? Except when he'd hugged her in a moment of weakness. That was something he wouldn't let happen again.

Did she know about his mom and dad? Is that what the OSI agent told her?

Swallowing his concern, he led her toward the exit.

A bulldog of a man rushed through the double doors of the base command. He wore the airman battle-ready uniform with a staff-sergeant insignia and the name

Dooley on the tag. The solid occupational badge marked him an engineer.

Westley swiftly maneuvered Felicity behind him. For all Westley knew, Boyd could be posing as an airman and using disguises to camouflage his appearance.

"Felicity!" the man exclaimed and hurried toward them. As he drew closer, Westley realized the man was older than he first appeared. Mid-to late-fifties.

Felicity nudged Westley aside. "Uncle Patrick."

Westley relaxed and stepped back, allowing Felicity room.

Patrick skidded to a halt and eyed Westley, saluted and then turned his gaze on Felicity. "Are you okay? I heard the Red Rose Killer is loose on base and that you were threatened."

"I'm fine, Uncle," she replied. "A little shaken, that's all."

"I would imagine so," Patrick said. "Colleen must be beside herself."

Felicity made a face. "I haven't told Mom and would rather you didn't as well."

Patrick smirked. "The last thing I want is to be the bearer of bad news to my sister." He gave a mock shudder.

"Uncle, this is Master Sergeant Westley James," Felicity said. "Westley, my uncle, Staff Sergeant Patrick Dooley."

"You're from the MWD training center, right?" Patrick asked. "I've seen you working the dogs."

"That's right." From Patrick's tone, Westley gathered the man wasn't a fan of the canines.

Patrick focused on Felicity. "It's not safe for you to

go home. You need to come stay with me. We're family after all."

The stiffness in Felicity's shoulders told Westley she wasn't keen on the idea. "She'll have all the protection she needs," Westley assured the man. "We're heading to the training center now to pick up a dog for her."

Felicity shot Westley a look that he couldn't decipher. He guessed she was thinking that it was against regulations for an MWD to be housed anywhere but in the kennels. He would have to explain when her uncle wasn't present.

Patrick's upper lip curled slightly. "Unacceptable. Your mother would never forgive me if I let something happen to you when I could keep you safe."

"I appreciate the offer, Uncle Patrick," she said. "But Westley will provide me the protection I need."

"I suppose you'll be safe at the training center as well." Patrick didn't sound mollified.

"Actually, I'm taking over the role of base photographer starting tomorrow," Felicity told him.

The man's eyes nearly bugged out of his head. "What? Whose crazy idea was that? You'll be out in the open. Exposed. Unacceptable!"

Though Westley agreed with the man's assertions, he remained silent. He would let Felicity fill in her uncle on Westley's role.

"The base commander's order," she said. "And Master Sergeant James will be with me."

Westley met Patrick's narrowed gaze. "You'd better keep her safe."

"I plan to," he replied.

Felicity let out a small huff of air. "We need to get back to the training center so I can collect my things."

Patrick walked outside with them. The temperature had risen on this April afternoon, warming the air to a nice muggy level that immediately dampened Westley's skin. Walking to the other side of base wasn't an appealing thought. "Patrick, would you give us a ride back to the training center?"

"Of course," he said and led them to a jeep parked across the road.

The vehicle smelled faintly of a scent Westley couldn't identify. He rolled down the window for fresh air. The ride to the center took all of four minutes.

Felicity gave her uncle a quick hug before he drove away, leaving them standing outside of the center.

"I didn't realize you had more family on base," Westley said as they walked toward the entrance.

"We aren't super close," she confessed. "Uncle Patrick and my dad used to be friends when they were young. That's how my parents met, but as Dad moved up through the ranks and into the OSI, he and Patrick grew apart." She let out a bitter-sounding laugh. "My parents grew apart, as well."

"Divorced?"

"Yes." She stopped to glance his way and shielded her eyes from the sun. "What about your parents?"

Acid churned in his gut. He had to ask, had to know. "What did Agent Steffen tell you?"

"Why do you assume he told me anything about you?"

"Because something he said upset you," Westley replied. "Something that you don't trust me enough to talk about, so I gathered that meant he warned you off of me."

Speculation entered her blue-green gaze. "No. What we talked about had nothing to do with you."

Relief swept through him. And he felt idiotic for his paranoia. "Good." He started walking again, intending to put the whole subject behind them.

She hurried to keep up the pace and put a hand on his arm before he could open the door to the training center. "But now I'm curious. You never talk about yourself. Why would I need to be warned off of you?"

Westley's mouth turned to cotton. Of course. The woman was curious. Felicity liked to talk and to hear others' stories. He'd seen and heard her on numerous occasions with the handlers that came to the training center and with the other trainers. She had a way about her that people found engaging and comfortable.

Right now, he felt anything but comfortable. He wasn't going to spill his guts about his past if he didn't have to. The things his parents had done didn't have anything to do with his present life. Nor with his ability to protect Felicity. "Sorry. Not going there."

"I know you're my superior, and I'm to follow orders," she replied, "but I figure since we're going to be stuck together for the foreseeable future, we may as well get to know each other a bit better."

He faced her. "There's nothing to know."

"Sure there is. Where did you grow up?"

The determination in her expression didn't bode well. The tenacity that would make her a great dog trainer one day also meant he wasn't getting out of this conversation easily. The only thing to do was give her the basics that anyone could read in his official personnel file. "I grew up in Stillwater, Oklahoma. My father passed on years ago." In prison, but he kept that tidbit to himself.

"And my mother is…" He didn't know where Lori Jean James was. Last he'd heard from her, she'd been in Nevada. "We aren't close."

"I'm sorry," Felicity said.

Her compassion annoyed him. He didn't want her pity. "Look. None of that matters. I have one focus right now. That is protecting you." He yanked open the door. "The first thing we need to do is find Glory. She'll be the best dog for you."

He didn't need to read Felicity's mind to know she wasn't pleased with him. It was written in the tiny V between her eyebrows and the irritation in her eyes.

Inside the center, Felicity went to gather her things from the locker room, while Westley headed for the dog kennels at the back of the building. He passed one of the long-time trainers, Rusty Morton. Westley liked the guy well enough.

Rusty paused to salute. "Master Sergeant."

Westley returned the customary salute. "At ease. How is it going?"

Rusty relaxed. "I'm headed out to see if I can find more of the dogs. Someone reported seeing some in the woods at the far edge of base."

That was concerning. Six hundred acres of rough terrain and steep canyons could pose a danger to the canines. He hoped nothing bad befell the dogs. "I'll be praying you find them." And praying the canines were unharmed. "I'll head out soon to search as well."

"Yes, sir." Rusty hurried away.

Why Westley clung to the faith of his childhood, he didn't know. Habit maybe. Or deep inside, maybe he still wanted to believe God answered prayers. So he prayed that Rusty and the other trainers out searching for the dogs had success.

Westley entered the large open space where numerous kennels lined the walls. Dogs barked in greeting. He was pleased to see so many of the dogs had been returned unharmed.

"We have about sixty dogs still missing," Caleb Streeter told him. The tall, muscular officer was refilling water bowls. Because Caleb and Westley were the same rank, they dispensed with the protocol of saluting.

Westley was surprised by the number and tried not to be disheartened. The dogs had to be somewhere on base. But where?

"I need Glory," Westley said as he stopped in front of her empty crate. "Where is she?"

"She's one of the sixty."

"No way!" Westley couldn't believe it. "Glory is a rock star. She'd come when called."

"I know. I don't get it," Caleb said. "Liberty, Patriot and Scout are missing, too."

"That's just weird." And worrisome. Westley rubbed the back of his neck, where tension had taken up residence. The four German shepherds were superstars in the making and very valuable to the military. They should have been easily recalled. He hoped and prayed they weren't hurt, or worse. Anxiety ate at his gut.

His gaze collided with the dark eyes of an all-black German shepherd named Dakota. A measure of relief eased some of the pressure knotting his muscles. Dakota was a good candidate for Felicity. The mature, multipurpose dog excelled in his training and had a good balance of aggression and excitability that was needed for patrol work. He'd been deployed with his handler on two missions overseas before coming back to the training center to be paired with a new handler after his handler had been injured. "You'll do nicely, Dakota."

The dog perked up hearing his name. Grabbing a lead, Westley released the dog from his kennel and latched the lead to his black collar. The dog was a two-year-old veteran well trained in protection. Westley was confident that Dakota would keep Felicity safe.

Westley explained to Caleb the situation of the Red Rose Killer and Westley's detail to Felicity's protection.

"Man, that's rough," the other trainer said. "What can I do to help?"

"I need you to take over the day-to-day tasks while I'm on this detail."

Caleb's blue eyes grew wide. "You got it."

Surprisingly, Westley didn't mind giving up control of the program. It was only temporary and he knew the dogs would be in capable hands. Taking Dakota with him, he went to find Felicity, who was talking with base reporter Lieutenant Heidi Jenks in the training center break room.

He saluted the officer while Dakota sat at attention.

"At ease," Heidi said as she returned the salute.

Turning his gaze on Felicity, he hoped she hadn't given away any details. "What's going on?"

Felicity smiled easily. "Just chatting. Do you know Heidi? She's my neighbor."

"Only by reputation," he replied.

Pushing back her long blond hair, Heidi said, "I was hoping you all could tell me about the missing dogs and the two trainers who were murdered here last night."

"No comment," Westley replied. "Felicity, we need to go."

Heidi scrambled from her chair. "Wait. Give me something. Do you have any info on Chief Master Sergeant Lockwood's murder?"

"Sorry, Lieutenant. You'll have to contact the base commander for information." He gripped Felicity by the elbow and hurried her out of the center. Once they were away from the reporter, he said, "What did you tell her?"

"Nothing," she replied. "I know better than that. My dad was OSI, you know."

"Right." He took his cell phone from his pocket and sent a text to the training staff telling them Caleb would be in charge and not to talk to the press.

"I thought you said Glory was the dog for me," Felicity said, petting Dakota. "Not that I'm complaining. I like this guy a lot."

Westley relayed what Caleb had told him as they hurried toward base housing.

"I have to believe we'll find the dogs," she said, though a thread of anxiety wove through her tone.

"Ever the optimist, aren't you?" he replied.

"Is that a bad thing?"

He shrugged. "It leaves you open to disappointment."

"Maybe. But if I go around expecting disappointment then I'm sure to find it."

He marveled at the way her brain worked.

"Would you mind if we say a prayer for the dogs' safety?" she asked, her eyes searching his face.

"Be my guest," he said. He'd like to think God would hear and deliver on their request. Maybe he would for Felicity.

She bowed her head. "Lord God, please watch over the missing dogs and bring them back safely. Watch over the whole base, Lord. Keep everyone safe from Boyd Sullivan. Amen."

"Amen," he mumbled.

When they reached her house, crime-scene tape fluttered around the mailbox, slamming home the reminder of the danger lurking on base.

Before Felicity could step inside, Westley halted her with a hand on her shoulder. "Let Dakota go first." If the Red Rose Killer was waiting inside, the dog would alert.

He unhooked the lead from the dog's collar. "Search," Westley told Dakota.

The dog went inside. Westley tensed, waiting for some sign of alert to trouble. A few moments later, Dakota returned without alerting.

"It's safe," Westley said.

Felicity stepped inside and let out an audible gasp.

Westley followed her, taking in the disarray of the living room. Either she was a messy housekeeper or someone had ransacked her house.

FOUR

Felicity clenched her fists at her sides, taking in the damage done to her house while she'd been at the briefing.

The stuffing from the couches littered the floor like little puffy clouds. All the books from the shelves were strewn about. Framed photos had been knocked off the walls, the glass shattered. A sense of violation seeped through her bones.

The blatant destruction was worse than the subtle signs of intrusion that had caused her to question her sanity. Now she knew without a doubt she wasn't going crazy. Someone had been in her house, searched her house. Was it the person who killed her father?

Dread nipped at her. Had the person found what they were looking for? Was it the evidence in her father's last case that had gone missing?

If so, then what chance did the OSI have of catching the person who took her father from her?

"I take it this isn't how you left things this morning." He took out his phone and reported the break-in to base security.

Westley's wry comment grated on her already taut nerves.

She whirled on him. "No. This is the work of a killer."

"Why would Boyd want to wreck your house?"

She snapped her jaw closed and clenched her teeth. Should she confide in Westley? The question poked at her like a cattle prod. Ian had said not to trust anyone.

Agitated, she hurried through the house, seeing the same sort of ransacking in every room, though her bedroom wasn't nearly as torn apart. But the majority of the chaos was concentrated in her father's office. His file cabinets had been emptied, his desk drawers dumped in heaps.

"Someone seemed to be searching for something important to them," Westley mused.

She wondered how much help he could be in figuring out the mystery. The man was smart.

Aware of Westley and Dakota dogging her steps, she wrestled with the need to tell Westley the truth. There was no reason why she shouldn't trust this man. Working for him for six months had shown her he was a man of integrity. Surely, he wasn't involved in her father's death. Yet, reluctance kept her silent.

He cocked his head and studied her. Dakota sat and mimicked the man. Felicity shook her head, amused despite the circumstances. Seemed like both males were analyzing her.

"What aren't you telling me?"

Westley's question jerked her gaze to meet his intense stare. Her heart pounded as her instinct warred with Ian's directive.

"Felicity, I can't protect you if I don't know what is going on."

True. Westley was the only one standing between her and a potential killer.

Two killers, in fact.

And if Westley didn't know there was more than one threat out there, then how effective could he be? And once Westley knew everything, he could help catch her father's murderer. She'd ask Ian for forgiveness later.

"This wasn't the work of Boyd Sullivan. At least, I don't believe so." There was the slimmest possibilities Boyd or his accomplice had trashed her home, though their motive was a mystery.

Westley's eyebrows rose. "Then who? Why?"

She inhaled, blew out the breath and then said, "My father's death wasn't an accident."

Westley frowned. "What do you mean? How so?"

Her stomach clenched. "Agent Steffen believes that the last case my dad was working on is why he's dead. My father had a lead on a hit-and-run off base. His case notes are missing."

"So that's what Agent Steffen wanted to talk to you about. He thinks your father's death was no accident. That he was…murdered?"

Bile rose to burn her throat. "Yes."

"Felicity—"

She could hear the need to comfort her that had been in his voice earlier, when he hugged her. "Don't. Please, Westley, just don't. Not now."

Westley rubbed a hand over his jaw. "Okay. Okay." He looked around the office. "So this was someone looking for the evidence your father had."

Grateful he was refocusing on something they could

both handle, Felicity blew out another agitated breath. "I believe so. The question is did they find what they were looking for?"

"This morning, when you thought there was someone in your house, there really was."

The grim reality of how vulnerable she'd been sent a shiver of terror down her spine. To cover her fright, she bent to pick up a broken picture frame.

"Don't." He echoed her plea; only from him, the word was a command.

She stilled.

"The Security Forces crime-scene techs need to dust for prints and look for particulates."

Of course. She straightened and stared down at the smiling face of her father, his arm wrapped around her on her sixteenth birthday. Tears burned her eyes. She held them back. No way would she cry in front of Westley. "I miss him so much."

"He was proud of you," Westley said.

She lifted her gaze to him in surprise. "That's kind of you to say."

"It's the truth. He came to the training center not long before his death and watched you putting Riff through his paces," Westley told her.

That's right. She'd been so nervous knowing her father was there. She'd tried extra hard to do everything perfectly. And Riff, thankfully, had cooperated on that day. She hoped someone found him soon and returned him to the training center.

"He asked me how you were doing. If I thought you were in the right place."

Her stomach sank. She braced herself. "And what did you tell him?"

"That you have the makings of a good trainer," Westley replied.

She swallowed the lump of emotion clogging her throat. "You did?"

"Yes. I could tell he was pleased."

Love for her father swelled in her chest. "Do you believe that I'll make a good trainer?"

"I do. In time."

She held his gaze as his words slid into her, bolstering her confidence. That was the closest Westley had come to giving her a compliment on her work. Being the youngest and newest trainer, she tried so hard to earn his approval. Instead, most of the time she earned only a scowl from the handsome, buttoned-down master sergeant.

He cleared his throat and averted his gaze but not before she saw a softening in his eyes that sent a flutter through her. He wasn't scowling at her now.

She swallowed and tried to make sense of the change in her boss. Well, he was no longer her CO. Now he was her protector.

Gesturing to the front door, he said, "Let's wait outside."

With Dakota at their heels, they walked out to the porch.

Felicity leaned against the railing and faced him. The need to make sure they were on equal footing forced words from her mouth. "I'm trusting you to keep me safe. I'm trusting you with the knowledge that my dad's death was more than it seems."

Westley braced his feet apart and returned her gaze. "I'm honored. On both accounts."

She narrowed her eyes. She toggled two fingers between them. "But this has to be a two-way street. You must trust me, as well. I'm not some wilting lily for you to prop up."

A small smile curved his lips. "Duly noted."

Annoyance buzzed around her head like a million tiny mosquitoes. It was like doing her absolute best to prove herself yet again and falling short.

A flush of frustration heated her skin. "I need to know that you won't keep secrets from me. If something comes up with Boyd or the investigation into my father's death, you can't try to protect me by not telling me."

All humor left his face. His jaw firmed. "If you need to know I'll tell you."

"No. That's exactly what I mean." She pushed off the railing. "If we're to do this, we're all in together. You don't get to decide what's right for me. Not you, or anyone."

"Aren't you tired of carrying that chip on your shoulder all the time?" he commented softly.

Her eyebrows shot up. "What do you mean? I'm just trying to do my best."

"But you don't have to do this alone," he countered.

"As my supervisor, I took instructions from you. But now, you're not my boss. I want to make sure we are clear on that."

"Crystal."

He stepped closer, forcing her to tilt her head to look up at him. She found herself fascinated with the little gold specks surrounding his dark irises, making the outer rim of blue even brighter up close. There was so much in his gaze that confused and confounded her. Determination. A spark of anger. And something else that had her pulse leaping.

What was going on? This was her superior. The man who never stopped watching her so he could find a fault.

"But make no mistake, Felicity." His deep voice commanded her attention. "My mission is to protect you. Whatever it takes. If I tell you to duck, you'd better duck. I refuse to have your stubbornness cost you your life."

Felicity swallowed hard. She hated the way his words wound through her, conjuring up horrifying images of death and destruction. "I am not stubborn."

His mouth softened and his eyes sparkled. "Your stubbornness is one of your most appealing traits."

He found her appealing? Whoa. That was unexpected.

She blew out a breath, unsure what to say or how to feel. The line between them that always seemed so clear at the training center was now blurring.

Before she could reply, several vehicles roared to a stop in front of her little house. Best to let his comment go. She didn't want to care what Westley thought of her.

But what she wanted and what happened were rarely the same thing.

Westley watched the play of sparks in Felicity's eyes and pressed his lips together to keep from grinning. He'd surprised her with his comment. Good. He wanted to keep her on her toes. She needed to stay sharp if they were going up against two deadly threats.

Turning his attention away from the lovely staff sergeant, Westley greeted Captain Justin Blackwood and the OSI agent, Ian Steffen, with a salute. Two base-security policemen followed with crime-scene kits in hand.

"What happened?" Justin asked. "Did Boyd Sullivan break in?"

Westley exchanged a quick glance with Felicity. A red rose and ominous note this morning and now an intruder in her house. It made sense the captain would ask about Boyd.

"We don't know, sir," Westley said. "Someone broke in and ransacked the place. It's obvious they were looking for something."

Justin pinned Felicity with a questioning look. "Any ideas what they were searching for?"

Felicity's gaze darted to Ian. Westley figured she was looking to the agent for permission to speak about their suspicions regarding her father's death.

Ian gave a subtle nod before stepping forward. "I can answer that, but first, please direct your men to process the scene. This is for your ears only."

Justin's gaze narrowed, but he motioned for the two MPs to proceed into the house. When the two men were out of earshot, Justin said, "Explain."

"Prior to OSI Agent Monroe's death, he was working on several cases that are still open," Ian said.

Justin swept a hand toward the house. "Then this isn't related to the Red Rose Killer?"

Ian shrugged. "Hard to say. From what I've read on Boyd Sullivan, this isn't part of his MO."

"Neither is taking jewelry from his victims," Felicity interjected.

All eyes turned to her.

"Maisy told me that her father's cross, the one he always wore, was missing when she found him."

Westley heard the subtle pain in her tone. She hurt

for her friend. He told himself the sharp constriction in his chest was for *both* women's losses.

"Captain Blackwood," Ian said, "I suggest conferring with the sheriff's deputy in Dill, Texas. The one who brought down Sullivan the first time around. She may have some insight into his psyche that might help us find him."

"Good idea," Justin said. His next comment was cut off when his cell phone rang. "Excuse me." He stepped away to take the call.

"Better to keep the focus on Sullivan," Ian said in a quiet tone.

Westley could only guess the OSI agent didn't want to advertise the fact that Felicity's father had been murdered.

If the killer thought he had gotten away with the break-in attributed to the Red Rose Killer, the more likely he, or she, would make a mistake. Westley sent up a silent prayer that God would let justice be done on earth for her father.

When Justin returned, his blue eyes were troubled. "We've got a missing cook. Airman Stephen Butler didn't show up to his shift in the commissary today. But his car was found in the driveway of his base housing."

"Are you thinking he's another of Boyd's victims?" Westley asked.

"We'll see. I'm headed over to inspect the car." To Westley, Justin said, "Keep in touch with me." His gaze slid to Felicity as he turned. "We'll see you both tomorrow morning back at base command."

Once Justin's vehicle disappeared from sight, Ian ushered them inside.

Westley kept Dakota at his side as the two crime-scene techs were packing up their equipment.

"Did you find anything worth noting?" Ian asked them.

"No, sir," the older of the two said. "We've collected prints and will run them through the databases and compare them to Agent Monroe and his daughter." He nodded at Felicity in deference.

She smiled back at him. "Thank you."

If they found prints that didn't belong to her or her father, then they could have a lead on the intruder. Westley hoped it would be that easy.

Once the two techs had left, the trio gathered in her father's office. Westley released Dakota. The dog sniffed at the floor and moved around, inspecting the room. A large mahogany L-shaped desk took up half the space and a large black captain's chair sat behind the desk. Filing cabinets and a bookshelf filled in the remaining space and more of Felicity's photos decorated the wall.

The pictures were good. Ian had been right. She knew what she was doing with a camera.

"Felicity has explained to you my suspicions about Graham's death?" Ian asked Westley as he hitched a hip on the edge of the desk.

"She has, sir." Worry camped in his gut. "Why hasn't there been an official investigation?"

Ian's expression turned even more grim. "There's no evidence to follow. Only my gut feeling that the case Graham was working on had turned deadly. I've tried to piece together what I can from the civilian police report."

"Which is?" Westley asked.

"In a rather suspect neighborhood of San Antonio, a motorcycle struck a civilian and left the scene. The bike had a Canyon Air Force Base sticker on the back. The witness could only say the rider was dressed all in black to match his bike."

"The victim?" Felicity asked.

"Broken back. Paralyzed from the waist down."

Empathy dampened her eyes. "That's horrible."

Westley hated the thought that someone from the base would be so dishonorable as to leave the scene. Unless the hit wasn't an accident. A foul taste rose from his stomach. "Was the victim targeted?"

"Not that I can tell," Ian said. "It seems more like a bad case of 'wrong place, wrong time' on both sides. The roads were slick from a recent rain. The streetlights were out when the pedestrian stepped off the curb into the path of the bike."

"Do we know what Agent Monroe's case files look like?" Westley asked as he picked up a stack of file folders. "Were they in a notebook or in a folder like these?"

"Dad kept meticulous records," Felicity said. "But I don't know how he managed his work cases." She looked to Ian. "Have you found my dad's laptop?"

Ian shook his head.

Felicity frowned. "I haven't seen his laptop here. I've been through his safe and nothing important was in there."

"We need to find that computer," Ian stated. "His notes and the lead he was working on will be on the hard drive."

Westley's blood pressure rose. "We're going to have to work on the assumption that this guy didn't find the computer based on the condition of the house. We need to keep her safe."

"Which is why you're here, Master Sergeant James."

Westley pulled in a bracing breath and met Felicity's gaze. She rolled her eyes in response. Oh, yeah. This was going to be fun.

Ian headed toward the door. "I need to focus on the hunt for Boyd Sullivan. I trust you two will be circumspect in searching for Graham's case notes and his computer. I hate to think someone in the OSI could be involved, but as far as I know Graham didn't share with anyone that he had a lead that would break the hit-and-run case."

"Yes, sir," Westley assured him. "We'll keep our investigation on the down low."

"You'll let us know if you hear any more about what Boyd is up to?" Felicity asked. "I'm praying he left the base now that everyone is looking for him."

"One can hope so," Ian said as he left the house.

When they were alone, Westley asked, "Where else could your father have hidden his laptop?"

Felicity thought for a moment. Her gaze lifted to the ceiling. "There's an attic crawl space used for storage."

"Let's go check it out," Westley said. "Dakota," he called to the black German shepherd who had taken an interest in her father's desk.

Dakota had dropped to his belly and crawled beneath the desk until only his tail poked out. When the dog tried to back out, the whole desk shook. Dakota growled, his paws digging into the carpet as he tugged.

Westley hurried over, kneeled and peered under the desk. Needing light, he took his Maglite from his utility belt and aimed it into the space. Felicity scooted in on her knees and pressed close to Westley. He had to fight to keep focused on the dog rather than on the soft curves melding into him and the vanilla scent of her hair teasing his senses.

Dakota's collar had caught on a metal latch in the side of the wood desk.

Felicity dropped onto her belly and wiggled her way farther beneath the desk.

"There's a secret compartment. Dakota must have followed my dad's scent under here," she said with excitement ringing in her voice. "But I can't release the latch or unhook his collar."

"Let me." Westley squeezed in next to her. "Hold this."

He handed off the flashlight. Her slim fingers closed over his, creating warm spots on his skin before she relieved him of the device. He flexed his hand and then grasped the little metal hook. The awkward position didn't make it easy, but he managed to unlatch the door which popped open, freeing Dakota. The dog quickly scrambled away from the desk.

Felicity shone the beam of light into the compartment.

"What's that?" Felicity reached past him to grasped what was in the secret cubby. They both shimmied out from beneath the desk.

Felicity held up her find.

A key with strange grooves along the blade and an oblong bow with a cutout in the center glinted in the light.

He met her confused gaze. "Any idea what the key opens?"

She shook her head. "I don't. But the key has to be important if Dad hid it."

Westley had to agree. Whatever the key opened would lead them to her father's killer. He knew it in his bones. But how would they find the lock?

FIVE

Shaken to her core at finding the key hidden in her father's desk, Felicity's fingers trembled. In them she held the one clue that could lead them to her father's murderer.

Westley helped Felicity to her feet. His big, strong, capable hands dwarfed hers, making her feel feminine and treasured. For a moment, she wanted to hang on to him in case she needed steadying. If she was honest with herself she'd admit she liked having him close after such a horrible day. He was solid and secure. And she found herself wanting to lean on him for support.

But she squared her shoulders, took a breath and stepped away from him, forcing him to release her. She had to stay strong. Not show any weakness.

He tucked his hands into the pockets of his uniform jacket.

Holding up the key to inspect it, she said, "I've never seen this before."

"Could it be to his desk at the OSI office?" Westley asked.

"Ian said Dad's desk had been emptied."

"Maybe a footlocker or gym locker?"

"Dad used the base rec-center gym, but the lockers there have combination locks on them." She walked to the office closet and opened the door. "Dad's old service footlocker is in here." She pushed back a rack of coats. "It doesn't have a lock on it, though."

"Maybe the key goes to something inside the locker?" Westley suggested.

"Maybe." She tugged the box from the closet. Westley hurried over to help her. His nearness did funny things to her insides. She should have felt crowded, but instead she was comforted by his presence. Maybe that was why she'd felt the urge to hang on to him when she stood. She was glad she wasn't going through this alone.

She lifted the lid and surveyed the contents. A folded flag, boxes holding her father's service medals and a stack of letters in her mother's handwriting bound by a rubber band.

Westley rocked back on his heels. "Would your father have stashed his laptop in here?"

"Doubtful," she said as she closed the lid with disappointment. "And if he had, the computer's gone now."

"We need to take the key to Ian," Westley said. "Do you want me to hold it for safekeeping?"

"We do need to take the key to him. But until then I'll keep it." Her father had hidden the key for a reason. Until she knew the reason, the key stayed with a Monroe.

She reached beneath the collar of her uniform and tugged out a gold chain with a delicate cross that her grandmother had given to her on her sixteenth birthday. She quickly undid the clasp and slipped the key onto the chain before rehooking the clasp. She let the necklace rest against her uniform.

Placing a hand over it and taking solace from the tiny reminder of Grandma Esther, she said, "Where I go, it goes."

A low growl emanated from Dakota seconds before they heard heavy footsteps in the living room.

With a hand on his sidearm, Westley positioned himself in front of Felicity. Dakota stepped in front of Westley, his tail up, his ears back. Tension radiated from the dog.

Felicity froze, once again wishing she had her own sidearm. She'd talk to Lieutenant General Hall about it tomorrow. For now, she stayed rooted to the spot behind her two protective males.

"Felicity!"

Recognizing her uncle's voice, Westley relaxed and gave Dakota the hand signal to stand down.

Pushing past Westley, Felicity called out, "Coming." She quickly tucked the necklace back beneath her uniform before hurrying out of the office. She didn't need to tell Westley not to mention the key. No reason to get her uncle needlessly worked up about her father's death when they had no hard evidence to prove he'd been murdered.

Westley and Dakota followed right behind her. They found Patrick standing in the middle of the living room with his mouth agape. He rushed to Felicity and pulled her into a crushing hug. "Are you okay? I heard something happened here. Who did this? Did the Red Rose Killer come back?"

"I don't know, Uncle," she said, her voice muffled in his shoulder. He smelled of the cigars he relished and Old Spice. His uniform was rough against her cheek.

"See, I told you, you need to come stay with me until

this madman is captured," Patrick said. He pulled back to stare at her with worry lines crinkling his forehead. "If anything happened to you—" He blew out a noisy breath. "My sister couldn't take the shock."

Felicity appreciated his concern but she didn't want to dwell on her mother's reaction. "Nothing is going to happen to me. As you can see, I've got protection. Dakota and Westley will keep me safe."

Patrick's lip curled as he eyed the dog.

"He's a good dog. Protective." Felicity knew from her mother that Uncle Patrick had had a bad childhood experience with a dog.

Patrick met her gaze. Concern darkened his expression. "You shouldn't stay here, though," he argued. "Look at this place. It's a mess."

"It's my home," she said. "I'll clean it up. I'm not letting the likes of Boyd Sullivan drive me out of the house I shared with Dad."

Patrick dropped his chin slightly. "Your father is gone, pumpkin. He wouldn't want you to risk your life by staying here out of sentimentality."

"It's not sentimentality," she replied. "It would be too hard to pack up and move. Besides, if Boyd is on base and watching, then he'd know where I was going."

Patrick frowned. "I don't like it."

"Neither do I," Westley said.

Felicity's gaze whipped to him. Figures he'd side with her uncle.

Westley held up a hand as if to ward off an argument from her. "But Felicity is correct. Any move would draw more attention to her. Dakota will be staying with her, and I'll be close by at all times."

She smiled reassuringly at Patrick. "See. I'll be taken

care of." It grated to say that. She could take care of herself. But then again…if she'd truly been Boyd's intended target last night at the kennels, she clearly needed the backup.

"If you're sure." Patrick rubbed the back of his neck. "I could stay here with you."

"No!" She practically shouted the word and then grimaced at the sound of panic in her voice. The last thing she wanted was to have her uncle fussing over her. He'd be pushy like her mother. "I mean…no, thank you. I don't want to put you out. I'll be fine."

Patrick glanced around and then his gaze settled back on her. "You have my number. If you need me for anything, you ring me. I'll check in with you often."

Deciding that was as good as she'd get, she nodded. "That would be great. I'll call if I need to."

"All right, then." Patrick narrowed his gaze on Westley. He spared Dakota a parting glance and a shudder, then said, "Promise me you won't let anything happen to her."

"I promise."

Westley's deep voice wrapped around her. He was a man who kept his promises, but how could he make this one when there was no guarantee he could keep it?

Felicity eyed the Office of Special Investigations. They were here to bring the key to Agent Steffen, though she wasn't sure that it mattered. She doubted Ian would know what the key unlocked.

They'd driven over in her two-door compact car with Dakota sitting on the back seat. Westley hadn't balked when Felicity had climbed into the driver's seat. She'd been half-convinced she'd have to argue with him to drive her own car, but instead he'd relaxed into the passenger seat after adjusting it to accommodate his long legs. His wide shoulders took up the whole seat and hovered close to her shoulder. If she leaned a little to the right, they'd be touching, which made her hyperaware of every bump in the road.

She'd parked in front of the building and now she hesitated. She hadn't been to her father's office since his death. Memories threatened to swamp her. She fought them back with as much energy as she could spare, afraid if she didn't keep them at bay she'd drown.

She forced herself to slip out of the car and meet Westley and Dakota on the sidewalk. She noticed that Westley's gaze scanned the area, his hands on his utility belt, before he gave her a nod to indicate she should go ahead of him.

The receptionist smiled softly at her with sadness filling her eyes. Felicity had known her since she was ten. The tears were hot on the back of her throat. She could feel Westley's gaze, but she didn't dare look at him or the tears would start flowing. She had to be strong. They had a killer to catch. And a mystery to solve.

She led the way down the hall. The building was quiet on this late Sunday afternoon. The carpet beneath their feet snagged at Dakota's nails.

Felicity stopped short outside a closed door halfway down the hall. Her father's name still graced the name plaque. A spasm of longing hit her. On a whim, she slipped the key from beneath her uniform jacket and took off the necklace.

"Worth a try," she murmured at Westley's questioning look. She put the key in the lock. It didn't fit. She hadn't really expected it to. If the key was so important that her father went to the trouble of hiding it in a secret compartment in his desk, it wouldn't be so mundane as to be a key to his office.

"Is the door locked?" Westley asked.

She tried the handle. It opened easily. She stepped inside and breathed in. She knew it was a trick of her mind, but she inhaled the lingering scent of her dad's citrus aftershave. Her heart ached and grief twisted in her belly.

The office walls had been stripped of the framed photos and certificates that had once decorated the space. The desk was bare and the filing cabinet drawers were open and empty. She wasn't sure why seeing the space so barren left her feeling empty and grief-stricken.

She guessed the reality that he was truly gone couldn't be denied here. At home, his things were still touchable, as if waiting for his return. Maybe her uncle was right. Maybe she was staying in the house out of sentiment.

Her friend Rae Fallon, a rookie fighter pilot, needed a roommate. Maybe Felicity should consider moving into Rae's apartment.

She shrugged off her thoughts. Right now, she and Westley had a task to do. She couldn't let herself fall down a rabbit hole of sorrow.

Turning to leave, she bumped into Westley. His hands steadied her. She couldn't deny she liked the way warmth seeped through her jacket to touch her skin. She looked into his eyes. The compassion in his gaze brought on a burn of tears. She blinked to keep them at bay.

"It's okay to grieve," he said. "You've been so strong this past month."

"I grieve," she said. "In private." Where no one could judge her for the noisy sobs and the red-rimmed eyes.

"I want you to know you don't have to keep everything in all the time," he said.

She shrugged away his hands. "You sound like a shrink."

His mouth lifted at one corner. "Doling out advice I was given a long time ago."

She recalled he'd mentioned his father had passed on. "How old were you when your father died?"

Westley stepped back, his expression closing like a door in her face. "Seventeen."

"Had he been ill?" she asked gently.

"Let's just say things weren't good and leave it at that." He gestured toward the door. "We need to see Ian."

Obviously, Westley had no intention of sharing his past with her. To him, she was an assignment. Nothing more. She couldn't help disappointment from burrowing deep inside, even though she knew it was silly of her to feel anything where Westley was concerned. Better for them both to remain detached.

Westley moved to the exit with Dakota at his side. He stopped in the doorway, looking both ways before allowing her to exit in front of him.

They knocked on Ian's office door. It whipped open and Ian's eyebrows rose in surprise. "Is something wrong?"

"We think we found something important," Felicity said and showed him the key while explaining about the secret compartment in her father's home desk.

He waved them inside the office and examined the key. "You have no idea what the key opens?"

"None," she and Westley said in unison. They stood shoulder-to-shoulder facing the older man.

"Neither do I." Ian handed the key back to Felicity. "It could be nothing."

She frowned. "But why would he hide this then?"

"I don't think that's relevant to your father's murder. For all we know the key could have been in the desk for years. The piece was an antique when he bought it, right?"

Her shoulders slumped. She hadn't thought of that. Maybe the key wasn't her father's. Her fingers closed around the piece of metal, the edges digging into her skin. She'd really hoped she'd found the means to uncover her father's murderer.

Ian picked up his jacket and shrugged it on. "Right now, I have to focus on the Red Rose Killer."

Her stomach knotted. "Has Boyd Sullivan struck again?"

By the grim set of Ian's jaw she knew the answer before he spoke. "We believe so. The commissary cook that had been reported missing this morning, Stephen Butler, is dead. His body was found in a trash bin of an off-base local restaurant. His uniform and ID weren't found at the scene."

"Boyd dressed like Stephen and used his credentials to get on base," Westley stated.

"That's the going theory," Ian replied. "I'm heading to the morgue to verify the cause and time of death." He met Felicity's gaze. "Be careful. I'll see you both tomorrow morning."

Felicity and Westley walked out with Ian. As they

entered the reception area a man rushed forward, holding a cell phone. Felicity winced at the sight of base reporter John Robinson. With his red hair and horn-rimmed glasses, he looked more like a caricature than a serious journalist.

"Agent Steffen," John said, holding out the phone with the speaker pointed at Ian. "What can you tell me about the Red Rose Killer? Have there been any more developments?"

"No comment," Ian said with a frown and continued walking.

John shoved the phone in Felicity's face. "You're a target. Why would Boyd Sullivan, known as the Red Rose Killer, want to hurt you?"

Following Ian's lead, Felicity said, "No comment." She and Westley pushed past the reporter.

"Aww, come on, guys," John complained as he followed them out to the sidewalk. "The base is in an uproar. The personnel deserve to know what's going on."

Westley put up a hand to prevent John from following them. "Lieutenant General Hall will make a statement when he is ready. Until then, back off."

John's mouth turned into a petulant scowl. "What is the lead MWD trainer and—" John flicked a glance at Dakota "—a guard dog doing in the OSI offices? Are you providing protection for Staff Sergeant Monroe?"

Westley stepped into John's space and stared him down. Dakota growled, clearly sensing his handler's tension. "I said back off."

John held up his hands and moved away. "Fine."

Felicity glanced at Westley, glad she wasn't the one at the wrong end of his anger. When he put his hand to the small of her back to propel her down the sidewalk, heat seared through her uniform to warm her skin.

"You handled him well," she commented.

Westley blew out a breath. "He's harmless, but I don't want him making a pest of himself to you. The last thing we need is a nosey reporter poking around into what we're doing. If we're going to find the lock that key belongs to, we need to fly under the radar with our investigation."

She paused to stare at him. "So you believe the key is important?"

He seemed to contemplate the question. "My gut tells me yes. But maybe it's wishful thinking."

That she understood. "I feel the same. The key looks old, but not like an antique."

"It won't hurt anything for us to keep our eyes open for a lock that it might fit," he said.

"Sounds good to me." She was glad to know he was on the same page as far as finding her father's killer. "The goal is to attract Boyd but not the attention of anyone else."

"Right." Westley's phone dinged. He checked the incoming text message. "A couple more dogs have been found."

"That's good." She sent up a prayer that all the animals would be recovered safely. "What is the total count now?"

"We're still missing over forty dogs," he replied. "I can't grasp that Glory, Patriot, Liberty and Scout haven't returned."

"That's strange," she said. Worry twisted through her. "You don't think anything bad happened to them, do you?"

"I hope not. The dogs are valuable. All of them," he said. "But those four are our cream of the crop."

In his tone she heard the same anxiety she felt. Before she thought better of it, she threaded her fingers through his and gave his hand a squeeze. "They will be found."

"I wish I had your confidence," he said as he paused to open the driver's side of her car. "I hope they didn't find a way off the base."

"That would be scary," she said.

A Security Forces vehicle rolled up behind them and Ethan Webb leaned an elbow on the open windowsill. "Hey, you two. Where are you headed?"

Felicity assumed they'd go back to her house, but then her stomach rumbled, making her aware she hadn't eaten more than a few bites of the lunch she'd grabbed at the training center before she and Westley had gone to her house. She wondered if Westley had eaten today.

"I'm starving," she announced rather unceremoniously.

Both men stared at her.

She shrugged. There wasn't much in the way of groceries at home. "I want tacos and chips and salsa from La Taqueria."

Westley chuckled, a sound that sent a little tingle down her spine. "Then the BX it is."

The BX was the base's shopping center filled with popular restaurants and dry-good stores.

"I'll join you after I kennel, my partner, Titus," Ethan said.

"We need to take Dakota to the training center as well, so he can have his dinner," Westley said.

"Meet you there." Ethan drove away.

Felicity drove to the training center. Once there, they fed Dakota and checked on the dogs. Then they met Ethan outside. He was talking to Rusty.

Westley returned the salute. "Caleb tells me you brought in Winnie and Lacy."

Rusty nodded. His hazel eyes were troubled. "Yes, sir. They were wandering around the church grounds. Pastor Harmon called."

"There are more out there," Westley replied, a note of anxiety threaded through his words. "We need to find those dogs."

"Yes, sir." Rusty hustled away.

"You could have told him he'd done a good job," Felicity said to Westley. "A little encouragement goes a long way."

Westley cocked his head and studied her. "You don't think I'm encouraging?"

She barely stifled a snort. "No. You tend to be direct with your criticism and withhold your praise. And frankly—" She lifted her chin. Time to stand up to him and say what she'd been holding in for months. "It bugs me. It would be nice if every once in a while you said 'Well done. Good job. Way to go. You did good.'"

Westley raised an eyebrow. "If I'm not correcting you, you're doing it right."

The urge to roll her eyes was strong but she resisted and smiled sweetly. "Sometimes it's helpful to hear some encouragement."

"I'll take that under advisement," he said in a tone that grated on her nerves.

Ethan's laugh reminded her they weren't alone. "You two sound like an old married couple."

Felicity shot Ethan a glare. "Not even."

"We're moving from hungry to *hangry*," Westley murmured.

She opened her mouth to ask him how he dared to say that, but then she realized he was correct. Her hunger was making her irritable. "You're right." She sighed. "Can we go now?"

"I'll meet you there," Ethan said and headed to his vehicle.

"Your chariot awaits," Westley said with humor in his expression as he gestured to her car. Her insides turned to liquid and her heart did a little two-step in her chest.

The old adage Be Careful What You Wish For came to mind as he grinned at her. She'd wondered what it would be like to see him really smile when the force of a small grin was like taking a set of paws in the gut. How on earth was she going to survive spending so much time with him if he could make her knees weak with one grin?

SIX

Sated, Westley pushed his empty plate away. He'd enjoyed this respite except for the weight of the missing dogs pressing on his mind. The restaurant was noisy with conversation and music playing from speakers in the corner. A television attached to the wall showed a muted soccer game. Every time one of the two teams scored, the crowd cheered. Westley and Felicity sat side by side with their backs to the wall. He liked being able to see who was coming their way and to observe the crowd.

Plus, he wouldn't deny he liked having Felicity within arm's reach. In case of a threat, he told himself. Not because she was a beautiful woman. Which wasn't the best path for his thoughts to wander down, especially after nearly telling her about his father.

That kind of slip wouldn't be productive. The last thing he wanted was her pity.

Her anger he could take. She could chew him out all she wanted about not giving praise. He'd turned out just fine without receiving any.

Ethan Webb and Linc Colson occupied the other two seats at the table. Linc had arrived a few minutes after them. Apparently, Ethan had called him on his way to the eatery.

Westley couldn't remember the last time he'd sat in a restaurant with those he considered friends. Most of his meals were frozen, microwavable dishes eaten in the training-center break room. This was a nice change. He only wished it hadn't come at the cost of so many lives.

"I heard you mention you had leave coming up," Felicity said to Ethan. "Any fun plans?"

"Nothing firm," he replied. "After being overseas, it will be good to relax."

Having never been deployed, Westley could only imagine Ethan's need for some downtime.

A tall muscular man stopped by their table.

"Hey, Isaac," Westley said, standing to shake the Senior Airman's hand. "I'd heard you were back."

Isaac Goddard was a former combat pilot recently returned from Afghanistan.

"Yes, it's good to be home." Isaac's green eyes rested a moment on Felicity. "Hello."

She smiled at him. "Hi. We haven't met." She held out a hand. "Felicity Monroe."

The two shook hands and a strange sense of possessiveness spread through Westley. He wanted to put his arm around Felicity and claim her as his. Instead, he said, "You know Ethan and Linc?"

The other men rose to shake Isaac's hand and clap him on the back.

"Welcome home," Linc said.

"I heard you're trying to bring home a dog from Afghanistan," Ethan said.

Isaac nodded, his expression haunted. "That's right. I filed the paperwork to have Beacon sent to me."

Curious, Westley asked, "Is the dog injured?"

"No, he's a hero." Isaac rubbed his chin. "He saved my life."

"What kind of dog is Beacon?" Felicity asked.

"A German shepherd. I really hope the brass will let me bring him to the States. I'm afraid of what will happen to him if he stays there."

"We'll pray you and Beacon are reunited," Felicity said in a gentle tone.

Tenderness filled Westley at her thoughtful comment.

Isaac gave her an odd look. "Okay. Anything that helps. I'll see you all around." He walked away and they took their seats.

Felicity leaned close. "Uh-oh, here comes Heidi."

Sure enough, the female base reporter weaved her way through the crowded tables, heading straight for them. "Incoming," he said to the others.

Ethan and Linc swiveled to see who was approaching. Because they were in a casual setting, they dispensed with the formal salute.

As soon as Heidi reached the table, Linc held up a hand to the base reporter. "No comment."

"I know, I know," she said and adjusted her dark-framed glasses. "You all can't talk about the Red Rose Killer. That's not why I'm here."

Westley wasn't buying it. "Then why are you here?"

Heidi pointed to Felicity. "I understand you're being reassigned to the photo lab."

"Where did you hear that?" Westley asked. It wasn't a secret, or at least it wouldn't be once Felicity started roaming the base with her camera. But it was still disconcerting to know the information was out there already.

"I never reveal my sources," she said. "Is it true?"

Felicity sighed. "Yes, it is. Lieutenant General Hall asked if I'd take on the position because the current photographer is transferring off base."

Heidi edged closer to the table and took a notebook and pen from her purse. "Felicity, is this reassignment really because you're a target of Boyd Sullivan?"

"Hey," Ethan objected. "Didn't we just establish we're not discussing him?"

Heidi's eyebrows drew together, but she didn't acknowledge Ethan's words. "What qualifications do you have to be base photographer? Formal training?"

"I've taken some photography classes," Felicity replied.

Heidi made a note. "Won any awards? Had your work displayed in a gallery?"

Felicity shook her head and a red flush crept into her cheeks. "No."

Sensing how uncomfortable Felicity was, Westley said, "Enough with the questions. Lieutenant General Hall feels she's a good fit for the job. That's all that matters."

Heidi hitched the strap of her purse higher on her shoulder over her standard blue short-sleeve service shirt. "And I'm trying to do my job."

Felicity put a hand on his arm. "It's all right." To Heidi she said, "I'll be photographing the BMT graduates and their families Thursday. You might want to come and see how it goes."

There was gratitude in Heidi's smile. "I will. Thank you." She glanced around the table. "Are you all going to the memorial service tonight at the Canyon Christian Church? I understand Pastor Harmon will be doing a special tribute to the victims."

Westley's gut clenched. Felicity's fingers tightened on his arm. He could feel the tremor traveling through her. He covered her hand, offering what little comfort he could.

"Yes," Felicity said. "We're going."

Ethan and Linc nodded also.

"Then I will see you there." Heidi pivoted on her black flats and wove her way out of the restaurant.

"How did she know you were here?" Ethan asked Felicity.

Felicity shrugged. "I guess the base grapevine is alive and well."

Westley signaled to the waitress they were ready for their check.

After paying their bill, Westley and Felicity left the restaurant.

"I'd like to go home and freshen up before the service tonight," Felicity said as she put her car in Reverse.

"Of course," he said. "Let's stop by the training center so I can do the same. Then we'll go to your place."

She pursed her lips. "You really aren't going to let me out of your sight, are you?"

"Not if I can help it." He was tasked with keeping her safe. More like he'd demanded the detail, but he didn't need to explain that tidbit to her.

The Canyon Christian Church pews were filled as Felicity, with Westley at her side, filed into the large sanctuary. Everyone was standing, with arms around each other, as they sang "Amazing Grace."

Memories of her father's memorial service played through Felicity's mind. She'd sat in the front row with her mother at her side. They'd held on to each other in their grief while Pastor Harmon had spoken about her father's years of service and dedication to his country and his family. Felicity's heart had broken over the senseless accident.

But it wasn't an accident. He'd been murdered.

Acid burned through her chest. She placed her hand over her heart, feeling the outline of the key beneath her dress uniform.

"This way," Westley whispered in her ear, drawing her back to the present.

He guided her to a pew on the right, where an airman shuffled over to make room for them. Westley stepped aside so she could move past him. She couldn't stop herself from giving him an appreciative glance. He wore his dress uniform well.

The navy jacket fit his broad shoulders and tapered down to his trim waist. She thought him handsome in his battle-ready uniform and in civilian clothes, but in the dress blues, he was hotter than the Texas sun in July.

She gave herself a mental head slap as she stood next to her friend Rae Fallon, a rookie fighter pilot. Rae smiled at her with sad eyes and put her arm through Felicity's.

Emotion welled within Felicity as Westley placed his arm around her waist. His compassion and willingness to comfort her in public sent surprise cascading over her, warming her from the inside out. But then the rational side of her brain kicked in. Everyone had an arm around the person next to them. He was simply following suit. She wouldn't read more in to it. Instead she focused on how good it was to be a part of something so much bigger than herself. And seeing the camaraderie among her fellow servicemen and -women gave her comfort.

When the music ended, everyone sat and Pastor Harmon approached the podium. On the big screens behind him, four images appeared—Airman Landon Martelli, Airman Tamara Peterson, Airman Stephen Bulter and basic military training commander Chief Master Sergeant Clint Lockwood.

Tears sprang to Felicity's eyes. Her heart hurt for the loss of the fellow MWD K-9 trainers, the commissary cook and the father of her friend Maisy.

After Pastor Harmon's touching eulogy for the murdered air-force personnel, Felicity and Westley left the church with the crowd.

"We'll head back to the training center to grab Dakota before going to your house," Westley told her.

She nodded. Her spirit felt heavy with the weight of grief and anger. Why had Boyd come back to the base to kill? Why hadn't he just disappeared once he escaped prison? She could only imagine how warped his mind was to make him risk returning to Canyon to spread his evil.

"Westley," Captain Justin Blackwood called from the sidewalk, where he stood with his sixteen-year-old daughter, Portia, who'd only a year ago come to live with Justin after her mother died.

Felicity and Westley veered off their path and stopped by Justin. "Sir," Westley said with a salute. Felicity followed suit.

Justin returned their greeting with his own salute. Felicity had to press her lips together to stop a smile when she noticed Portia roll her eyes and duck her head to stare at her phone.

Felicity remembered what it was like to be the daughter of an officer in the United States Air Force. All the protocols, the pomp and circumstance, that to a young girl seemed over-the-top. But Felicity had grown to appreciate the steady nature of the military. She hoped one day Portia would as well.

"How are we with the dog situation?" Justin asked.

"Rounding up more every hour, sir," Westley replied.

"Good." He rubbed a hand over his jaw. "Now if we could only find Boyd Sullivan. We found out how he got on base."

"We heard," Westley said. "But once on base, someone had to have hid him. Do we know who yet?"

"Unfortunately, no. But we're still combing through the personnel, looking for anything that might point to his accomplice."

"Did someone talk to his half sister?" Felicity asked.

"She's been questioned. She admitted to visiting her brother in prison but denies helping him in any way. Do you know her?"

"We've met briefly, but no, I don't know her," Felicity replied. Even though the base could feel small and isolated at times, there were too many people on base to become friends with everyone.

Justin nodded, his gaze going to something over her shoulder. She turned to see Heidi standing close by. Boy, she never gave up.

Felicity turned back toward the captain and noticed the other base reporter, John Robinson, lurking by the lamppost, obviously trying to eavesdrop on their conversation. They clearly had a tag team going. She nudged Westley and directed his attention to John.

Westley shook his head. "Vultures. Sir, we should table any more discussion until the meeting tomorrow."

"Agreed. Good night. Be careful," Justin said before turning away and ushering his daughter to the parking lot.

Because the church was only a few blocks from the training center, they had parked there and, walked over. Now twilight had slipped to night. A million stars twinkled in the sky and the moon rose in a crescent over the base. In some ways so ordinary. A typical night in Texas. However, today had been anything but ordinary.

Four people were dead.

A killer was on the loose.

And she'd learned her father's death had been murder.

Tension coiled through her as she walked. Her pace picked up.

"Eager to get home?" Westley murmured as he matched her stride.

"Eager to put this day behind me," she replied.

He snorted his agreement and slipped a warm hand around her elbow. It was a gentlemanly gesture. Protective. Possessive.

Her heart fluttered.

In a panic, her gaze leaped to the stop sign ahead as if her brain was sending her a warning.

Don't go any further with that train of thought.

Letting herself believe his actions had any deeper meaning beyond protecting her from Boyd Sullivan was foolish.

The crowd from the church thinned the farther away

they walked from the building. They passed the dentist offices and rec center. The veterinarian clinic's lights were on and Felicity waved to the receptionist in the window. As they crossed the parking lot for the vet clinic, the sound of an engine turning over marred the quiet night. Odd. The streetlamp that normally kept the lot lit up at night was dark.

"Hurry," Westley said.

Sensing his tension, she quickened her pace even more. Tires squealed as a car shot forward. Felicity caught a glimpse of a chrome grill before Westley's arm snaked around her waist and he lifted her off the ground.

With her wrapped in his arms, he dove out of the way seconds before the vehicle roared past, barely missing them. They landed hard on the pavement, Westley taking the brunt of the fall, Felicity landing on top of him. For a long, silent moment neither moved.

Heart in her throat, she said, "Are you okay?"

He grunted in reply. "Up."

Realizing she was squishing his midsection, she disentangled herself from his hold and rolled to the side in a sitting position. In the dark, she reached for him, finding his shoulder as he sat up.

"That was close."

She sucked in a breath at his words. Too close. Someone had tried to run them down. "That was a base vehicle. One they use to move the planes."

"We need to alert security."

"Can you stand?" she asked.

"Yes," he barked out.

She didn't take his tone personally as she rose and helped him to his feet. He was allowed to be cranky after dodging a speeding truck. "Thank you for saving my life."

"Saved both our bacon," he said. "That maniac would have mowed us both over."

"True," she said past the tension lodged in her chest like a rock.

Only when they were inside the training center did she see that Westley's uniform jacket was ripped at the elbow and blood seeped from a scrape. While he made the call to Security Forces, she went in search of gauze and alcohol wipes.

She ran in to Bobby Stevens, an airman and new trainer who'd only been at the center for a month.

"Hey, Bobby," she said.

He saluted. His gaze took in the items she held. "Everything okay?"

"Westley's injured," she told him. "I got it."

"What happened?" Bobby followed her to Westley's office, where he was still on the phone.

Not sure she if should say anything, remembering Ian's warning of not trusting anyone, she fudged. "A little mishap, that's all."

Westley ended his call and said, "Bobby. How are the dogs?"

"Good, sir," Bobby replied with a salute.

Westley returned the salute with a wince. No doubt from his injured elbow. "Make sure to let the vet know if any of the dogs seem off. You never know what any one of them could have eaten."

Bobby nodded and hurried away.

To Felicity, Westley said, "Let's get Dakota and go."

She frowned and held up the gauze and wipes. "Let me dress your wound."

"Later." He came around his desk and went to a closet, where he grabbed a duffel bag. "Let's go."

By the time they made it outside with Dakota trotting alongside them, two Security Forces vehicles rolled to a stop. Linc hopped out of one and Justin out of the other.

Justin strode to their side. "What happened?"

After Westley explained, Felicity spoke up. "I recognized the vehicle as one of the trucks that push the planes around the runway."

"Did you get the license number?" Linc asked.

"It had been removed," she told them.

To Linc, Justin said, "Put out an alert. Anyone sees one of those trucks missing a plate needs to report in." Linc nodded and headed back to his vehicle. To Westley and Felicity Justin asked, "Any chance you saw the driver?"

They both shook their heads.

"We were too busy diving out of the way," Westley remarked drily.

Justin rubbed his chin. "Last we heard, a civilian reported spotting Boyd a few hours away. But that person could be mistaken and he could actually be on base."

"Or the driver could be someone else," Felicity said. Her gaze met Westley's.

"The one who ransacked your house?" Justin looked thoughtful. "Why try to hurt you?"

She didn't have an answer. It was one thing to think the villain was searching for the file on the hit-and-run. Now was he trying to kill her?

A shiver of fear went through her. Dakota edged closer and touched his nose to her hand. The dog apparently sensed her upset.

"I'm taking Felicity home," Westley said. "Dakota and I will be on twenty-four-hour duty."

Felicity wanted to say that it wasn't necessary, but she wasn't about to put herself in a vulnerable position just because she was uncomfortable with the idea of Westley in her home.

Though *uncomfortable* wasn't exactly the right word. More like she'd be hyperaware of him and that would mess with her head. She was struggling as it was to keep her feelings from veering into territory she'd rather not explore. Yet, she couldn't come up with a logical protest that wouldn't reveal her feelings.

"All right then. Stay safe." Justin drove away, as did Linc.

Deciding it would be better to take the small SUV Westley used for transporting dogs across base, they left her car parked in the lot. They loaded Dakota into the back and then both climbed in the front. After buckling up, she turned to Westley. His strong jaw was set in a tense line. His capable hands gripped the steering wheel.

Emotion clogged her throat. He'd risked his life for her. And she had no doubt he would do so again if necessary.

"Thank you again. I appreciate your willingness to see to my safety." Inwardly she groaned at the stiff and formal way she spoke when she was nervous.

Westley sat silent for a moment, then he looked at her. "The truth is I should have known that car was there. I should have been prepared for something to happen. I won't be caught unaware again."

"Please, you couldn't have foreseen the near miss with the base truck. I didn't see it."

"But it's my job to see the threat before it gets to you."

"You're not a superhero," she said.

He snorted. "Maybe that's what you need. Someone else who will protect you better."

A flutter of panic hit her out of the blue. "Stop it. I want you to protect me. Now start this car and get us home." She sat back and tried not to think about how true those words were. She couldn't imagine putting her life into anyone else's hands.

But what about her heart? Was that safe as well?

I want you to protect me.

As Westley sat on the leather couch in the living room of the Monroe home, Felicity's words reverberated through his mind.

She had no idea how much those words rocked his world. No one had ever wanted him for anything. Not his father or his mother. Not the foster parents he'd been sloughed off to after his mom had dumped him off at child protective services. Okay, that wasn't totally accurate. There had been one foster mother who had treated him with kindness, but then he'd been yanked from the home after a fight with another foster kid.

He'd hardened his heart long ago against the need to be wanted.

But with those words Felicity had turned him to mush.

As he helped her put her house back in order, he'd tried to keep an emotional and physical distance. He'd been relieved when she'd finally bid him good-night and had gone upstairs.

Above his head a floorboard creaked. He was hypersensitive to every movement she made as she settled in for the night.

He leaned back against the cushion. From this vantage point he had a clear view of the front door, the back door and the door to the garage. Dakota laid down across the threshold to the stairs after he'd done a perimeter check. They were on guard and ready, should any danger appear.

Felicity was as safe as they could make her.

Even still, Westley sent up a prayer that God would surround the house with protection. The thought of how easily that truck could have taken out Felicity pierced him with an unnerving fear of losing her.

Of failing her, he amended.

When no more noise came from upstairs, Westley heaved a relieved sigh and hoped she would be able to rest after the day she'd had. Being a target of the Red Rose Killer, then discovering the awful truth that her father had been murdered and then someone trying to take her life—it was more than most people could handle in such a short time. Yet, Felicity was strong in spirit and personality. Stronger than he'd ever given her credit for. Her father would be proud of her.

Westley was proud of her. His respect and admiration for her had increased tenfold. How could he go from thinking she was annoying to realizing she was so special? Special and beautiful. Kind and smart.

Just because he was noticing her good qualities didn't mean he had any intention of becoming romantically involved. He wasn't looking for a romance with the pretty staff sergeant.

In fact, any sort of relationship would only end in disaster. He believed that with his whole being.

He wasn't cut out for commitment. He wasn't the kind of guy a woman should pin her hopes on. According to his mother, he had too much of his father in him.

And too much of his mother.

Both were scarred and dysfunctional. Stood to reason that he was damaged goods, too. He'd promised himself long ago he would never saddle another person with his horrible baggage. And the last person he ever wanted to dump his past on was Felicity. She deserved better than the likes of him.

He would protect her with his life.

But he had a sinking feeling protecting his heart wouldn't be as easy.

SEVEN

In the bright morning light that had her squinting, Felicity followed the smell of brewing coffee and spicy sausage into the kitchen. She halted on the threshold.

Her sleep-fogged brain processed the sight of Dakota lying by the back door. He lifted his head from his chew bone and wagged his tail in greeting, while Westley stood at the stove wearing her father's black barbecue apron over his battle-ready pants and a white T-shirt that molded to the hard planes and angles of his chest and back. His dark hair was spiky on top and his strong jaw was shadowed by stubble.

The pull of attraction zinged through her veins. Beneath her fresh battle-ready uniform, a blush warmed her skin.

He glanced her way. Appreciation gleamed in his blue eyes and he flashed her a crooked grin. "Hope you like chorizo and eggs. It's all I could find that was edible in your refrigerator besides salad dressing."

"Smells delicious." Stifling the urge to flip back her hair, she walked to the coffeemaker and poured herself a mug before taking a seat at the counter. "I haven't been shopping in a while."

"We'll remedy that today," he commented as he turned off the flame beneath the fry pan.

Having only seen him eat prepared meals, she said, "I didn't know you cooked."

"I can on occasion." He dished out the steaming scrambled eggs and sausage onto two plates.

"My dad taught me the basics, enough that I can get by." She let out a wry laugh. "I'm still not comfortable with a steak or fish."

"I can show you how to grill a flawless steak or poach a fish to perfection."

Somehow his words didn't strike her as a boast, but were simply a statement of fact. The man knew how to do things.

"That would be great." The idea of him giving her a cooking lesson thrilled her more than she cared to admit. "Did your mother teach you?"

Westley set a plate in front of her along with a fork and stared at her a moment before replying. "One of my foster mothers was a gourmet chef and she made it a point to teach each kid that came through her home how to cook. She made cooking fun and interesting. She let us experiment with food and spices and such."

Absorbing his words, Felicity wasn't sure what to say. Remembering how he'd shut her down yesterday when she'd asked about his father, she hesitated probing further. But then again, he'd volunteered the information. She could hear the fondness in his voice as he spoke of the foster parent who'd taken the time to teach him to cook, but she couldn't help but hurt for his lack of a normal childhood. "How many foster homes were you in?"

Carrying his plate, he came around the island and sat beside her. "Four."

Her hurt for him quadrupled. "How old were you when you entered the system?"

"Ten."

But his father hadn't passed on until Westley was seventeen, she recalled. Obviously, there was more to the story there. Curiosity drove her to ask another question. "What happened to your parents?"

"Let's bless this food and eat it before it gets cold," he said.

She bowed her head. "Dear Lord, bless this food to our bodies and our bodies to Your service. Amen."

When she raised her gaze, she found Westley staring at her.

"My dad's blessing," she explained.

"I like it." He shoveled a forkful of egg and sausage into his mouth.

He wasn't going to make it easy to get him to open up. And for the life of her she couldn't understand why it was so important that he did. Granted, they would be together, close together, for the foreseeable future and she was putting her life in his hands. Trusting him to have her back.

Getting to know each other better seemed logical. Practical. It would deepen the trust between them. But she could be patient. Letting the subject drop for now, she ate, enjoying the heat of the meat-infused eggs.

After her last bite, she sighed with contentment. "My dad would make this combo on Saturday mornings. My mom didn't like the spiciness. But I love it. Thank you so much."

"I guessed as much last night when you asked for extra jalapeños in your tacos. And you're welcome."

She grinned. "I own stock in antacids."

His laugh was rich and deep and shuddered through her with a delicious wave of warmth.

His cell phone rang. He set his fork on his empty plate and excused himself to take the call. He opened the back door, letting Dakota outside while he stepped onto the porch. Felicity could hear the low murmur of his voice as she washed their dishes and the frying pan, then set them on the drying rack next to the sink.

Westley returned to the kitchen. "That was Justin. The meeting has been moved up. We need to get to base command pronto."

"Let me just brush my teeth and I'll be ready to go." She hurried upstairs, forcing from her mind all thoughts of cooking lessons, foster homes and delicious male laughter. She needed to stay focused.

After securing her hair into a regulation braid with the ends tucked out of sight under her beret, she finished getting ready. She paused on the landing to the stairs. Below, Westley had squatted down to Dakota and was rubbing him behind the ears. The dog's eyes practically rolled back into his head with pleasure. Her insides melted a little at the show of affection between dog and man. And some part of her yearned to have that same sort of attention directed to her.

She nearly snorted aloud at the ridiculous thought. *Get a grip*, she told herself. Just because Westley was being nice to her while he was forced to have her underfoot didn't mean she had to go all mushy about him. Still, she couldn't deny the tender feelings growing in her heart. She ached at the thought that he'd grown up in foster care. She wondered why. What had happened to put him in that position?

Patience, she reminded herself. Her father always said she had a gift for getting others to open up. She'd redirected that ability to the dogs while working with them. Eventually, she'd crack Westley's hard shell and work the story out of him. She only hoped she was brave enough to handle whatever she found inside.

Westley held open the door to base command for Felicity to enter before him. Carrying her camera bag over her shoulder, she smiled her thanks to him as she passed to enter the building. She had a great smile that reached her blue-green eyes. Something he'd tried hard in the past not to notice because he'd been her commanding officer.

Right now, though, he let himself take all of her in, including the vanilla scent wafting from her hair. This morning when she'd come downstairs for breakfast she'd worn the long strands loose and swinging before she'd braided it and tucked up under her beret. He liked that she wore a minimal amount of makeup, just enough to highlight her already pretty features.

He gave himself a mental shake as they were ushered into the conference room. He needed to keep his head in the game and ignore the attraction and affection for Felicity building in his chest. He couldn't believe he'd confessed he'd been in foster care. Revealing such intimate details of his past hadn't been intentional, yet talking about the woman who'd taught him to cook to Felicity had come easily. It distressed him how easy a lot of things were with Felicity.

The conference room was filled, every chair at the

table taken. Ian leaned against the wall and nodded in greeting as Westley and Felicity took positions beside him. Base commander Lieutenant General Hall seated at the head of the long table, held up a hand to gain the room's attention.

To the right of the lieutenant general sat FBI agent Oliver Davison and to the lieutenant general's left was Justin. Also seated at the table were Linc, Ethan and several other members of the Security Forces.

Westley was surprised to see Ethan Webb's ex-wife, Jillian Masters, seated at the table as well. She wore her US Marine dress uniform and a scowl on her face. Apparently, she wasn't on base by choice. Westley met Ethan's gaze. The tension in his friend's eyes was palpable.

Also at the table, seated next to Justin, was a pretty redhead dressed in civilian clothes and clearly very pregnant, while a tall, imposing man, also a civilian by the looks of his Western-style jeans and button-down shirt, stood behind her with his hands on the back of her chair.

"Let's get this briefing going," Lieutenant General Hall said. "I'd like to introduce Deputy Sheriff Serena Hargrove and her husband, Jason Hargrove, former Dallas PD. Together with Deputy Hargrove's K-9, they brought down Boyd Sullivan the first go-round."

A murmur rippled through the room. Westley had read the news reports of how the deputy and her K-9 partner, an English springer spaniel trained in wilderness air search, had tracked Boyd to a remote cabin in the Texas Hill Country. He'd like to talk to the officer about her canine and look in to adding the specialized work to the training center. But that would have to wait until life returned to normal. As long as Sullivan was on the loose, Westley's focus was to protect Felicity.

"Deputy, what can you tell us about Boyd?" Lieutenant General Hall asked.

The woman's lips twisted. "He has a sick mind, but make no mistake, he is intelligent and sly. He doesn't do anything without careful planning. And his ego is as big as the State of Texas."

Lieutenant Preston Flanigan, one of the Security Forces members, leaned forward. "How did *you* manage to catch him?"

Preston had been in the last K-9 training session. Westley thought the young cop was a bit too impatient, but hoped the guy would chill eventually. He'd have to if he hoped to be a K-9 handler.

Serena spared him a glance then focused back on Lieutenant General Hall. "Boyd hadn't expected my partner, Ginger. She's small, but mighty. She caught him by surprise and distracted him long enough for me to apprehend him."

"I was there," Oliver said. "I can vouch that Serena and her little dog acted bravely. The arrest was a good one."

"Do you think that's why he messed with the kennels and released all the dogs? Hoped we'd be too busy recovering them to search for him?" Linc said.

Jason Hargrove spoke up. "Having spent more time with Sullivan than I care to ever repeat, I can tell you he believes he can outsmart anyone. I have no doubt he thought the chaos would afford him time and opportunity to move freely."

"Which it did," Justin stated. "Did Boyd have a partner in Dill?"

Serena shook her head. "Not that we know of. There was no indication of one."

Lieutenant General Hall's gaze zeroed on Ian. "What about the cook?"

"The medical examiner says cause of death was strangulation," Ian replied.

"Stephen Butler's ID badge was used to gain access at the south gate at oh-four-hundred," Justin explained. "We're still working on how Boyd got off the base after the attacks."

"Are we sure he left?" Ethan asked. "Just because the news reported sightings of him, we can't know for sure if he's off base or not." His gaze slid to his ex-wife and then away.

Jillian's lips twisted, but the woman made no comment.

Justin nodded. "That's true. Which is why the base is on high alert with extra security at the gates. And Baylor Marine Base is also coordinating their effort with ours to find the escaped prisoner before he hurts anyone else."

Lieutenant General Hall rose. "I want Sullivan found. And the person who is helping him. Am I clear?"

A chorus of "Yes, sir" filled the room.

"Dismissed," Lieutenant General Hall said. He turned to the two civilians. "Thank you for coming all this way."

"I wish we could be more help," the deputy said as her husband helped her to her feet.

Felicity leaned close to whisper in Westley's ear. "We should talk to her about wilderness air-search training."

Having her echo his earlier thought made him grin. "Good idea."

She held his gaze for a moment. Something flared in her eyes before she quickly looked away. A slight pink tinged her cheeks. He wasn't sure what he'd seen. Approval? Attraction? Disconcerted, he pushed aside the thought and followed the Hargroves out of the conference room.

After introducing himself and Felicity, he said, "I would love to hear about the wilderness air-search training you did with your K-9 partner."

"If you give me your contact info, I can put you in touch with the trainer that we used," Serena said.

"I'd appreciate that." He gave her his cell-phone number and email address then bid them goodbye.

Westley escorted Felicity to the photo lab for her new assignment.

"Deputy Hargrove looked like she was uncomfortable," Felicity said. "She has to be close to her due date."

Westley made a noncommittal noise. He didn't know anything about due dates or pregnancies in humans. Dog gestation periods he understood.

Setting her camera bag on an empty desk, Felicity peered at him with curiosity shining in her eyes. "Do you ever think you'll have your own kids?"

"Me?" He nearly choked on the word. "No. What about you?"

She shrugged. "Maybe. If I find the right man to share my life with."

He told himself to forget it. It was none of his business but the words flowed off his tongue before he could stop himself. "Ever been close to walking down the aisle?"

She let out a laugh that was half bitter and half self-effacing. "Hardly." A flicker of hurt crossed her face before she turned away to busy herself unpacking her bag. He didn't like to think some guy had caused her pain.

"Why do you say it like that?"

She shrugged. "I haven't found anyone I click with, I guess. The men I've dated were disappointing." Her lips twisted. "Or rather I was the disappointment. Maybe my expectations are too high."

He couldn't imagine anyone being disappointed in her. She was fun and smart, and pretty. "You have criteria?"

She smiled faintly. "Yes. I want sparks," she said. "I want to be loved as I am. I want to share my faith as well as my life with the man I give my heart to."

"Those sound reasonable," he murmured. He wondered if she felt the sparks that he did whenever they were together. Probably not.

It was best not to let himself put too much stock in his attraction to the lovely sergeant. Their situation was temporary. They both had jobs to do. And when the killers—Boyd and the person who murdered her father—were arrested and locked away, Westley and Felicity would return to the training center and life would resume as before. And if he kept telling himself that eventually he'd make it happen.

She peered at him with curiosity shining in her eyes. "What about you?"

He should have expected the question. His stomach twisted. "Marriage isn't something I plan on tackling."

She frowned. "Why not?"

How could he explain he was afraid his father and mother's pattern of behavior would somehow play out in his life? That he wouldn't ever risk letting anyone close enough to find out?

The door to the photo lab opened and Commander Lieutenant General Hall walked in, saving Westley from replying. Westley and Felicity snapped to attention and saluted.

Lieutenant General Hall returned the salute. "At ease."

Relaxing, Westley moved aside to allow the lieutenant general to address Felicity.

"I see you're settling in," Lieutenant General Hall commented.

"Just starting to, sir," she said.

"You know your assignment?"

"Take as many photos as possible all over base in the hope I capture Boyd's image," she replied. "Or his interest."

Westley's gut clenched at her words. He'd be with her, by her side to protect her, but it didn't make stomaching the fact that she was being dangled out like a piece of squid to hook a shark any more appealing.

Lieutenant General Hall clapped her on the shoulder. "You've got heart, Staff Sergeant Monroe. Your father would be very proud of you."

Surprise marched across her face before her expression softened. "Thank you, sir. That means a lot to me."

Westley wondered why she always appeared amazed when anyone mentioned her father's pride in her.

"Sir, I'd like to carry a service weapon," Felicity said.

Lieutenant General Hall frowned. "Only Security Forces personnel are allowed to carry on base. It would raise too many questions if the base photographer carried."

Westley sensed her frustration. He could appreciate

her need to have a sidearm. But she would have to be content to have him and Dakota at her side.

"Master Sergeant James," Lieutenant General Hall said, focusing his eagle-eyed gaze on Westley. "I trust you and your dog will keep Staff Sergeant Monroe from harm?"

Squaring his shoulders, Westley met Lieutenant General Hall with a level gaze. "Of course, sir. With our lives."

Westley heard Felicity's sharp inhale but he kept his attention on Lieutenant General Hall.

"Very good. Keep my office informed and be careful." Lieutenant General Hall left the room.

Once the door closed, Felicity stepped close and scrutinized him with a pinched brow. "Did you mean that?"

He blinked, unsure what she referred to. Was she jumping back to their conversation about marriage? "Excuse me?"

"That you'd protect me with your life?"

Relieved by the question, he nodded. "Absolutely."

Looking pleased, she grabbed her camera. "Then we'd best get to it."

Felicity had been the base photographer for two days and she loved it. Some of the photos would be used for PR, others for the base newsletter, website and social media.

She loved the freedom to roam unfettered, to capture moments that might otherwise go unnoticed. Loved the joy of not having to be exacting with the lighting and the composition of the shots, but rather catching unposed, unscripted action shots of airmen going about their day, or contemplative images of the various personnel across the expanse of the base.

And having Westley and Dakota at her side, knowing they had her back, allowed her to focus on the camera.

They stopped at the edge of the training obstacle course, where a basic military-training unit ran through the obstacles. She adjusted the f-stop and clicked off a multitude of shots. And she knew that some were spectacular. Not all, but there would be some she'd be proud of. Over the last two days it seemed she'd taken more pictures than she had her whole life. The SD card was nearly full. They'd taken a few breaks to eat lunch, to let Dakota rest and to use the facilities. Soon they would stop for the day and head back to base command.

A gust of wind whipped her hair into her eyes. Her braid had completely fallen apart over an hour ago, so she'd tied her hair back with a rubber band, but the ends were still giving her grief in the Texas breeze.

"Here. Hold this." She handed her camera to Westley so she could free up her hands. Then she adjusted the strap of her camera bag across her body into a more comfortable position.

After securing her hair into a bun at her nape, she took the camera back and lifted the lens to her eye, clicking through more shots. Something in the background moved in the woods beyond the young airmen. She zoomed in.

A tan dog peeked out from around the trunk of a tree. Her heart rate ticked up. "Westley, there's a Belgian about forty meters straight out behind the tree with the crooked top."

She handed him the camera so he could use the lens to see what she had. "Niko."

Taking the camera back, she said, "You should go get him."

"*We'll* go get him," he countered. "Come on."

Inordinately pleased by his inclusion of her even though she knew he simply wanted her near for her safety, she jogged with him and Dakota to the wooded area that made up the back part of the base.

Westley whistled, catching the dog's attention. "Niko. Come."

The dog hesitated. Felicity was afraid the dog would bolt. From her camera bag she grabbed the banana she'd taken from the commissary at lunch. She unpeeled the fruit and then broke off a piece. Holding it in her hand so that it was visible to the dog, she dangled it low against her thigh. "Come. Treat."

Niko's nose twitched, then he was loping toward her, clearly wanting the offered banana. As soon as his mouth touched the fruit, Westley grabbed Niko's collar.

Westley met her gaze. "Well done."

She blinked. For a moment her old defenses rose, making her wonder if he was mocking her after the tirade she'd heaped on his head about being stingy with his praise, but his expression was open and his approval appeared genuine. She grinned. "Thank you."

Westley threaded Dakota's lead through Niko's collar so the two dogs were tied together. "Let's get this guy to the vet and make sure he's okay."

They loaded the dogs into Westley's vehicle and drove to the other side of the base. The vet checked out the dog and declared him slightly dehydrated but otherwise in good health. Felicity was thankful. She worried about the remaining missing dogs and prayed they would be found soon.

"They'll start making their way back. Just like Niko did," Westley told her as if he sensed her anxious thoughts.

Strange that in such a short time they would be so connected, she thought. "I'm sure you're right."

After dropping Niko off with Caleb at the training center and feeding Dakota dinner, Felicity was anxious to get the photos uploaded so she could go home and put her feet up.

Once they arrived back at base command, she made quick work of uploading the images and sending them to the FBI database. As she settled into the passenger seat of Westley's vehicle, she yawned.

"Don't fall asleep on me yet," Westley told her. "We've got to go to the BX and buy some more groceries."

She groaned. "Can't we order something to go?"

He let out a scoffing laugh. "I have a feeling you do that often."

"It's easier," she admitted. Most nights she was too tired to bother with making her own food.

"Fine. How about a hamburger and fries?"

"I'll take a hamburger and a salad," she countered.

They drove to the nearest burger joint located near the BX, ordered and headed back to her house. He unpacked the takeout bag while she filled glasses with water and snagged her favorite salad dressing from the refrigerator. Westley blessed their meal, and then dug in to his burger and fries.

She shook the bottle of dressing before pouring a generous amount over the lettuce and assorted vegetables.

Westley raised an eyebrow. "Drowning your greens, huh?"

A low rumble emanated from Dakota's throat. His gaze was on Felicity. She made a face. "What's he doing?"

"I don't know," Westley said. "Dakota, sit."

The dog continued to stare at her while he obeyed the command.

Stabbing her fork into the salad, she took a bite.

Dakota barked and jumped onto the table. Using his nose, he knocked her salad to the floor, making a huge mess.

"Hey!" she protested.

Dakota put his nose to Felicity's mouth and whined. She held herself still, unsure what was happening. Would the dog attack? She couldn't wrap her mind around his strange behavior.

Westley scrambled out of his chair and grabbed Dakota by the collar and yanked him to the floor. "I've never seen him do that before."

Felicity's stomach roiled. Sweat broke out across her body. "I'm going to be sick."

She clamped a hand over her mouth and swallowed convulsively.

"Felicity!"

She heard Westley's voice, heard the panic, the fear, but she couldn't respond as the world titled, swam out of focus. She listed to the side, sliding off the chair onto the floor, but the impact barely registered. Her mind screamed a warning. Something was wrong. Very, very wrong.

EIGHT

Heart pounding in his ears, Westley dove to his knees beside Felicity where she'd fallen to the kitchen floor. Dakota whined. He'd dropped to his belly, his nose stretched out to Felicity.

Her eyes were closed. Westley couldn't tell if she was breathing.

Please, Lord. I can't take another death.

Lungs frozen in dread, he pressed his fingers against the tender skin of her neck. He felt the steady thrum of her pulse beating there. She was alive. The tight vise that had gripped his chest expanded, allowing him to breathe. Had she had a seizure? That would explain Dakota's behavior. Some dogs had the uncanny ability to sense an oncoming seizure. Westley had never seen it happen and hadn't known Dakota was that sensitive.

He yanked his phone from his pocket and dialed 911. He quickly explained to the dispatcher the issue and gave the address. Keeping the line open, he set down the phone and placed a hand to Felicity's cheek. Her skin was clammy.

The pungent odor of the salad dressing invaded his senses. His mind replayed the scene in his head. Dakota had acted strange immediately after Felicity had opened the dressing bottle. If the dog's disobedience wasn't enough, he'd attacked her salad bowl, sending it flying.

A knot of apprehension twisted in Westley's gut. His gaze flew to the dressing bottle still standing on the dining table. Had the contents been tampered with? Had Dakota picked up a deadly scent?

Fear sidled up and choked him.

The sound of sirens rent the air. He jumped to his feet and ran to the front door, opening it wide and urging the paramedics inside.

"She's got a pulse but it's weak," he told them. "I think she may have been poisoned."

"Westley?" Justin rushed to his side. "I heard the call come in."

Glad to have his captain's support, Westley told him what had happened while the paramedics tended to Felicity. "The dressing. It needs to be tested for poison."

"I'll take care of it and Dakota," Justin said. "You go with Felicity."

Westley nodded and hustled after the paramedics as they loaded Felicity into the back bay of the ambulance. Taking a seat on the bench next to her, he took her hand. "Felicity, stay with me, okay?"

She looked so vulnerable lying there with an oxygen mask covering half her face. He hated seeing her like this. He wanted her to wake up and chew him out again. He wanted to see her smile and hear her laugh. Feelings he'd been trying to contain bubbled up, escaping the compartment he'd stuffed them into. If he was being honest with himself, he would admit that he'd grown to care for the young staff sergeant. No, *care* wasn't the right word. He was falling for her in ways that terrified him. He lifted her hand to his lips and kissed her knuckles. She had to be okay.

He bowed his head and silently prayed like he'd never prayed before.

At the hospital, Felicity was whisked away behind the closed doors of the emergency room. Westley was barred from following. He paced the waiting area as frustration and fear spiraled through him.

He spotted First Lieutenant Vanessa Gomez at the nurses' station and rushed over. "Lieutenant Gomez."

"Master Sergeant James." She acknowledged his salute. "Can I help you?"

"Yes." He told her about Felicity. "Can you check on her? Please?"

"Of course." Concern laced Vanessa's voice. Without another word, she hurried through the swinging door and disappeared.

An interminable amount of time ticked by as Westley continued to pace until Vanessa finally returned. "Dr. Knight will be out shortly to talk to you."

"Is she…" He couldn't get the words to come out.

"They are working on her." Compassion shone in her eyes. "You have to trust she'll be okay."

He nodded. He wanted to trust that God would save her. Westley hated the feeling of helplessness stealing over him.

Finally, a doctor in a white lab coat approached. The name tag on his breast pocket read Dr. Trevor Knight. "Are you Master Sergeant James?"

"Yes." Westley's heart stuttered as he waited to hear the news. "How is Felicity?"

"She's going to be fine," Trevor assured him. "Because of the suspected poison, we administered activated charcoal and pumped fluids to flush her system. We heard from Security Forces that the tainted salad dressing contained crushed hemlock leaves. Very toxic and fast-acting. If you hadn't reacted swiftly..." The doctor didn't say it, but Westley knew the potential outcome. "But the staff sergeant ingested such a small amount that there shouldn't be any residual aftereffects."

"Thank you." Palpable relief coursed through Westley's veins. "When can I see her?"

"She's resting now, but you're welcome to sit with her," Trevor said. "Follow me."

He led Westley to a private room. Felicity was lying in the bed, a blanket tucked around her as she slept. Her loose, light brown hair spilled over the pillow, making his mouth dry. He moved to sit beside the bed and brushed a few stray strands of hair from her face. Dark lashes rested against her cheeks.

He took her hand, so soft and warm, and settled back to wait for her to wake up, though he had no idea how to proceed from here. He'd grown attached to this beautiful, spirited woman. But how could he ever act on his feelings when doing so would jeopardize both of their careers in the air force? No, he had to find a way to stuff his emotions back into their boxes and maintain a professional distance from Felicity.

Unfortunately, he had a feeling that might be as easy as bottling her laughter.

"You're going to be okay."

Felicity pressed her lips together to keep a chuckle from escaping. From the moment she'd awoken in the hospital with Westley holding her hand, he'd been comforting, soothing, and had assured her that she hadn't ingested enough of the poison inside the tainted bottle of salad dressing to cause any permanent damage. "So you've said for at least the tenth time."

After being discharged, Westley had brought her home and insisted she rest on the couch. He'd put an afghan over her, fluffed a pillow behind her head and brought her a tall glass of water.

She should be annoyed by his incessant need to treat her like an invalid except the relief, concern and tenderness in his eyes made her heart pound. She couldn't deny she liked having his attention, the good kind, lavished on her. He made her feel special and cared for. His haggard appearance was testament to having slept by her bedside in the hospital last night. Only a man who cared would do that, right?

She had no idea what to do with the thought, so she tucked it away for safekeeping.

"Sorry. I'm hovering." He frowned, clearly befuddled by his own behavior.

She captured his hand and gave a gentle squeeze. "It's all right. I'm sure it was scary. I'm grateful for Dakota or I'd have kept eating the salad."

"He's a hero."

She turned her focus to the dog in question. He sat next to the couch with his nose resting on her knee. "You're a good boy, Dakota."

His tail wagged.

"He must have smelled the hemlock in the dressing," she said.

"A good thing, too. His sensitive nose saved your life."

She'd seen dogs turn away from tainted food before, that wasn't something that needed to be trained into a dog. She was glad that Dakota was watching out for her welfare.

The house phone rang. Westley brought her the cordless handset. She glanced at the caller ID and sighed inwardly when she saw it was Dr. Flintman, the base therapist. No doubt he'd heard about her trip to the ER. "Hello."

"Felicity," the doctor's deep, kind voice boomed in her ear. She held the phone slightly away from her. "You haven't been in to see me."

She smiled wryly. "No. I've been a bit busy."

"I've heard. Very traumatic. How are you coping? Are you still having nightmares?"

She could honestly say she hadn't had one for the past few nights. First, because she'd felt safe with Westley downstairs, and then, of course, last night was spent in the hospital. "I'm doing okay. I haven't had a nightmare in a few days."

"Hmm. You really should come in to the office. I have some medication I think will help to keep you doing okay."

"Like I said before, I'd rather not take anything. If things get bad again, I'll call."

"Well, I can't make you, but I'm here if you need me." The doctor hung up.

Felicity placed the handset on the end table and met Westley's curious gaze. He'd taken a seat in her father's recliner. It was nice to see him sitting there. Her father wouldn't have minded.

"Nightmares?" Westley asked.

She'd been worried that Westley would find out about her visits to the base therapist. Now, though, she had no choice but to tell him the truth and hope he wouldn't think differently of her. "After I found my father, I started having really bad dreams. I sought help with Dr. Flintman."

"Ah. Good for you."

The approval in his eyes pleased her, and she felt relieved. "It helped a bit to talk about it. He offered to prescribe some medication that he thought I'd benefit from but I'm holding off taking it."

"I understand. But if things get bad—"

"I'll reconsider," she said.

"Okay." He leaned back. "Lieutenant General Hall said you are to rest today and we'll get back to work tomorrow."

"Did you sleep at all?"

"No."

Tender empathy crowded her chest. "I think we could both use the rest." She rubbed Dakota's head. "We've got an alarm right here." She could tell Westley wanted to protest. "Please."

He nodded. "I won't be any good if I'm asleep on my feet." He pulled the lever that elevated his feet and reclined the chair back. He cocked an eyebrow. "Aren't you going to rest, too?"

She did chuckle then. "Yes, I will."

She stretched out on the couch and turned on her side to face him. After a moment, she closed her eyes, sure she wouldn't fall asleep with him so close by.

But it was two hours later when a pounding noise woke her up. Her eyes popped open in time to see Westley vault from the recliner, his hand on his sidearm. He blinked several times as if getting his bearing.

Sitting up, she said, "Someone is at the front door."

He strode across the living room and pulled open the door. Tech Sergeant Linc Colson stood there.

"The captain asked me to swing by and check on you two," Linc stated.

Westley stepped aside so he could enter. "We were resting."

Linc came all the way into the living room. "It's good to see you're doing well," he said to Felicity.

"Thanks." Deciding this would be a good time to freshen up, she stood up. "I'm going upstairs."

Westley hurried to her side as she headed to the staircase. She leveled him with a pointed look. "I don't need you hovering."

He raised his hands. "My bad."

She couldn't resist touching a hand to his chest. "You're a good man, Westley James."

His blue eyes darkened with something that made her pulse skip. She jerked her hand back and fled upstairs before she gave in to the dangerous urge to kiss him.

It took all of Westley's self-control not to chase her upstairs and tug her into his arms and kiss her. He'd seen the yearning on her pretty face and felt the answering longing deep inside of himself. If they'd been alone…

Wow. He was in so much trouble.

Kissing Felicity would be…amazing. Not to mention reckless.

And knowing that she'd felt it, too, sent joy soaring through him. He quickly wrestled the wayward attraction into a far corner where it wouldn't see the light of day again. Or at least where he could pretend it didn't exist.

He had to keep his head and his heart on the path before him. Logically, he understood his emotions were heightened from nearly losing her. They were both running on intensified feelings that had no place in their world.

Linc's rumbling laughter tightened Westley's shoulder muscles. A flush of embarrassment heated his face. He couldn't remember ever feeling so... He wasn't even sure what the term for it was. Vulnerable? Out of control?

Calming his racing emotions, he turned to face his friend. "What are you chuckling about?"

"You." He gestured to the stairs with his chin. "And her."

"I have no idea what you mean." Westley walked into the kitchen and poured himself a glass of tap water. He drank it as though he'd been stranded in the desert. The cool liquid helped to center his thoughts. His job was to protect Felicity, not pant after her like a lovesick teen. "Help me throw out every scrap of food in the house. I don't know what else might have been tampered with and I won't take any chances with her life."

"Why don't we have the crime-scene techs test everything?"

"It will be more expedient to just clear out the cupboards and fridge, then start over with sealed goods."

"Why would Boyd Sullivan put poison in her food?" Linc shook his head. "It doesn't fit."

Westley contemplated telling Linc about Agent Monroe's murder. Not that he didn't trust his friend, but Westley decided it would be best to keep that information in a close circle. Less chance to tip off the murderer that way.

"Do you think you two should even stay here?" Linc asked.

"I don't know if she'll leave." Westley spread his hands. "Besides, where would we go?" It occurred to him he'd automatically included himself. But for now they were a package deal. Until the threat to her life was neutralized, he wasn't leaving her side.

"There's base housing near the command center."

"I'll talk to her about it." He tossed a box of cereal into the garbage can. "How is the investigation coming? I assume Sullivan hasn't been found or I'd have heard."

"Unfortunately, we're no closer to catching him than we were yesterday. But we do have a lead."

That comment raised the hair at his nape. "What do you mean?"

"Someone is revealing information about the investigation to an anonymous blogger. Information that we haven't made public and weren't intending to."

"That sounds dangerous." Westley thought for a moment. "Could it be one of the base reporters? They've been sniffing around, asking questions, showing up everywhere."

Linc shrugged. "Maybe. Whoever the person is revealed that Zoe Sullivan visited her half brother just two weeks before his escape. Very few people knew that bit of info. Now the base is speculating she's helping her brother."

"Do you think she is?"

"I'm not sure, but I'm keeping an eye on her. She's cagey. Something's definitely up with her. Frankly, I don't trust anyone related by blood or friendship to Boyd Sullivan."

"I don't blame you there," Westley said. "Although innocent until proven guilty."

"Right." Linc checked his watch. "Hey, I have to go. Zoe's teaching a class and it ends soon. We can't have her walking around base unattended."

"Be careful," Westley told him.

Felicity stepped into the kitchen, blocking Linc's path, and looked at Westley. "What are you two doing?"

Westley paused with a bag of spaghetti hovering over the garbage can. She looked so pretty wearing jeans and a long-sleeve button-down top in a kelly green that deepened the color of her eyes. She'd twisted her hair at the back of her head, exposing the creamy column of her neck. But it was her eyes that caught his attention, eyes that sparked a warning he was beginning to know—and appreciate—well.

"Getting rid of any more potential hazards to your health," he stated and dropped the spaghetti into the garbage.

"I guess that's the best thing to do." She reached up to finger the key hanging around her neck.

Linc peered closer at the key. "You ride?"

"Ride what?" she asked.

He pointed at the key dangling from the chain. "That's a key to a BMW 2-series motorcycle. Vintage. Probably late sixties."

"Are you sure?" Westley exchanged a glance with Felicity. The hit-and-run her father had been investigating involved a motorcycle. Could they have the key to the one that hit the pedestrian? Literally the key to a big chunk of the mystery?

"Yes." Linc shrugged. "I like motorcycles. Do you

have the bike? It would be worth some money. A collector's item."

She tucked the key inside her blouse. "No. Just a memento."

"Ah. Well, I'm outta here." He shook Westley's hand. "Let me know if you need anything."

"We will." Westley walked him to the living room door. "Thanks, man."

As soon as the door closed behind Linc, Felicity said, "Did you hear that?" Anticipation echoed in her tone.

"Let's not get too hopeful," he said. "Even if that is the key to the motorcycle that your father was investigating, we still have no clue where it could be stashed."

"True. We need to get back out there," she said.

"Tomorrow is soon enough."

She nodded. "You're right. You know, I've been thinking. We never did search the attic. Maybe Dad's files are there."

"Are you up for it?"

"I am. The rest helped."

"Let's do it." Abandoning the kitchen, they rushed upstairs, stopping beneath the attic access door with a step stool she'd retrieved from her father's room.

Placing it under the hatch in the ceiling, he climbed up and lifted the door. Grasping the lip, he pulled himself up then reached down to lift her through the opening. The unfinished space ran the length of the house. Rafters provided support for the pitched roof. And stacked boxes provided many places where her father could have hidden his files.

"Most of this is my mom's stuff," Felicity said. "After the divorce, Dad put everything she'd left behind up here."

"Is this going to be painful for you?" Westley asked. He knew the agony of having to deal with the remains of a parent's things. After his father had gone to prison, his mother had tasked him with the job of packing away his dad's things. Westley had refused, which had earned him a beating, ironically with one of his father's belts. Despite the lashing, he hadn't touched his father's belongings.

"I don't think so," she replied. "It will be harder to pack up my dad's things."

His gut clenched. "Yes, it will." He'd admired and envied the love between Felicity and her father.

She lifted the flaps of a box to rummage inside. "Was it hard for you to deal with your father's possessions?"

"Hardly," he said. He moved a box closer to her to look through. He didn't feel comfortable searching through her mother's stuff. He doubted they'd find anything up here. All the boxes had layers of undisturbed dust.

"Will you tell me what happened to him?"

He really didn't want to. Dredging up the past wouldn't serve any purpose. But maybe if he told her, then he wouldn't have to worry about her falling for him. Once she knew the type of gene pool he came from, she'd want to keep far away from him.

"My father was a murderer."

NINE

She couldn't have heard him right. A murderer? Unease slid down Felicity's spine. She inhaled the musty odor of the attic, taking in some dust, and coughed. Catching her breath, she asked, "What happened?"

He sat on a trunk and dropped his head into his hands. There was a long moment of silence. She waited, hoping he would let down his walls and fully open up. He couldn't leave her hanging with such a shocking revelation.

"It was my fault."

His despondent tone broke her heart. She absorbed the blow. "Help me understand."

He lifted his gaze to meet hers. Torment swirled in the blue depths of his eyes. "I was ten when it happened."

So young.

"We were in a busy restaurant," he continued, his gaze dropping to his boots. "My feet were big. Too big. I was awkward, gangly even."

She couldn't imagine him clumsy and self-conscious. When Westley ran alongside the dogs during training he was nimble, but his six-foot frame contained the same sort of coiled power the dogs had. Unlike Felicity, who had cornered the market on gawkiness.

"I tripped over my feet, knocking a man's drink into his lap. He said something harsh to me and my dad took exception." Westley let out a mirthless laugh, a sound she didn't understand.

"They got in a fight. Dad punched the guy hard, he went down and hit his head on the metal foot of the table and died."

Her stomach knotted. What a horrible incident for a child to witness.

"My dad had a long rap sheet for assault and battery so the judge gave him a ten-year sentence for first-degree manslaughter. He died when I was seventeen."

Stunned, she reached out to touch his arm. "I'm sorry."

He shook his head, stopping her from touching him. "No reason for you to be sorry. He was a hothead who couldn't control his anger. It landed him in prison, where there were bigger, angrier men. I'm just surprised it took so long before someone beat him to a pulp."

The breath left her lungs. His callous words echoed with an underpinning of unfathomable pain. She'd had no idea Westley had a traumatic past. And she had no words of comfort to offer. The urge to wrap her arms around him and hold on tight gripped her, but doing so wasn't a good idea for either of them. They had to maintain a professional demeanor if they hoped to work together at the training center in the future. A future where, God willing, the Red Rose Killer was once again behind bars and her father's murderer would be brought to justice.

Despite her warning, she moved closer to sit beside

him and put a hand on his strong shoulder, now bowed with undeserved guilt. He made a distressed sound, as if her offer of comfort hurt him. Her hand floated to her lap.

A thought intruded as she recalled his earlier reaction to remembering the event that led to his father's incarceration and a cold sweat broke out over her skin. "Was your father violent with you? With your mother?"

He stood and paced away. "He was rough. On both of us."

Her heart contracted painfully in her chest with empathy and sorrow. Was that why Westley was so self-contained and unwilling to show emotion? The man had rarely smiled in the six months she'd been under his command. Not for her lack of trying. She'd assumed all this time he was displeased to have her in the training center. Could it be his attitude was more of a shield he hid behind rather than a reflection of his feelings for her?

She'd have to process this at another time. Right now, with him looking like he'd rather be anywhere but here, she sought to ease the hurt stirring within him. "You can't blame yourself for something that was out of your control. You were a child. They were grown men who made the choice to fight."

"Logically, I know that, but that doesn't stop my mother from blaming me. It's why she left. Why I was sent to live in foster care."

The injustice of it all made her so sad and angry that she couldn't ignore her emotions. Professional demeanor could take a flying leap. She went to him and put her arms around his waist. He tensed, holding himself ramrod-straight, his stiff arms at his sides. Frustration pulsed through her. He'd offered her comfort when she'd needed it, yet refused to take it from her.

"Westley," she said, her tone half plea, half censure.

The tension suddenly drained from him and he wrapped his arms around her, drawing her closer. She laid her cheek against his chest. His aftershave—spicy, woodsy and masculine—teased her senses. His heart thudded in time to her own.

His strong arms made her feel safe, cherished even. It was a feeling she could get used to if she allowed herself. She should step back, break the contact before her emotions got too tangled up with him. But she had no willpower. Nor the desire to step away.

He used the crook of his finger to lift her chin and draw her gaze to his. The tenderness in his eyes made her breath hitch, but it was the flare of attraction she saw in them that sent her pulse skyrocketing.

He dipped his head but halted inches from her lips, giving her the choice.

She didn't have to think about it. She wanted him to kiss her. Had for so long, even though she would never have admitted it to anyone, least of all to herself.

Had her former irritation and annoyance with Westley been more about an attraction she hadn't wanted to acknowledge?

Deciding to stay in the moment rather than analyze the past, she rose on her toes, closing the gap, and pressed her mouth to his. His lips were warm and firm, yet so gentle.

One hand stayed at the small of her back, while his other cupped the back of her head.

A low growl filled her head. It took a moment for her to register the sound. Dakota. They'd left him on guard duty in the hall beneath the attic opening. Was he protesting being left out?

Westley drew back. Their gazes met, and questions ricocheted through her mind. What did the kiss mean? Did she want it to mean something? Did he?

Dakota's growl turned into a bark of alarm, sending apprehension cascading over her limbs.

Westley nudged her behind him and leaned cautiously over the side of the attic opening. Unwilling to be coddled, Felicity dropped to her knees beside him to see for herself what had upset the dog. The hall was empty, but Dakota faced her father's room, his tail erect, his ears back and teeth bared, guarding them from an unseen threat.

Westley grabbed Felicity's elbow and tugged her behind him as he reached for the weapon holstered at his thigh. "Stay here."

In a move that was both athletic and fluid, he dropped quickly through the attic opening, landing soundlessly beside Dakota. Frustrated to be sidelined again, Felicity watched the pair advance down the hall, two warriors on the hunt. Dakota's growls and barks bounced off the walls.

Felicity's fingers curled into a fist. Adrenaline pumped through her veins. She needed a weapon.

She'd understood Lieutenant General Hall's refusal to let her carry. It would draw attention to her and make Boyd less likely to attack. Not that Westley and Dakota weren't enough of a deterrent. At the moment, she could only pray for Westley's safety.

Dakota erupted in a barrage of vicious barking.

"Halt!" Westley's shout came from her father's bedroom.

The sound of several gunshots rang out. A canine yelp punctuated the air.

Felicity's heart jackknifed. "Westley!"

Fearing the worst, she scrambled out of the attic, landing ungracefully with a jarring thud on the carpeted hall floor. As she regained her balance, she sent up a prayer, asking God for Westley and Dakota to be all right.

Cautiously, she made her way to the entrance of her father's bedroom, pressing her back against the wall. Anxiety clogged her throat, her mind already preparing her for devastation. She flashed back to the day she found her father's motionless body, and a shudder of dread worked over her flesh. With air trapped in her lungs, she peered around the doorjamb.

Inside the room, she found Westley holding Dakota, praising him with soothing words and a gentle tone. The dog panted at a fast clip. She hurried to their side. "What happened?"

"The intruder got away," he said. "I nicked him in the arm. But Dakota's been hit." His voice shook with emotion. "There's so much blood I can't tell how bad it is."

Her gaze lurched to where Westley's hand gripped Dakota's hind end. Crimson blood seeped through his fingers. She grabbed a pillow from the bed and stripped off the case. "Here." She shoved the wadded-up material at him. "Use this and apply pressure. We have to get him to the vet clinic."

He took the pillowcase and pressed it against Dakota's wound. "Dakota managed to get a piece of the intruder's pant leg."

She followed his gaze to a ragged-edged piece of dark cotton material lying on the carpet.

"Now we at least have his scent as well as his DNA." He gestured to the windowsill, where a smear of blood marred the white molding. "We'll call Security Forces, but right now we have to get Dakota to the vet." He rose, lifting the dog in his arms. "Call Dr. Roark and tell him we're coming."

Worry for Dakota churned in her gut as she made the call to the vet, who promised to be ready for them.

She prayed Dakota's injury was only a flesh wound as she hurried ahead of Westley and opened the front door.

"You drive," Westley said, heading to her car. "I'll hold him."

As soon as she got in the car she placed a call to Security Forces, and someone assured her they'd be at her house promptly to collect the evidence.

The short drive to the clinic seemed to take forever. When they arrived, the doors to the veterinarian hospital wing of the training center were open and Captain Kyle Roark, DVM and head of Canine Veterinary Services at CAFB, stepped out along with a female tech dressed in green scrubs.

"Follow me to exam room three," Dr. Roark said briskly and led the way.

Inside the room, Westley placed Dakota on the metal exam table. The dog tried to stand. Felicity jumped to subdue him at the same time as Westley. Their hands tangled together as they maneuvered Dakota successfully to his uninjured side.

"Good job, you two," Dr. Roark said. "You make a good team."

Felicity's cheeks heated. She met Westley's gaze, noting the appreciation in his eyes.

"Let's see what we have here," the vet said. "You two keep him still while Airman Fielding and I tend to his wound."

As the vet and the tech washed the wound, Felicity leaned in to Dakota's ear. "You're going to be okay."

The dog turned his head and licked her face. A good sign, she hoped.

"Well, now," the vet said. "Looks worse than it is."

She was so thankful to hear those words, Felicity's knees weakened. She could see the pronouncement had the same effect on Westley.

"The bullet grazed his upper thigh. He'll need a couple of stitches but he'll be right as the Texas rain within no time at all."

"That's good to hear, Doc." Westley's voice was filled with relief and gratitude. The lines of worry etched around his mouth eased.

"Airman Fielding will give you detailed instructions on how to care for the wound and a bottle of pain relievers," Dr. Roark said when he was finished administering to the dog. He clapped Westley on the back. "You all should get some rest."

"We will. Thanks." Westley picked up Dakota, cradling him to his chest.

Felicity took the instructions and the meds from the vet tech and then followed Westley outside. "Do you think we should take him to the training center instead of my house?" she asked.

He nodded. "He'll be comfortable in his kennel. And it will keep him from popping a stitch."

Westley headed toward the door that would take them through the back of the center. They entered the kennel room and a barrage of barking ensued. Most of the crates were filled with dogs. The empty ones made her stomach knot. There were still many dogs missing.

She quickly commanded, "Quiet" and the dogs in their kennels obeyed. She was sad to see Riff's crate still empty. She hoped the young Belgian Malinois would be found unharmed.

"You and I will stay here with Dakota," Westley said as he placed the dog gently into a crate and shut the door. "I think it would be safer for all of us."

"I agree," she said, hating to think the intruder might return to her house.

"There's a room here with a cot. We'll take shifts sleeping."

Not the most comfortable situation. But better than the alternative.

"Tomorrow we can figure out new housing," Westley said.

"We can take my uncle up on his offer to stay with him."

"That's one idea," Westley replied.

She chose to let his noncommittal answer go. "Obviously the guy hasn't found what he was looking for." She fingered the key beneath her uniform. "We need to find the motorcycle the key belongs to. Then we'll find my father's killer."

He brushed a stray strand of hair off her cheek, causing a shiver to trip over her skin. She had to look frightful. Just as he did with his uniform smeared with blood. Yet he looked at her like he approved of what he saw. "First things first. Your safety is my priority."

She'd never been anyone's priority. Her mother had been too busy with her law practice and her father too dedicated to the OSI. She'd always felt like an afterthought, unless of course she messed up, then she got their attention. Not the kind of attention she wanted growing up. She liked the idea of being Westley's priority way more than she probably should.

"Let's get back to your house and see how the crime-scene techs are doing." He stepped back. "And you can pack a bag."

They left the training center after checking in with Caleb Streeter, who promised to look in on Dakota. When they arrived at her house, the crime-scene techs were packing up their things and Special Agent Ian Steffen was on scene.

When he saw Felicity he hurried down the walkway, intercepting them. "I was worried about you two." He gave them each a once-over. "I take it neither of you has sustained injuries."

"No, we're good," Westley replied.

"We were in the attic when Dakota alerted us to the intruder," she told him.

Ian's eyebrows rose. "Did you find anything related to the case your father was working on?"

"Unfortunately, no," Westley responded.

But Felicity had learned more about Westley and her own feelings, so not a total loss.

"But hopefully the evidence collected will reveal the intruder's identity," Ian said. "If it was Boyd then we'll know for sure he's still on base."

Felicity didn't believe this was the work of the Red Rose Killer. "We think the intruder was looking for this key." She slipped it from the collar of her uniform.

"Maybe." Ian frowned.

She didn't understand why he refused to consider the key as important. "We have it on good authority that this is a specific type of motorcycle key. Possibly the motorcycle used in the hit-and-run."

That grabbed his attention. "If that is the case, then I should take it for safekeeping."

"But you're not officially working her father's murder," Westley stated. "Won't there be questions if you log the key into evidence for a nonexistent case?"

"I can handle that," Ian said.

"We'll keep the key," Westley said flatly.

Did Westley not trust Ian?

"I'll open an official investigation as soon as I can." Ian's tone held a note of defensiveness.

Westley's hands fisted at his side. "We have to find this guy now. Not later."

"Right now all available resources are on the Red Rose Killer case," Ian said. "That's why you have been detailed to Felicity's protection."

"Last report we heard, Boyd's not on base," Felicity said.

"There have been sightings in multiple places at multiple times. It's like sorting sand for a specific granule," Ian replied, sounding harassed. "The sightings could be to confuse us. To keep us from looking on base."

She could only imagine the pressure Ian was under. They all felt it to some degree.

"Plus, we're working on ferreting out Boyd's accomplice. Interviewing every single person on base, double-checking alibis and looking for any connections to Boyd." Ian wiped a hand over his jaw. "The more time goes by, the more the trail goes cold. Everyone is on high alert." He pinned her with his gaze. "We had the photos you've taken analyzed. But there's no sign of Boyd."

Felicity's stomached knotted. Her priorities were split between justice for her father and helping to capture the serial killer. "I'll be ready to resume taking pictures tomorrow," she promised.

Westley put his hand on her shoulder. "You were poisoned. If you need more time, you'll take it."

The gruff tone would have set her defenses on edge in the past, but she'd come to realize his default mode when struggling with his emotions. Stifling the urge to give him a reassuring smile, she simply said, "I'm feeling fine."

"Then I'll see you both tomorrow," Ian interjected. "Be safe."

When Ian got into his vehicle and left, Felicity turned to face Westley. "You don't completely trust him, do you?"

Westley shrugged. "I'm not sure what to think. He claims to want to catch your father's killer yet…he's not acting like the threat to your life is important."

"I don't believe that's true. With Boyd Sullivan on the loose, the OSI is stretched thin. Ian has no way to prove my father was murdered. And he's counting on you to protect me."

The skepticism in his eyes said he wasn't convinced. "Which I will," he assured her.

"I know." And that pleased her to no end.

They went inside the house. He followed her to her bedroom, where he inspected her corkboard, which was filled with photos and memorabilia, while she packed a duffel bag with a few days' worth of clothes. She didn't know how long they would stay at the training center, or if they'd move to her uncle's or other base housing.

"You were a cute kid," Westley commented with a smile.

She made a scoffing noise. "Hardly. I was gangly, self-conscious and an easy target."

His eyebrows pinched together. "You were bullied?"

"A little." She didn't like thinking about the laughter of her schoolmates when she'd trip on her way to her desk. Or dropped the beaker full of vinegar in science class. Or when she got so excited during choir because she'd finally hit the right note only to knock three people off the risers, causing bruises and hurt feelings.

She zipped her bag with more force than necessary. "I was mostly uncoordinated. Clumsy. My mother was forever lamenting to anyone who would listen that she didn't dare put out any fragile or breakable keepsakes because the 'little whirlwind' would destroy them."

"You've grown out of that phase," he said as he came up behind her. "Yes, you're enthusiastic, but it's part of your charm. Not to mention you're beautiful, smart and brave."

His words burrowed deep into her soul, soothing the sore spots she long thought healed. Her mouth went dry. She sent up a plea to God above that this was real. That Westley truly saw her how he claimed to.

He moved closer to her, his warm breath ruffling her hair. So close every cell in her body reacted, drawn toward him as if he exuded some magnetic force. She turned slowly to stare up into his handsome face, the memory of his kiss so fresh in her mind.

"You're very distracting," he said as he stepped back slightly.

"You say that like it's a bad thing."

"It has been. We work together. You know the air-force policy on fraternization."

"I'm not under your command."

"Not now, but you will be again." He headed to the door. "We shouldn't linger here."

She knew he was right, of course. Once the threat to her was neutralized, she and Westley would resume their roles at the training center. Which was what she wanted. Right?

"Let me just grab my bagful of lenses." She headed to the closet and went up on tiptoe to reach the box where she kept an assortment of different types of lenses for her camera. Her fingertips clutched the edge and she worked to slide the box from the shelf.

"Here, let me help you." Reaching over her head, Westley grabbed the sides of the box just as she backed up to make room for him. She stepped on his foot, stumbling against him. Reflexively, she fought for balance. Her elbow connected with his midsection as she tried to keep from falling. And succeeded in unintentionally knocking him off his feet. He landed on his backside while the box flew from his hands, the lid flying off and spilling the contents onto the carpet.

Mortified, her face flamed to what she was sure was a bright shade of red. "I'm so sorry."

He stared at her with surprise on his handsome face then he burst into laughter. The deep sound resonated within her chest, eliciting a giggle. Thankfully he wasn't angry at her clumsiness.

The release of hilarity at the situation freed some of her tension. She enjoyed the sound of his laugh and for a moment they were insulated from the dangers of the outside world.

She dropped to her knees beside him to collect her lenses and stared at the small electronic tablet.

She stilled. Her good humor faded, was replaced with a mix of anticipation and dread.

Her gaze lifted to meet Westley's. "I think we've found what the intruder was looking for."

TEN

Westley's laughter died as Felicity's words reverberated through his brain.

I think we've found what the intruder was looking for.

He sat straighter. His ribs were sore from where her boney elbow had made contact, reminding him of his tumble and that for a few minutes he'd let down his guard and enjoyed the moment. He seemed to let loose a lot around Felicity. There was something about her that freed him in ways he hadn't experienced before. Best not to read too much into it, he decided. Instead he focused on her words. "What did you find?"

Felicity pushed aside a lens lying on the carpet to reveal a black tablet the size of a small notebook. "That is not mine."

That piqued his interest. He studied it. "You think your father put it there?"

"I don't know how else it would have gotten into my lens box." She flicked a finger at the device. "This has to contain the evidence that will lead us to my father's killer. This is most likely what the intruder was searching for. He must have only done a cursory look inside this box and since the tablet was at the bottom he missed it."

The same intruder who'd shot Dakota. Thankfully the dog's wound had been superficial, and he was now resting in his kennel. Westley rubbed his chin, contemplating their next move. Should he call the OSI? The crime-scene techs? So far the perpetrator had left no prints, only his DNA through the blood left after Westley wounded him. "We need to see what's on the device before we alert Agent Steffen. Let's take it to the training center and look at it there. I'm not comfortable lingering here."

They collected her lenses and bags then headed out the door. The small hairs at his nape quivered with a sense of foreboding. He glanced around, assessing the area for a threat as he ushered Felicity to the vehicle. Were they being watched?

He couldn't see anyone, but that didn't mean he wasn't out there. Boyd Sullivan, aka the Red Rose Killer, had targeted Felicity. Westley doubted the man would give up easily. Yet, Sullivan wasn't the immediate threat. Whoever killed Felicity's father had also tried to harm Felicity by poisoning her. All in an attempt to keep her from finding the tablet?

When they arrived at the training center, Westley put Felicity's things into the small room they used for the overnight-shift staff. He made a mental note to look at the schedule to coordinate the sleeping arrangements. This wasn't ideal, but would have to do. Keeping Felicity safe meant making the best of the situation.

"I need to check in with Captain Blackwood," he told her.

"I'm going to check on Dakota," Felicity said. "Don't look at the tablet until I can join you."

"I wouldn't dream of it," he assured her. He watched her walk away, feeling like she'd taken the sun with her. He nearly laughed out loud. When had he become poetic?

Disliking having her out of his sight, he followed her to the kennels. He greeted the trainers, who were busy taking care of the dogs. Felicity had kneeled down beside Dakota's crate and was petting him through the metal rungs. The dog licked her hand.

"I gave him his pain meds," a rookie trainer, Lila Fields, told them. "He was whimpering."

"Thank you," Westley said. He liked the single mom. She was competent and compassionate, and very interested in working with dogs suffering from PTSD, though she'd made it clear she didn't want to discuss why she had the special interest.

Felicity glanced up at him with surprise in her eyes. "I thought you were calling the captain."

"I will, but I wanted to see Dakota, too."

She searched his face as if trying to decide if he was telling her the truth. He arched an eyebrow. He did want to make sure the dog was resting but that wasn't his only motivation. But he certainly wasn't going to cop to needing to keep her within arm's length, even though they were safe within the confines of the training center.

A slow smile teased the edges of her mouth and a twinkle appeared in her eyes. She went back to talking to the dog. Did she suspect his true reason for following her? And if so, what did she think? Judging by the smile, she wasn't displeased. His heart rate kicked up

a notch. For the millionth time he admonished himself
for his base reaction. *Now is not the time.*

Then again, he could be completely wrong about
what she was thinking. She wasn't as easy to read as
he apparently was.

After a few minutes, Felicity rose and they went to
Westley's office and switched on the tablet.

It wasn't password-protected. "That's weird," Felicity said. "Why wouldn't he use a pass code?"

Westley pressed the button for the home screen.
There were no apps or email icons, only several folders. All untitled.

"That's so not like my dad. He's usually so organized. You know, 'a place for everything and everything in its place.'"

"Let's have a look at file number one." He clicked on
the icon. An album of photos spread across the small
screen.

Felicity gasped. "These pictures are from my parents' wedding." She touched the screen, her finger hovering over her parents' images. Her mother looked so
pretty in her white wedding gown, her hair piled upon
her head and surrounded by a pearl-trimmed veil. Her
dad looked handsome in his mess-dress uniform. "I'd
only seen the portrait of my parents' wedding day that
used to hang in the living room."

"Your parents look happy," Westley said.

They did. Both were smiling. Dad's arm was wrapped
around her mother's waist while she held a bouquet of
white gardenias. Her mother's favorite flower.

Felicity double-tapped the photo so that it took up the
whole screen. As she peered closely at the image staring back at her, a knot formed in the pit of her stomach.

Her mother had a distinct bump in her belly. "She was pregnant with me."

Westley tilted his head. "How can you be sure?"

"Look. Can't you see it?" She paced away from his desk, the confines of the office suddenly closing in on her. "This explains so many things." Like why her mother was always hypercritical. And the lectures about making good choices and the consequences of poor choices. "My mind is blowing up."

"Let's not be overdramatic."

"Overdramatic?" She stared at him. "Are you kidding me?" She made a slashing gesture with her hand. "You don't get it. My whole life my mom told me to wait for love. To not get serious about a guy too soon. That every decision I made needed to be well thought out. Not something done in haste or in the heat of the moment." She shook her head at the irony. "Now I understand. Makes total sense. She acted in the heat of the moment and regretted it. Regretted me. No wonder I can never get her approval. She didn't want me to begin with."

Westley came to her side and took her hands. "Look at me," he said. "You can't think that."

"But it's obvious, isn't it?" She felt like the world was crumbling under her feet. "They had to get married. My dad was an honorable man. Of course he married her."

"They had to have loved each other," Westley insisted. "They wouldn't have stayed together for as long as they did if they hadn't loved each other on some level."

"Maybe. But they eventually did divorce." She wanted to believe him. She wanted to believe that her parents had loved each other. Doesn't every child want that?

She didn't question her father's love. He had made it clear every day of his life. But her mother... All the doubts and fears that she had as a child rose to the surface. She'd tried so hard to make her mother happy and proud. But she'd been doomed from the get-go. "I was a mistake." Numbness stole over her heart.

"Don't say that. Don't let this define you or define your relationship with your mother."

She met his gaze. "But how can I not?"

Determination lit the depths of his eyes. "You can talk to her," he suggested, his tone gentle.

"Like that's going to happen." Just the thought of asking her mother such intimate questions about her life and her marriage made Felicity's insides clench. "You don't know my mother. She can be intimidating at the best of times. I shudder to think how she would react if I asked her if she regretted having me or if she regretted marrying my father. We don't talk about things like that."

Westley drew her to his chest, wrapping his arms around her. "You're right—I don't know her. But she can't be all that bad, because I like her daughter a lot."

He liked her? A lot? The admission surprised her, pleased her. Stirred up all the emotions she'd been trying to ignore. She liked him a lot, too. More than liked him, if she was being honest with herself.

But where could their relationship go? Their future in the air force depended on not becoming involved. There were lines they shouldn't—couldn't—cross.

As much as she wanted to see where this attraction would lead, she knew the best thing for them both was to deny the connection they both obviously felt for one another.

They had a purpose that needed their attention.

She stepped back, took a deep breath. "Let's look at the other files." She wanted to forget what she'd learned, but doubted that knowledge would ever go away. For now she stuffed it into a box within her and hoped the lid would stay shut. "One of the other files has to be related to the case my father was working on."

On the tablet, Westley closed the open file of wedding photos, and then clicked on the next file. More photos appeared. These were of Felicity as a child, and shots of her father and her uncle mugging for the camera. There were photos of her mother as well, looking beautiful and serene sitting on the sand beneath an umbrella. Felicity vaguely remembered going to a Corpus Christi beach. She still had a collection of seashells in her room from that trip. Her mother did look happy here in these photos, she noted.

"These aren't helpful," she said. "Try that one."

Westley exited the file and clicked on the next one. A window popped up and asked for a password. "This has to be it," he said. "Any idea what your father would use as a password?"

"I haven't a clue," she said.

"I'll try your name."

No go.

"Try Colleen," Felicity said. "My mom's name."

That didn't work, either, and neither did the other obvious passwords they tried. He closed the folder and powered down the device before handing it to her. "Hopefully Cyberintelligence can crack the code."

"We have to take this to Ian in the morning," she

said. She tucked the device in the deep pocket of her uniform pants. "This may be the evidence he needs to open an official investigation into my dad's death."

Westley's gaze narrowed. "I hope we're not making a mistake by trusting the man."

"We're not." At least she prayed they weren't. But could she trust her judgment? After learning the circumstances behind her parents' marriage, she found herself doubting everything.

Everything? she asked herself. Even her growing feelings for Westley?

The rising sun shone bright over the Texas Hill Country, washing Canyon Air Force Base in shades of gold. Felicity loved this time of day. The world seemed fresh and alive, though she felt a bit wilted from lack of rest. Taking turns on the cot in the training center hadn't provided her much sleep. She feared Westley hadn't received much shut-eye, either.

Only Dakota seemed to have much energy this morning. If his hindquarter wasn't sporting a bandage, she wouldn't have known by his even gait and wagging tail that the dog had been recently hurt.

As Westley drove them back to the OSI offices, with Dakota in the back seat, Felicity glanced out the passenger window at the horizon and sent up a prayer. She had much to pray for. Strength, both physical and mental. Closure for her father's death. Boyd's capture. An untangling of her confusing emotions for Westley.

She told herself she had to be patient. The promise of Romans 8:28 came to mind.

And we know that all things work together for

good to them that love God, to them who are the called according to his purpose.

She had to trust that God knew what was needed and He would provide as He saw fit. She filled her lungs with a deep, settling breath. She might not have had the rest she needed, but she felt renewed.

They arrived at the building and rushed inside to Ian's office, but he wasn't there. They backtracked to the front desk.

"Agent Steffen is off base following a lead on the Red Rose Killer case," the woman at the desk told them.

"Can you tell him to contact one of us as soon as possible?" Felicity tried to hide her disappointment. She was anxious to see what was in the password-protected file.

The electronic tablet burned a metaphorical hole in the pocket of her uniform pants. But she couldn't do anything with it until Ian's return. Meanwhile they needed a distraction. "The BMT graduation is this afternoon. I'd like to get some photos of the setup."

With Dakota at their heels, they went to the photo lab, where she picked up her camera. On the way out they ran in to Yvette Crenville. The base nutritionist paused to salute. There were dark circles beneath her eyes, and she looked like she'd lost weight.

"Are you okay?" Felicity asked, worried for the younger woman. They were both targets of Boyd Sullivan. In fact, Felicity figured Boyd would have more reason to feel slighted by Yvette since the woman had made their breakup very public.

Yvette patted her utility cap as if checking to be sure

she'd put it on. "I've been so stressed. This whole thing with Boyd is too much."

"You'd feel better if you had a protection detail," Westley stated.

Felicity certainly did.

Yvette rolled her eyes. "Please. I go to the hospital and my apartment. If I'm not safe at either of those two places, then there is nowhere on base that I'd be safe."

"Having a dog and a handler with you, getting there and back, will give you peace of mind," Felicity told her.

Yvette eyed Dakota and his bandaged hip. "What will give me peace of mind is Boyd back in jail." She adjusted her uniform jacket. "I've been called in to talk to Captain Blackwood again. Like I would help Boyd?" She huffed. "As if. If you ask me, it's Zoe Sullivan they should be questioning. Gotta go." She hurried past them.

Felicity watched Yvette disappear inside the command building. "Do you think she's right? Zoe does seem the most likely to be Boyd's accomplice."

Westley shrugged. "If she is, Linc will find out."

They spent the rest of the day in and around the BMT graduation events. The crush of people made Felicity nervous at first, but with Westley and Dakota watching her six, she relaxed into the process and enjoyed herself, capturing the day's memories. This photography gig wasn't half bad. In fact, she could see herself doing this long-term. Which she would be doing until Boyd was caught.

As dusk settled over the base they returned to where they'd parked the SUV at the back of the lot near the north woods.

She stopped and gripped his arm as dread made her skin prickle.

"Boyd was here." She pointed a shaky finger to the front windshield.

A red rose was tucked under one of the wipers. A small square piece of paper was plastered to the glass.

Westley plucked the note from the windshield, careful to only touch the edge.

"Let me see," she said.

Together they stared at the words typed across the paper.

I'll get you yet.

Her stomach lurched. Boyd was on base. And close.

Anger twisted in Westley's gut. He scanned the area for the fiend, but with so many people milling about, there was no way to tell if Boyd was out there among them.

"I feel so exposed here," she whispered.

He did, too. Despite the fact that they were on a military installation on high alert, somehow Boyd Sullivan managed to move around at will. They could even be in his crosshairs right now. "Don't touch anything. I'll call the captain from the center I need to bag this evidence. Then we're out of here."

From the back compartment of the SUV where he kept supplies, he grabbed a brown paper bag and a set of latex gloves. With the gloves on, he slid the rose and note inside the bag. He placed the offending evidence in the glove box, then opened the doors to let Felicity and Dakota into the SUV. As she passed him to climb in, he touched her arm. "I'm not going to let him, or anyone else, hurt you. Not on my watch."

The look of trust and tenderness in her eyes sent his pulse racing. "I know."

He couldn't stop himself from leaning in and placing a quick kiss on her sweet lips. Her quick inhalation nearly made him steal another, but not now. If ever.

When he closed her door, he shook his head, marveling at the way life was spinning in a direction he'd never expected. From the moment he'd learned that Felicity was in danger, his world had changed. No longer was the future clear. No longer did he know with crystal clarity what he wanted and didn't want in life. He'd thought he had it all mapped out. He'd work at the training center until they forced him to retire. Then he'd open his own dog-training facility. But now he couldn't envision the path before him. Not without Felicity.

He told himself there was only one thing he needed to concentrate on—keeping Felicity safe.

Keeping an alert eye out for any threat, he climbed into the vehicle. He put the key in the ignition, then hesitated. "Why would Boyd leave a note and rose now?"

"Because he's sick?"

"Are we sure Boyd placed them there?" An itch he couldn't name niggled at him. "What if the intruder placed those there to throw us off?"

"To make us think Boyd was the one who poisoned me and broke into my house?" she said. "But we know it wasn't Boyd. It was whoever killed my father." She patted the tablet. "The person is after this."

"Right." His mind whirred with possibilities. Why would the intruder use the note and rose to scare them? Or had Boyd really set them on the hood of Westley's vehicle?

"Don't you think it odd that this note was typed while the first one was handwritten?" Felicity asked.

"It does seem strange." Westley's unease intensified. "Though if you think about it, for the first note he probably didn't have access to a computer and printer."

"True. And whoever is sheltering him has both. I still can't believe anyone on base would help the likes of Boyd."

"People do strange things." Vicious things. Deadly things.

"That's true." She sighed. "Only God knows what really goes on in someone's heart."

Apprehension slithered across his shoulders. He gazed out the front windshield, staring at the dark woods. If Boyd wanted to shoot them he had perfect cover within the trees, yet they sat here unharmed. "We need to get out of the vehicle now."

He didn't wait for her response but hopped out and quickly came around to her side to open her door.

She climbed out. "You think he booby-trapped the car?"

He released Dakota. "I'm not taking any chances."

The dog circled the SUV then dropped to his belly near the front end, his nose aimed toward the undercarriage. A menacing growl filled the air.

"What's he doing?" Felicity asked.

"He sees or smells something that has his hackles up," Westley replied. "That's not his normal alert signal."

Waving Felicity back a safe distance, Westley crawled beneath the vehicle to look for signs of sabotage. A pack of C-4 had been strapped to the undercarriage. There'd been no attempt made to hide either the explosive or the remote detonator blinking a red warning light. Westley froze. Fear like he'd never experienced before blasted through his body.

Felicity's cell phone rang, sending him scrambling out from under the SUV. The look of horror on her pale face matched the sickening dread filling his veins.

She held the phone from her ear. "He says he'll blow up the car if we don't hand over the tablet."

ELEVEN

Felicity's heart stuttered within her chest. Her feet rooted to the spot, she was too afraid to move, afraid if she and Westley and Dakota ran, the man on the phone would detonate the bomb. Westley stepped to her side and took the phone from her hands.

"Who is this?" he demanded. He listened for a moment, his gaze scanning the tree line. "What makes you think we haven't made a copy?"

Still holding the phone in one hand to his ear, Westley grabbed the back of her uniform jacket and pulled her farther away from the vehicle. He let out a shrill whistle and Dakota came running. "Not going to happen, man."

He closed the phone, then yelled, *"Run."*

Galvanized into action by the flood of adrenaline released at his command, Felicity whirled away from the vehicle and ran as fast as her legs could go.

"Get back!" she yelled to the other people going to their nearby cars. "Bomb!"

People scattered, fleeing the area.

When she and Westley, with Dakota at their heels, were a safe distance away, Westley called Security

Forces, alerting them to the bomb strapped to the undercarriage of the SUV.

"What did the man say to you?" Felicity asked after he hung up with the Security Forces dispatcher. She glanced nervously over her shoulder at the SUV, expecting it to explode at any moment.

Westley shook his head. "Nothing for you to worry about."

She gripped his arm in frustration. "Don't do that." She wasn't going to take being coddled.

With a wry twist of his lips, Westley said, "Sorry. He claimed he could get to you at any time and if we didn't leave the tablet and all copies of its contents in your mailbox—without overwatch—tonight, he'd kill you."

A shiver of apprehension wormed its way over her flesh. She was thankful she had two earthly protectors and God watching out for her. And equally grateful Westley told her.

Within minutes the area was evacuated and the bomb squad arrived along with the base's ace bomb-sniffing bloodhound, Annie, and her handler, First Lieutenant Nick Donovan. Felicity and Westley saluted the lieutenant.

Two explosive-ordinance-disposal techs, wearing bombs suits to protect them from the potential blast, approached the vehicle.

Felicity put her hand to her throat, fingering the cross on her necklace, and held her breath.

Within a matter of minutes the EODs had the bomb deactivated and disassembled.

"A crude design," Nick told them. "Amateurish."

"That was a lot of C-4," Westley said.

Nick shrugged. "I'm not saying it wouldn't have fulfilled its purpose."

Which was to kill her and Westley and destroy the evidence in her pocket. She shivered with a ripple of anxiety.

"As a precaution," Nick said, "Annie and I will take a tour of the lot."

"Good idea, Lieutenant," Westley said.

As the explosives expert and his canine walked away, Captain Justin Blackwood arrived. Westley updated him.

"What can you tell me about the caller?" Justin asked.

"Not much," Felicity said. "He sounded muffled, like he had something over the phone." Something niggled at her mind, clamoring for her attention. She tried to hold onto it but whatever her subconscious was trying to say remained elusive. "Maybe the voice sounded vaguely familiar."

"It could have been Sullivan or his accomplice," Justin said. "You may know his accomplice."

"We may *all* know his accomplice," Westley said. "But I'm not convinced this was Sullivan."

Justin peered at him speculatively. "But he left a rose and note on the hood of your vehicle. If it wasn't Boyd or his accomplice, then who?"

Felicity met Westley's gaze. There was no mistaking the question in his eyes. Did they tell the captain about her father's murder?

She nodded. This latest attempt on her life could have ended so badly, not just for her, Westley and Dakota, but also for a multitude of innocent people. They needed to voice their suspicion before it was too late.

"We have something to tell you," Westley said. "But not here."

"I'll drive you back to the training center," Justin said. "You can explain on the way."

They hopped into Justin's vehicle. Dakota nudged his way next to the captain's canine partner, a Belgian Malinois named Quinn. Felicity sat in the back, Westley in front. She sat forward, putting her hand on Westley's shoulder. "Let me explain."

Westley nodded.

"We believe my father was murdered," Felicity informed the captain as he drove. She told him everything Ian had told her and all they knew so far.

Justin glanced sharply at her in his rearview mirror. "So the break-in and the poisoning—those weren't Boyd?"

"No, I—we—believe the man responsible for my father's death was looking for the evidence my father collected during the investigation he was conducting at the time of his death."

"We found an electronic tablet hidden in Felicity's bedroom," Westley told him. "It's what the bomb perp is after."

Not the key they'd found in the desk, just as Ian had predicted.

"How did he know we have it?" Felicity asked. "We haven't told anyone, not even Ian."

"He had to have bugged your house," Justin said.

"We need to do an electronic sweep of the place," Westley said.

"Don't we have an electronics-sniffing dog?" Justin asked.

"We do. She's in training." Felicity couldn't keep

the excitement from her voice. "Senior Airman Chase McLear and Queenie, the cutest little beagle ever, have been in training only a couple months in this new specialty, electronic detection."

"I'll talk to Chase," Westley said.

Justin nodded. "Report back to me tomorrow," he ordered when he pulled over at the training center.

"We will, sir," Westley said as he opened the door. He let Dakota out of the back seat, while Felicity stepped out of the car.

Westley held open the training-center door for Felicity to enter. "You must be exhausted," he said. The warmth in his tone soothed her more than her favorite chocolate melting on the back of her tongue.

"It's been a trying day," she said. "But you must be just as tired."

"I won't lie, I didn't get much sleep," he told her.

"Then I should bite the bullet and ask my uncle if I can stay with him, or rather, if we can stay with him," she said.

He brushed back her hair from her face. "I have the feeling that will be hard for you."

She shrugged. "I don't like asking for help. But I have to get over myself."

He smiled and his approval warmed her heart.

"That's my girl."

His words thrilled her. Was that how he saw her? His girl? She arched an eyebrow. "Girl?"

He made a face. "Please don't take offense."

"I'm teasing you," she said with a grin. "I don't mind being your girl."

Westley's eyes widened and a slow smile spread across his face. "Duly noted."

Heat infused her cheeks. A niggling little voice reminded her that even though he wasn't currently her superior, one day they would go back to the training center and resume their positions within the working-dog program, which meant this thing between them had nowhere to go. Even knowing that, she couldn't muster up regret for the flirty words.

"Let's see if we can find Chase and Queenie," Westley said. "If they have time now, let's go over to the house."

They found Chase, a tall, gentle giant of a man, and his comparatively small beagle in the center of the training ring working with the specialized trainer, Special Agent Denise Logan, on loan from the FBI K-9 Unit. Agent Logan had helped successfully train the FBI's electronics sniffer dogs.

Westley explained what they needed.

"We're game," Chase said, his gaze going to Denise.

The stocky brunette considered the idea as she twisted her wedding ring. "All right. Let's see what Queenie can sniff out. But don't get your hopes up too high. We haven't attempted a listening device."

Felicity sent up a prayer that Queenie and Chase would come through for them. She didn't like the idea that someone had been listening to her every word. The invasion of privacy was somehow worse than having her home ransacked.

Accompanied by Dakota, Westley and Felicity led the way to her house. They went by foot because the evening air had cooled off and she only lived a few blocks away. As they approached, the door of the adjacent house opened and reporter Heidi Jenks stepped out. She waved and hurried down the walkway.

Westley groaned.

"It's fine," Felicity told him and quickened her pace to head off Heidi.

"What's going on?" Heidi asked. She obviously was in for the evening because she had on yoga pants and a T-shirt. But her sharp-eyed gaze took everything in.

"Out for a stroll," Felicity said, skirting the truth. Westley hustled Chase, Denise and the dogs past at a fast clip.

"Looks like something serious is going on," Heidi countered.

"Nothing worth mentioning," Felicity assured her, hoping she'd take the hint.

Heidi pressed her lips together. "I thought we were friends."

Felicity's heart sank. She didn't want to hurt Heidi's feelings. "We are. It's just some things are not for public consumption."

"Not you, too." Heidi huffed. "I did not post the blog."

It took a second for Felicity to connect what Heidi meant, then she remembered that an anonymous blogger had leaked the information about Zoe Sullivan visiting her half brother, Boyd, in prison. "I know you didn't." At least Felicity hoped not.

Westley caught her attention with a wave from the porch of her house, where he and Dakota kept watch. Her heart did a little jig in her chest. She had to admit she didn't mind having the two males worry over her.

"Look, I've got to go." She strode away, aware of Heidi's gaze.

When she reached the porch, Westley slipped his

hand around her elbow. "Was she fishing for information?"

Wanting to protect her friend, she said, "She's curious. Wouldn't you be if you saw all of us coming down the street?"

"I don't know if I trust her," Westley said. "She could be Boyd's accomplice for all we know."

"I highly doubt it," Felicity said. "Heidi may be ambitious, but she's not corrupt."

He lifted a shoulder. "You never know."

She didn't like the doubt he'd planted in her mind. She glanced across the side yard separating the two houses. Heidi remained on her porch watching them, but Felicity refused to believe ill of her neighbor.

Wanting to redirect their focus, Felicity said, "Let's see how Chase and Queenie are doing."

Inside the house, Denise put her finger to her lips, indicating they were to remain silent while Chase and Queenie worked. As the dog sniffed around the couch and coffee table, Westley and Felicity stood back with Dakota sitting in front of them, his dark eyes watching the other dog.

Queenie sat by the end table, her tail wagging. Chase gave the dog a treat, then kneeled down and felt the underside of the small table. He smiled and peeled away a small, round device and held it up.

Felicity couldn't believe it. She had actually been bugged. Westley's grim expression told her he'd expected as much.

Denise took the device and inspected it, then nodded before placing the electronic bug into an evidence bag. Then she made a motion for the pair to continue on.

They all followed as the beagle led them down the hallway to Felicity's bedroom.

Felicity winced as the pair entered the room. She and Westley and Denise filled the doorway to watch Queenie sniff the bed and the floor around the closet, then finally come to a halt at the dresser. Chase opened the bottom drawer. Queenie sniffed but didn't alert. Two more drawers were opened before the beagle alerted. Inside the top drawer was a listening device. It was the same drawer that had been open the morning Felicity had awoken to find someone at the foot of her bed. She shuddered with revulsion. The intruder had been spying on her. That was how he known about the tablet. But did he know about the key? Was the key even significant?

Chase and Queenie checked the rest of the house and found no more devices.

Denise took the evidence bags and set them outside before coming back into the house. "I'll have those sent to the FBI lab for analysis." Then she turned to Chase. "This was a successful test," she said, obviously pleased. "I'm proud of you both."

Despite the sick roil in her belly from having been bugged, a smile tugged at the corner of Felicity's mouth at the sight of the red creeping up Chase's neck at the compliment. She slanted a glance at Westley. He raised an eyebrow at her. She wanted to poke at him about how easy it was to give praise, but decided she didn't need to point out the obvious.

"Good job," Westley told Chase. Felicity couldn't stop the grin this time. And she hadn't had to say a word. Okay, maybe she'd given him a look but still... he could learn. That warmed her heart.

Chase shrugged. "It wasn't me. Queenie did all the sniffing."

Westley clapped the other man on the back. "We appreciate it just the same."

Looking decidedly uncomfortable, Chase tugged at the collar of his uniform. "We'll head back to the training center now if you don't need us anymore."

"No, you're good," Westley said.

Chase, Queenie and Denise left the house, taking the devices with them.

"Now what?" Felicity said. "Do you think it's safe to come back here?"

"Not yet," he said. "I want to install a security system before you do. Tonight we'll bunk with your uncle and then tomorrow I'll make this house a fortress."

She appreciated all he was doing for her. "Thank you. I don't know if I could handle all of this without you."

A frown formed on his handsome face. "You're strong, Felicity. I have no doubt you can handle anything life throws at you."

His words sent pleasure sliding through her. She had the strongest urge to kiss him, but considering they were standing on her porch beneath the light, where anyone could see them, she refrained. Instead, she focused on the job they still had to do. "We need to get the tablet to Ian before anything else happens."

"You're right," Westley said. "Why don't you call and see if he's back on base?"

"Can do." Felicity fished out her cell phone from the pocket of her uniform pants and dialed the OSI office. On the third ring, the receptionist answered.

"He's in a meeting with Lieutenant General Hall and Captain Blackwood," the woman said when Felicity asked for Ian. "I'm sure he'll contact you when he's done. I gave him your earlier message."

Felicity thanked the woman and hung up. She related the information to Westley. "I hope this means there's been a break in the Red Rose Killer case. We'll all sleep better once Boyd is back behind bars."

"This is true," Westley agreed. "But I won't sleep at all until the maniac who killed your father is captured." He curled his fingers around her hand that held the tablet. "We need to get this to a secure place until we can pass it off to Agent Steffen."

"It would be safe with you," she said, willing to let him carry the burden.

"I have an idea," he said. "There's a small safe in the office of the training center, where we keep the paperwork on the dogs and an emergency stash of their medication. The tablet will be safe there tonight."

"Good idea." She held his gaze. The tender expression on his handsome face made her pulse jump.

She knew she could count on him to protect her and find a solution to any problem. He was a man of honor and integrity. A man worthy of loving.

Her mouth went dry at that thought. Was she falling in love with Westley?

She had to admit that maybe she was.

It was such a strange sensation, considering not that long ago she wasn't sure she liked him or that he liked her. But things had changed between them at a rapid clip.

A pang tugged at her heart. She didn't see a way for them to ever be a couple. Not if they hoped to continue to train the dogs, with her under his command.

Best to put any thoughts of romance out of her mind and close off her heart before they both got hurt.

Felicity stepped back, putting space between her and Westley. He could sense her withdrawing from him emotionally. He wasn't sure what thought had crossed her mind to make the small *V* appear between her eyebrows. For a moment there, as they stood beneath the glow of the porch light, he'd seen the spark of attraction that seemed to simmer within her and flared occasionally when he least expected it. He savored those moments. Even though he knew there could never be anything real or long-lasting between them. Still, it was nice to pretend for a second here and there...

"I should call my uncle," she said, her voice tight. "See if we can stay there tonight."

"Right." It was the right call. Her uncle was family. They would both be more comfortable there than taking shifts on the cot. "Let's go to the training center and take care of the tablet, then you can call him."

They walked back, Dakota trotting beside them. Westley wanted to ask her if she was okay, but that seemed like a dumb question considering all that had transpired. Of course she wasn't all right. She had to be stressed and scared, and was putting up a brave front. No, not a front. She was brave. And kind and so much stronger in spirit than he'd given her credit for in the beginning.

He admired and respected Felicity. Enough to know that he had to keep his emotions in check so as not to ruin her career or her life.

At the training center, they tucked the tablet into

the small safe located in the desk cabinet. Then Felicity called her uncle.

"Thanks, Uncle Patrick, we'll see you soon," she said as she hung up. Then she looked up at Westley. "He's happy to be of help."

"I hope he won't mind Dakota staying with us," Westley said.

Felicity pulled a face. "Uncle Patrick isn't fond of dogs."

"So I noticed," Westley said. "But he'll have to deal with it."

Felicity scratched Dakota behind the ears. "Uncle Patrick just has to get to know you. He'll see not all dogs are scary."

She grabbed her bag from the cot room and followed Dakota and Westley outside to the parking lot. Westley had the keys to the vehicle used by Caleb Streeter because Westley's SUV was now in the custody of Security Forces.

They drove to the set of apartments at the north end of the base, where her uncle had a unit on the fifth floor. They took the elevator up and knocked on her Uncle Patrick's door. He opened it immediately. He stood in the open doorway in his socks, regulation sweatpants and a T-shirt stretched over his broad shoulders.

Dakota emitted a low growl. Westley glanced at Dakota. The hair along his back raised in a ridge. His tail was up, his ears stiff. What was that about?

Patrick's gaze bounced from Felicity to Westley and then landed on Dakota. "Oh, no. He's not staying."

"Only way Felicity and I stay is if Dakota does," Westley stated firmly. He wasn't going to trust anyone, not even himself, with Felicity's safety without extra protection.

A deep scowl created lines along Patrick's forehead. "I don't like dogs."

As if he understood the words, Dakota bared his teeth in a snarl and lunged at Patrick, sending him stumbling backward with horror on his face.

TWELVE

"Dakota, no!" Felicity's heart slammed against her chest. What was going on? She'd never seen the dog go into attack mode without provocation. The only times she'd witnessed Dakota's true fierceness was in demonstrations where Westley or one of the other trainers wore a padded bite suit. She hurried across the room to stand in front of her uncle. She held a hand to Dakota. "Stop!"

Westley reeled in Dakota and grabbed his collar, holding back the snapping and snarling dog.

"Stand off! Heel!" Westley commanded in a loud tone that reverberated through the apartment.

Dakota slowly complied and sat, but his intense focus was trained on Patrick. His teeth were still bared but he'd quieted down to a low, ominous growl.

"Put that away!" Westley said, his gaze on something over Felicity's shoulder.

She whirled to find her uncle holding his service weapon in shaky hands. Thankfully the barrel was aimed at the floor.

"Get that beast out of here or I'll shoot it!" Uncle Patrick yelled. Sweat gleamed on his forehead.

"Whoa." Felicity held up both hands, now needing to protect Dakota. "Uncle Patrick, lower the weapon. Westley will take Dakota back to his kennel."

Uncle Patrick didn't seem to hear her. His fear-filled gaze was on Dakota.

Afraid the situation would career even further out of control, Felicity faced Westley. "Take him back to the center."

"Felicity—" Westley warned, even as he tugged on Dakota's leash, forcing the dog to retreat into the hallway. Felicity hurried to the door. She closed it to a crack, her gaze on Westley. "I'll be fine."

"I shouldn't be leaving you."

"It's okay. I'll be fine. He's my uncle, after all."

"I'll check on you after I get Dakota settled." He shook his head. "I don't get what got him so riled up."

"He must sense Uncle Patrick's animosity toward dogs," she said. Why else would Dakota go into full attack mode?

Westley nodded but he was clearly perplexed and upset by the situation. So was she. They trained for these variables. They couldn't have an unpredictable dog in the program. She only hoped this was an anomaly and not a new pattern of behavior for the German shepherd.

She shut the door and leaned against it. Her pulse galloped along her veins. She took several calming breaths, glad to see her uncle had set the gun on the dining-room table. He crossed to the bar and poured himself a tumbler of amber liquid. He held up the glass. "Want a drink?"

She shook her head. "No. Thank you." She blew out

a breath. "I'm not sure what got into Dakota. He's not like that normally."

"Mongrel beast should be put down," Uncle Patrick growled.

"No!" The thought of Dakota being euthanized because he'd thought he'd been protecting her nearly made her knees buckle.

Patrick downed his drink in one long swallow then poured himself another and moved to sit on the couch. "I hate dogs."

Trying to understand the virulence in Patrick's voice, she moved to sit across from him. "Mom told me you had a horrible experience with a dog once. What happened?"

Patrick leaned his head back against the couch and stared off as if remembering. "When we were kids, your mom and I would get off the school bus in the neighborhood before ours because it was quicker to walk home across the Moselys' field than wait a half an hour for the bus to circle around to our house. Mr. Mosely kept the field mowed but that spring he'd died and the field became overgrown. Still, we made a path through the tall grass and weeds." He sipped from his drink.

"One day a large mutt charged through the grass, barking and snarling." He shuddered and took another drink. "He belonged to Mr. Mosely's adult son."

"How old were you?"

He glanced at her. "Ten. Your mom was eight. She was a couple feet ahead of me on the path. I yelled for her to run but she froze." He rubbed a hand over his jaw. "I still can see her standing there. The look of terror on her face. That dog closing in on her. I reacted. I pushed her out of the way in the nick of time." He lifted his pant leg to reveal his calf muscle. "They're faint now, but I carry the scars of that dog's teeth."

She winced. No wonder her uncle had freaked out at Dakota's behavior. Felicity's heart hurt for her uncle and her mother. She could imagine the horror the two children experienced. "You saved Mom. You were a hero."

Patrick snorted. "Yeah. That's what everyone said. It didn't make the pain or the fear or the nightmares go away."

She could relate to lingering fear and nightmares. "I'm sorry. If I had known, we wouldn't have brought Dakota over."

He swirled the last of his drink before gulping it down. "Just keep the beast away from me."

"I will." She stood and picked up her bags by the front door. She needed to freshen up and have a moment alone. "Where shall I put my things?"

He waved toward a short hallway. "You can take the bedroom. On the right. Bath to the left. I'll sleep out here on the couch. And the master sergeant can use a bedroll when he returns."

She carried her bag to the bedroom and sank onto the edge of the bed. Propping her elbows on her knees, she dropped her head into her hands. Life had become a roller coaster. She was ready to jump off and be on even ground.

Her cell phone rang. She fished it from her pocket.

"Hey, you okay?" Westley's deep voice filled her head.

Relaxing back on to the bed, she replied, "Yes. Boy, oh, boy. What a day." She told him about the dog attack her uncle had suffered as a child.

"That explains your uncle's reaction, but not Dakota's. I've asked Dr. Roark to take a look at him when he has a free moment to make sure there's nothing medically wrong."

She sat up. "Oh, I hope that's not it." Or maybe she did hope so because then they could treat him. "Is Dakota calm now?"

"Not really. He hasn't been aggressive at all but he can't seem to focus and he keeps pacing back and forth in his kennel. Frankly I'm afraid to leave him until Dr. Roark can take a look at him. He did not want to leave your uncle's apartment complex. I practically had to drag him to the vehicle and then had to pick him up and put him in because he wouldn't jump in himself."

"That's so weird. There's no need for you to return here tonight. Stay with Dakota."

"Are you sure?"

"Yes, I'm safe here."

"Before I forget to tell you, Rusty found Riff and brought him in."

Her heart lifted. "That's good news."

A photo album on the bottom shelf of the bedside table caught her attention. She took it from the shelf and set it on the bed.

"On another note, I have a security company coming tomorrow morning to arm your house. Once they have the system in place you can return home."

"That's good." She flipped open the photo album. She wouldn't have pegged Uncle Patrick as the sentimental type to keep pictures in an album. The first page was of a bald-headed baby lying on a blanket. Uncle Patrick, she assumed. He was a cute baby. "I'm sure Uncle Patrick will be more than happy to have his bedroom back after he spends the night on his lumpy-looking couch."

Westley chuckled. "Couldn't be much worse than the cot at the center."

"Or the barracks," she countered. She flipped through the pages, smiling at the baby pictures of her uncle.

"True. I don't miss those bunks."

She ran a finger over the image of her mother as a baby. "Do you ever think about giving up your studio apartment for a house?"

"Someday."

When he had a wife and family? The thought snuck up on her. She wondered what it would take to make this man settle down. Did she have what it took to be the one he settled down with? Did she want that? A quiver of nerves ran through her as she realized there was a part of her that very much wanted a future with Westley. But how could she and still hope to work with the dogs?

"I should let you get some rest," he said. "I'm staying at the center a little longer. With Dakota behaving the way he is, I think I'd better keep an eye on him until he's less agitated. If you need anything, call me and I'll be right there."

"I will. I promise." She hung up and scooted to the head of the bed to lean against the wall. She continued to look through the photo album. There were many pictures of her uncle and mother as they grew up together. It was fun to see her mother going from a gap-toothed child, to a girl, to a teen, and finally to a young woman. The last few pages of the album held photos similar to the ones on the tablet.

One image held her attention. It was the same picture

of her father and Uncle Patrick that was on the tablet, but in this one, they were sitting on motorcycles. Two black bikes. And both men were dressed in black leather and holding black helmets.

Her hand went to the chain around her neck. Did the key belong to a motorcycle her father had once owned?

She scrambled off the bed, taking the photo album with her. In the kitchen she found Uncle Patrick drinking a beer and eating smoked salmon.

"Are you hungry?" he asked as she entered.

Taking a seat at the counter, she answered, "A little, actually." She laid the photo album open on the granite top. "I didn't know you and Dad rode motorcycles."

Patrick flicked a glance at the album. "Yep. Those were the good old days."

"Whatever happened to my dad's bike?" She'd never seen him on one.

"Colleen didn't like it, so he sold it."

She studied the motorbike in the photo. Remembering Linc's certainty of the type of bike the key on her gold chain fit, she asked, "Was Dad's motorcycle a BMW 2 series?"

Patrick's shoulders visibly stiffened. He slowly turned toward her. "Why would you ask about that specific bike?"

The coldness in his tone sent a chill sliding down her spine. Her mind scrambled to see why her question would upset him. Should she tell him about the key? She couldn't see what harm it would be to show him what she'd found. She tugged the chain out from beneath her uniform top and held up the key. "I found this in Dad's desk."

Patrick took a long swig of his beer and wiped his

mouth with the back of his hand before setting the bottle on the counter and closing the distance between them to stare at the key. He crossed his arms over his barrel chest. "No. Your father rode a Ducati."

"Oh." She wasn't sure what to make of Uncle Patrick's strange reaction to the key. Her gaze strayed back to the picture. The two bikes did look a bit different. She lifted her gaze. "Was your motorcycle the BMW?"

"It was."

Her heart beat a bit faster in her chest. "Where's the bike now?"

"Scrap yard."

"A long time ago, right?" She hoped, because the thought forming in her mind was causing distress to strangle her from the inside out. Uncle Patrick couldn't be the rider of the motorcycle that had struck the pedestrian and left him paralyzed, could he?

"Where's your father's tablet, Felicity?"

Her breath hitched. She strove to keep her cool as panic flared in her gut and lit a hot path to her brain. Oh, no. No, no, no. Uncle Patrick couldn't be her father's murderer. He couldn't be the one who'd tried to poison her. The one who had shot at Westley.

Oh! Lungs tight from lack of air, the world tilted as the realization slid home. Dakota had snapped at the man who'd shot him.

"Where is it?" Patrick demanded again.

Sliding from the stool, Felicity faced her uncle. "You killed my father."

Patrick's eyes narrowed. "He fell off the ladder."

Anger infused her. "Did he? Or did you stage it to look that way?"

Lips thinning, Patrick stepped closer. "Don't mess with me."

Refusing to be intimidated, she stood her ground. "You were the one riding the motorcycle that hit the young man and then rode away."

"He stepped out from between two cars," Patrick said, his words an admission and an excuse.

"Then why didn't you stop and help him?"

"That's exactly what your father asked."

"It's a valid question." Her gaze went to the beer bottle then back to him. "You were drinking."

"I'd had a few. I didn't see the guy. It wasn't my fault. But your father demanded I turn myself in." He let out a bitter laugh. "Like that was going to happen."

"So you killed him?" Her heart bled with grief over the senselessness of it all. If Patrick had just owned up to his crime, her dad would still be alive.

"Graham wouldn't listen." Patrick moved toward her. "I want that tablet, Felicity. And any copies you made."

She narrowed her gaze. Copies? "You're the one who planted the bomb in Westley's vehicle and called me. I knew I recognized the voice." And Dakota had recognized his scent on the explosives.

His face twisted. "I should have just blown you all up."

"Why did you leave the note and rose?" She let out a humorless laugh. "Oh, I know, to pin your crime on the Red Rose Killer."

"I'm still going to pin my crimes on that maniac."

Her stomach knotted at the implication in her uncle's words. "I'm leaving."

He grabbed her arm. "No. You're going to give me that tablet."

"I don't have it." She jerked her arm from him and backed away. Her gaze landed on the dining room table a few feet from her, where her uncle's service weapon still sat. If she could get to it... She edged toward the table.

Patrick lunged forward, knocking her to the side and pouncing on his gun. She regained her balance, but he swung the barrel toward her.

She stilled, her hands up. Her heart plummeted. Fear turned her blood to ice, making her ache with dread. "Don't do anything rash."

"Where's the tablet?" He advanced on her.

"At the training center where all those *beasts* are." She had the satisfaction of seeing her uncle blanch.

She sent up a silent plea to God that somehow, someway, Westley would be able to disarm her uncle before he killed her or anyone else.

"There's nothing medically wrong with this dog," Dr. Roark told Westley. "His wound is healing nicely. His heart rate is normal and so is his temperature."

Motioning for a much calmer Dakota to jump off the exam table, Westley said, "That's good to know but it doesn't explain his strange aggression toward Felicity's uncle."

Dr. Roark pumped hand sanitizer on his palm and rubbed his hands together. "Had he and Dakota ever met?"

Westley thought about that. "Yes." Patrick had shown up at Felicity's house. "But Dakota hadn't reacted at all then."

"Something must have happened between then and

today," the doctor suggested. "Something that made Dakota want to lash out?"

But what? Westley hadn't seen her uncle again until a little while ago. Could it be that Dakota had sensed the other man's fear and reacted? No, Dakota wouldn't have shown such extreme hostility because of the other man's fear.

It was a puzzle that Westley intended to unravel because he couldn't have an undisciplined dog in the program. He would have to do some research and see if there was something in Dakota's background before he came to Canyon that might explain his behavior.

With Dakota by his side, they left the vet clinic and headed along the now darkened street toward the training center. When they reached the edge of the parking lot, Westley stopped short. A thought rammed into him with the force of a missile.

What if Dakota had reacted so violently because he recognized the scent of the man who'd shot him?

The realization made Westley stumble, and nearly go to his knees.

Felicity!

He had to get to her. To warn her. To protect her. From her uncle.

At a run, he led Dakota to one of the training-center vehicles. He had keys to all the SUVs on his keychain. Quickly, he and Dakota jumped inside. He fumbled to find the right key and stuck it into the ignition.

Headlights cut across the parking lot as one of the maintenance trucks pulled in and came to an abrupt halt. The driver's door flew open, and Staff Sergeant Patrick Dooley hopped out, a gun in his hand.

Dakota let out a snarl.

"Quiet," Westley admonished, not wanting to alert the other man to their presence. Breath lodged in his throat, he watched Patrick motion with the gun and Felicity climbed out of the vehicle.

Westley's heart stuttered to a crawl. Patrick was forcing Felicity to turn over the tablet. But what would Patrick do when he realized she didn't have the combination to the safe?

Holding his breath, Westley waited until Felicity and her uncle disappeared into the training center before he and Dakota jumped out of the SUV and raced to the door.

There was no time to call for backup. Westley had to get inside before Patrick did something drastic.

Swallowing back the fear of losing Felicity, Westley felt determination burn through his gut. He would do anything to save the woman he loved.

THIRTEEN

With the barrel of the gun pressing hard against her ribs, Felicity led the way through the training center toward the back office. The muted sound of dogs barking from the kennel filled the hallway.

Glancing at her uncle, she noticed the beads of sweat on his brow and the tightness around his mouth. He was nervous. After hearing of his horrific ordeal when he'd been attacked by a vicious dog, she wanted to feel sorry for him, but any sort of tender emotions toward her uncle were gone.

He'd basically admitted to killing her father, who'd supposedly been his best friend, and trying to kill her, his own niece.

Her mother was going to be devastated.

Felicity's heart hurt for her mom.

As they passed the break room, Lila Fields stepped out, nearly ramming into them.

"Oh, I'm sorry," the rookie trainer said, almost dropping the plate in her hand along with a buttered bagel.

"No problem." Felicity tried to keep her voice neutral and not let the panic show.

Lila's curious gaze landed on Patrick. "Hello."

Felicity gritted her teeth. The last thing she needed was Lila asking questions or becoming suspicious that something was wrong. She didn't want anybody else's life in danger. She needed Lila to go about her business so that Uncle Patrick wouldn't feel the need to harm the woman.

Hoping to keep her voice free of the fear making her heart boom in her ears and her fingertips tingle, she said, "Lila, this is my Uncle Patrick. We're looking for Westley. Is he in his office?"

"No, I believe he took Dakota to the vet."

Felicity's stomach sank. She wasn't sure what to do now. When Uncle Patrick realized she didn't know how to get into the safe, he would go ballistic. She had to figure out a way to overpower him. A dismal prospect. He outweighed her by half, at least.

"We'll wait for him, then," Uncle Patrick said. "In his office."

He gave Felicity a nudge with the barrel of the gun, effectively keeping the weapon out of sight, and kept his fingers tightly around her biceps.

Leaving Lila with a nod, they continued down the hall. Once inside the office, Patrick gave her a little shove, forcing her to the middle of the room, while he shut the door.

"Where's the tablet?"

"It's in the safe." She visually swept the room, searching for something to disarm him with, or to knock him out.

Anger for all he'd done—a hit-and-run, killing her father, trying to kill her—burned like a torch inside of her. But there was nothing within reach to use as a weapon. Frustration beat against her temple. Her fingers curled at her side.

Waving the gun, Patrick said, "Where's the safe?"

Felicity swallowed back the anxiety dampening her anger. "In the desk cabinet to the right."

Uncle Patrick moved to inspect the cabinet. Taking advantage of his distraction, she edged toward the door, hoping to make an escape. If she could get to the kennels, she could let the dogs loose. Uncle Patrick might run away.

Or shoot one of the canines.

On second thought, she couldn't put the animals at risk, either.

"Take one more step and you'll regret it," Uncle Patrick said, aiming the weapon at her head. "Open the safe."

"I don't have the combination." Holding up her hands, she spoke calmly, much more calmly than she felt. "Only Westley does."

She wasn't sure if that was true. She supposed Caleb Streeter had access, but she wouldn't volunteer that information. Who knew what Uncle Patrick would do.

Uncle Patrick plopped down into one of the two side chairs and put his feet up on the desk. "Then we'll wait for Master Sergeant James."

Apprehension bubbled up in her chest. She wished there was a way to warn Westley. She hated the thought of him walking in blind to the situation.

She remained standing where she was between Uncle Patrick and the door, hoping that when Westley came in she could provide a shield. She could only pray that Lila would see Westley before he headed to the office and tell him they were waiting.

At least that would give him a heads-up. But it wouldn't tell him to be cautious. He had no idea her uncle was the one behind her father's murder and the attempts on her life.

She hoped Westley would cooperate with her uncle because she couldn't stand it if anything happened to him.

Deep inside she had to admit her concern for Westley's welfare not only stemmed from the fact that they were friends and worked closely together, but also because her feelings for him had morphed into something that left her breathless.

She loved Westley.

If the circumstances weren't so dire and precarious, she'd sink to the floor with the knowledge that she'd fallen in love with the one man she shouldn't. Not if she hoped to return to the training center under his command.

It was a problem she had no idea how to resolve. She prayed there would be time to figure it out.

Westley kept Dakota at his side as they eased into the back entrance of the training center. The overhead light revealed the hallway was empty. Knowing Felicity's uncle would go nowhere near the dogs, Westley figured they had headed to the office. He needed to get there before anything happened to Felicity. With caution tightening his shoulder muscles, he and Dakota hustled to the office. The door was closed.

Dakota sniffed the edge of the door. The hair on his back raised, alerting to the fact that the dog smelled the enemy. Westley gave Dakota the hand signal used by soldiers for combat silence and then motioned for the dog to take up a position on his belly to the side of the door out of the line of sight.

Feeling the need to ask God for help, Westley sent up a quick prayer. Hope that the Lord above would hear his plea bolstered his resolve. He dug his phone from his pocket and put it on silent, then dialed Captain Blackwood's cell.

Leaving the line open, he tucked the cell into his breast pocket and reached for the door handle. On a deep breath, he swung the door open, careful to keep to the side in case Patrick had a twitchy trigger finger.

Felicity stood in the middle of the room, her surprised gaze meeting his. She mouthed, *He's got a gun.*

Giving her a nod, Westley decided to play ignorant. "What's going on?"

"Come in, Master Sergeant," Patrick drawled from the chair facing the desk. "Put your hands in the air."

Complying, Westley walked through the door and moved to stand next to Felicity. "What's with the gun, Staff Sergeant Dooley?"

Patrick's feet hit the floor. "I want the tablet."

"Okay. I'll give it to you." Obviously the man wasn't thinking clearly. There was no way he'd walk out of here unscathed. They were in a public place. One yell and reinforcements would come. But Westley had questions, and the best way to learn the answers was to appease him. "Tell me why you've been trying to kill your niece."

"It's that serial killer's fault," Patrick said. "He targeted Felicity. I knew once that happened there would be extra scrutiny on her and eventually there'd be questions about Graham's death. Agent Steffen was sniffing around, trying to reopen the investigation. I had to make sure there was nothing left of Graham's investigation to point to me."

"Are you admitting to killing Agent Monroe?" Westley asked him.

"I'm not admitting anything."

"But my father's case notes will convict you of the hit-and-run," Felicity said.

"I told you that was an accident," Patrick said.

"And poisoning Felicity? Was that an accident?"

"It would have worked if that dog hadn't intervened," Patrick groused. "Everyone would have thought that psycho had made good on his threat. And then I could have found the tablet."

Felicity took a step forward. "What did you do with my father's laptop?"

The older man snorted. "It's at the bottom of the Gulf of Mexico." Patrick waved his gun. "Now give me that tablet! Once I destroy the thing, there won't be any evidence."

Afraid that Patrick's agitated state would lead to him shooting Felicity, Westley tucked her behind him, where he could protect her. "Once we give you the evidence, then what? Are you going to kill us, too? Both of us?"

A scowl wrinkled Patrick's forehead. "I'll have to, won't I? Even if you couldn't prove what happened was my fault, you'd make my life miserable. But I'll make sure to blame it on the Red Rose Killer."

The man was definitely unhinged if he thought he'd get away with his scheme. Keeping a hand on Felicity and forcing her to move in tandem with him, Westley edged slowly around to the other side of the desk, leaving a clear path from the doorway to Patrick. "Boyd Sullivan is a convenient scapegoat."

"You won't get away with it," Felicity said. "Agent Steffen will discover your crimes."

"He hasn't yet," Patrick said. "Now, open the safe."

Knowing they had one shot at this, Westley tugged Felicity into a crouch in front of the safe. In a loud, clear voice, Westley yelled, "Get 'em!"

Dakota sprang into action, charging into the room and going straight for Patrick's leg. His powerful jaw latched on. Patrick let out a yowl of pain and terror. Westley jumped up and vaulted over the desk, grabbing the gun and wresting it away from the other man.

Aiming the weapon at Patrick's chest, Westley gave the commands, "Out! Heel!"

The dog immediately let go and backed up to a sit beside Westley. But Dakota's body was tense and poised, ready to attack if given the command.

Patrick crumpled to a heap, his hands holding on to his leg. Felicity grabbed the desk lamp and lifted it high over her uncle's head.

"Felicity, no. It's over," Westley said, afraid she'd follow through on the intent in her eyes. He didn't want her to have that regret. "I have him covered. He's not going anywhere."

Slowly, her gaze cleared and she lowered the lamp, setting it carefully back on the desk. Stiffly, she moved to stand next to Dakota. She put a hand on his head. "Good dog."

The sound of pounding feet filled the room and a moment later several Security Forces officers stormed in with weapons drawn. Then Captain Blackwood stepped inside, followed by Ian.

"It seems you have everything under control, Master Sergeant James," the captain said. Holding up his phone, he added, "We heard everything."

Lowering the gun and handing it to Security Forces, Westley told Felicity, "I dialed the captain's cell before I entered."

She blinked up at him with surprise lighting the depths of her eyes. "How did you know?"

"I realized that Dakota was reacting to the scent of the man who'd shot him when he went into attack mode back at your uncle's apartment," he explained. "I should have figured that out right away. I'm so sorry you had to go through this."

"I didn't see it at first, either," she told him. "He's family." She watched as the Security Forces officers dragged her uncle from the room in handcuffs. Westley put his arm around her shoulders, offering her what comfort he could. It took every ounce of willpower he possessed not to gather her in his arms and hold her close and never let her go.

"I thought I could trust him." She shook her head, sadness pulling at the corners of her mouth. He wanted to kiss away her disappointment and hurt.

"I found a photo of him and my dad on motorcycles," she said. "That's when I realized he was the one whom my dad was investigating for the hit-and-run." She let out a bitter sound. "He said my dad had wanted him to turn himself in, but Uncle Patrick refused. Instead, he killed my father and made it look like an accident."

"You can rest easy now," Ian said.

"No," Westley countered, his heart rate jumping. "She's still a target of the Red Rose Killer."

"Of course," Ian stated. "That's not what I meant at all. We have closure now on Agent Monroe's death. The family of the hit-and-run victim will appreciate knowing the man who paralyzed their son will be charged with multiple crimes and spend the rest of his life in prison."

It was justice. But it would be painful for the Monroe family.

"What is the latest intel on Sullivan?" Westley asked.

"There have been reported sightings all over the state," Justin answered. "We're not sure of the reliability of any of the information. Our best guess is Boyd is paying people to claim they've seen him."

Westley's gut clenched. She was still in danger. Not only from the maniac serial killer known as the Red Rose Killer, but also from Westley's feelings for her. He didn't know how he could continue to be detailed to her protection while keeping his love for her a secret. He wasn't that good at subterfuge.

He was going to have to trust that God would watch over her and arrange for someone else to be assigned to her protection detail. For both their sakes.

"You're what?" Felicity stared at Westley. Sunlight filtering through the blinds of the photo lab gleamed in his dark hair. His beret was tucked into the pocket of his battle-ready uniform as he stood with his hands stiff at his sides, and his strong jaw was set in a determined line. Beside him Dakota tilted his head, his dark-eyed gaze bouncing between them.

"You can't asked to be rotated off my detail," she stated flatly.

Why would he do that? Her pulse pounded with adrenaline as if she'd run a marathon. Every vital system in her went on alert at hearing such disturbing news.

"It's a good idea if we don't spend as much time together," he said in a rush.

Disbelief washed over her. "You don't want to spend time with me?"

He grimaced. "No. That's not it."

"I'm pretty certain that is what you just said."

"I'm botching this."

She planted her fists on her hips. "You think?" A ribbon of frustration wound around her heart.

Rolling his shoulders, he said, "The training center needs me."

"I thought Caleb was handling things there."

"He is."

"But you're not happy with his work?"

"No. I mean, that's not what I'm saying."

Her head was spinning. She wished he'd be clearer. "Then…?"

"Caleb is doing a great job, but there are just some things that need to be taken care of, that need my attention. And still so many dogs are missing. I need to focus on finding the dogs."

She wasn't quite sure she believed that excuse. Yes, the dogs were a priority. One she could help him with. She really didn't want to take offense at him basically standing here telling her he didn't want to be with her, but she couldn't help the sense of betrayal. Hurt. Disappointment flooded her veins. The training center had been running fine for the past week, and would continue to. But that really wasn't the issue, was it?

She'd thought she and Westley had come so far. She'd thought he felt the same way toward her. She'd hoped he'd fallen in love with her the way she'd fallen in love with him. Apparently, she was wrong.

"You don't want to protect me anymore." The words tasted bitter on the tongue. "Okay, I get it. You didn't want the detail in the first place. I don't even know why you agreed to it."

She walked away from him, stopping at the desk to picked up her camera. She fiddled with the lenses, trying hard not to let the tears burning the back of her eyes fall. Her heart crumbled, the pain sharp.

He came up behind her, awareness seared her clean through. His hands rested lightly on her shoulders and gave her a gentle squeeze.

"Felicity, it's not that I don't want to protect you. I do, but I can't."

She didn't understand. He wasn't making sense. He'd done a wonderful job so far. He and Dakota.

She turned around and stared into Westley's handsome face. There was distress in his eyes.

Was this because of her uncle? Her heart hurt to think that Westley still believed he'd somehow failed by letting her uncle get so close. "This mess with my uncle was not your fault." She implored him to understand. "You have to accept that. There was no way for you or anyone to suspect Uncle Patrick killed my father and was the one trying to kill me."

A tender smile played at the corner of his mouth. "I do know that. I just wish I'd caught him sooner so you wouldn't have had to go through all of this."

"I'm okay and he's in custody. He won't hurt me again, not from prison."

A pang of sadness for her mom thrummed through Felicity. The conversations Felicity and her mother had

had over the past few hours had been tense and tearful, but better than any conversations they'd had before. Felicity felt they'd turned a corner in their relationship. Her mom had asked if Felicity would come to San Francisco for Christmas this year. She'd agreed.

"Boyd Sullivan is still out there." Westley stepped back, putting distance between them. "You're still a target. You need protection 24/7. I can't provide that for you anymore."

She stepped toward him. "Why? Why can't you?"

He spread his hands wide, as if encompassing the obviousness of it all. "We will have to work together again one day. I'm not going to risk your career because I can't control my feelings for you."

Her heart skipped a little bit. He *did* care for her. A smile spread through her, from the top of her head to the tips of her toes. "You *do* have feelings for me," she nearly whispered.

He ran a hand through his hair. "Of course I do, Felicity," he huffed. "But if I stay close to you…"

Her mouth went dry. "Westley."

He took another step back. "I will not act on my feelings. There's too much at stake. Your career. My career."

Her heart beat hard in her throat. She moved a step closer. "What if I told you I have feelings for you, too?"

He held up a hand as if to ward her off. "No, no. We can't go down that road."

"But what if I want to?" She made up the distance with two steps. He stepped back again. This dance was taking them across the room toward the door. She frowned. "What are you afraid of, Westley?"

"I can never be the man you need." The words were harsh, as if torn from him.

Absorbing his statement, she shook her head, denying his claim. "Of course you are. Don't you understand? I'm in love with you, Westley."

The color drained from his face. "You can't be."

"But I am and you're going have to face the fact that you love me, too." She prayed her words were true as she stepped closer and grasped the sleeve of his jacket. The cotton fabric was soft and crumbled easily beneath her fingers. The man wearing it was the polar opposite. "Do you deny loving me?"

His gaze fixated on her hand then rose to meet hers. There was so much torment in his eyes that she hurt for him. And she hurt for herself, because she knew he would never own up to his feelings for her. She just didn't understand why.

He gently pried her fingers loose and held her hands in his. "Felicity, I care for you more than I've ever cared for anyone else."

That gave her a spurt of hope.

"But the United States Air Force is our lives. Our careers. I will not allow anything to derail your career."

"That's not your choice to make."

He let go of her hand and took two steps back this time. His hand grasped onto the doorknob. "I'll talk to Lieutenant General Hall. I'll have Caleb and maybe Ethan and Linc, or whoever else I can get from Security Forces to rotate in."

Her fingers curled into her palms. He wasn't giving her a chance to choose for herself.

"I'm not saying I won't be there for you, Felicity. I will, but I just can't do it around-the-clock. It's too painful."

He opened the door and gave her one last longing look that broke her heart in two. "I'm sorry."

Motioning to Dakota, he said, "Stay. Guard." Then Westley disappeared out the door.

Felicity staggered to the desk and sank onto the chair. What just happened? He didn't give them a chance. He didn't give her a chance to tell him that she'd... That she'd what? What she would do for them?

She looked around the photo lab, taking in the pictures hanging on the walls that she'd shot over the last week, and realized with certainty she enjoyed this job and would gladly stay in it, if that meant she and Westley could be together.

But obviously he didn't want her to be with him. Or maybe he did, but he was too scared. Either way, the outcome was the same. He'd walked away from her. From them.

A little voice inside her challenged, *What are you going to do about it, Felicity?*

She rose and walked to the window to stare out at the late April morning enveloping Canyon Air Force Base in a warm glow. She contemplated the question.

What could she do? She'd told him she loved him and he still left. Did she chase after him like some crazy stalker?

No. He didn't want her.

She would just have to learn to live without him.

FOURTEEN

Westley stared into the depths of his root-beer bottle. Around him conversation and laughter abounded through Canyon Air Force Base's popular diner. He sat at the counter because the thought of a table for one didn't appeal.

He ached from head to toe. Not from physical exertion, though he'd run the dogs and handlers hard the last two days in between searching for more of the missing dogs. No, he hurt because he missed Felicity and Dakota.

Lieutenant General Hall had agreed to let Westley rotate out of Felicity's detail and leave Dakota in place for her security.

Knowing Dakota was keeping watch over Felicity gave Westley some comfort, but he missed her laughter and the joy on her face as she captured images with her camera. And while he hated for her to experience it, he also missed the sorrow that at times darkened her eyes when she didn't think he noticed.

He noticed everything about her. And loved everything about her.

I'm in love with you, Westley.

Her words were sweet torment.

But it was for the best that he kept a distance between them, for both of their sakes. And if he kept reminding himself of that fact, at some point it had to become true, right?

A hand slapped him on the back of the shoulder. "Drowning your sorrows there, Westley?"

Westley slanted a glance sidewise to see Special Agent Ian Steffen sliding onto the stool next to him. He sat up straight. "No, sir." He winced. "I mean, yes, sir."

Ian waved off the formality. "Relax. We're just two guys sitting at a counter having a soda." Ian gave the amber bottle nestled in Westley's hand a once-over. "Root beer. Okay. I'll take one of those," he told the waitress who came over. She nodded, grabbed a bottle from refrigerator, popped off the top and plunked it down on the counter in front of Ian before walking away.

Westley sank back into his dejected mode. Funny how easy it was. He'd thought he'd long ago shaken off feeling sorry for himself, but without Felicity in his life, he felt lost and adrift. The future he'd once seen so clearly had dissolved into mist. He didn't know what to do now. It all seemed so bleak.

"Cyberintelligence cracked the pass code on the folder in Graham's tablet," Ian told him.

Westley gave the man his attention. "And?"

"As we thought, it contained all of Graham's case notes on the hit-and-run, including incriminating evidence against his brother-in-law," Ian replied. "Not that we need the evidence with all that transpired."

"But at least we know for sure," Westley said. He peeled at the label of the root beer bottle. He was glad for Felicity's sake that she had closure on her father's death.

After a beat of silence, Ian asked, "What ails you?"

Westley shrugged. "It's been a long week." Actually a long few days. Days without Felicity in his life.

"You want to tell me why you asked to be rotated off Staff Sergeant Monroe's protection detail?"

Should he confess to the OSI agent that he'd grown fond…no, *fond* wasn't the right word. Grown to *love* his charge?

If he did, there would be no going back.

"Personal reasons," he finally said. He wouldn't put either of their careers, especially Felicity's, in jeopardy.

Ian gave him a dubious look. "Right. I think you've fallen in love with the pretty staff sergeant and are afraid to do anything about it."

Westley choked on a sip of root beer. He cleared his throat and took probably one of the biggest gambles of his career by looking the agent in the eye. "Excuse me?"

Ian grinned. "Man, it's obvious." His dark eyes actually twinkled with certainty. Westley couldn't decide if the roiling in his stomach came from relief or terror. "I remember that feeling from long ago when I first met my late wife."

"Do you regret falling in love?" Westley asked. The thought of losing Felicity terrified him. But so did living without her. He couldn't win.

It was Ian's turn to stare into the abyss of his root-beer bottle. "I learned along the way that regret only breeds discontentment. You do what you do, with the most information you have at the time, and sometimes it works great." He lifted a muscular shoulder. "Sometimes not so much, but at least you did something." He stared Westley in the eyes. "Running away isn't doing something. It's chickening out. Running away is not what we do in the US Air Force."

Westley straightened. "I'm not running away."

"Looks that way to me."

"I don't want to do anything to jeopardize her career. She wants to be a dog trainer. We can't be in the same chain of command."

Ian arched an eyebrow. "You could move over to Security Forces and be a dog handler. You could leave the service and go into civilian law enforcement."

Westley had thought of those same options. "I don't know what would be the right decision." He blew out a breath and pushed back against the counter. "Frankly, I don't feel worthy of her love."

Ian shook his head. "I never pegged you as insecure. Get over yourself. Does she love you?"

A tremble coursed through Westley. "She said she did."

The man scoffed. "What are you sitting here for? That's where you start," Ian insisted. "All the rest of the decisions will work themselves out."

Could it be that simple? "I wish her father was here so I can ask for her hand, because he would either give me his blessing or tell me to get lost."

"Still sounds vaguely to me like you're looking for another excuse to bolt. But that's just me." Ian shrugged.

Westley shook his head. "Agent Steffen, don't go easy on me, or anything—"

"Okay, okay." Ian laughed, holding up his hands in mock surrender. "Just saying…" He trailed off, then eyed Westley speculatively. "She has a mother, you know."

"Yes, yes, she does."

"Colleen Monroe is a tough and shrewd woman. If you can obtain her blessing then you're set."

Westley swigged the last of his root beer and contemplated everything the agent had said. He did need to get over himself. Felicity loved him despite his family history. He'd left his parents' failings behind when he joined the air force.

Of the options available to him, he realized it didn't matter what he did. The only option he couldn't live with was not having Felicity in his life. "You're right, Agent Steffen," he said with determination. "I need to go after what I want."

He wanted Felicity in his life as surely as she was in his heart.

Ian tipped his root beer bottle toward Westley's. Westley clinked his bottle against Ian's.

"Here's to going after what you want," the agent said.

"Aim high—" Westley began the USAF motto.

"Fly, fight, win," Ian said, finishing his sentence.

Sliding off the bar stool, Westley said, "I'd better go make a phone call."

With a nod of thanks, Westley headed out the door with purpose in his stride.

Felicity arrived home three nights later, escorted by one of the base MPs and with Dakota trotting alongside her. The dog had been her constant companion even as the detail changed every eight hours. Westley had been true to his word that she would be protected around-the-clock. She was grateful. She really was, but she missed him. Missed the way his eyes crinkled at the corners when he was amused. Missed the way he made her feel safe and cherished.

Shoulders slumped, she was headed up the walkway toward her front door when Heidi stepped out of the house next door and called her name.

Needing a friend right now, Felicity hesitated. Many people on base believed the reporter to be the anonymous blogger leaking information to the public. Could Felicity trust her?

Only one way to find out. Felicity did an about-face and moved past the guard. Dakota stayed right at her heels. She met Heidi at the shared property line.

"Hi, Heidi. How are you tonight?" Felicity asked, careful to keep the despair she clinging to her from tingeing her voice.

"Better than you, I take it," Heidi said. "You look like somebody kicked your dog." Heidi smiled at Dakota. "But he looks okay."

That's kind of how Felicity felt. Except Dakota was right here, healthy and strong and willing to protect her even when Westley wasn't willing.

Her hands tangled in Dakota's fur. She dredged up a smile for Heidi. "I'm okay. Still trying to process everything."

"I'm so sorry about your uncle," Heidi said.

"Thanks. Me, too."

Heidi glanced toward the security guard. "I thought Westley was detailed to your protection."

"He needed to do some things at the training center," Felicity said. The ache in her chest intensified. "He'll rotate back in at some point." At least she hoped so. Then they could talk and resolve some of their issues. Or not. It had been three days since he walked out of her office in the photo lab. Three days with strangers following her around base, sleeping on her couch, watching out for Boyd Sullivan. Three days with her wishing Westley was there beside her. Only the presence of Dakota brought her any peace.

Depression and exhaustion set in. "I need to go get some rest," she told Heidi. "We have new recruits coming in tomorrow and I want to catch them as they get off the bus."

Heidi smiled gently. "Sure, no problem. I'll talk to you later."

"Thanks." Felicity hurried into the house, the young guard following her. "Make yourself at home," she told the MP.

She went to the refrigerator and grabbed herself a ginger ale to settle her upset stomach. Then she and Dakota headed upstairs. He was the only one she let witness her tears.

"Master Sergeant James, what can I do for you?" The clipped female voice on the other end of the phone line had Westley straightening his spine and squaring his shoulders. He stared out the window of his small studio apartment in base housing. From this vantage point he could see the parade grounds, where several vintage planes were on display, a sight he never tired of.

Taking a breath and gathering his courage, he said, "I am calling to ask for your permission to marry your daughter."

Colleen Monroe's voice dipped. "Excuse me? You want to marry Felicity?"

Though they were miles apart and he couldn't see

her, he recognized the strength in her voice. This was a woman used to intimidating others.

"Yes, ma'am, I do. I'm in love with your daughter."

After a heartbeat of silence, she asked, "How well do you know my daughter?"

"I know her very well. We are stationed together at Canyon Air Force Base."

"I owe you a debt of gratitude, Master Sergeant James," the woman said, her tone soft with emotion. "Felicity told me how you saved her life on several occasions. You have my permission to ask her to marry you." There was a smile in her voice.

Tension drained from his shoulders. "Thank you."

Now to convince Felicity to give him another chance.

Felicity hurried down the hall toward Lieutenant General Hall's office. She'd been summoned a few minutes ago from the photo lab, where she was busy uploading today's photos to the FBI database. Thus far she hadn't captured any images of Boyd Sullivan.

She knocked on the lieutenant general's door and heard a male voice say "Enter."

Pushing open the door, she stepped inside and froze. Lieutenant General Hall sat behind his desk, but it was the sight of Westley standing in front of the desk that made her pulse race. She drank up the sight of him. He wore his semiformal dress uniform, the dark navy coat looking sharp over his broad shoulders and tapered waist. His creased navy pants and black shoes made him appear taller. Formidable.

The moment his tender gaze met hers, her mouth dried like the desert.

"Come all the way in, Staff Sergeant," Lieutenant General Hall instructed.

Buying herself time to process the situation, she closed the door, adjusted her uniform coat and patted her braided hair before turning back around and walking slowly toward the two men.

She drew herself to attention and trained her focus on the lieutenant general. She saluted. "Sir?"

"At ease," Lieutenant General Hall said. He stood. "I'll give you two the room."

"Sir?" Confusion ran rampant through her system.

Lieutenant General Hall rounded the desk and stopped beside her. He put his hand on her shoulder. "Your father would be proud of you, Felicity."

Her mouth dropped open as the lieutenant general left the room. Then her gaze sought Westley's. "I don't understand."

He stepped close and took her hands in his. "I can explain but first I want to know if you'll give me another chance."

She inhaled sharply. "Are you ready to give us a chance?"

"I am," he said. "You were right. I was afraid. Afraid of failing you or disappointing you."

Tenderness filled her.

"But as someone recently told me, I need to get over myself and go after what I want."

"What is it you want?"

"You. Us." He lifted her hands to his lips and kissed her knuckles. "I love you, Felicity. I want to spend the rest of my life making you happy. Keeping you safe. Loving you."

Her breath held in her lungs. Excitement bubbled inside her chest. "What are you asking me, Westley?"

"Will you marry me?"

Elation engulfed her, making her head swim. "Yes. Yes, I'll marry you."

He let out a shout of joy and clasped his arms around her and swung her off her feet into a dizzying circle. When her feet touched the ground she leaned toward him, needing a kiss.

But he held back. His face was serious as he looked at her. "Are you sure?"

Was he still so unsure of her, unsure of her feelings for him?

She laid her hands on his chest, feeling his heart beating in double time. She would spend the rest of her days making sure this man knew her love was true and forever. "Yes, I am sure. I want to marry you. I want to spend the rest of my days with you and, God willing, there will be many, many days."

She fought back the specter of Boyd Sullivan and his horrible roses and notes. She wouldn't allow him and his threats to crowd in on her happiness.

A grin spread across Westley's face. "Close your eyes," he said.

"What?"

"Trust me. Close your eyes."

She closed her eyes. He wrapped an arm around her waist and turned her around. "We're walking," he said.

Chuckling, she allowed him to lead her forward. She heard the office door open. Then they were walking on the carpeted hallway toward the entrance of the building.

"How much farther?" she asked.

"Just a bit," he said. "No peeking."

"I won't." She heard the click of the outside doors opening and then they stepped out into the evening breeze.

"Stairs," he told her. He led her down the steps in front of the command building and then across the asphalt of the driveway.

Her feet sank in the grass. Overhead the flap of the American flag let her know they were standing beneath the flagpole in front of the command center. She heard a chuckle, but not from Westley.

"Don't open your eyes until I say so, okay?" Westley asked.

She sighed. "Okay, fine."

He moved away from her, leaving her standing there alone. But she wasn't afraid. She knew she was safe. Westley was close by.

"Open your eyes," he said.

She blinked against the setting sun as her eyes focused. People stood at the edges of the lawn, but it was only the two males directly in front of her that held her attention.

Dakota sat next to a kneeling Westley, a large bow decorated the German shepherd's neck. Her gaze locked on the small little silver box dangling from the ribbon. Her heart fluttered with delight.

"Surprise," Westley said.

"Is that…?" She swallowed.

Westley undid the bow, letting the little silver box drop into his open palm.

She edged closer. Her body quivered with excitement.

He opened the box and held it up for her to see a

beautiful marquis solitaire ring nestled next to a braided gold band.

"Felicity Monroe, will you please do me the honor of becoming my wife?"

She went down on her knees in front of him, her hands closing over his. "Yes. A thousand times, yes."

He slipped the diamond ring on her finger.

Dakota let out a happy *woof.* A cheer went up from the spectators. She lifted her gaze to see that so many of their friends had gathered to witness the proposal. She grinned.

Westley touched the braided ring still nestled in the box. "This is for the ceremony and for you to wear whenever you don't want to wear the diamond. It's not safe to wear the diamond when you're working with dogs."

One of the issues they needed to resolve. She closed the box. "I'm the base photographer."

"Only until the Red Rose Killer is caught."

"What happens after that?"

"Once you are no longer in danger, I will give up my post and go into civilian law enforcement."

She shook head. "Unacceptable. The only way this will work is if you stay at the training center."

He opened his mouth to argue, but she put a finger to his lips. "Don't you see? This way I get the best of both worlds. You stay at the training center and I can come visit you and the dogs anytime I want. You do your dream job and I get to be a photographer. A dream I never even realized I wanted."

His lips split in a broad grin. "I love you."

"Good. I'll need to hear that a lot." She held up her hand, admiring the sparkly ring on her finger. "I will wear this diamond with pride and joy. But more importantly, I will love you for always."

He cupped her head and kissed her. Another cheer went up. Dakota wedged his way between them, breaking the kiss. The dog licked her face. She and Westley laughed with happiness. And they would be happy. Despite Boyd, despite her uncle and despite any threat to try to come between them.

Westley helped her to her feet. "How soon should we do this?"

"As soon as Pastor Harmon is available," she said.

Westley waggled his eyebrows. "I was hoping you'd say that. We have him booked for tomorrow afternoon."

She giggled. "You don't waste any time."

"I don't want to spend another moment without you by my side."

"By your side is where I want to be. Always."

"It's been a month, people," Lieutenant General Hall said as he stood at the head of the conference table. Concern and displeasure were etched in his face, causing tension to ripple through the room.

Westley exchanged a quick glance with Felicity. His wife. Joy filled his heart. He took her hand beneath the table. They could face anything together.

They'd married in an intimate ceremony at the Christian church on base with Pastor Harmon officiating. Felicity's mother had flown in and Ian had walked the bride down the aisle. Lieutenant General Hall had stood up as Westley's best man, while Felicity's friend Rae Fallon had been her maid of honor.

Westley and Felicity decided to postpone a formal honeymoon until after all the dogs were safely returned and Boyd Sullivan imprisoned once again. Westley moved his belonging from his studio apartment to Felicity's house. He'd thought it would feel odd to live in the home she's shared with her father but it wasn't at all. In fact, he wanted to believe that Graham Monroe would have approved.

Felicity continued on as the base photographer, and Westley, with Dakota by his side, kept her safe 24/7. He still kept tabs on the training center, though Master Sergeant Caleb Streeter was in command. And he still worked to find the dogs that remained missing. Thirty-two dogs were still unaccounted for, including the prized four German shepherds. Searching for the dogs and protecting Felicity kept him busy. Guarding Felicity around the clock brought him immense joy marred only by the anxiety of the missing dogs.

This morning, Lieutenant General Hall had called this meeting out of well-known frustration. Boyd Sullivan was still at large. And the identity of his accomplice, someone here on base, remained a mystery.

"Special Agent Davison," Lieutenant General Hall said as he turned to the man on his right. "Please update us on the Red Rose Killer."

FBI Special Agent Oliver Davison stood to address the room. "We have conflicting reports all over the state of sightings of Boyd Sullivan. Now we're getting reports of him being as far away as Louisiana."

A murmur went through the room.

Lieutenant General Hall pinned his gaze on Captain Justin Blackwood. "And his accomplice?"

Justin planted his hands on the table and said, "We are doing our best to find the person who helped Boyd gain access to the base, sir."

Lieutenant General Hall's jaw tightened. "Someone had to have seen something or knows something." His gaze swept the room, landing briefly on each Security Forces member present. "I want answers, people. I want the base turned inside out and upside down if need be."

Everyone nodded.

One of the Security Forces members, Lieutenant Preston Flanigan, spoke up. "I still say Zoe Sullivan, Boyd's half sister, is his accomplice."

Tech Sergeant Linc Colson leaned forward to stare at the other man. "I'm on it," he said in a warning tone that left no doubt he was telling the other MP to back off. "If Zoe is his accomplice I will find out."

Lieutenant General Hall nodded his approval. "All right, then. Dismissed."

Westley and Felicity filed out with everyone else.

"I need to grab my camera," she said.

They linked fingers and headed to the photo lab. Once inside he shut the door and took her fully into his arms.

"Another day in paradise," he said with a smile.

She wound her arms around his neck and pulled him closer. "Every day is paradise with you. And I know here, in your arms, I'll always be safe."

"On my watch. Always."

And she kissed him.

* * * * *

Valerie Hansen was thirty when she awoke to the presence of the Lord in her life and turned to Jesus. She now lives in a renovated farmhouse on the breathtakingly beautiful Ozark Plateau of Arkansas and is privileged to share her personal faith by telling the stories of her heart for Love Inspired. Life doesn't get much better than that!

Books by Valerie Hansen

Love Inspired Suspense

Emergency Responders

Fatal Threat
Marked for Revenge

Military K-9 Unit

Bound by Duty
Military K-9 Unit Christmas
"Christmas Escape"

Classified K-9 Unit

Special Agent

Rookie K-9 Unit

Search and Rescue
Rookie K-9 Unit Christmas
"Surviving Christmas"

Visit the Author Profile page
at Harlequin.com for more titles.

BOUND BY DUTY

Valerie Hansen

God is our refuge and strength, a very present help in trouble. Therefore we will not fear.
—*Psalms* 46:1–2

Special thanks to former air force sergeant Nancy N. for her advice and to our pastor, John, who also served, as did his son.

Terri Reed, Dana Mentink, Maggie K. Black, Lenora Worth, Lynette Eason, Laura Scott, Shirlee McCoy and I all did our best to support each other's efforts and learn proper air force protocol for this series. It was difficult but we gave it our all.

God bless the men and women of our current military who daily give far more, and those who have sacrificed in the past to keep us free. We are grateful beyond words.

ONE

She was being watched. Constantly. Every fiber of her being knew it. Lately, she felt as though she was the defenseless prey and packs of predators were circling her and her helpless little boy, which was why she'd left Freddy at home with a sitter. Were things as bad as they seemed? It was more than possible, and Staff Sergeant Zoe Sullivan shivered despite the warm spring day.

Scanning the busy parking lot as she left the Canyon Air Force Base Exchange with her purchases, Zoe quickly spotted one of the Security Forces investigators. Her pulse jumped, and hostility took over her usually amiable spirit. The K-9 cop in a blue beret and camo ABU—Airman Battle Uniform—was obviously waiting for her. She bit her lip. Nobody cared how innocent she was. Being the half sister of Boyd Sullivan, the escaped Red Rose Killer, automatically made her a person of interest.

Zoe clenched her teeth. There was no way she could prove herself, so why bother trying? She squared her slim shoulders under her blue off-duty T-shirt and stepped out, heading straight for the Security Forces man and his imposing K-9, a black-and-rust-colored rottweiler.

Clearly, he saw her coming because he tensed, feet apart, body braced. In Zoe's case, five and a half feet was the most height she could muster. The dark-haired tech sergeant she was approaching looked to be quite a bit taller.

He gave a slight nod as she drew near and greeted her formally. "Sergeant Sullivan."

Linc Colson's firm jaw, broad shoulders and strength of presence were familiar. They had met during a questioning session conducted by Captain Justin Blackwood and Master Sergeant Westley James shortly after her half brother had escaped from prison.

Zoe stopped and gave the cop an overt once-over. "Can I help you with something, Sergeant Colson?"

"No, ma'am."

A cynical smile teased at one corner of her mouth. "Oh? Then why is it you're always following me? Don't you ever get a day off?"

"Just doing my job, Sergeant."

She knew he was right, but it galled her to be the object of futile efforts when base Security Forces could have been using their manpower to figure out who at Canyon Air Force Base was *really* cooperating with Boyd. How long were they going to continue disrupting her life and work? A wryly humorous thought intruded, and she chuckled.

Colson stared. The muscular K-9 at his side tensed. "What's so funny?"

Zoe waved her hands in dismissal as best she could with the canvas grocery tote handles looped over her forearms. "Relax, Sergeant. I wasn't laughing at you.

I was just picturing you guys trying to track me when I'm giving flying lessons. How are you at piloting a T-38 in close formation?"

She was relieved to note he was having difficulty containing his own smile. His mouth stayed put, but there was no denying a spark in his green eyes.

"I'd wait for you on the ground," he said. "Or outside the simulator."

Sobering, Zoe shook her head slowly, her light brown ponytail swinging. "I don't suppose it would do me any good to take an oath that I haven't seen Boyd since the last time I visited him in prison."

"That's not for me to say."

"No, I don't suppose it is." An eyebrow arched above her hazel eyes. "What if it were? Would you be willing to at least give me the benefit of the doubt instead of condemning me outright?"

To her surprise and disappointment, he said, "No."

"So much for the famous air force camaraderie," Zoe muttered. Louder, she said, "Fine," shouldered past him and started up the sidewalk toward Base Boulevard.

He turned slightly as she passed. "Those bags look heavy. Why didn't you call a cab after you bought so much?"

"It's a beautiful spring day in the heart of Texas," she snapped back. "Walking is a pleasure."

"If you say so."

Righteous indignation surged, and she picked up her pace. She couldn't stop the base cops from shadowing her, but she didn't have to make it easy. If her conscience hadn't kept kicking up, she would have enjoyed her impromptu plan to ditch this one even more.

Instead of looking back to see how far ahead she was

getting, she checked the reflections in the rear window of a bus that was unloading green recruits, probably for a tour of the impressive shopping facilities at the Base Exchange.

It looked as if Sergeant Colson was trailing her by at least a hundred yards. *Good.* Her smile returned. She shouldered her way through the milling group of men and women gathered on the sidewalk, then ducked in front of the idling bus, keeping it between her and the K-9 cop for as long as she could before darting around the far end of the stores in the Exchange and breaking into a run.

The moment she saw the warehouse complex behind the stores she knew exactly what to do next. She slipped between two of them and paused to catch her breath. Yes, the K-9 could and would track her. But in the meantime, she intended to enjoy thwarting his handler for a few minutes. Let Colson wonder where she was and what she was up to. Base personnel had already painted her as a clever criminal, a person to be avoided and mistrusted. A contrary side to her nature insisted on payback.

She ducked around a second corner, tried a side door to one of the warehouse buildings, found it unlocked and bolted through, lowering her sacks of groceries to the floor as she pressed her back to the inside of the steel door.

Breathless, Zoe stared into the darkness of the vast windowless storage area and waited for her night vision to improve.

This is wrong, her conscience insisted.

Was she finished playing games? *Not quite.* Leaving behind her purchases, she flipped the lock on the door to secure it and began to edge past pallets of boxes stacked in rows, looking for a different exit.

The sudden whirring of a motor stopped her in her tracks. Somebody was raising the overhead bay doors at the far end. Light crept below the broad edge of the moving panels. Then they stopped, leaving a gap of about three feet between the floor and the base of the door.

Zoe didn't move. Hardly breathed. Had Sergeant Colson located her already? Wow, he was good at tracking. Or, at least, his dog was. She was preparing to step forward and reveal herself—until she realized she wasn't seeing a K-9.

Instead, a man in camo and combat boots and a woman wearing a skirt and high heels ducked beneath the hanging door. All Zoe could see clearly was their feet and lower legs, but it was obvious she'd given Colson too much credit. He hadn't found her. This was probably nothing more than a lovers' tryst.

Voices reached her but were too muted to understand. She was about to back away and give the couple privacy when she saw a muzzle flash and heard the reverberation of a gunshot.

Instinct made her duck and cover her ears. Self-preservation kept her down while every hair at the nape of her neck prickled and her body trembled, willing her to run yet keeping her feet leaden. She could barely breathe.

The female figure was crumpling to the floor. Zoe could see blood spreading across the back of a reddish-haired woman's light-colored blouse. The shooter bent over her, his gun at the ready, a black ski mask hiding his features.

Help! She had to get help. Trembling, Zoe pulled her cell phone from the pocket of her PT shorts. Its lit screen and beeps of dialing were her undoing. As the victim lay still, bleeding and perhaps dying, the assailant straightened, wheeled to face the noise and started to move toward Zoe.

He was coming for her. She was next!

Linc Colson was concentrating, his jaw clenched, every nerve taut, as he followed K-9 Star. The rottweiler was as good as they came, and he trusted her tracking skills implicitly. That was why when she began to bark and paw at a closed warehouse door, he drew his sidearm and immediately tried the handle. Locked. And far too sturdily made to kick open.

He'd reached for the mic clipped to his shoulder, intending to report the evasive actions of his assigned suspect when a C-130 passing overhead forced a delay. He could hardly hear Star's barking over the roar of those engines, let alone hope to be able to transmit clearly. He just hoped Sergeant Sullivan hadn't run off to meet her murderous brother.

Linc jiggled the door handle again to no avail. He had just let it go when the heavy door swung open and a body slammed into his chest. *Zoe Sullivan!* Pushing her away, he commanded Star to sit and stay while one hand hovered over his holster and he faced his quarry.

Gasping, she raised both hands, palms out. "Don't shoot. It's me."

"I can see that." He had to shout at her to make himself heard over the fading roar of the cargo plane.

When she reached out to him, he took additional evasive action. "Stay where you are."

"No! You don't understand."

Her voice was shrill. Different than before. She sounded frightened. Well, too bad. "If you didn't want to get in more trouble, you shouldn't have tried to ditch me." He peered past her. "Where's Boyd?"

"How should I know?"

Judging by the way she kept shaking her head, waving her hands and gaping at him, she'd scared herself more than she'd worried him. Good. It served her right.

"I'm sorry. I promise I won't do it again, but..."

"You sure won't." He signaled his dog to stand guard. "No more special courtesy for you, Sergeant Sullivan. From now on, I'm your shadow. You got that?"

"Fine. Then follow me."

She turned and ducked back through the open door so quickly only Star kept up. Linc shouted, "Stop!" But the flight instructor kept right on going, stumbling when Star got in front of her to try to block her progress.

Linc grabbed a fistful of the back of Zoe's shirt and yanked her back outside. "Oh, no, you don't!"

She struggled against his hold. "Let me go. She may not be dead yet!"

"*Who* may not be dead? What kind of games are you playing now?"

"No games. I saw a woman get shot." Staggering to keep her balance, she pointed with her whole arm. "Right in there. The shot echoed. You must have heard it, too."

"Not over the engines of a C-130." Linc drew his gun and took a defensive stance. "If you're lying..."

"I'm not. I saw the shooting with my own eyes. When I tried to phone for help, the killer spotted me. I had to run for my life." Her lips trembled. "And, no, it wasn't Boyd. At least not this time."

Either the flight instructor was telling the truth or she deserved an Oscar for acting, Linc decided. Not only was she shaking all over, his own nerves had begun firing wildly. The back of his neck tingled and he sensed danger the way he had in combat when trying to outwit a hidden enemy.

Pushing her aside with his free arm, he aimed blindly into the dark warehouse. "How could you see a thing in there?"

"The—the loading door at the other end was partly open when it all happened. The guy must have closed it after he shot her."

Linc reached for his radio, reported the possible crime and was assured of backup, then instructed Zoe. "You stay out here. I'm going in to see if I can find the lights."

"No way. Suppose the shooter gets behind you."

"Star would alert me."

"I still think I should go along. I can help."

"The dog can do it better," Linc insisted.

"I give up. I'm scared, okay? My little boy needs me, and you know I'm unarmed. The shooter knows I saw him. I don't want to wait out here by myself."

He could hear her rapid breathing, feel her fear. "That's the first totally honest thing I've heard you say," Linc replied. "All right. But stay close behind me in case I have to fire."

"Gladly."

Stepping inside, Linc placed each boot as silently as possible. He moved ahead in a half crouch in order to present a smaller target. Star preceded him. Zoe followed.

A swishing, fluttering noise from above startled all three of them. Zoe let out a tiny gasp but didn't scream, impressing him, despite his lingering anger at her foolish tricks. Star paused for a moment, then looked forward again. "A bird in the rafters," Linc whispered.

Although his human companion didn't react, he continued to feel her presence, as if his actual shadow had substance. He'd have waited for backup if Sullivan hadn't mentioned a victim. Given that complication, he needed to reach the scene and assess any injuries. Quickly.

Pausing, Linc waved his palm in front of Star's nose, then held it up to stop Zoe, too. "Stay here. The panel for the lights is right ahead. When I turn them on, I don't want you to be out in the open."

"Will your dog panic and bite me if you leave?" Zoe whispered.

Under other circumstances Link would have chuckled. "Not unless I tell her to, so don't run away again."

Sergeant Sullivan's muttered reply faded to nothing as Linc moved forward. His sight had adjusted to the darkness enough to tell where he was but not enough to spot hidden attackers.

He reached for the panel and flipped the switches. Banks of overhead fluorescent lights flickered, then steadied, illuminating the entire warehouse.

Linc's first act was to ensure that there was no imminent threat. His gaze swept the building contents, then came to rest on Zoe. Star was seated at her feet, panting and totally unconcerned, meaning she sensed no danger lurking nearby.

In contrast, the flight instructor was standing there with her hazel eyes wide and her mouth hanging open, looking as though she was about to keel over.

Linc followed her line of sight to the base of the roll-up door. The concrete was spotless.

No dust.

No blood stain.

And no body.

TWO

Zoe took a shaky breath. "That's impossible!" She wanted to explain what had happened but couldn't. She had seen the shooting with her own eyes. Had watched the victim fall and bleed. So where had the injured woman gone?

Her companion reached for his mic. "Colson here. False alarm at the warehouse."

Watching his expression removed all doubt that he blamed her for the false alarm. Only it wasn't her fault. It hadn't been. She knew what she'd seen, how she'd felt when the assailant had turned and come toward her. Imagination or hallucination or whatever a person wanted to call it was not enough to scare her that much.

The K-9 handler raised a dark eyebrow. "Well?"

"Oh, no. You're not going to blame me for this, Colson. I don't know what really happened, but I am not making anything up. I heard a shot. I saw a victim fall and watched a red stain blossom on her back. There is no way this floor can be this clean and dry after that. Not this fast. There has to be a logical explanation."

"I'm waiting for it," he said.

Zoe took a deep breath and exhaled noisily. Slowly

shaking her head, she glanced down at the imposing patrol K-9. "I'd rather try to explain it to your dog. She looks more likely to believe me."

"Don't let her temporary relaxation fool you. One word or signal from me and Star will be a formidable adversary."

"I know. It's just that sometimes I tend to relate to animals better than I do humans. And see her cute tan eyebrows? She's not scowling at me the way you are."

"Maybe that's because you didn't lie to her."

"I didn't lie to you either." Zoe knew there was pathos in her tone, but she didn't try to hide or excuse it. "There has to be a clue here. A drop of blood or something. Please. Bring in somebody who can test the area for it. At least give me the benefit of the doubt."

"So you can waste our time and resources?"

Her voice became strident. "*Me?* You're the ones who are wasting time by focusing on *my* life when you should be trying to track down my stupid half brother before he does something else too horrible for words. I haven't seen him since before he escaped, and I only went because I felt sorry for him. I don't want to see him on the outside of prison walls. I have my little boy to protect. Do you think I want Boyd anywhere near Freddy?"

"Why not? You sure visited him plenty."

"That's different. Boyd's all the family I have left since Dad died. I suppose I should have stayed away, but I kept hoping he was worth redeeming."

"By you?" She heard him huff.

"No. By God and Jesus," Zoe said, and this time there was new gentleness in her speech.

"Some people aren't worth it," Colson countered drily.

"I disagree. *Everybody* should have the chance to reform, no matter what they've done." Her heart clenched. Too bad it was too late to help Freddy's daddy.

That all-encompassing statement apparently convinced the cop to turn away and once again use his radio. "Give me Captain Blackwood," he said. After a short pause he followed with, "Linc Colson here, sir. I'm at warehouse W-16 behind the BX. Sullivan insists she saw a crime committed and is requesting a tech team. Do you want me to stay here until you give me further orders or shall I relinquish the scene?"

Zoe couldn't hear the reply because the sergeant was wearing an earpiece, but judging by his grim look, he wasn't happy with the captain's decision. She waited expectantly for him to end the call and explain.

"They're coming," he grumbled. "You win. This time."

"I'm not trying to win anything," she insisted. "I just don't want a criminal to get away with murder."

"Right."

Zoe could have brought up the sacrifice of personal happiness she'd made when she'd turned in her former husband, John, for possible espionage, a transgression, which may have been responsible for his untimely death, but since those records were sealed, she figured it would be best to keep that part of her past to herself. Her rotten brother was plenty for now. Between relatives she couldn't help knowing and choosing the wrong man to marry, her record of discernment was pitiful.

She decided to try changing the subject. "So, Linc

is what the *L* on your name tag stands for? Is that short for Lincoln?"

"Not anymore. It's just Linc now."

"Why?"

"Because I got tired of being called Abe. Nicknames are bad enough in the air force. They were lots worse when I was a kid."

She had to smile at him. "Gotcha. Boyd liked to call me Baby Sister, and the kids in the neighborhood and at school picked it up. Thankfully, it didn't follow me into the air force, even if my brother did."

"You got off easy when he washed out." He gestured to some cardboard cartons piled near the open bay doors. "We might as well sit down."

"Your *dog* is tired, right?"

One corner of his mouth twitched for a moment as if a smile was trying to get out before he regained control and answered, "Right. My *partner* is."

"Sorry." Zoe led the way to the stack and tested it to make sure the carton was strong enough to support her before sitting. "I had forgotten you guys considered your K-9s partners."

Linc took a seat with Star between them. "We're classified as teammates. She's an MWD, Military Working Dog, and I'm her handler."

Zoe gazed down. "She's beautiful."

"And intelligent and trained to be lethal if necessary," Linc cautioned.

"I don't doubt that for a second." Meeting Star's upturned face with a tender look of her own, Zoe dangled the tips of her fingers over the edge of the box. The dog noticed but didn't seem upset, so she took a chance and wiggled them.

Star had apparently realized she wasn't a danger, because she sniffed Zoe's fingers, then gave them a quick lick.

Zoe giggled. Linc did not. "It's a good thing for you that Star has been socialized more than some of our other dogs or she'd never put up with that. What are you trying to do, recruit her over to the dark side?"

That opinion deserved a hearty laugh. "Not at all. Actually, I'm very impressed with Star. She's a lot smarter than you Security Forces people are. She's already decided I'm one of the good guys around here."

"Then it's a good thing she's not the one in charge."

Linc was not pleased by Zoe's conclusion, but he had to give her credit for having a kind enough heart to make an emotional connection with the dog, despite the fact that such interactions were usually unsuccessful. Nevertheless, that didn't prove her innocence. She'd already admitted having a soft spot where Boyd was concerned. She could have helped him sneak on and off the base at the very least, although Linc couldn't imagine why she would, particularly since she seemed worried about the safety of her little boy.

Truth to tell, Zoe may not have had anything to do with an actual crime or with Boyd's latest victims, other than the fact that they were all connected to Canyon. Two dog trainers, a basic training instructor and a base cook had all died during the previous month and warning notes had been delivered to other potential targets. The trainers and one other, Chief Master Sergeant Clinton Lockwood, were found with red roses the way past victims had been. Boyd could have done all that himself and probably had, particularly if he was actually inside the base's perimeter fence as they suspected.

Which brought Linc's musings back to Zoe Sullivan. She might have helped her half brother gain access if she thought she was doing the right thing and could handle him. There was certainly a stronger possibility for *her* to have given assistance than there was for any of Boyd's former cronies who were still serving at CAFB to do so. They might have supported his illegal activities when he was still enlisted, but those who had stayed on after his discharge and had advanced in rank now had promising careers to consider.

Linc's pondering was interrupted by the arrival of Captain Justin Blackwood, accompanied by a lone evidence technician and base photographer, Staff Sergeant Felicity James. Linc snapped to attention, as did Zoe. Blackwood returned the salute. "As you were."

"I didn't mean for you to bother about this personally, Captain," Linc told the captain.

"I wanted to see the scene for myself." Blackwood was eyeing Zoe as if he expected her to say or do something odd. "Show me what you found."

"It's more what we didn't find." Linc stepped forward with Star, angling so he could also keep an eye on Zoe. "Sergeant Sullivan said the shooting happened here. She insists there must be evidence."

When he pointed at the base of the door, she spoke up. "I was in the back of the building, sir. I couldn't tell exactly how close to the opening the two people were standing, but I could judge left and right. I put the shooting victim a foot left of center with the shooter to the right of that. Any blood spray patterns should be near the bottom edge of the door."

The Captain looked to the tech, who was opening a forensics test kit. "Okay. Colson will run the door up a few feet so you can check the cement apron, too, and Sergeant James can snap a few pictures for the record."

Complying, Linc wished he had thought of that. Normally, he would have, but he had been so sure the Sullivan woman had fabricated her story he'd been lax. That wasn't good, nor was it fair if she was telling the truth.

Which she isn't, he assured himself. He wasn't sure exactly what her motives were. He didn't have to know. All he was supposed to do was follow her in case her murderous brother tried to make contact.

That was a task he relished. Capturing an escaped serial killer was worth working overtime and putting up with a clever woman's tricks. In a way, it was too bad that Sergeant Sullivan was using her superior intelligence and quick mind to thwart the law. Given different circumstances, he would have admired her.

Watching Captain Blackwood oversee the testing of the base of the roll-up door, Zoe felt her confidence waning. Clearly, they weren't finding the clues she had expected.

When the tech straightened, picked up his gear and shook his head, she knew she'd been bested. But by whom? By what? She was positive she'd witnessed a shooting. The chances of such a violent act leaving no trace were slim to none. There had to be something there. There simply had to be.

Unfortunately, she wasn't trained to find it. She was trained to teach basic flying. Period. Frustration brought unshed tears to her eyes, and she fought to remain stoic. "I saw two people. One shot the other. A body fell."

Linc's left brow arched. "You're sticking to that fairy tale?"

"No, I'm sticking to the truth as I know it. There's a big difference."

Although rancor in Colson's expression was evident, he didn't counter. Instead, he turned to his superior and apologized as if the callout was his own error.

"Sorry, Captain. This false alarm was my fault. The subject was out of my sight for a few minutes, so I can't verify anything that took place during that time."

"Well, see that she isn't again, Colson."

"Yes, sir."

The look that the K-9 cop shot her gave Zoe the shivers. She didn't know how her surveillance could get any worse but figured she was about to find out.

She desperately wanted to counter with a statement of her own but managed to hold her tongue. It was doubtful that either man would believe she'd merely been blowing off steam and overreacting in righteous anger regarding the unfair surveillance situation.

Someday, perhaps she'd have a chance to speak her mind, but this was certainly not it. She was already in enough trouble due to her relationship with her nefarious brother, however strained. Considering all the pressure she'd been under lately, there was also a one-in-a-million chance she might have been imagining things. There had been times recently when confusion over minor things had worried her.

If there was a chance that her mind was playing tricks again, her wisest choice would be to let everyone continue to believe she had made up the shooting story as a distraction. Otherwise, someone might deem her unfit—both as an aviation instructor and as Freddy's mother. No way was she going to allow that to happen. Her job was important, yes. She loved her country and was eager to serve. But her little boy was everything.

THREE

"I can call a cab and escort you home," Linc told Zoe after the captain and tech left.

"That won't be necessary."

"You're right. It isn't. But if you're really as upset as you've been acting, it's sensible." He could almost see the wheels turning in her brain before she nodded.

"I'll walk. But I would like the company, just in case. I have to stop at the side door and pick up my groceries."

The change in Sullivan's demeanor bothered him, not because she had stopped arguing but because she seemed so downtrodden. Still, she'd fooled him before, much to his embarrassment, and could easily be acting again. Making comparisons to her criminal brother was natural. Boyd had been charming when it suited him, then he'd changed into a self-serving killer.

Not that Linc believed Zoe was that bad, he assured himself. But it would behoove him to remember she was kin to a serial killer. She and her brother had had the same father, so there was a chance she had inherited whatever genes that made Boyd so dangerous. That judgment wasn't a lot different from their process of choosing likely candidates for K-9 service. The tendencies for action had to be there before training began or efforts for tight control over those instincts might be time wasted.

Ahead of him, Sergeant Sullivan paused to reclaim her grocery totes and started out the door. Linc tensed, wondering if she'd try more evasive tactics and was mildly surprised when she waited for him to clear the exit with Star and fall in beside her.

"You were right," Zoe said with a sigh. "I should have driven. I'm suddenly exhausted." She paused for a heartbeat. "And, no, I'm not asking for that taxi or hinting that I want you to help carry anything while you're on duty."

Linc harrumphed. "It takes a lot out of you to evade the police, huh?"

"Dodging you wasn't the smartest thing I've ever done."

"They why did you do it?"

"Frustration, I guess. I got tired of being treated like a criminal and decided to rebel a little."

"Not a good idea."

She sighed again, this time more loudly. "Yeah. It seemed kind of okay at the time. At least until the shooting."

Pacing her by shortening his strides, Linc remained silent and waited to see if she'd confess more. Instead, she gave him a cynical glance and said, "I really goofed. I liked it better when you and your cohorts were hiding and just shadowing me."

"You may have seen us once or twice, but most of the time we were out of sight."

She laughed.

Linc was not amused. "Are you insinuating you knew we were keeping you under constant surveillance?"

"Absolutely. For one thing, the fact that I was being watched made me edgy, made my senses tingle the way a hare reacts to a hungry coyote." Pausing, she blushed. "Why do you think I started keeping my blinds closed?"

"Because you were hiding something."

"Yeah, my private life."

"We watched the doors for signs of your brother. We weren't peeking in your windows."

"Says who?"

"Says me. You don't have a very high opinion of our Security Forces, do you?"

They had reached Zoe's four-story apartment building. She stopped at the foot of the concrete walkway to answer. "I think the police, both civilian and military, do an amazing job keeping order and tracking down criminals. What I *don't* like is being considered one of the bad guys."

Linc had to admit she had a point. Assuming she was innocent, of course. He nodded in tacit agreement. "I get that. I do. But suppose you were positive a student pilot was unstable. Would you allow him or her to fly or would you wash them out?"

She made a face. "I've washed out more than one."

"Because that's your job as a flight instructor."

"Yes."

"Then bear with me here," Linc said. "Watching you for clues to finding your brother, Boyd, is my job. Even if you haven't been helping him since he escaped from prison, you can't be certain he won't show up looking for you. We know he or someone mimicking him has been on base or we wouldn't have had threats and killings identified by red roses and predictable notes."

He sensed he was getting through to Zoe. "Do you plan to spend the rest of the afternoon at home, Sergeant Sullivan?"

"Yes. As soon as I send the babysitter home, Freddy and I are going to play a few games."

"All right. I'll go up with you and check the place over."

"Seriously? You want to search my apartment?"

"Unless you refuse permission. If you do, that points to culpability. My CO can always ask for a search warrant."

"I know. Actually, given the morning I've had, I'd almost welcome it. Just don't scare my little boy. Or the babysitter."

"I'll try not to. I was kind of surprised to see who you got to watch him."

"Portia Blackwood, you mean?"

"Yes." Line had been shocked to see Justin's daughter show up. "Does her father know she's here?"

"I assume so. Captain Blackwood posted a notice asking parents to consider Portia for babysitting to give her something constructive to do now that she's living with him. I called and left a recorded message and she got back to me."

"I can't believe Blackwood gave her permission to sit for you in the first place, considering the possibility of your brother showing up."

"Oh, dear. I didn't think to ask when she called. Maybe she went behind his back." Zoe lowered her voice. "I'm not sure she'll work out anyway. She didn't seem very enthusiastic when she arrived." She shrugged. "Doesn't matter. My Freddy normally spends a lot of his time at the day care and preschool on base and he's perfectly happy there."

"I can't understand why you called Portia in the first place." Following closely, always on alert, Linc climbed the stairs to the second-story apartment with Zoe and Star. "I hear the captain has his hands full with her."

"Well, that's to be expected," Zoe countered. "He wasn't on scene often until Portia's mother passed away." Linc saw her cheeks redden. "Sorry. That sounded too harsh. I shouldn't be gossiping. I don't know the facts firsthand."

"I'm sure my captain did the best he could in a difficult situation."

"I'm sure he did."

Linc noted she had not locked her apartment door and remarked on it. "I'd really be more careful if I were you."

"I usually am. I guess I figured Portia would lock it when I left." She stepped inside and called, "I'm home!"

Linc saw a barefoot child hurrying toward her, arms open wide as if he hadn't seen her in months. The little boy's grin was a mile wide, and his hazel eyes that matched Zoe's twinkled. His hair was curlier and more blond than light brown, but otherwise he was the spitting image of the staff sergeant.

When she dropped her groceries to scoop the toddler up in her arms, Linc was oddly touched. This was a personal side of her he had not noted. The mutual love was so evident, so strong, it seemed to fill the tiny living room.

Zoe kissed Freddy's cheek as he wrapped his pudgy arms around her neck and shouted, "Mama!" Seconds later, he noticed the dog and started to squirm. "A puppy!"

"Whoa. Hold on, honey. That's not a puppy you can play with. That's a member of the air force, just like Mama is. The dog is working right now."

"That's right," Linc said. "Star and I are going to go check your house while you and your mother wait right here. We'll be back in a few minutes and then I'll introduce you. Okay?"

The eager child was nodding. "Uh-huh."

"Good." Linc looked around. "Where's your baby-sitter, Sergeant Sullivan?"

"Beats me." She turned to her son. "Where's Portia, Freddy?"

"She has time-out."

Zoe was obviously confused. That made two of them. Concerned and on high alert, Linc gave her a hand signal to wait, then took Star and began to work his way through the apartment, room by room. Only one door was closed.

He placed the heel of his hand on the grip of his holstered pistol, prepared to make entry and threw open the door.

Portia's ensuing scream was loud enough to be heard over the roar of a jet engine.

Zoe clasped Freddy tightly and took cover behind the kitchen island. It wasn't until she heard the clicking of Star's nails on the hardwood floor that she raised enough to peek over the top. There was her so-called babysitter, clasping an iPad to her chest and breathing hard. Linc and Star were herding her ahead of them and it was evident she was one unhappy teen.

Rising, still holding her son close, Zoe scowled. "Where did you find her?"

"Sitting on a bed with the door shut, so she could instant message her friends without being disturbed." He gave the girl a light tap on the shoulder to urge her to fully face Zoe and the boy as he continued. "I'm glad you weren't gone long, Sergeant. If you had been, who knows what might have happened."

"I agree." Swallowing her anger, Zoe spoke as sternly as possible while her insides quaked with fear for Freddy's welfare. "I'm afraid I won't be able to use your services again, Portia. I'm sorry."

"Whatever." The sullen teen flipped her long blond hair back defiantly.

"We're both fortunate that the person who scared you just now is one of the good guys," Zoe said. "It could have been anyone."

Portia huffed. "Here? We might as well be in jail."

"Normally, I'd agree with you," Zoe said, eyeing Linc for clues to his opinion of how she handled the situation and feeling assured they were both on the same page.

She addressed the girl. "I put aside two hours' wages for you before I went to the store to make sure I had the right change." She sat Freddy on the counter and steadied him while she reached up to open the overhead spice cabinet. "It's right—"

Stunned, Zoe stopped with her hand raised. "I know I put it here. I remember doing it."

Linc spoke quietly. "Is it possible you only meant to leave the money and it slipped your mind because you were distracted?"

"I don't think so." Zoe was beginning to wonder herself, although there was no way she'd admit it, particularly not to him. "All right, Portia," she said, reaching into her pocket and pulling out a handful of bills. "Here. If this isn't enough, I can write you a check."

The girl grabbed the money without counting it. "I don't need your check. I only took this job in the first place to get out of the house." Still clutching her iPad, she hurried to the door and let it slam behind her.

"Whew." Zoe let out a breath. "I wouldn't want to be that girl's father. It's hard enough being a single parent without stumbling into the job late the way the captain did. It's too bad he wasn't able to be a stronger presence in the girl's life when she was younger."

"Yeah. Deployment can mess up families." Linc eyed the half-open kitchen cabinet and scowled. "You know, you have been under a lot of stress lately."

"Meaning?"

He shrugged. "Maybe it's finally getting to you. You're all by yourself with a child to worry about. You're under suspicion. Your convict brother could show up here at any minute and you still have to perform your normal teaching duties. That's a lot to process."

"Why don't you just spit it out?" Zoe demanded. "You and your boss are sure I imagined the shooting and now you're suggesting I'm losing it over little things, too."

"Are you?"

"No." It was almost a shout and frightened her son into reaching for her. Penitent, Zoe lifted him into her arms and stepped back. "I'm sorry if I scared you, honey." Looking at Star, she asked Linc, "Did you mean it when you promised he could pet your partner?"

"I did." To Zoe's delight, the man even smiled slightly, although it didn't quite reach his eyes.

"Let's go into the living room where we can be comfortable," Linc said, leading the way. "I normally don't take Star's vest off when we're working, but I'll make an exception today." He sat on one end of the small sofa with his K-9 at his feet and proceeded to unbuckle her harness.

"Where should we sit?" Zoe asked, realizing that whatever Colson said, she'd end up close to him. There was no way she was going to get one inch away from her three-year-old son in the presence of a trained attack dog so, like it or not, she was going to have to grit her teeth and cozy up to the security man.

"Right here is fine," he said, keeping his attention focused on Star while indicating the empty end of the settee.

Yup. Really close, she thought. *Oh, well, I can do anything for Freddy's sake. I certainly don't want him to grow up scared of authority or become a criminal like his uncle, Boyd.* Boyd's latest crimes made her almost wish she hadn't taken back her maiden name. Given the treasonous acts associated with her late husband and her plans to make the air force her career however, it had seemed the lesser of two evils. She supposed it still was.

To Zoe's surprise, the cop seemed to mellow as he relaxed and petted the rottweiler. His voice was low, his expression appealing. When he spoke softly to Star, the K-9 gazed into his eyes with total adoration. The pair had gone from imposing threats to friendly neighbors in the blink of an eye. Why couldn't Sergeant Colson act this way when he was shadowing her? She would have liked him a lot better if he had.

That thought stopped her heart. Liked him? Her? No way. He was just another problem to face, another hapless bird sucked into her jet intake, ready to cause a crash. So why was she having such a hard time continuing to dislike him?

Because he was being so kind to Freddy, she answered easily. A big scary cop and a trusting little boy were relating to each other as if they were meant to be best buds.

Linc held out his large hand and Freddy grasped it without hesitation. The sight of the man safely guiding her son's little chubby fingers toward a dog powerful enough to harm them touched her heart. Her son had never known his father, never had a male role model. And until that moment, Zoe had not realized the enormity of what he'd been missing.

FOUR

Linc wasn't surprised by the way Star treated the trusting little boy after a proper introduction, but his own reactions to the situation gave him pause. A feeling of tenderness he had not anticipated flowed over and through him, leaving a sense of peace and rightness behind. What was that all about? He didn't even like kids. At least he didn't think he did. Truthfully, his experiences with small children were limited, and he'd always viewed them as sort of alien creatures. Cute but unknowable. So how had he apparently managed to connect with this one?

He cast a sidelong glance at Zoe and was awed by her expression, as well. The way she was gazing at her son left no doubt of her love and devotion. From what Linc could recall, nobody had ever looked at him that way, not even his own mother, and as far as his dad was concerned, he might as well have been invisible—unless he'd misbehaved. Then his father had taken plenty of notice and dished out serious punishment.

Such thoughts pulled Linc from his earlier calm and left him wondering what Freddy's father had been like. There wasn't much background information in Sergeant

Sullivan's personnel file, but since she'd chosen to re-
vert to her maiden name, he figured there must have
been notable conflict.

"You're doing fine," Linc told the child. "Just pet her
gently. She likes her ears scratched like this." He demonstrated, then laughed when Freddy tried it. "Not so
hard, okay? Star wants to keep her ears attached to her
head. She needs them to hear with."

Freddy giggled. "Silly."

Linc's grin was genuine and widening. He really got
a kick out of this kid. "Here. Let me tell her to lie down
and you can scratch her tummy. She loves that, too."

Instead of bending over Star as she dropped to the
floor and rolled onto her back on command, Freddy
threw himself down beside her and reached across her
body to wiggle his fingers in her short soft hair. "Tickle,
tickle."

She turned her head without rising and gave his
cheek a lick. Childish laughter filled the room, and the
boy put his hands over his face. "Eww. She kissed me."

"Because she likes you," Linc replied. He looked at
Zoe. "I hope you don't mind."

"It does my heart good to see Freddy so happy. If
it takes a little dog slobber to make that happen, how
can I mind? Besides, the newest info on keeping kids
healthy is to raise them with animals and let them build
up resistance to germs."

"Good to know." Linc startled slightly when his radio
went off, and he cupped a hand over his earbud, listening to the dispatch coming over his radio.

Zoe gently touched his forearm. "Is everything okay?
It's not Boyd, is it?"

"No." Linc put on his blue beret and gave Star's leash

a tug. "We have to go downstairs for a few minutes. A couple of our dogs that were still missing after they were all released last month have been sighted coming this way. I'm supposed to keep an eye out and try to capture them."

It was all he could do to avoid looking at the place where her hand still lay. The sensation was electric. When she withdrew her slim fingers, he almost wished she hadn't.

"We won't go far," he said, rising. "Hand me your cell phone and I'll enter my number. We'll be right downstairs if you need anything."

"I can manage my brother if he does show up," Zoe countered, complying anyway. "He doesn't scare me."

"Well, he should." Linc gave her back her phone and paused just long enough to put his dog's working vest back on her. That also gave him time to be certain Zoe was taking his warning seriously. When she sobered, he was satisfied.

Star accompanied him to the door, tight at heel position. Linc glanced back. "Lock this after me."

"I will."

"Now," he added, when she didn't immediately act.

"Yes, sir," she said, giving him a smile and a mock salute.

More chatter was coming in over his radio. Linc keyed his mic. "On my way. I'll meet you in the street."

With a last look at the woman and child, he turned on his heel and left. Normally, he would have waited until he was certain she had locked her door, but the last messages indicated that several of the missing dogs were nearby. His plan was to position himself on the lawn of the apartment building and wait, hoping that

Star's presence would draw the others in. Many of the highly skilled K-9s had been found and returned to the CAFB training facility, but there were still thirty-two dogs missing, including four special animals. He wanted to find all the dogs, of course, but locating Glory, Patriot, Scout and Liberty would be a real coup.

A Security Forces SUV was approaching slowly, driver and passenger scanning the area. Linc waved them down.

"I haven't spotted any loose ones yet, but I just got down here," Linc called.

Novice trainer Bobby Stevens, the driver, nodded and glanced up at the apartment windows. "We have an audience. Did they see anything?"

Linc followed the same line of sight and felt his heart skip like a flat stone thrown onto the surface of a placid lake. Zoe and Freddy were peering out their open window, watching the drama in the street unfold.

"No. I was working up there with Star when I got the call. We were all sitting in the living room."

The SUV passenger, Master Sergeant Caleb Streeter, chuckled wryly. "Must be nice getting to sit around all day, Colson, while the rest of us bust a gut chasing reports of dogs."

Under different circumstances, Linc might have returned the taunt. Instead, he chose to tamp down his pride and stay silent. The most important task was catching the Red Rose Killer, and as long as Zoe Sullivan was on base, she was still their best, most important lead.

In the shadowed corners of his mind lurked the realization that he also wanted to keep her safe. Her and her little boy, a child whose openness and charm had touched his heart in a way he couldn't begin to explain. Maybe it was Freddy's lack of a father that made him identify with the boy, Linc mused, remembering the shame his own dad had brought upon him and his mother by going AWOL, becoming a thief and finally being arrested and jailed.

That was one thing he unfortunately had in common with Zoe. Neither of their families was anything to be proud of. And neither of them could do a thing about changing the past. Linc had spent his adult life trying to rise above the stigma of his untrustworthy, unreliable father.

The comparison between his situation and Zoe's struck him like the blast from a jet engine. He was not a bit like his father, so why did everybody seem to think Zoe Sullivan would side with her brother, given the opportunity?

Because she'd kept in such close touch with Boyd, he reasoned, clenching his jaw. That was the difference, and it was a big one.

His eyes were drawn to the apartment window again. As a single mother who had the responsibility of caring for Freddy, would she jeopardize his well-being for the sake of a killer? Approaching the question logically, Linc didn't think so. The trouble was Boyd had always been good at hiding his true nature, at least at first. The women who had refused to date him and men who had somehow crossed him had paid the price for thwarting the emotionally twisted man. Could his seemingly innocent sister be the same kind of person?

A loose German shepherd, tail flagging and ears erect, drew Linc's thoughts back to the current task.

The dog was trotting toward Star, panting as if smiling and acting ready to play.

Linc crouched down. "Come here, boy. That's a good boy."

Although the dog slowed and lowered its head as if deciding whether or not to flee, it continued in their direction, then stopped nose to nose with Star. Linc's hand moved slowly, surely, until he was able to slip a looped leash around its neck. The shepherd wore no collar or ID band but since each member of the training project had been microchipped, he knew the dog would easily be identified.

Streeter had left the vehicle, and Linc handed him the dog he'd caught. "Looks like this poor guy missed a few meals. Do you want me to hang around down here a little longer, just in case others show up?"

Streeter shook his head. "No. I'll load this one and cruise the rest of the neighborhood."

"Copy," Linc replied. He didn't particularly like taking orders from a sergeant who was technically not his boss, but it was a reasonable request. Besides, he wasn't eager to return to the Sullivan apartment until he'd figured out why being there had rattled him so.

He'd realized he'd carelessly let down his guard. That was a mistake. A huge mistake. One he would not repeat.

"Look, Mama. Another puppy!" Freddy was peering through the screen as Zoe steadied him.

"I see them. Looks like your friend Star has somebody to play with."

"I wanna go play, too."

"Not now, honey. The policeman is working and so is his dog. We have to stay up here and just watch."

"Aww."

"No whining." Zoe tried to distract him. "How about a game on the iPad? You can make some doggies wag their tails."

"Naw. I wanna watch real puppies. They're soft. I love them."

"Not all dogs are as nice as Star," Zoe warned, "and she might not be fun if Sergeant Colson didn't tell her it was okay. You need to be very careful with all dogs. Ask permission before you try to pet them. Promise?"

Freddy nodded vigorously, but Zoe had doubts he'd take her advice until he was older and wiser. That was the trouble with small children. Until they'd had experience, they were willing to try just about anything. After today, she would have to be doubly vigilant about his interactions with strange animals.

A noise behind her caught Zoe's attention. Frowning, she froze. What was that? It sounded like the squeak in the hallway floor. Listening intently, she didn't hear it repeated. Nevertheless, she started to glance over her shoulder.

Nothing there. She began to feel foolish. *Boy, am I jumpy.* She was turning back to the window when she sensed more than saw movement in her peripheral vision. Instinct made her tighten her hold on her son. Was there actually somebody there?

An instant later, she whirled and put substance to her jitters. A figure in a dark hoodie was tiptoeing across the far end of the small living room!

Zoe thrust Freddy behind her and held him there, hoping and praying she didn't look as scared as she was. With the hoodie masking the side of his face, there was no way to identify the intruder. One thing was certain—he was too slightly built to be Boyd.

"Get out of here," Zoe ordered, relieved that the quaking of her insides wasn't reflected in her voice.

The figure stopped dead. Nobody moved. Zoe could feel the pounding of her pulse in her temples.

A weapon. She needed a weapon. Anything with which to defend her innocent child. But what? The only people on base who were armed were members of the Security Forces and posted guards. Casting about, she saw nothing usable. That left bravado as her only option, and lots of it.

"I said get out of here." It was a commanding order, almost a shout, and Zoe felt her son grasping her legs from behind, the way he did when he was frightened.

A hand with slim but masculine fingers rose to pull the sides of the hood closer. The man dipped his head, averted his gaze momentarily, then pulled something from his pocket.

A knife!

Zoe gasped. Her resolve deepened, hardened, became the wall she needed to protect her little boy. She dropped into a combative stance, feet apart, arms extended and ready to fend off the coming attack. No lowlife with a blade was going to get past her. Not if she had anything to say about it.

Freddy had backed off and begun to cry as she'd prepared to do battle. The attacker turned to the boy for an instant, then focused back on Zoe.

She grabbed her jacket off the couch and wrapped it around one forearm, never letting her concentration stray. The man seemed hesitant, as if having trouble choosing his next move. That was to her advantage. She didn't want to face him hand to hand but intended for him to believe she would.

Her mouth was so dry she couldn't swallow, let alone muster a convincing threat. So there they stood as the seconds ticked off, Zoe braced and ready and her adversary hesitating until the hand with the weapon began to visibly shake.

She had him worried. Good. Now all she needed to do was force him to bolt. Would a charge do it? Maybe. And maybe it would trigger his predatory instincts and drive him toward her.

Before she could decide, Freddy touched the back of her leg and whimpered. "Mama?"

Habit caused her to react. She eased her stance momentarily and lowered one outstretched hand toward the boy. That was all the opening her enemy needed. He leaped at her, falling short because she dodged just in time.

With a guttural roar, she charged, coming in low and catching him at the waist the way a football player would take out an opponent.

The man stumbled backward and fell.

Zoe went for the knife and managed to grab his wrist before he threw her off and started to scramble away with his weapon.

She raised the hoodie-wrapped forearm in case he chose to turn and slash at her. Time seemed to slow to a snail's pace. He flipped onto his hands and knees, combat boots slipping on the slick flooring, and crab-walked until he could regain his footing.

Zoe screamed, afraid he was going to detour toward her son.

Freddy was already at the window, waving his hands and yelling, "Help," in his screechy little voice.

The attacker threw the bolt and jerked open the door. Momentum carried him into the hallway.

Breathless, Zoe followed, inhaled as deeply as she could and let loose with a blood-curdling shriek. "Colson! Stop him!"

FIVE

Linc was moving toward the apartment building before he knew what was happening. Star ran ahead of him, barking.

He took the stairs two at a time, reaching the second floor and immediately spotting Zoe braced in her open doorway.

"What's wrong?"

She gestured with her arm. "A man. That way. Down the back stairs. Camo pants and a dark hoodie."

Star was straining at her leash. Linc drew her in and hesitated only long enough to ask Zoe, "Are you okay?"

"Yes! Go! Don't let him get away."

He would have given Star a tracking command if he'd felt it was necessary. In this case, she was clearly on the fresh trail and needed no more encouragement. Had Zoe forgotten to lock her door after him? Worse, could he have overlooked someone hiding in the apartment? He'd checked it thoroughly.

Except for the room where Portia had been, Linc added, berating himself. Careless. Unprofessional at best. He had allowed himself to assume that the teenage girl was alone when she may have had company.

She wouldn't be the first babysitter to entertain friends when she should have been minding a child. The instant messaging beeps from her iPad and the absorbed look on her face had thrown him enough that he'd never thought of checking the room further.

But he'd surprised Portia. How would a friend have had time to hide? More important, where was the guy now? Star was still straining at her leash, but there was nobody in sight.

They reached the rear parking area just as a motorbike roared off. Star might have been able to keep up for a short distance if Linc chose to release her, but there was no use endangering the K-9's welfare when he wouldn't be there for the takedown and arrest.

Linc shaded his eyes, trying to make out details of the bike and its rider. But the sun was too bright.

"Star. Out," he commanded forcefully.

Although she remained excited, acting eager to continue her pursuit, she obeyed. Linc knew that his primary task was watching and monitoring the actions of Sergeant Sullivan. Given the state she'd been in as he'd passed her door, he figured it was best to return for an explanation. Assuming she'd offer one.

It bothered him that he still doubted her, yet what choice did he have? She was who she was, the sister of a convicted murderer. Anything beyond that fact was only relevant to where it led them in locating Boyd Sullivan and halting his latest killing spree. Part of him felt sorry for Zoe and her little boy, while another part kept warning him to keep his distance, particularly emotionally. There was no room for sentiment in his job. No place for opinions not based on hard evidence.

And right now, the evidence kept indicating that Sergeant Sullivan was trouble with a capital *T*.

Zoe had kept watch at her door, just in case. Plus, she wanted to be ready to identify whomever the cop and his dog captured. When she saw them returning alone, her heart fell.

"He got away? How? You had to be right behind him."

"Motorbike," Linc replied. "Star could have kept up on foot for a short distance, but I couldn't have."

"You let him go? Just like that?" Wheeling in a huff, she reentered her apartment and scooped up Freddy, holding him close and murmuring words of comfort.

"What happened anyway? Where did the guy come from?" Linc asked.

"I don't know. I'd locked the door like you told me to, so I guess he was inside all along." Her eyes narrowed on Linc, and she grimaced. "I can't believe you missed him when you checked."

"Neither can I. Stay here a sec while I take a second look."

"Better than the first time, I hope." She knew she was being hypercritical, but someone had just threatened her child and her mother-tiger instincts were still strong.

As soon as Linc and Star returned to the living room, Zoe apologized. "Look. I'm sorry I snapped at you, but that guy was scary. He had a knife."

"What? You didn't tell me that."

"You didn't give me a chance. Besides, I wanted you to hurry up and catch him."

"All right," Linc said, sobering and pulling a small

notebook and pen from a deep pocket on his ABU. "Start at the beginning and tell me everything."

By the time she was finished relaying the basics of her scare, Zoe felt exhausted. She yawned. "Sorry. I guess the rush of adrenaline is wearing off."

"You're not on duty today?"

"No. I had planned to shop, as you already know, then do some housecleaning and relax with Freddy."

"What about tomorrow?"

"We usually go to church on Sunday mornings. If you're still assigned to watch me then, I think you're allowed to bring the dog inside."

"I am. I just don't usually go to church."

"Why not?" Zoe smiled. "Afraid the roof will cave in if you show up?"

"Something like that. I wouldn't want to shock your pastor."

"I think Pastor Harmon will be okay with it. He's a seasoned preacher." Sobering, she added, "I'm starting to appreciate your diligence more than I did before. I really would feel safer if you—or another officer—were with me. With us."

Watching Linc nod, she wondered if the concern she was sensing was real or imaginary. His expression was hard to read when he was at case. The way he had looked as he and K-9 Star had dashed past her in the hallway, however, was quite memorable. It would be a long time before she forgot his intensity or the way his courageous actions had made her feel. Being married to John Flint had not imparted that kind of cosseted feeling, although belonging to the air force had given her security and a stable place to call home. At least until her brother had been dishonorably discharged, arrested and convicted as a serial killer. Those events had changed everything.

Oh, her job had continued afterward and she'd managed to retain rank, but there had been a subtle shift in the way she was perceived by her fellow airmen. Her troubles had actually begun even earlier when she'd discovered that her late husband had been disclosing details of base operations to unnamed parties. Zoe had taken the proof of it to her superiors immediately. It had been the right thing to do, yet she'd been so mortified she'd almost resigned. If not for the assurances of her officers and thanks from the Department of Homeland Security, she just might have crawled off to lick her wounds and given up the career she loved.

And now Boyd was back.

Yes, she had her son and the best job in the world, but what would keep her brother from spoiling the life she'd hammered out for herself?

Listening to Linc as he reported the incident and requested a tech team to dust for fingerprints, Zoe shivered. Just when she'd thought things couldn't get any worse, they had done just that. As one thing led to another, she felt surrounded by so many unknowns—it was mind-boggling. Being so beset by problems also made her dredge up past failures. Normally, she wasn't so hard on herself, but these current circumstances were enough to cause her to question her choices the way she used to. That not only wasn't good, it wasn't fair to herself or to those around her. Freddy needed a strong, capable parent, not a whimpering, worried mama. She would give him what he needed if it killed her.

In the hidden corners of her subconscious, there lingered the notion that she might be more right than she wanted to be. Her stalker might very well bring death. And then who would look after her son?

Linc left Star sitting with the Sullivans as he welcomed the tech team and their evidence gathering equipment. "There was definitely an uninvited guest in here," he told them. "According to the sergeant, the guy was too slightly built to be Boyd Sullivan, but treat this scene as if it could have been him just the same. No sense taking chances."

The lead tech was the same one who had inspected the warehouse for him. "You sure this time?"

"Sure enough," Linc replied. "He was apparently hiding in the bedroom, and she saw him trying to sneak off. Star and I chased him out the back. He rode away before I got a look at him, but this was no figment of Sullivan's imagination. Star was hot on a trail."

"Gotcha. We'll start in there."

Zoe had been waiting in the background while Linc spoke. He caught her studying him when he turned. The expression on her pretty face didn't suit him, so he approached. "Look, Sergeant, I understand how all this can seem a bit overwhelming but we'll get to the bottom of it eventually."

"Not if people keep insinuating it's all in my head." She sighed. "At least I know your dog believes me."

"I have no doubt you saw somebody."

"*Saw?* I had my hands on him."

"You what?"

"You heard me. When he acted as if he was going to go for Freddy with that knife, I rushed him." She pointed. "We crashed to the floor together right over there. I had hold of his wrist, but he threw me off and ran. I guess I should be thankful he didn't decide to cut me on his way out."

"Stay right there. Don't move. Don't touch anything," Linc ordered. It was only a few strides to the hallway and bedrooms where he called, "One of you get back in here and check for trace evidence. Now!"

His next words were for Zoe. "What else are you withholding?"

"Nothing. I wasn't withholding that." Her hands were clasped in front of her. "Look. I was in combat mode, okay? Details were fuzzy. Some still are. All I know for sure is that I charged him when I thought he was going on the attack."

Linc glanced over at her son. "At least one of you had the presence of mind to call for help."

"Did he? Good for Freddy. That didn't register with me either. Nothing did except the fight I was in. I do remember screaming, probably at you, come to think of it."

"Maybe." Linc shook his head. "You were certainly hollering something when I hit the top of the stairs. Are you always so excitable?"

"Only when somebody is threatening to kill me," Zoe countered. She rolled her eyes. "You don't need to act as if I'm a hysterical female, okay? I'm actually very levelheaded and sensible. Most of the time. I'd have to be to have dealt with the significant others in my life."

"Your brother."

"And my late husband. But that's a story for another time." She stood still as evidence techs inspected her hands and stroked her skin with sterile cotton swabs. "I can't imagine that there's anything there."

"Maybe not," Linc said. "But when there is even a remote chance of touch DNA, it makes sense to take samples." He addressed the technician. "Check her clothing, too. She says she grappled with the prowler, so there may be something stuck to her body, as well."

"I wish you'd been this thorough in the warehouse," Zoe drawled. "There had to be some kind of evidence there."

"Yeah. From any one of the hundred or so people who had passed through in the last few weeks," Linc countered. "This is different. You and Freddy are the only ones living here. If anything from the attacker rubbed off on you, we'll detect it."

"Who do you think it was?" she asked.

"Well, I'm beginning to doubt it was your brother if that's what you're asking," Linc said. "Knowing that he pulled a knife on you and you tackled him changes everything. If it had been Boyd, I imagine you'd have tried to talk him down." It amused him to see her rolling those warm hazel eyes again, and he chuckled softly. "Hey, I just tell it like it is."

"No," Zoe countered, "you tell it like you think it is. There's a huge difference."

He decided to humor her now that the techs had stowed their samples and returned to the bedroom where the man had probably been hiding. "Okay. Here's what I think happened. You hired Portia to babysit, and she invited a young man to keep her company. When he heard you come home, he probably thought you were alone and he hid. Then, when I checked the bedroom and rousted Portia, I failed to let Star search the rest of the room. That's on me."

"You think he was here all that time?"

"Yes, unless you left your back door open."

"Never. There's a dead bolt and chain on it so Freddy won't wander out on to the deck."

Linc shrugged and spread his hands. "There you have it. You probably scared that guy so badly he'll never come around again." To his relief, Zoe began to smile.

"I sure hope so. He scared me plenty."

"Are you okay now?" Although he expected her to affirm her well-being, he hadn't imagined she would be so candid.

"Yes," Zoe said, her smile softening. "I'm okay. You're here."

She averted her gaze, but not before Linc noted the glistening of unshed tears and felt his gut clench in empathy.

SIX

"I don't care what some anonymous blogger wrote. There's no way Zoe Sullivan faked a prowler to try to distract us from the search for her brother," Linc told Captain Justin Blackwood. "For one thing, I saw a guy fleeing." They and others were gathered in the Security Forces headquarters for a meeting of the team assigned to bring down Boyd Sullivan. Besides the regular air force members, there was Oliver Davison of the FBI and Special Agent Ian Steffen from the Office of Special Investigations.

Blackwood nodded. "All right. We'll go with that conclusion. I've talked to my daughter about the incident, and she's denied having anyone in the Sullivan apartment with her, but I've done enough interrogating to suspect she may be lying." He shook his head slowly. "Makes me wish I hadn't deployed so often when she was growing up. I hardly know her."

"We can't go back," Master Sergeant Westley James chimed in. "If we could, I'd save the lives of my two murdered team members." He cleared his throat. "Of course, I did end up marrying Felicity after successfully protecting her, so some good did come out of the Sullivan incursion."

"True." Blackwood addressed the group. "Any other leads on our escaped felon? I want to hear your ideas even if you don't think they're relevant." He was quite serious when he added, "Remember, besides the murders, Boyd Sullivan's the reason we're still missing so many valuable K-9s."

Special Agent Davison spoke up. "Some of my people participated in a ground search for your dogs, as you know. Senior Airman Ava Esposito helped organize the grid and worked with her search-and-rescue K-9, Roscoe. One of the others said he was the survivor of a chopper crash."

Linc nodded. "Probably Senior Airman Isaac Goddard. He's trying to bring a heroic German shepherd home from Afghanistan and adopt him, so I know he has a heart for dogs."

"Anything else?" Blackwood asked, scanning his team in the conference room.

Linc cleared his throat. "Well, sir, it's not directly related to the missing dogs, but there is something odd Sergeant Sullivan said recently. I checked her file again and didn't find much about John Flint, her late husband. What's the deal on him? Could he have had any connection to her brother?"

Hesitating long enough to make Linc uneasy, the captain said, "Some of her personal information has been redacted. It's my understanding it was done as a reward for actions she took on behalf of Homeland Security, but there's no way I can access their sealed files. If you want to know more, I suggest you ask her directly."

"Do you think she'll tell me?"

"If you get closer to her, she might," Sergeant James interjected. "I hear she's already beginning to rely on you and Star. That's good."

Uncomfortable with the direction the conversation was taking, Linc cleared his throat. "Are you ordering me to make this personal?"

"I can't do that, Sergeant. But I can tell you it's important that we put an end to the Red Rose Killer's actions both on and off the base. If Zoe Sullivan holds the key to doing that, I expect you to take every advantage offered, even if it means sacrificing some personal comfort."

"She seems good at heart," Linc argued.

"Then it won't hurt you to befriend her, will it? I'll make it easy for you. Except for required days off, she'll be your only assignment. Make the most of it. Since you two already seem to have a slight bond, I'm going to rotate your relief so she concentrates more on you. The new duty schedule will be posted this afternoon."

"Yes, Master Sergeant. I'll do my best."

And he would. Linc wasn't thrilled with the suggestion that he pretend to become personally involved with Zoe and her son; he was simply resigned to the need for it. As assignments went, it wasn't bad as long as he kept a tight grip on his feelings and guarded his heart well enough. He'd do it for the air force, for his country. The way he viewed it, he wouldn't be doing anything wrong as long as he didn't lead Zoe on or let her believe he was romantically interested in her.

The trick was going to be convincing himself that subterfuge was a necessity and that he wasn't becoming the kind of lowlife his father had been. He'd spent most of his adult life living down that odious man's sins, and

any inkling that his own honor might be at risk gave him
a sense of foreboding. Linc knew he was as human as
anyone, but he had long ago vowed that he would never
display even the slightest hint of dishonesty. He would
not follow in his thieving, lying father's footsteps. Ever.
Neither would his loyalty ever come into question. Not
if maintaining it literally killed him.

Zoe had Freddy up and dressed for Sunday services
in plenty of time. She had seen a dark-colored SUV
parked in the street below her apartment and assumed
it belonged to the Security Forces. Was Linc in it? Part
of her yearned to see him again, while another part of
her worried that she might be starting to get too depen-
dent upon him—and his K-9 partner.

Freddy had no such qualms. "Is the doggy going
to church with us?" he asked, bouncing on his tiptoes
with excitement.

"I don't know, honey. It's possible."

"You asked. I heard. So he's going, right?"

Zoe had to smile at the child's expectations of the
perfect day. "The Security Forces man may bring Star
if they're on duty today. We'll have to wait and see."

"They could come anyway."

"I know. I know." But the chances of that were probably slim, she added to herself. No telling why Linc had
acted so put off when she'd suggested he accompany
them to church, but she didn't think it had anything
to do with her or Freddy. No, it was something else.
Something deeper. He wouldn't be the first soldier to
turn from God after experiencing combat, although of-
tentimes the reverse was true. Strong Christians could
be formed in the trenches, too. It all depended on the

man or woman and their willingness to trust in a higher power rather than relying only upon themselves. Bowing a knee could be tough for someone who had always felt totally self-reliant.

Or for someone who simply chose evil over good, as her brother had. Sadly, she was beginning to lose hope that Boyd would ever repent. At this point, the most she could hope for was that he'd stop hurting others and be brought to justice. As much as she'd loved the boy he'd been when they were growing up, she could not accept his adult self. Whatever goodness was still inside him had been masked by a blackness that encompassed his heart and made him a different person. Someone who had to be stopped. In that regard, she almost wished he would contact her, because she wouldn't hesitate to turn him in.

A small head ducked beneath her hand and she felt Freddy's silky hair. "Don't be sad, Mommy. If the doggy doesn't come, you can pet me. See?"

Laughing, Zoe gave his hair a gentle tousle. "Okay. But you have to promise to behave in church and not bark."

The child's eager "Ruff, ruff" made her chuckle more.

"Careful or you'll be eating kibble instead of cookies."

He giggled, eyes sparkling. "I'm not really a dog. Little boys need cookies."

"Okay." She smoothed the skirt of her dress and patted her knot of hair that she'd twisted neatly and clipped at her nape. "You ready?"

"Uh-huh." Freddy grasped her hand.

"Then let's go."

The closer Zoe got to the street, the more butterflies there were cavorting in her stomach. Would Linc be waiting? Would he go to church with them? She kept telling herself he wouldn't, but in the back of her mind was the hope he would. Why it mattered, she wasn't sure, but she desperately wanted him with her. Going to services was a step in the right direction, and perhaps she was meant to be the catalyst that led him back to the fold.

Yeah, right. Some Christian disciple I am when all I can think about is how safe he will make me feel, she countered. That was the basic truth. She wanted Linc and Star with her for protection far more than for altruistic reasons, and it was just as well to admit it. Matter of fact, she was going to tell him the same thing the first chance she got.

Which was about to be…later, Zoe realized as an unfamiliar enlisted man got out of the SUV and greeted her.

"Good morning, Sergeant Sullivan," the younger airman said with a broad grin. He gestured at the car. "I'm here to give you a ride to church."

"No, thanks. We usually walk."

He sobered. Seemed nervous. "Sorry. I was told to drive you, and if you don't want me to get busted, I'd appreciate it if you'd get in."

Zoe noted that his neck and face had reddened and he was breaking a sweat. "Who did you say sent you?"

"Um, Tech Sergeant Colson."

"I see. You have written orders then?"

"No, ma'am. It's just a *ride*."

If the young airman hadn't sounded so unsure and acted jittery, she might have got into the car without question. Looking around her, Zoe noted others passing by on the sidewalk and in the street. At least she and Freddy weren't isolated there. Once she entered the vehicle, she'd be hidden behind its tinted windows and lose any advantage she had now.

Despite the fact that the driver opened the rear passenger door for her, Zoe didn't get in. Instead, she slowly backed away. Her eyes narrowed, taking in everything about the airman and committing his features to memory. The trouble was, he looked a lot like every other immature green recruit. Acted it, too.

"You'll—you'll be late for church," he said with a wheedling tone.

"If I am, I am." Still balancing Freddy on her hip, Zoe took her cell phone out of her purse and quickly found the number Linc had entered the day she'd chased away the prowler. In seconds she had him on the line.

"Colson."

"This is Zoe Sullivan. I want to thank you for sending a car for me, but it's really not necessary."

"What did you say?" His shout was loud enough that she eased the phone away from her ear. By the time Linc added, "I didn't send anybody to get you," his words were practically broadcast volume.

Zoe saw the driver's face pale. "It—it was just…" he began before wheeling, jumping into the car and hitting the gas. The tires slipped and screeched on the pavement. Holding her son close, Zoe stepped up on the curb and melted into a small crowd of onlookers.

Her phone was still on, Linc's voice strident. "Where are you now?"

"The street in front of my apartment. He drove off. I don't know who he was. He said you sent him and I—"

"Stay there. I'm on my way," Linc ordered. She heard the roar of a motor in the background as he added, "ETA less than five. Are you and the boy all right?"

"We're fine. I didn't fall for the trick."

"Can you ID the vehicle or the driver?"

"It looked like one of your black SUVs. The driver was just a nervous kid."

"The same one you caught in your apartment?"

"I don't think so. This guy was shorter. And less belligerent." She pulled Freddy closer and backed farther from the curb until she was partially standing behind the trunk of one of the cottonwoods lining the street. "How much longer before you get to me?"

"You should be able to hear my siren. I'm only a couple blocks away, turning off Canyon Drive and passing the Base Command Office."

"Copy. We'll wait right here."

As the wailing of Linc's siren grew louder, Zoe's fear waned. She had thwarted an enemy once again, and her knight in shining armor was about to ride up on his prancing steed and protect her.

On second thought, she didn't need any knight. She needed information, some of which her so-called *knight* might be withholding, she realized, because he didn't trust her. Maybe now he'd open up more. As long as she was even partially in the dark about what was going on behind the scenes, she was more vulnerable.

A chill chased up her spine as she thought about their near abduction. Only common sense and a niggling warning in her subconscious had kept her from believing the clean-cut young airman and getting into that car. How many other traps were waiting? How many more dangers would she have to identify and avoid before this nightmare was over?

A black SUV that was the twin of the first one rounded the corner on to her block and skidded to a halt, its siren winding down like a balloon losing air. Zoe had no doubt who was behind the wheel of this one. The sight of Linc Colson leaping out and releasing his K-9 from the rear brought immense relief. It also brought unshed tears to her eyes, tears that were quite embarrassing.

She blinked them away before Linc got close enough to notice. Smiling, she looked up at him. "You made good time. Where were you?"

"Waiting at the church. What happened to your assigned guard?"

"Beats me." She shrugged. "At first, I thought it was the kid who said he was here to pick me up. But when he got out, I could tell he wasn't part of the security team."

"Who was he?"

"I've never noticed him before. This is a big base. I could have walked right past him—and a hundred just like him."

"I have my people looking into it," Linc said. "Part of this is my fault. I thought your night guard would escort you as far as the church. He said when he saw the car pull over and park, he assumed I was picking you up and he left. That kind of mix-up won't happen again."

"I certainly hope not." Zoe spoke from the heart. "I suspect the problem is that you people aren't watching me for my sake. You're here because you expect Boyd to show up."

"Granted. That doesn't mean I'm going to take your reports of trouble lightly."

"Honest?"

"Honest," Linc promised. "If we manage to apprehend the airman who was here this morning, will you be able to ID him?"

"Yes. As soon as he began acting suspicious, I paid special attention to his face. Trouble is, I couldn't read his name tag and he resembles half the guys on base. How did he manage to get the keys to one of your SUVs?"

"That's another very good question."

Zoe sighed as she helped Freddy into the rear seat of Linc's vehicle and, in the absence of a car seat, fastened his seat belt. "In retrospect, this guy seemed more scared than menacing, as if he knew he was in the wrong and didn't want to be there."

"Interesting. Do you think your brother would be capable of fooling a clueless recruit into doing his bidding?"

"My brother again? Why do you keep blaming everything on Boyd? I mean, if he wanted to talk to me, he could just call."

"On the burner phone you smuggled to him in prison?"

Astounded, Zoe gaped at him. "What are you implying?"

"Master Sergeant James and I paid a visit to the prison and spoke with a cell mate of your brother's. He told us Boyd had a burner phone in his possession before his escape."

She stood tall, shoulders back, chin up, and faced him. "Well, he didn't get it from me."

Noting Linc's sigh, she wondered if she might be getting through to him. He did nod. "Okay. Then where do you think it came from?"

"How should I know? You're the security guy. Was I the only one who visited the prison?"

To her relief, Linc shook his head. "No. One of our aircraft mechanics was there, too. Jim Ahern."

"I think my brother had mentioned him before."

"He may have. They were buddies before Boyd was dishonorably discharged."

"Then why all the interest in me? Why don't you put a watch on Ahern, too?"

"We're not ignoring that possibility," Linc said. He started to reach for the front door on the passenger side. Zoe stopped him. "I'll ride in the back with Freddy, if you don't mind."

Although Linc easily acquiesced, she could tell he wasn't thrilled that she'd refused to sit next to him. Well, too bad. Every time she began to think he might be on her side, he came up with another accusation and proved the opposite.

When Zoe admitted to herself that she wished he wasn't going to church with them, her conscience reared up and gave her a swift kick. Just because somebody was a thorn in her side, that didn't mean that person didn't need the Lord. Maybe Linc was more in need of God's mercy than she was.

Her glance caught his in the rearview mirror, and she was surprised to sense actual concern. Long after he broke eye contact, she continued to observe him. Analyze him. Admire him, despite his contrariness. There was something about the sergeant that impressed her in a way she didn't understand. Moments ago, she'd been wishing he wasn't there, yet now his presence was giving a lift to her spirits and bringing peace to her heart.

That was crazy.

It was also patently true.

SEVEN

Seated in the last church pew with his charges, Linc was fine as long as he kept his focus on doing his job, which meant not allowing himself to relax and enjoy Zoe's or Freddy's company. Star, on the other hand, was having no such qualms and was leaning against the boy's tennis shoes, panting.

The K-9 didn't have Linc's background to create bias. Lies had cost him the lives of men in his former unit, something he would never be able to forget, and more lies threaded through his memories of his father. The parent he'd believed to be a hero had turned out to be nothing more than a thief and a coward, a familial sin he was still doing penance for in his own way.

His father was a lot like Boyd Sullivan, he thought. Slick on the outside and rotten to the core. It wasn't until Zoe nudged him and asked, "Did you have dill pickles or lemons for breakfast?" that he realized his disturbing thoughts were being revealed in his expression.

"I feel as though I've been making a steady diet of sour lemons," Linc replied, "in the form of unanswered questions and out-and-out lies."

"Not to mention the stuff that's been happening to me while you've been assigned to watch me."

Linc saw a scowl beginning to knit her forehead beneath her bangs, so he continued. "It's all part of the same package. If—and that's a big if—you happen to be telling me the whole truth, we have more than one problem to solve."

"Duh. You think?"

A hush was coming over the congregation. Linc laid his index finger across his lips. "Shush. We'll talk about this later."

"Guaranteed," Zoe said. As the congregation rose, she pulled a hymnal out of the rack on the back of the pew in front of them and expertly thumbed to the called-for page.

Linc did not intend to sing along. He hadn't been in a church since the deaths of some of his best friends and he was far from comfortable. Nevertheless, the music tugged at his boyhood memories of standing in a worship service beside his mother and following her lead as she gave voice to her strong faith. In that respect, Zoe kind of reminded him of his mom. Her pitch was perfect, her tone both soothing and inspiring.

When she extended one side of the open hymnal toward him, he grasped the edge and made a small effort to join in. The more he sang, the more poignant the song seemed. For some reason, words that were familiar suddenly took on deeper meaning, each phrase drawing him closer to the faith he'd once professed.

Linc resisted the inner call. He continued to sing until a catch in his throat made his voice crack. Keeping his eyes forward, he released the hymnal to Zoe and stood at attention. He was a soldier. A member of the elite Security Forces. His own man and afraid of nothing. He didn't need the crutch of religion. He didn't need anything or anybody except his badge and his dog.

As positive as those thoughts were, they weren't enough to banish the tightness in his throat or the sense that he was missing something vital. Something that was almost within his grasp.

Zoe usually felt at home in church, though she might not be at ease in any other group. Even her personal friends had acted rather distant since they'd learned who her brother was and what had been occurring ostensibly because of him. Although she would have liked to come up with a reason to deny some of the charges against her sibling, she knew without a doubt that he was capable of killing on a mere whim. He'd proved it to judge and jury. As much as she wished she could, there was no way to convince herself he might be innocent this time, either.

She had some fond memories of her big brother looking after her when they were children growing up in Dill, Texas. She'd idolized him, following him everywhere when she was a little girl, but current events were undeniable. Boyd had not only confessed in court, he'd acted proud of his crimes and justified for committing them. Therefore, she had no rebuttal for those who blamed Boyd for the terrible things occurring since his escape. He was intelligent yet behaved in a way she couldn't fathom, couldn't identify with. The youth who had stood up for her against playground bullies had chosen to become an abusive adult rather than continuing to champion those who needed help. If he had stayed on the side of law and order, he would have made an excellent military officer or policeman.

As for the personal problems she was currently facing, however, Zoe doubted Boyd would bother to create that kind of chaos. Not only was it unlikely that he'd have known she'd duck into the warehouse in time to see that supposed shooting, he wouldn't have sent an enlisted man to do his bidding that morning when he could easily have contacted her himself. Not to mention whoever had been lurking in her apartment, particularly since Portia had vowed she knew nothing about the prowler and had convinced everybody she was not responsible. That made the whole scenario much, much more terrifying.

Zoe's thoughts were cut short when the service ended. Everyone stood. Zoe let Freddy climb up on the bench beside her, so he'd be at eye level and she turned to speak to Linc. "We usually go out for lunch on Sunday after church. Is that all right?"

"You don't have to ask me," he said flatly. "If you aren't too worried about being out in public, then go."

"I'd almost rather be out and about than back in my apartment, wondering who else is hiding there, ready to pounce. How about the Winged Java for lunch? You're coming with us, right?"

"Absolutely. I have the day duty. Let's get back to the car so I can check my messages in private. I want to see if they managed to nab your SUV driver."

She shuddered. "He's not *mine*. In fact, I hope I never run into him again." Falling into step with Freddy propped on her hip, she said, "By the way, I keep imagining I'm catching glimpses of the shooter from the warehouse. I know it has to be impossible to tell, because his face was covered, but… I don't know. I keep seeing guys who move the way he did, and it gives me the jitters."

"What about his supposed victim? Any sightings of her?"

"No. That actually should be easier because she had reddish hair, but I haven't noticed anybody who looks like her."

"Any more thoughts about the guy in your apartment?"

"I'm just glad he didn't show himself sooner and hurt Freddy," Zoe replied. "Or Portia. Now that I think about it, he probably wasn't one of our airmen. His face was shadowed by the hoodie but it looked grubby, as though he might be growing a beard. Airmen are always neat and their uniforms make them look so handsome."

"You in the market for another husband?"

Cheeks warming, Zoe shook her head. "No way. I've had my fill of smooth talkers and romance. Been there, done that, have the T-shirt and the scars to prove it."

"You mentioned your late husband before. What was the deal with him anyway? I can't find much on file. That is, if you don't mind talking about him."

They had reached the SUV and Zoe had helped Freddy get settled before climbing into the front seat. Linc had briefly checked his messages, then pulled into traffic and was heading for the café before she chose to answer.

"His name was John. John Flint. We met in basic and by the time we were both E-2s, we'd fallen in love and decided to get married."

"I figured out that much. What happened to him? I was told he died in an auto accident, but there are no details on file and all I could find for a cause of death is *unknown*. Did he die of his injuries?"

Hesitating, Zoe studied Linc's profile. As much as she wanted to deny it, there was something about him that inspired confidence. As long as she didn't reveal the specifics of John's crimes, she supposed it wouldn't hurt to clue him in a little.

"There are questions, suspicions surrounding the accident," Zoe said, keeping her voice soft so Freddy wouldn't overhear. "Officially, the accident caused his death. The reasons behind that crash are something else. I inadvertently unearthed evidence that my late husband had committed crimes and I turned in the evidence. The authorities began to speculate that perhaps he had been...terminated after that, because he knew too much and his usefulness had ended."

"Usefulness to whom?"

"Good question. If they ever did figure it out, I wasn't told."

"Who are *they*?"

"The case eventually made its way to Homeland Security. They're the ones who sealed the files." She noted Linc's scowl and the way his fists gripped the steering wheel. Little wonder. Mention Homeland Security and walls shot up. That agency was the be-all and end-all of national defense. The very fact that it had become involved marked John's death as the act of subversives. Or worse.

"What did you find that implicated him?"

"They asked me not to divulge those details," Zoe explained. "I'm not sure what investigations grew out of the info they got from his laptop, but it no longer matters. John may not have directly murdered innocent people the way my brother has, but he was not the kind of man I thought he was when I married him. If he hadn't died, I'd probably have divorced him when I learned what he'd been up to."

"Could any of that background be influencing what's happened to you lately?"

"I can't see how. It's been years." Sighing deeply, she leaned against the seat. Bothered by the knot of hair at her nape, she pulled the pins that held it in place. Shaking out her tresses, she raked her fingers through them. Linc was watching her out of the corner of his right eye and that much intensity made her nervous. "What?"

Color rose to infuse his cheeks. "Nothing."

"You may as well say it," Zoe grumbled. "Boyd and Freddy's daddy—the men in my life. I can really pick 'em, huh?"

"You didn't pick your brother. He came as part of the family package. My lineage isn't much better."

"Really?"

"Really. Listen, if I tell you something in confidence, will you promise to keep it to yourself?"

"You'd trust me that far?" Her eyebrows arched theatrically. "Maybe you'd better not confess anything. I don't want to be responsible if your deep dark secret gets out."

"It's not about me. It's about my dad. He was in the air force, too, only his record was far from honorable. They caught him stealing and drummed him out of the service. After that, his personal life fell apart and he left my mother. She raised me alone." He leaned his head back, gesturing toward the back seat. "Kind of like you and Freddy."

"Is that why you seem to understand him so well?"

"I don't know. Maybe. What I'm trying to say is, don't beat yourself up about your past. We all make mistakes. It's part of life. The good news is we can turn it around and make amends, because you and I are still alive and kicking."

What was he alluding to? Did he think his speech about his father was going to loosen her tongue? Sure sounded like it. She steeled her nerves and cleared her throat. "Listen, Colson, I went to my commanding officers and did all I could to make things right after John died. And I would do the same now if I had any clues about Boyd. Is that clear?"

"Crystal." Linc slowed as they passed the distinctive Winged Java café with its white coffee mug mural and lit red, white and blue decorative wings. There was a line of customers out front waiting for a chance to enter. "We'll starve before we get a booth in there. What do you say we pick up a pizza from Carmen's instead and eat it back at your place?"

Zoe wanted to argue. She really did. But his suggestion made perfect sense, and she knew Freddy had to be hungry, even if her own stomach was too crowded with butterflies and angst to leave room for food. "Fine. I was going to invite you in, anyway. It looks as if this afternoon is going to be a hot one, and I see no reason to make that poor dog suffer in the heat."

"Can I come in with her?"

Zoe huffed and nodded. "Yes, as long as you behave. No jumping on the furniture—or jumping to conclusions."

"Promise. And maybe if we go back over the recent incidents involving you, we can find some kind of pattern. It's worth a try."

"I've been over and over it. There are no logical connecting factors."

"Only because we haven't discovered them yet," he argued.

"It's not my brother," Zoe told him flatly. "Boyd may be a lot of things but subtle isn't one of them. If he wanted to punish me, he'd come right out and do it. No. Whoever's been messing with me is someone other than him." She lowered her voice. "I'm actually more afraid of the unknown than I am of Boyd. I keep remembering the man in my apartment who pulled the knife on us."

Linc wheeled into the drive-through lane under a red-and-white awning outside Carmen's Italian Restaurant. "Funny you should see it that way," he said. "The same possibilities occurred to me."

She couldn't suppress a relieved smile. "Hooray. Finally. Now we're getting somewhere." The reserved look on his handsome face told her Linc had not come as far in his reasoning as she had. That was okay. At least he'd made a baby step in the right direction.

And for now we're reasonably safe, she added, swiveling to grin at her cute little boy. Being committed to the air force meant she wasn't free to go on the run from her enemies, nor was there any place on the base where she could hide. Not for very long at any rate. That meant standing her ground and bravely facing all foes just as the military she honored did, at home and around the globe.

It might sound clichéd to outsiders, but she was a part of the best fighting force in the world and proud of it. So was the man who sat beside her and imparted both courage and strength. Linc Colson may not feel that close to her as a person, but she was ready to stand by

his side against anyone and anything. What she could
not accomplish on her own was more than possible with
his support. They would succeed and get to the bottom
of all that had been happening. Together.

Full realization hit her like a rocket ignition. Zoe's
pulse sped, pounding until she wondered if the beats
were audible. She had just mentally joined herself to
Linc Colson in a way that surpassed anything in her
past. The sense that they were already a functioning
couple, standing as one, was so strong it left her breathless.

Her first instinct was to deny those conclusions and
banish any notions of partnership. But she didn't. She
couldn't. Like it or not, she wanted him beside her, now
and for as long as unknown foes kept coming at her.
So far, they had found no victim of the shooting she'd
seen. The person in her apartment had escaped. And
she had thwarted this morning's effort to coax her into
the wrong vehicle. So far, so good, but how long could
that last? Considered together, those instances were
enough to set her on edge and keep her looking over
her shoulder all the time. Plus, there was the question
of the whereabouts of her murderous sibling. Every day
brought more angst and increased her fear. Only one element brought relief, and she was most grateful.

*Thank You, Lord, for sending Linc and his K-9 into
my life,* Zoe prayed silently. *I don't care why they're
here. I'm just thankful they are.*

EIGHT

It didn't take long to get to the Sullivan apartment with their food. Linc let Zoe handle the pizza box and shepherd her child while he and Star took point. The K-9 began straining at her leash as soon as they reached Zoe's second-story apartment.

"Whoa. Wait," Linc ordered sternly. "I thought I'd convinced you to lock up."

"I did." She leaned to peer past him.

"Well, the door's not even closed all the way, so something happened."

His outstretched hand became a barrier. "You stay out here with the boy while I check inside."

To his dismay, Zoe disagreed. "How do you know this isn't a ploy to get you to leave us alone out here in the hallway so we're vulnerable?"

"That is a valid point," he said. "Okay. Slip inside after I give you the okay and do your best to secure this door. It doesn't look like it's been jimmied so the lock should still work."

"How could—"

"I don't know. One thing at a time, okay? I'm going to make an entry and let Star tell me if there's anybody in here who doesn't belong. I'll leave the door open and signal you to follow as soon as I'm sure it's safer in than out."

Satisfied by her nod, Linc gave the door a push, stood aside with the K-9 and called out, "Security. Anybody in here?"

Star seemed relaxed enough that Linc quickly motioned to Zoe and Freddy to follow him in. They stopped as ordered and waited. The little boy was behaving with extraordinary restraint, probably because he was picking up vibes from the adults.

Linc once again made a barrier with his outstretched arm to keep his charges in place. "Stay here and look around the room. Does anything look different or missing?"

"I think the sofa was moved. It looks farther to the right than I left it. But why would anybody move furniture?"

"Maybe you did it while you were cleaning and forgot."

"Sounds like my whole life lately. My possessions seem to have a mind of their own. I put my purse on one table and it ends up somewhere else when I look for it. Stuff like that."

"Do you think you're just rattled because you're worried?"

"It's possible." She shivered and pressed her back to the closed door while Freddy hugged her knees.

"We'll talk about all that later." Linc gave Star the command "Get 'em" and let her leash extend.

Nose to the floor, the K-9 began to sniff. She coursed back and forth in the living room a few times but surprisingly she alerted on nothing, then proceeded to the kitchenette and then down the only hallway. A few minutes later, she was heading back to the entry.

Linc gave Zoe a shrug and a slight smile as he followed his dog back through the living room. "Nothing positive. Not even a stray prowler."

"Not funny," she said, making a face. "The last time took ten years off my life."

"You can spare them." He unleashed his dog, relieved Zoe of the pizza box and strode toward the small kitchen. "If I hadn't seen your file, I'd have thought you were still a teenager."

"There are times when I feel twice my twenty-six years," Zoe replied. "How old are you?"

"Four, in dog years, if you count them the old way. There's a new complicated formula that's supposed to be more accurate but seven to one is a lot easier."

"Hmm, twenty-eight. I'd have guessed you were older. Sorry."

He had placed the box on her kitchen counter and was washing his hands at the sink. "Not a problem. Looking more mature helps in my job. Besides, there are plenty of miles on me."

"Hard ones?"

Zoe was sponging off Freddy's hands and prepping him for a messy meal, so she wasn't watching Linc when she'd posed the question. He was glad. For an instant, he suspected his face had displayed some of the latent pain and grief he still carried. He'd told her about his father, which was more than she needed to know. He did not intend to brief her on the loss of his human friends or the subterfuge that had cost them their lives.

"Relatively hard," Linc said, working to keep his

tone casual. "I did a tour overseas before coming back stateside and joining Security Forces."

"Did you work dogs over there?"

He shook his head. "No, but their training impressed all of us. That's why I applied to become a handler myself when I came home."

"You seem to be a natural," Zoe told him as she lifted Freddy into his booster seat at the small table. "I used to have a dog when I was little."

Seeing her smile fade and hearing a telling sigh, Linc waited until she'd got drinks for all three of them and was seated before he sat down and continued that line of conversation. "My dad would never let me have a dog, so I mostly hung out with the ones in the neighborhood. Even when they disobeyed their owners, they usually listened to my commands. Labs were my favorite. What breed did you have?"

"Trixie was just a little white mutt, but I loved her," Zoe said without looking at Linc. Her somber mood caused him to reach out. She permitted him to lay his hand over hers where it rested on the table next to her paper plate, and he could feel a slight tremor. "She disappeared."

"You never found her? I'm sorry."

Although Zoe raised her chin and squared her shoulders, he could tell it was an effort for her. When she said, "I think my brother got rid of her because he was mad at me," Linc was dumbstruck. His fingers tightened around hers and Zoe squeezed back. What could he possibly say to help her heal from a trauma like that? A child losing a beloved pet was bad enough. Suspecting that her own brother was behind it had to ache all the way to her core.

Linc placed his other hand over their joined ones and simply waited. This was a truly amazing woman. She had been hurt and had suffered loss repeatedly, yet she'd insisted that there was something inside Boyd worth saving. Was that forgiveness or naïveté? Maybe it was both. And maybe she was relying on her Christian faith for the strength to not only face each day but to soothe the wounds of the past.

He had been counseled to do the same. He knew it would help him cope. But he wasn't ready to forgive the lies that had led to the loss of his friends in combat or the woman who had told them so convincingly. And that didn't include his father's betrayal of their family and the bevy of falsehoods that man had spewed.

Zoe was a better Christian than he'd ever be, Linc ultimately concluded, meaning she was probably telling the truth about Boyd, too. The main reason he hated to admit that was because it meant he was further from apprehending the escapee than anyone had anticipated.

And more innocents were probably going to die.

Staring at their joined hands, Linc promised himself he would not let one of those victims be Zoe Sullivan.

During most of the meal, Zoe had concentrated on Freddy rather than pretending to be upbeat. She did manage to eat a little, but her appetite was nil. Neither she nor Linc had talked a lot, although he had made a few attempts at casual conversation. Freddy, on the other hand, was his usual loquacious self.

"Don't try to talk until you swallow, honey," she prompted. "It's not polite."

"Mmm." His grin would have been edged with tomato sauce if she hadn't been wiping his face frequently as he ate. "When can I play with the puppy?"

"After we're done," she said. "And no feeding her from the table. Dogs don't like pizza."

"Yes they do." To prove his point, the boy leaned to one side and let Star lick his messy fingers.

Linc stopped him firmly. "Don't. Please. Working K-9s are not supposed to take food from anybody but their handlers. You need to help her keep the rules, okay?"

"Okay." Subdued, Freddy straightened while Zoe cleaned the hand that had been offered to Star. "I'm done. Can I play now?"

"After we wash you with soap at the sink," his mother said.

Linc stood first. "I'll take care of him for you. Finish your meal. You've hardly eaten a thing."

She didn't argue. Excuses were unnecessary. The man was observant enough to tell she'd lost her appetite and to no doubt guess which part of their earlier conversation had caused it. Most of the time she was able to keep her unhappy past at bay, but once in a while, like today, it reared up and bit her hard enough to draw figurative blood all over again.

Watching him scoop up a messy Freddy and hold him at arm's length, Zoe was touched. Her son was giggling instead of fighting the cleanup and Linc was grinning as if he, too, was having fun. Soapy water splashed the counter and Freddy's shirt, but Linc dried everything off before setting the boy on the floor and telling Star it was okay to play.

When he resumed his seat at the table, Zoe took a

bite of her now-cold pizza just to please him. "I'm really not hungry."

"Well, maybe you will be later. Want me to slip the leftovers into your fridge?"

"Sure. That would be fine. Don't bother wrapping them. They never last long enough to get stale."

Linc had put the pizza away and was straightening when she saw him pause and apparently listen to his earpiece. He touched the mic on his shoulder. "Copy. Did you take a report?"

Again, he listened, making Zoe curious. It wasn't until he had ended his one-sided conversation that she asked, "More trouble?"

"Not about your brother, if that's what you mean. Do you know Yvette Crenville? She's the base nutritionist."

"I think I may have met her. Why?" Zoe held her breath, hoping he wasn't going to cite more mayhem. "Is she okay?"

"Yes. But she reported harassment, so I wondered if there might be any connection to your problems."

"Who bothered her?"

"I suppose it won't hurt to tell you since she says it's already shown up on that unauthorized base blog we've been trying to silence."

"The one that claims to have all the inside info on Boyd and blames me for keeping his whereabouts a secret?"

"Yeah, and insists your encounters with prowlers are fake and meant to distract us from tracking him. Whoever's been writing it apparently keeps shutting down in one place and popping up in another before we can get a handle on the location. I suppose if the brass gave it high priority, they could stop it, but so far it's proved fairly unimportant. It is bothersome, though."

"No kidding. What's the story on Yvette?"

"She says she's afraid of one of the aircraft mechanics. Jim Ahern."

Zoe smiled slightly. "That guy may think he's a priceless gift to all women, but he seems pretty harmless."

She had expected Linc to ease up and was taken aback when he frowned instead. "What's wrong?"

"Ahern was one of the only other people who visited your brother in prison. We checked him out thoroughly, but since his name has popped up again, maybe we need to keep a closer eye on him." He sat down at the table opposite her, his eyes never leaving hers. "Remember I told you I found out from one of Boyd's cell mates that he had a burner phone? A lifer named Johnny Motes. He told us that the calls Boyd had made sounded more businesslike than romantic, so we figured he was contacting cohorts on the outside."

"What makes you believe anything a convict says? He could have lied."

"Yes, he could have. But Motes was negotiating for a better pillow and five hundred bucks in his commissary account, so we figured he was probably on the up-and-up. If I hadn't been so sure he was being truthful, I wouldn't have come up with the five hundred myself."

"*You* paid it?"

"It was that or not get the whole story. I thought it was worth taking the chance, and the air force didn't agree."

"So, was my brother contacting Ahern? He's here on base. He could easily have helped Boyd."

"True, but the unproven suspicions regarding Ahern are for petty crimes and vandalism. Besides, as you said, he's a great mechanic. Why would he risk his air force career?"

"Him?" She jumped to her feet. Anger had taken over. "What about *me*? I love the air force. I worked hard to get to where I am, and I intend to stay until retirement. Why would I do something that would cost me so much?"

"Whoa. Calm down." Speaking quietly, Linc joined her and reached for one of her hands.

She jerked it away. "Why should I calm down? The whole base has been treating me like a leper ever since Boyd showed up and started doing his Red Rose Killer act here. You Security guys have made me the main focus of your investigation. All that does is convince everybody that I'm a part of his crimes."

"It isn't just that. Really. Listen to me. My assignment may have started out as a normal surveillance of your activities but it has turned into more, at least for me."

Once again, he reached for her hand, and this time Zoe didn't pull away. "Explain."

"It's beginning to look as though you may be the target of some dirty tricks, okay?"

"You mean like opening my apartment door and leaving it ajar?"

"That and maybe the guy with the knife, not to mention your fake chauffeur this morning."

"Have they located him?"

"No, but one of the cars had additional miles on it so we had it dusted for prints. It had been wiped down."

"Wonderful. Just like my apartment and that warehouse door. Why can't crooks be as dumb in real life as they are on TV?"

"They all make mistakes eventually. The trick is never giving up and following every lead."

Zoe couldn't help being bummed. "I suppose nobody is looking for the redheaded shooting victim I saw."

"Not that I know of. Do you think that was a setup, too?"

"It almost had to be to leave no clues. I've been over and over what happened that day and I still can't figure out why anybody would want to stage a fake murder or would have known I was in that warehouse and in position to see it."

"We came to the same conclusion."

"Unless you weren't the only one following me."

"Star never alerted."

"Yeah." She sighed noisily and gestured around the room. "Like in here, this morning."

"Not exactly. She did seem to hit on trails, but they were pretty much all over the place."

"Could she have been mistaken?"

Zoe felt his fingers tighten around hers and noticed a hardness in his gaze that indicated intensity she couldn't explain until he said, "No. I think she was picking up the scent of somebody who had been walking around inside your apartment and had covered a lot of ground." He paused, then added, "I suspect whoever has been in here may have been doing things to try to convince you you're losing your mind."

"Gaslighting me? Why would they do that? Are you joking?"

The somber way Linc shook his head told her otherwise. "No. The more I think about it, the more sense it makes. I want you to start keeping track of every time you notice an anomaly. I don't care how insignificant it is. Write it down along with the time of day and the date. We need to see if there's a pattern."

Zoe would have pulled her hands free and gone to get a pen and paper right then if she hadn't been so comforted by Linc's touch. A few more seconds of drawing strength from him wouldn't make any difference in the long run. Some of the instances of confusion were etched in her memory while more minor ones had been forgotten. They could start with her stronger memories and build from there.

Raising her gaze to his, she was met by a softening of his green eyes and the promise of a smile. Her lower lip trembled, as did the hands he was grasping.

"It's going to be all right," he told her.

When he put it that way and looked at her with such gentle strength, she didn't doubt him for a second.

His lips were so close, his manner so inviting, she had to struggle to keep from rising on tiptoe and kissing him. Their clasped hands formed a barrier between them that was helping to keep them apart, until he released her and bent to close the distance.

Zoe closed her eyes and gave in just as Linc apparently gained control of himself and pulled away. To her embarrassment, she almost staggered forward to kiss empty air.

He caught her shoulders, righted and steadied her, then smiled sadly as if he'd read her mind. "Not a good idea, I'm afraid."

Moritified beyond belief, she shook loose and denied everything with a quick reply. "I have no idea what you're talking about."

His laughter as she stomped away grated like spinning tires throwing up loose gravel.

It wouldn't have been so bad if he hadn't been right.

NINE

Star was napping on the sofa beside Freddy, but Linc was so uptight by the time Zoe finished relating all the questionable instances of the past few weeks he had to pace.

Reaching the boundary of the small living room, he spun around to face her and pointed at the tablet on the kitchen table in front of her. "I can't believe you didn't bother to mention all this."

"Most of it could have been my imagination. You said yourself that I've been under a lot of stress."

"Forget that. Think. See yourself as the victim and assume all these things were done to unsettle you. Who would be that vindictive?"

She huffed and arched both eyebrows. "Lately? There isn't enough paper on this pad to list the names of all the people who seem to be upset with me. Ever since Boyd showed up at Canyon Air Force Base and my name was linked with his, I haven't even had an invitation to go out for coffee."

"You're exaggerating."

"I wish I were. I go to work, do my job, come home

to Freddy, then do it all over again the next day. My social life is the pits."

"Unbelievable."

"Yeah?" She rolled her eyes. "Believe it, Colson.
Sharing this pizza with you is the closest I've come to
having company in weeks." He heard her huff before
she continued. "But at least that beats being hit on by
airmen who think that just because I'm a single woman
I must be ready for romance."

"There is the problem of crossing ranks being for-
bidden. Don't they understand how much trouble you'd
be in if you accepted dates with them?"

Zoe chuckled. "Yeah, well, it doesn't seem to bother
them to try. I think it's probably a challenge to see if
their macho appeal is enough to get me to step over the
line. Most of them are pitiful."

"Gotcha." Linc rejoined her, sat with his elbows resting on the table and pulled the list to him. "I suppose
there's no way you can recall names, is there?"

"Mostly, no. A lot of the offenders were my students
of course, because I have the most one-on-one contact
with those. I think a few even thought they could over-
turn my decisions to wash them out by romancing me.
There were times when it was actually hard to keep a
straight face."

"Maybe you're selling yourself short," he said quietly, watching her for clues to her innermost feelings.
"There are lots of men on base who would count themselves fortunate to get a date with you."

To his chagrin, she laughed. "I don't see them lining up because I'm such a great catch. And that's for
the best. I already told you. I have no intention of get-

ting involved. I have my job and Freddy. That's plenty for a satisfying life."

"I've enjoyed being with you today. That's not a bad thing, is it?"

His ego took a jolt when she looked him straight in the eyes and said, "You're here because you're working. Nothing more, nothing less. When the job is over, you won't give me or my son a second thought, and you know it."

Mentioning their "almost" kiss seemed inappropriate in view of her candid opinion. Besides, Linc began to wonder if the physical attraction between them was merely a result of proximity. After all, he was a normal man and Zoe was a beautiful woman. There was bound to be at least a little overt interest. He certainly couldn't deny that he admired her. She was beyond strong willed and intelligent, not to mention she had integrity.

Finally, he could admit he believed her when she insisted she'd had no recent contact with her nefarious brother. And he also believed that someone was trying to convince her she was mentally unbalanced. Given what she'd already weathered in life, he had to assume she was smart enough to discount such blatant maneuvering. Perhaps it was time to tell her so.

Linc reached across the table the way he had when she'd needed comforting during their meal. Once again, Zoe let him touch her hand. "Look," he said, "I know this is a rough time for you. And I don't deny there's tension when I'm working with you. But that doesn't mean I can't enjoy your company, too. The more I learn, the more I trust you."

"Really?"

"Yes, really. We'll still be keeping an eye on you in

case Boyd shows up, but I believe you when you say you had nothing to do with his escape or presence here."

Glistening unshed tears made her eyes sparkle. The urge to reach out with his free hand and cup her cheek was so intense Linc almost acted on it. He thought he'd regained his self-control until a solitary tear slid down her cheek.

Before he could stop himself, he'd brushed it away with his thumb. The sight of the vulnerable, innocent woman reached inside his heart and settled in as if making a home there. This kind of pure empathy was beyond his ability to resist. Without meaning to get in this deep, he had carried out his captain's orders to befriend her. Boy, had he.

The biggest problem Linc had now was how he was going to keep his emotions tamped down enough to properly do his job. This was why family members were seldom assigned together. They mattered too much to each other. And right now, right here, Zoe Sullivan meant more to him than was good for either of them.

His relief K-9 officer showed up on time, removing his reason for staying. Linc was not happy that the night watch had fallen to a rookie. Nevertheless, it was not his place to question his superiors' decisions, so he checked in with the airman, then headed for his quarters with Star.

It was going to be a long night.

The sensitivity Linc had shown when they'd been together in her kitchen had stuck with Zoe long after he'd left.

He'd taken copies of her lists with him, promising to check which of her possible suspects may have been off duty when the majority of her home invasions had taken place. Given the number of them, such a search was going to take time. In fact, she began to wonder whether one perpetrator was responsible for everything. The more she mulled over her life, the more people she noted who were not happy with her.

Such was the lot of a dedicated instructor whose final decisions about a candidate's flying abilities and reasoning in a crisis could make or break his or her career. The percentage of female pilots she had washed out was about the same as male. Although, with fewer women applying for flight school, the actual numbers were smaller. Then there was the gender bias some of the students had against her. Yes, this was the twenty-first century but old habits died hard, even now. Life off the base in rural Texas was proof of that, although since she rarely ventured into nearby towns, she hadn't often run afoul of good old boys and their antiquated attitudes.

Deep sleep came more easily than Zoe had expected. Freddy had been so tired after the stimulating Sunday he'd had that he'd gone to bed without argument and she had soon followed.

Morning light was beginning to filter through the blinds in her bedroom when she finally stirred. Stretched. Swung her legs over the side of the bed, onto the floor and felt…

Bolting upright, she gasped. Lifting her bare feet, she looked down and her eyes widened with shock and fear. The soles of her feet were covered in a warm, sticky red substance.

Blood.

The smell was so cloying. She started to gag, then

forced herself to calm down. To take stock of the situation. *Am I hurt? No.* Nothing physical seemed to be wrong with her. But then where had the pool of blood come from? Whose could it be?

"Freddy!" Zoe leaped up and dashed toward her son's room with no thought of the bloody footprints she was leaving in her wake. A scream lodged in her constricted throat, kept there by sheer force of will as she braced herself to face the worst nightmare of her life. She slid to a stop at her son's open door, one hand on the jamb to steady her trembling body and keep her knees from buckling.

A sigh replaced the scream in her throat when she found Freddy lying on top of the covers in his pajamas, soundly asleep and clearly unhurt. As she watched, he made a sound like a sleepy kitten and rolled over to face her. He was fine.

"Thank You, Jesus," she whispered breathlessly.

Zoe knew he'd be terribly frightened if he saw her feet, so she edged away and turned back, retracing her crimson footprints. The blood wasn't from her or Freddy, so where had it come from? Why hadn't she awakened? Moreover, who had managed to invade her privacy once more to carry out such a heinous act?

Fear-based adrenaline had borne her to her son's room. Now, though, she shook so badly she could hardly continue to move. She leaned on the walls, working her way along until she was back in her own room.

The foul puddle remained beside her bed and she could see where she had initially stepped. A strong urge to wipe up the mess almost overcame her before she reached for her cell phone instead. She must not touch anything. She had to summon help. To call…

Linc Colson. No one else would do, not even others on the Security Forces.

Hand still extended, she struggled to subdue her tremors enough to properly pull up his number and prayed that the strong stomach on which she prided herself wouldn't fail her. An unexpected vibration almost caused her to drop the phone before she could dial. She was receiving an incoming call. From Linc!

All self-control fled the moment she heard his voice. Before he could finish his good-morning greeting, she was shrieking unintelligibly. It was the closest she could come to shouting, "Help me!"

Linc had been standing in the street observing her apartment window when he'd called. There was no way to tell what Zoe was trying to say, but he didn't need words. Her shrillness and sobbing were plenty.

"I'm coming!" Phone pressed to his ear, he straight-armed the outer door and raced up the stairway. Star was way ahead of him. He noted a fleeing figure dressed in black at the far end of the hallway and made the split-second decision to drop the leash, point and command, "Get 'em!"

Training dictated he must follow his K-9. And he would have. If Zoe had not appeared in her doorway with both feet covered in blood.

Linc's heart and gut clenched simultaneously. Sliding to a halt he shouted, "How bad?" as he eyed her from head to toe, expecting to see injuries. Would his skills be sufficient to save her life if she was bleeding out?

"It's—it's not mine," she stuttered. Arms extended, palms up, she simply stood there as if in shock.

"What do you mean it's not yours?" Linc's already-taut muscles knotted more. He could barely get "Freddy?" out or believe Zoe when she shook her head.

"No. Not him either."

"You *sure*?"

"Yes. I just checked. I don't know where this awful stuff came from. There's a big puddle of it in my bedroom."

Linc saw her start to waver as if she might faint. He reached out, ready to steady her if need be, yet failing to fully grasp her explanation. She was panting as though she'd just finished a marathon and her eyes weren't focusing well. They were wide and glassy.

He reached for her. She started to pull away and staggered. Linc caught her by the arm. "You need to sit down." Truth to tell, so did he.

"I—I—I woke up and…"

"This happened while you were asleep?"

Another nod.

"Did you see anything, anybody?"

"No. I'm a sound sleeper except for sometimes when Freddy makes a noise at night. I never heard a thing."

"Okay." He guided her all the way inside, preparing to close the door behind them.

She started to fight him. "Let go. I need to wash. I have to get this off me!"

There was panic in her tone. Little wonder. Though Linc commiserated, he stopped her. "No. You can't wash until the crime scene techs get here. We'll need pictures of everything in situ. I mean, where it is now."

In the background, he heard Star barking ferociously. She had someone cornered. "I need to go help my dog. Will you be okay?"

Zoe nodded and leaned against the doorjamb. "Yes.

Go. Catch whoever did this and bring him back so I can take a good swing at him."

"Atta girl. I mean, affirmative, Sergeant."

Star's barking reached a crescendo. Linc knew that as soon as it stopped she'd capture her prey with a painful bite and be holding fast until given the command to release.

His boots hit the floor hard, the sound echoing along the empty hallway, reminding him of a beating heart. His own was pounding, more from seeing what had been done to Zoe than from actual exertion.

Star gave one last intense growl before a human screamed. She had him! *Good girl*, Linc thought. *Hold.*

The screams turned to curses. Almost to the corner where he'd last seen his K-9 partner, Linc heard a scrambling sound followed by Star's yip. Then all was silent.

He whipped around the corner so fast he almost lost his footing.

For the second time in minutes his heart stopped. There lay his dog, alone and prostrate. It took several more seconds before Linc was close enough to tell she was still breathing. Falling to his knees beside her, he gently touched her quivering side.

"I should have stayed with you," he whispered haltingly. "I'm so sorry, Star."

TEN

Mayhem reigned in and around Zoe's apartment. When Linc didn't return quickly, she'd put in a call to Security Forces and reported all she knew, including the sounds of human and dog doing battle. That would certainly explain why Linc and Star had not come back yet.

Further proof was the arrival of other K-9 teams. Among them was Master Sergeant Westley James, handling an all-black German shepherd, another man with *Watson* on his name tag and what looked like a Belgian Malinois, and a stern-looking guy in a dark windbreaker displaying *FBI* in large white letters across the back.

Zoe stayed out of their way while being examined by ambulance personnel. She'd kept her head enough to insist on photos before allowing the first responders to check her from head to toe. While a young female airman kept Freddy occupied and isolated, crime scene investigators had taken samples from Zoe's bedroom and had bagged everything before allowing her to shower in private.

Getting clean had never felt so wonderful. If she hadn't been so worried about Linc and his dog, she would have felt total relief. No one was telling her a thing. After having got used to the way Linc had begun treating her, she was taken aback by the cold shoulder she got from both his team and other investigators.

Emerging in clean, dry PT clothing and with a towel around her wet hair, Zoe recognized Captain Blackwood from the warehouse investigation. When her eyes met his, she was not soothed in the least.

Nevertheless, she approached him and saluted. "Captain."

His blue steel glance was almost enough to give her the shivers. "Sergeant Sullivan. I'm told you can't explain what took place here this morning."

"Only that I woke up and stepped in—" Zoe swallowed hard "—blood. I have no idea when it was put there or who did it. I didn't see a soul." She watched a shepherd dog leaving with its handler. "Did the dogs turn up any clues?"

"Some. Whoever supposedly attacked you is most likely the same person Star apprehended. A scent trail led from here to the spot where the dog was injured."

Zoe's heart skipped a beat. "She's going to be all right, isn't she? Nobody will tell me a thing except that she's alive."

"I don't have the veterinary report yet, but she was conscious when she was transported."

Clasping her hands, Zoe felt tears welling. "Oh, thank God. Literally. I've been praying for her to be okay."

Blackwood didn't seem impressed by her spirituality. "I would think, Sergeant, that you would put your son's welfare first and stop resorting to cheap tricks. Believe me, we will not be distracted that easily."

"What do you mean, *tricks?*"

"You know as well as I do that the red substance was not real blood."

"What? It wasn't?"

"No. It was not."

"Then why did you take so long examining my apartment?"

"Obviously something occurred here. If you didn't set up this fiasco to throw us off your brother's trail, perhaps you would like to stop withholding information about the person or persons who have been harassing you."

"Is that what you call it? I call it attacking me, especially this last time. That stuff sure felt real. How was I to know it was fake?"

He studied her as if she were a slide under a microscope before saying, "We're running tests on it to see if it can be traced, not that that will help much."

Zoe didn't try to suppress a shiver. "There's nothing more I can tell you, Captain. If I'm free to leave, I plan to drop my son at day care early, then begin conducting my regular classes. Any objections?"

"Not from me. When you're not teaching, Master Sergeant James will make sure you're covered until Sergeant Colson is able to resume his regular duties."

"Will that depend on Star? I mean, does she have to be well before he can come back to watch me?"

"That will be up to Sergeant James. As long as Sergeant Colson isn't involved in aggressive tracking or apprehension, I see no reason why he'd be sidelined until his K-9 is fit for duty."

"Thank you." Zoe truly meant it. The captain might not be smiling but at least he was speaking to her. She thought of teenage Portia and felt a twinge of empathy. It was hard for her, being of a lower rank, to speak openly with Blackwood. What must it be like to be his daughter and be forced to get used to his stern demeanor as part of daily life at home? Nightmares were made of notions like that. Although, given her own dad's overly permissive attitude toward his only son when Boyd was a naughty child, she guessed she'd rather have a strict father like the captain.

"Too bad we don't get to choose our parents," she murmured as she headed for her room to dress for work. In a way, she could choose another parent for Freddy, couldn't she? By finding a suitable male role model for her son while he was young and impressionable, she could help him mature into a far better man than her brother ever thought of being.

So who's a good candidate? It didn't take a heartbeat for her to picture Linc Colson. *Except I'm never getting married again*, she insisted. *Never, never, never.* Freddy can have mentors without her marrying them. Besides, limiting his exposure to one man was too exclusive. He needed to meet lots of strong, honest, sensible yet gentle men.

And there it was again. The image of Linc burning brightly in her thoughts and memories.

Logic intruded to dampen her mood like a summer thunderstorm in the dry Texas hills. Colson was only hanging around because he had orders to. Now that he'd been through trials with her, seen her looking her worst and had his dog injured to boot, she'd be the last woman he'd be able to look at romantically, even if she so desired.

Which I do not, Zoe insisted, hoping that stating the obvious would help her accept it. If she ever did decide to remarry, she knew she would choose a man a lot like Linc. *Except with a more trusting nature*, she added quickly. She might have a ton of baggage left over from childhood, but Colson wasn't empty-handed either. They were both toting enough excess to fill the cargo hold of a C-130.

Little feet pattered. Freddy ran to her as soon as she entered his room. He tugged on her skirt. Zoe bent down. "What, honey?"

"I'm hungry."

"I know you are, Freddy. What do you say we go out for breakfast today?"

"Why?"

"Um, because the house is a mess and there are lots of people here."

"I saw. They made me stay in my room." He brightened. "You can make pancakes for them, too!"

"No, thanks." Zoe helped him put on socks and shoes, then lifted him into her arms. "We can stop and buy breakfast on the way to see Miss Maisy at day care, okay? You can order whatever you want."

"Where's Star?"

Zoe had been hoping he wouldn't ask, but she wasn't going to lie to him. "Star got a little boo-boo so she's at the doctor's."

"Will he give her a shot?" The child's fearful expression was so comical she almost laughed.

"I don't know, honey, but if she does get a shot, I'm sure she'll take it like a good airman."

"Yeah. She's real brave."

Braver than I am sometimes, Zoe thought with chagrin. While she'd been standing there feeling sorry for herself and inadvertently distracting Sergeant Colson, that amazing K-9 was chasing down whoever had messed with her. If she were authorized, she'd award Star a medal.

Even though the blood wasn't real.

At the Military Working Dog Training Center, in the veterinary hospital wing that was an integral part of the installation, Linc's injured rottweiler lay stretched out on a steel table in an exam room. She was conscious and panting but not her usual energetic self.

Linc hovered in the background while Captain Kyle Roark, DVM and head of Canine Veterinary Services at CAFB, went over Star, wet black nose to stubby tail. One young female tech dressed in blue scrubs stood by, waiting for orders while another was preparing a gurney.

"I've given your dog a mild sedative and painkiller," Roark said, turning a sympathetic gaze toward Linc. "Her overall condition is good, but her respirations are a little fast and shallow." He was using a light but firm touch to examine Star's body. "I don't feel any broken bones, but I'm going to have Airman Fielding take her down to X-ray to make sure her ribs aren't cracked. Why don't you come with me and get a cup of coffee while we wait for the results of the films?"

"I thought they were digital these days."

Roark chuckled. "They are. It's an old habit to refer to plates and actual film." He stripped off latex gloves and dropped them in a refuse bin before taking Linc by the arm and steering him out of the exam room.

"I should stay with Star," Linc said. "She needs me."

"What she needs is rest, which I will see she gets while she's here. Don't worry. My people know what they're doing. Fielding may look young and afraid of her own shadow sometimes but she knows her job and does it well. You need to back off and settle down before your dog picks up your nervous vibes and gets upset herself."

Although Linc walked the hallway with the doctor, his heart remained with his K-9. "It's all my fault," he said solemnly when they reached the break room. "I stopped to check on a human victim and let Star go on alone. I should have stayed with her until we'd apprehended the suspect."

"Not if you thought you had a victim at the scene already. You know the dogs are trained to bite and hold on. The fact that Star took a couple of hits before he stunned her and escaped proves how good that training is."

"There's nothing wrong with my dog," Linc said, grimacing. "It's *my* training that needs refreshing."

The dark-haired veterinarian chuckled and clapped him on the back. "Don't be so hard on yourself. She's going to recover. The X-rays are just to be on the safe side. If it is cracked ribs, it's nothing life-threatening."

"If I ever catch up to the lowlife who kicked her, there'll be something life-threatening for him. *Me.*"

"Spoken like a dedicated K-9 handler." The vet approached a coffee urn and slipped two Styrofoam cups off the stack, handing one to Linc. "Help yourself. Creamer and sugar are over there."

"Thanks. I didn't get my usual shot of caffeine this morning." He filled his cup. "I was planning to have coffee with Sergeant Sullivan."

"I gather there's a big mess over there?"

"Yeah." Linc was shaking his head as he followed

Roark to a small table, plopped into a folding chair and wrapped both hands around his steaming cup. "I thought the sergeant had been cut to pieces when I first saw her." He suppressed a shudder.

"So I understand." The captain's dark gaze narrowed on the sergeant. "What's the deal with you and her, anyway?"

"Sullivan? Nothing special. Master Sergeant James ordered me to stick close and see what I can learn by finessing information out of her."

"Uh-huh." Folding his muscular arms across an equally strong chest, Roark began to grin. "You sticking with that story?"

"It's true."

"Right. And I'm the commander in chief." His expression of good humor softened. "There's nothing wrong with two sergeants becoming involved. At least you're not breaking any rules if you decide to date her."

"It's not like that. I'm just taking most of the daytime watches so she'll get comfortable with me and open up." He made a face into his coffee cup instead of looking at the captain. "I have decided she's not hiding info about her brother."

"So you trust her?"

"Enough. She's got a little boy. I don't think she'd do anything that might put him in jeopardy." A flash of pain crossed the vet's face so briefly that if Linc had not been looking straight at him he would have missed seeing it. "Hey, sorry, Captain. I wasn't thinking."

Roark shrugged nonchalantly, but Linc wasn't fooled. The memory had hurt. "It's okay. It happened a long time ago."

Knowing that the man had lost both his wife and

a young daughter—and during the Christmas season to boot—Linc decided to change the subject. "What's the prognosis for Star? Do you think she'll be sidelined long?"

"I doubt it. If nothing's broken, she should get over any soreness in a few days or so. Even with cracked ribs, she can do light duty." His smile returned. "I don't recommend you send her on any more solo chases for a while, though."

"Yeah. My fault entirely."

"What about Sergeant Sullivan? Did she sustain any injuries in the attack?"

Linc shook his head. "That's the crazy part. Whoever broke into her apartment apparently did it to unhinge her. I'm actually surprised that she recovered enough to function this morning."

"Women are not the weaker sex, in case you haven't noticed. We may be physically stronger, but they have us beat when it comes to rolling with the punches. Look at how she refuses to be cowed by a murderous brother. I'd have my back to a wall and be locked and loaded 24/7 if Boyd Sullivan came from my family. My older sister is bad enough." His smile spread to a grin. "She's a major in the army."

"Wow. I see what you mean."

Relaxing in the chair and stretching, Roark asked, "What about your kin, Colson? Are they military, too?"

Linc wished he could find a hole in the floor and dive through it. "One was. We don't talk about him."

"Don't worry about it," Kyle Roark said. "Every family has its unsavory relatives. You just have to dig deep enough and there they are."

"Yeah." Thinking of Zoe, Linc asked, "Do you know

anything about Sergeant Sullivan's late husband? His name was Flint. John Flint."

"Not offhand. Why?"

"It's not important. Apparently, he wasn't the finest representative of the air force either."

"We take what we can get," the vet replied. "Some recruits are better than others. Take Airman Fielding, for instance. At first glance, she seems a bit on the flighty side, but she's the best tech I've had in years."

"What's her story?"

Roark shrugged. "Beats me. She's not a typical chatty female. When I'm doing surgery that's a plus, believe me."

Linc stood, disposed of his empty Styrofoam cup and waited for his companion to join him. "I'm ready to go back and see about Star."

"Okay, okay. We've had a long enough break, anyway." He clapped Linc on the shoulder. "Remember what I said about women. It's okay to take up with somebody of equal rank. You won't lose stripes over it."

"That's not what's stopping me."

"Oh?" They proceeded down the short hall together. "Marriage is not for me. Never was. Never will be."

"Sounds pretty final."

"It is. Just because I believe she's been truthful about her brother doesn't mean I trust her regarding all the harassment she's receiving. She keeps insisting she has no idea who's doing this to her, yet it seems irrational that she wouldn't have at least a glimmer of a clue."

"You've classed her as an honest person, right?"

"Right." Not sure what the captain's point was, Linc waited for more.

"Then maybe she's too forthright to recognize lies

coming from those around her. I've known people like that. They have trouble seeing beyond the good and grasping the bad in others."

"Naive, you mean?"

Sobering, the captain led the way into his office and gestured toward a leather chair. "Have a seat."

"What about Star?"

"They'll notify me when she's ready for further examination. I want to talk about you for a minute." He circled his desk, sat down, pushed aside a short stack of files and clasped his hands atop the blotter.

"Okay." Given no other choice if he intended to see his K-9 soon, Linc eased into the chair Roark had indicated.

"Tell me about your combat experiences."

"Whoa. Where did that come from?"

"I'm getting the idea that there's more to your decision to stay single than you've admitted, that's all. Would you like to talk about it?"

A wall immediately rose around Linc's emotions. He knew he could refuse to discuss his past, and seriously considered doing so, yet there was something about Kyle Roark's manner and voice that urged him to open up. If the captain had pressed him, he was positive he could have held out. Since Roark merely waited and seemed relaxed about it, he decided to reveal a little.

"I lost part of my unit in Afghanistan."

A nod. "Understood."

"We were acting on bad intel and walked into an ambush. I barely got out alive. Some of the guys didn't."

"Not your fault, was it?"

"Not directly. We'd been befriended by the most beautiful dark-eyed woman I'd ever seen. Even with her hair covered, she was a stunner." Swallowing hard, he struggled to go on. "I wasn't the only one who fell for her lies. She was easy to believe."

"Again, that's not your fault. I'm sure she was well trained in fooling the enemy."

"Well, she was good at it. We followed her advice and walked right into a trap."

"You can't classify all women as liars because one tricked you. That's a lousy reason to reject romance."

"It's not just her," Linc countered. "It's a lot of things. My dad was the best liar I've ever known. He had everybody convinced he was some kind of hero when he was anything but."

"Sociopathic, maybe?"

"Maybe." Getting to his feet, Linc began to pace. "Look, I appreciate your concern, Doc, really I do, but all I want to do is be the best at my job and handle the best dog. Star and my badge are all I need. Deeper involvement with a subject I'm assigned to watch would be idiotic."

"So, how about somebody else?"

"Not interested."

Chuckling, the veterinarian rose and followed Linc to the office door. All he said was "Uh-huh. That's what I thought."

ELEVEN

Wearing her spotless dress uniform instead of her camo ABU, Zoe squared her shoulders, briefcase in hand, smoothed her blue skirt below the white blouse and strode from the parking lot to her classroom, expecting it to already be at least half-filled with students. Instead, it was empty.

Confusion momentarily halted her in her tracks. Where was everybody? Surely, she hadn't made a mistake about her duty schedule. That was impossible.

A tall, distinguished lieutenant general in uniform, his chest heavy with medals, appeared behind her at the door and cleared his throat. Zoe turned and snapped to attention with a brisk salute. "General Hall."

"As you were, Sergeant Sullivan. I came by to tell you we won't be needing you here today, or until whatever problems you have with your stalker are resolved."

"But, sir—"

"No buts. I sent you a memo after the final decision was made, but I thought it only fair to deliver this news in person, as well. You're officially relieved of duty until further notice."

Zoe was stunned. She hadn't done one thing to deserve being sidelined. Not one thing. Except be an innocent victim. Didn't the brass realize that?

There was nothing to do but submit, like it or not. "Yes, sir. What's my alternate assignment?"

"You have none. Not for the present. You're free to go wherever you wish on base. Just don't leave."

Realizing that she was gaping at the officer, she snapped her jaw closed. Clearly, there was going to be no chance to present an argument. She saluted again despite her disappointment. "Yes, General Hall."

"That's all. You're excused," he said before turning on his heel and leaving.

Zoe stood there, still and mute, while her temper threatened to come to a boil. The brass were blaming her, too, same as the enlisted members did. Everybody and his brother thought she was breaking rules and running amok when all she was trying to do was live a peaceful life and teach to the best of her ability. Only now they weren't going to allow her to do that either, were they?

She internally shook herself, refusing to be a victim of crime or of her superiors' decisions. What steps she would take next were unknown. The only thing she was sure of was that she wasn't going to sit on her hands and stew when she could be taking action. *Any* action. If she had to poke around in the lives of those she suspected might be holding a grudge and reveal who her nemesis was without help or sanction, then so be it. As long as Colson continued to accompany her, she figured she'd be safe enough leaving familiar surroundings.

Zoe didn't know where she'd have to look or who her snooping might upset, nor did she care. She was already persona non grata on base. A few more ruffled feathers wouldn't hurt a bit.

Heels clicking on the hard floor, briefcase swinging at her side, she waited until she was out in the warm sunshine before making a call on her cell phone.

Linc Colson answered almost immediately.

"This is Sergeant Sullivan," Zoe said. "Sorry to bother you. How is Star? Freddy's worried." She paused, then finished with the full truth, "So am I."

"I'm still at the vet hospital waiting to hear," Linc said. "Captain Roark thinks she may have cracked ribs, but otherwise she's looking pretty good."

"When will you know for sure?"

"Soon. Why? Has there been more trouble?"

"Yes, in a manner of speaking. I've just been relieved of duty. No more teaching or anything else until we figure out who's been making my life miserable."

"You're not teaching any classes today?"

Zoe could tell by his tone that he was worried and she understood why. She wasn't exactly fond of the decision to sideline her either. "Not today or anytime in the foreseeable future according to Lieutenant General Hall. It's the pits."

"Where are you?"

"I just left my empty classroom. Why?"

"Because you need protection, especially if you're going to be wandering around the base. I'll call my headquarters and arrange an escort until I get through here."

"I don't need a guardian to just go home." Hesitating, she said, "Tell you what. Why don't I come to you? That way I'll know how Star is as soon as you do, and we can leave there together when you're ready."

"I don't know. It might be hours."

"Ha! As if I had plans." Shaking her head even though he couldn't see her doing it, she added, "I'd rather hang out with you than have to break in a new bodyguard."

His muted chuckle came through. "*Break in?* Is that how you see our interaction? I'm not sure I like that opinion, Sergeant. It's not very flattering."

"Okay. How about if I admit how scared witless I was this morning and appeal to your sympathetic nature? I desperately need a friend—or at least somebody who doesn't view me as crazy or dangerous. Or both." Zoe lowered her voice and softened the tone. "I can't explain it any better than that, Colson. This hasn't been the worst day of my life —yet—but it's running a close second or third."

"All right. Do you know where the base dog-training complex is located?"

"Yes."

"I'm at the vet hospital between it and the enlisted rec center. You can't miss it. And don't try to walk all this way no matter how much you love Texas weather. Take a cab."

Smiling into the distance, Zoe could barely glimpse flags flying on the far side of the base. If she'd been clad for running or PT, she might have left her car behind and considered a brisk walk. Dressed in her uniform and the matching pumps that the outfit called for, however, she was far less inclined to go for a long hike, even on sidewalks.

"No worries," Zoe told Linc. "I drove over here this morning so I could drop off Freddy at preschool."

The temporary silence on the other end of the line

gave her pause. She scowled when Linc said, "Tell you what, either I'll come pick you up or you need to take a cab."

"Why? I told you I have my car."

His sigh was audible. "Yeah. You parked it there, right?"

"Of course, I did. I couldn't very well stuff it in my briefcase and carry it into class with me."

"Meaning it has sat unguarded for how long?"

"Just a few minutes." She looked at her watch. "Maybe fifteen at the most."

"Call a taxi."

The finality of his command jolted her rather than inciting anger. "You think somebody did something to my car? Why here? Why not back at my apartment?"

"One, we kept an eye on it there and two, that parking lot is always real busy. The place you parked this morning is far more isolated." He cleared his throat. "Humor me, Zoe. Be on the safe side. Call a cab. And do it now, before word gets around that you've been relieved of duty and your enemies start to figure out your new behavior patterns."

"I really hate feeling so vulnerable."

"I know. And I'm sorry. I'd be there right now if Star hadn't got hurt."

"I'm the one who should apologize. You're worried sick about her, and here I am causing you even more problems. I'll be there ASAP. Watch for my taxi."

"Thanks," Linc said.

She could tell he meant it. "No, thank you, Sergeant. You may be the only one on base who believes in me. I do appreciate it."

"The cab," he said gruffly.

"Gotcha. Hanging up now and dialing a ride."

Despite the first pangs of an impending headache, Zoe did as she'd promised. Then she slowly approached her parked sedan and gave it a once-over, even leaned sideways to peer under it. Nothing seemed tampered with or added.

Before her life had been so disrupted, she might easily have pulled out her keys and driven despite Linc's dire warning.

Now she wouldn't touch that car if her life depended upon it. She straightened, fighting an unexpected wave of dizziness. And little wonder. If Linc was right, her life actually might depend upon following his orders. She wasn't about to ignore his advice and test the concept.

When Linc completed the call, he noticed Captain Roark's arched eyebrows, so he explained. "Sergeant Sullivan is coming here since I can't go to her right now."

Roark shrugged. "You could, you know. Star is in good hands."

"I suppose so," Linc said, "but my CO told me to stay with her until I could make a detailed report on her condition. We assumed Sullivan would be secure while she was teaching."

"I take it she isn't?"

Shaking his head, Linc said, "She may be safe enough but she isn't teaching. They relieved her. I don't understand why. She hasn't done anything wrong. Everything's circumstantial."

The veterinarian grinned. "Never try to reason out

orders from up top, Sergeant. You'll drive yourself crazy if you expect them to always make sense."

"Gotcha." He eyed the doorway, wishing the tech would hurry up with those X-rays. "What's taking so long?"

"Tell you what. Why don't you go wait out front for Sergeant Sullivan while I see about your dog? If I need you, I'll send for you."

"That makes sense, I guess." There was no way Linc could divide himself in two, so tending to one task while Roark followed up on another seemed the wisest choice.

Taking a deep, settling breath of fresh Texas air once he reached the sidewalk, Linc was struck by the conundrum he'd just acknowledged. A few weeks ago, there would have been no hard choice to make. He would have opted to remain with his K-9 partner and let someone else fill any other gaps.

Now, however, he saw that his loyalties were being divided, and he didn't like it. In his mind, he visualized being at war with himself, as if he were both friend and foe in an ongoing battle in which there could be no clear-cut winner. If he directed all his energy toward Star and neglected taking care of Zoe and her little boy, he chanced letting harm come to them. If, on the other hand, he concentrated on the woman and child too much, he could lose Star, as present circumstances painfully demonstrated.

Almost convinced to turn and go back inside, he spotted an approaching taxi. To his chagrin, his heartbeat increased in speed and he felt beads of perspiration welling on his forehead. If Zoe was in that cab, then he'd know she was okay. What if she wasn't?

Keying his mic, he radioed Captain Blackwood and

identified himself. "I'm still at the vet's. They're taking X-rays of Star. Roark thinks she's okay."

"Good. Call me back when you know for sure."

"I will. But there's been another development," Linc said. "Sullivan has been relieved of duty. She's on her way to join me here."

"What? Why weren't we notified?"

"I imagine we will be. I just thought it best not to wait for the information to go through channels. When she told me, I instructed her to come here instead of my going to pick her up."

"Good. When I told you to get close to the sergeant, I certainly didn't mean for you to abandon your K-9 in a crisis."

"Affirmative. One other thing, Captain. Sullivan's leaving her private vehicle in a parking lot near her classroom."

"Why? Wouldn't it start?"

Linc felt his muscles tighten as if readying for hand-to-hand combat. "That's not the problem. I figured, given the incident at her apartment earlier today she shouldn't try to drive. She was away from the car long enough for it to have been tampered with."

"Now who's paranoid?" Blackwood asked. "What do you expect me to do about it?"

"I was hoping you'd ask Nick Donovan and his bomb-sniffing K-9, Annie, or somebody from ordnance to take a look. Maybe have it towed to a safe holding area?"

"You honestly think there's a chance it's rigged with explosives?"

"There's a chance of anything at this point," Linc said firmly. "Until we uncover the reasons for the strange attacks on her I think it's prudent to take precautions." He paused. "Listen, she's here, so I have to go. If anything changes, I'll let you know."

"All right. And, Colson?"

"Yes, sir?"

"Keep working on her about her brother. There's a fair chance he's the one behind the weirdness."

"I'll keep that in mind."

"Okay. Now, go see to your dog."

"I will."

Linc smiled and held out a hand to Zoe as she climbed out of the taxi. Her fingers were cool yet as soft as he remembered, her eyes sparkling with delight and her lips lifting in the smile that often graced his dreams of late.

She glanced at the mic clipped to the shoulder of his ABU. "Did you just get another call?"

"No. I was reporting in. Security hadn't been informed of your duty change yet, and I wanted to be sure my bosses were up to speed."

"Good old bureaucracy," she said, grinning up at him. "The news will probably reach interested parties at about the time regular base gossip does."

"Or after." Linc held the glass door to the building open for her. "No troubles getting here?"

"Other than having to abandon my wheels, no," Zoe replied. "I realize that old beater isn't much, but it gets me around okay. I'd hate to lose it."

"I'm having it checked for you," he said. "Until it's cleared, I'll drive you wherever you need to go."

"Thanks." She sobered as they proceeded down a long hallway. "How's Star?"

"No report yet, but it shouldn't be long." Ushering

her into the office where the head veterinarian sat behind his desk, Linc saluted and said, "Captain Roark, this is Staff Sergeant Zoe Sullivan."

The captain rose and returned the salute as Zoe did the same. "My pleasure. I understand you've had a rough morning."

"Yes, sir. You could say that."

"Well, if you need a break, we can always provide puppy therapy."

"Sir?"

Roark chuckled. "It's a standing joke around the kennels. Five minutes sitting in a pen of happy puppies is our standard cure for the blues. Works every time."

"My son would love it."

"I'm sure he would." The vet sobered and gestured toward a gurney being guided past the open door. "There's Star now. Follow me."

They joined the dog in the closest exam room where Roark displayed the X-rays on a monitor. "Star's X-rays show that nothing is broken, but she was so sore they had to administer a light sedative in order to get her to lie still for clear pictures. She's still pretty groggy."

Linc was surprised when Zoe dropped her briefcase, beat him to the sleepy canine, caressed her head and bent to kiss her muzzle. "Poor baby. I'm so sorry, Star."

Not only did Linc's eyebrows arch, Roark's did, too. The captain spoke first. "I wouldn't try that when Star is fully conscious if I were you, Sergeant Sullivan. She might take your nose off."

"Besides, we don't want her too well socialized," Linc added. "It can take the edge off protective responses."

Zoe backed away, blushing. "I'm sorry. She just looks so pitiful lying there."

Linc huffed to cover his own tender feelings toward the injured dog. "Yeah, well, she won't once the sedative wears off." He looked to Kyle Roark. "How long will she be sidelined?"

"I'd like to keep her here for a day or so, just to be on the safe side. Internal tissue injuries don't show up on X-rays, and since she is indicating pain, I want her monitored."

"Okay. What now?"

"I'll have Airman Fielding take her to Recovery. You can accompany them if you wish, Colson."

"I don't know. I…" His troubled glance lit on Zoe. "Is there anywhere you need to go now that we know Star's going to be all right?" he asked her.

"Yes," she said with a gentle look and slight smile as she stroked the rottweiler's shoulder. "I want us to go with Star, so you can be there to comfort her when she's fully awake."

The surprised glance the veterinarian shot Linc was nothing compared to his own awe. Despite all her problems and the way most of the base had rejected her, Zoe Sullivan's heart remained kind and caring. She'd realized how much he wanted to stay with his K-9 partner and was facilitating it for his sake. And perhaps for Star's well-being, too.

"Lead on," Linc told the vet tech. "We'll follow you."

As Zoe leaned down to retrieve her briefcase, Linc took it from her, then clasped her hand. She didn't try to pull away. Instead, her fingers laced through his. As far as he was concerned, he'd gladly stay connected like that for the rest of the day.

TWELVE

Seeing Star acting so weak made Zoe want to sit with Star on the folded blanket in the kennel run and cradle the poor dog's massive head in her lap. Only her dress uniform stopped her.

Happily, Linc had no such reservations in his ABU and sat beside his groggy dog, legs crossed.

Zoe leaned against the open gate. "Do you want me to close this?"

"Not yet. After she's back on her feet, we'll shut it and leave so she'll rest. Doc says that's what she needs most."

Studying the row of runs she could see from where she stood, Zoe asked, "Is this where all those loose dogs came from?"

"Some of them. We have a lot more room in the Military Working Dog Training Center next door. There are indoor and outdoor housing areas."

"I saw you catch that one dog. How many are still missing?"

Linc continued to stroke and comfort Star. "At last count, twenty-eight. Since almost two hundred were released in the first place, that's a fair capture rate, but nobody understands why four of the best trained K-9s have remained missing. We're all worried about them."

"What I don't understand is why they didn't all just come home. I mean, they're fed and cared for right here. Why run away and stay gone?"

He shrugged. "The theory in some cases is that since they're not well socialized before training and a few are also suffering from PTSD, the wilds of the base beyond our developed areas appealed to them. Remember, dogs are basically pack animals. If they have a strong pack leader, they'll follow him pretty much anywhere."

"But the base is fenced and patrolled."

"True. But we do get an occasional stray coyote inside the perimeter, so it's possible our missing dogs were able to slip out. Or they could be hiding in or around small caves in the rougher terrain the way Westley James thinks they are. There's also thick woods on base. It's been searched, of course, but so far that hasn't helped." Looking up from Star, he caught Zoe's concerned gaze and added, "We'll catch up to them all eventually."

"Will they still be useful after turning feral?"

"I wouldn't worry about overcoming that. Our trainers are the best in the business. They'll be able to handle any setbacks. It'll just take time and patience." He continued rhythmically stroking his dog's shoulder.

"Do you and Star train all the time?" she asked him.

"Practice, you mean? We do our share. Maintaining the K-9's proficiency is one of the requirements for being a handler. We never stop testing our dogs. Everyday patrols and assignments like the one I have watching you are only part of the picture."

He fell silent and concentrated on soothing Star. Zoe listened and heard a rumble. "Is she *snoring*?"

Linc rested his hand lightly on the rottweiler's head and began to grin. "Uh-huh. She's had a rough day." As he slowly got to his feet and backed away, he laid one finger across his lips. "Let's go and let her sleep."

Whispering, Zoe questioned that decision, "I thought you wanted to stay with her until she woke up."

He eased her out and closed the gate behind them. "That was when she was groggy from the anesthetic. This is pure sleep. See how her breathing has changed? Deepened? And watch her muzzle."

Zoe had to cover her own mouth to keep from giggling aloud. "Her lips flap!"

"I know. I've spent so much time with her I can tell how she feels by observation. She's exhausted but doing okay. And her gums are nice and pink. That's a good sign, too. According to Captain Roark, that means she's not bleeding internally. If she were, it would be evident by now."

Zoe let him cup her elbow and direct her away from the kennels. Their slow passage didn't rouse many of the other patients housed there. They were out of the veterinary hospital before she asked, "Where are we going?"

"First, I'm taking you home and waiting while you change, since you're not on duty anymore. Then I thought we'd go see one of the women your brother threatened."

"I hope she's here on base, because General Hall ordered me not to leave."

"She is," Linc replied. "First Lieutenant Vanessa Gomez is a nurse at the base hospital, and I want to pick her brain about something."

"Really? What?"

He didn't answer until they were in his SUV and had pulled into traffic. "We got a preliminary report on the substance that was found at your apartment this morning."

"They already told me it was fake blood. It was, wasn't it?"

"Yes. Mostly water and corn syrup with red food coloring and a little chocolate syrup to mute the bright crimson."

"Sure had me fooled when I stepped in it. I even imagined it smelled like the real thing."

"Me, too, at first glance. Very realistic. It made me wonder why the person who left it settled for a substitute. I'd think if he wanted to really freak you out, he'd have used the genuine article."

"Maybe it was hard to come by."

"That's one of the details I want to double-check. If Boyd wasn't behind it and the guy who is didn't want to harm anyone, he might have tried to steal blood from the hospital. I actually hope he did because that could give us some clues."

Zoe's eyes widened. "Of course! Why didn't I think of that?"

"Because you teach flying and I'm the cop. Our forensics team figured out what they were dealing with the minute they walked in. Your apartment smelled more like pancakes to them than it should have."

She smirked at him. "So, cop, what can a nurse tell us that we don't already know?"

"Since she was threatened by the Red Rose Killer, I thought she'd have some personal insights, maybe something more than the hospital administration gave us. It is in her best interest to speak freely, especially if she knows of a gap in their blood distribution system."

"Why take me along? I mean, unless you still think I'm hiding something and want to make me feel guilty, there's no real reason for me to meet this nurse."

"No, there isn't. But you do have to stay with me, and I have a few loose ends I can hopefully tie up without the use of my dog, so you're coming along. I can't just sit around and wait. It's driving me crazy to be idle."

"I understand," Zoe said, averting her eyes to stare out the window as they turned and crossed Canyon Drive. "I don't want you wasting time with me when there are bigger fish to fry. It's just embarrassing to talk to people my brother has hurt or threatened. I hate that I'm related to a serial killer."

"That's definitely not the reason I want you to go," Linc said. "Two heads are always better than one when it comes to spotting anomalies and picking out which ones may be of interest. And you need something to think about besides your own troubles. I figured a diversion might give your brain something to do while your subconscious works on the rest of our unanswered questions."

Zoe had to chuckle. "Sergeant, if my brain got any busier, my head might explode."

"Which reminds me," he said lightly, keeping the conversation from becoming somber, "after giving it a quick look, the bomb boys didn't find anything wrong with your car, but they did tow it in for further examination."

"I hope I can pick it up soon." Linc's SUV was coming to a stop at the curb in front of her apartment and she reached for the door handle.

"Whoa. Not so fast. I'm going to check your apartment before you go inside."

"Why? Your evidence people were still here when I left for work and probably stayed most of the time I was gone."

"Most of the time isn't good enough. I'll go in first, do a walk-through, then give you the all clear."

She shuddered, thinking of the way her home had looked the last time she'd seen it. "I hope they took away everything that was soiled. I mean, I'd hate to go back up there and find the same awful red mess I left behind—even if it is fake."

"Tell you what," Linc said. "If there are places that need TLC, I'll take care of those while you change. We can leave the hall door open so we don't start any rumors."

She was touched. And wryly amused. "After everything that's happened to me lately, I imagine my reputation is already trashed. Thanks for trying to protect me from gossip, but I'm less afraid of that than I am of finding another attacker lying in wait. You are more than welcome to inspect the apartment and wait there with me, whether my front door is open or closed."

"Thank you," Linc said.

"I'm serious. I trust you implicitly." Zoe realized she meant that from the bottom of her heart. There might be nobody else she could truly count on except Linc Colson. But that was enough. He was enough.

Watching him don his official blue beret as he circled the vehicle to open her door, she had to fight to keep from once again enumerating his many virtues. This was a good, good man. An admirable member of the Security Forces that kept the base safe. Not only could he be relied upon in a crisis, his presence gave comfort when all was in chaos.

Zoe clasped the hand he offered and carefully climbed down from the truck. His touch was warm, steady, welcome. It seemed as natural as breathing to slip her fingers between his. It was a pity that this kind of supportive contact would cease once Linc's assignment was over.

Given that nebulous peek into the future, she decided to make the most of these brief moments of closeness. He never needed to know how special he was becoming to her, nor did she intend for their camaraderie to blossom into something more, something deeper. She'd been married once. That was enough. God had rescued her in the nick of time or she might have ended up blamed for John's illegal transfer of classified data simply because she was his wife.

Thoughts of marriage melded with images of the strong man walking beside her and she nearly panicked. She gently slipped her hand from his.

It wasn't a lack of interest that caused her to withdraw. On the contrary. She'd broken their physical bond because she did care for him. Far, far too much.

The steps leading to the second-story apartment looked clean to Linc. What they'd find when Zoe opened her door was what worried him. Even if the evidence techs had gathered up all the throw rugs, there were likely to be signs left behind. How involved the cleanup would be depended on how much Zoe had tracked through the rooms while she'd waited for the authorities.

His jaw clenched as he turned the knob. The door was locked. "Do you have your key?"

"Yes." She produced it from a small handbag tucked inside her briefcase. "Do I have to wait out here, or can I follow you in like before and see what's what?"

"You can come. Just hang back and let me clear all the rooms before you get too curious."

"Yes, Sergeant."

"You may as well call me Linc," he said, stepping over a tacky partial footprint on the hardwood floor. "Where do you keep your cleaning supplies?"

"You—you don't have to mop this up." She was speaking to his broad back as he walked away.

"Do you want Freddy to come home to it?" Linc called from the direction of the bedrooms.

"Of *course* not."

Linc returned and said, "Then stop arguing and get me some rags, at least. Your room is actually the cleanest of all. I guess they took everything from in there as evidence. It's the hallway and this floor out here that caught the worst of the footprints."

"Do we need bleach, too?" Zoe asked.

"That would probably help lighten the red food coloring if it left stains, but the syrup should wipe up easily. I'm truly sorry this happened to you, Zoe."

"Yeah. Me, too."

Linc's gut twisted as he recalled his first impression of her when he'd seen her in her doorway that morning. The sight had stolen his breath and left him temporarily stunned. That was another reason why he hadn't immediately pursued Star. Concern that Zoe was injured had kept him with her. Wrong or right, it had happened, and

Linc wondered if his commanding officers suspected the fault in judgment.

Someday he would have to admit what had been behind his mistake. Hopefully, nobody would ask him to explain further. If they did, he was going to have to admit that his personal feelings had got in the way of doing his job at a most critical moment.

That was bad. Really bad. If it happened again and was reported, he could lose a stripe. Or, worse, he could lose his coveted position as a handler.

Linc sighed. Star—his Star—would be given to someone else.

Zoe took the time to spruce up the bathroom where she had showered earlier, careful to leave no trace of red. By the time she donned jeans and a T-shirt and returned to the living room, there was nothing left to mar that scene, either. She smiled at Linc. "Good job. Thanks."

"You're welcome. Ready to roll?"

"I guess so. I'll take my cell in case Maisy Lockwood calls from her preschool and day care. She's a wonderful teacher, but Freddy sometimes begs to come home early and I have to reason with him on the phone."

"You'd think he'd be adjusted by now. How long has he been going to that place?"

"Most of his life. It's not that. It's the rumors flying around. Even the littlest kids pick things up from parents or other caregivers. With Boyd, the talk of the base, I think Freddy's overheard plenty and he's afraid for me."

"He's not the only one," Linc said. "We'll go over

your list of possible suspects again when we break for lunch."

"Okay. Can I ask you a question?"

"Sure."

"Are you going to get in trouble for taking me with you?"

"I don't see a problem." Linc eyed her up and down, bringing a new warmth to Zoe's cheeks. "Dressed like that and with your hair down, nobody who doesn't already know you is going to suspect you're Boyd Sullivan's sister."

She smoothed the powder blue shirt over her jeans and turned in a circle. "You think? I figured since I wasn't on duty, this would do."

"Nicely."

Zoe caught the hint of a blush on his face, too. They were acting more like lovesick teenagers than responsible adults, weren't they? "I can change if you want. Maybe put on an ABU?"

"Nope. No camo. You're fine like you are." He led the way to the exit, and Zoe could have sworn she heard him mutter, "Very fine," before he opened the door and stepped out into the hall.

After that, there was no way she could suppress a grin and the incongruity struck her as ironic. Here she was, the sister of an escaped serial killer, the object of some madman who was bent on trying to drive her crazy, relieved of duty and under the thumb of Security Forces, who had blamed her for crimes that had no connection to her normally placid life. So why was she feeling almost elated?

Because Linc had promised to keep her by his side. There was no other plausible answer. He could have requested a replacement, yet he had not. Therefore, he wanted her there, wanted to be with her.

Looking heavenward, Zoe silently asked God what was going on. She didn't have to wait for an answer. It already lay in her heart. Like it or not, she was falling for Linc Colson. Hard and fast. And there wasn't a thing she could do about it.

THIRTEEN

Linc had no trouble locating First Lieutenant Vanessa Gomez in the critical-care unit of the base hospital. The insignia on his beret and his telltale sidearm and other official gear allowed them to pass through locked doors without delay.

A nod and salute were his reintroduction when he spotted Vanessa. Seeing the petite dark-haired nurse in her element gave him a more favorable opinion of her inner strength.

Vanessa stripped off latex gloves, disposed of them and quickly joined him. "Good to see you again, Sergeant Colson. I hope you've come to tell me the danger is over."

"Sorry, no," Linc replied. He inclined his head to Zoe. "This is Staff Sergeant Sullivan. Zoe, Lieutenant Vanessa Gomez."

The nurse froze. "Sullivan? You're the sister I've been hearing about?"

"Unfortunately," Zoe said with a huff. She offered her hand and Linc was relieved to see the nurse accept and shake it.

"Sorry." Vanessa was frowning when she looked

back at Linc. "Okay. If it's not good news, then give me the bad."

"Actually, in regard to Boyd, there's really nothing new. I came to ask more about blood."

"Blood?" The scowl deepened.

"Yes." Zoe explained, "Somebody sneaked into my apartment this morning and poured fake blood on my floor."

"Fake? That's not a surprise. Getting your hands on the real thing can be harder than robbing Fort Knox."

Linc asked her to go over the details for them.

"Sure. It's a real pain. First, we have to log every drop that comes in and goes out, and there's computer cross-checking. Even after the doctor orders a transfusion and a patient signs a consent form, it takes two of us to access supplies. Before blood is administered, everything is rescanned with the patient's records to prevent errors and verified electronically."

"That basically agrees with the info we got from hospital administration, only you provided more details. Thanks." Linc scanned the quiet unit. The air smelled like antiseptic. Privacy curtains were pulled between each bed and patients were eerily quiet while machinery hummed and beeped. The scenario reminded him of the hospital where he and his injured comrades had been taken after the ambush. Lives were on the line here, too. It wasn't fair. Dedicated men who gave their all for a just cause should never be buried under beeping, flashing machines, tubes, wires and white sheets.

He felt a light brush as Zoe slipped her fingers between his and clasped his hand. Hers was tiny compared to his and her grasp was gentle, yet it wasn't just her skin he felt—it was her emotional support. Had his morose thoughts been that evident? Apparently. And as opposed to shunning him as so many other women had when he'd acted depressed, she had reached out. Lifted him with a mere touch. The simple gesture hit him so hard he wanted to weep.

Instead he gave her hand a squeeze and squared his shoulders, reminding himself that he was on duty and the nurse was a target of the Red Rose Killer. This was not the time to let his mind wander or allow painful memories to take over his thought processes. He had a job to do.

There had been a time, years ago, when Linc would have followed that internal affirmation with a short appeal to a higher power for the ability to triumph. He'd stopped doing that when so many prayers had gone unanswered. Like the time he'd prayed for the welfare of his buddies before and after the ambush.

I should have suspected, he insisted for the thousandth time. *Should have had some inkling that it was a trap.*

Ideas swirled in the back of his mind like a tornado of dust rising from the desert. Had he wondered? Doubted? It was not his practice to accept intel without checking its validity. But they'd been ordered to complete their mission ASAP, and there hadn't been time for many precautions.

And since then? Linc asked himself. Since returning stateside and becoming a member of the Security Forces, he'd occasionally wished he had someone close who understood him, who could empathize without pity.

A shiver shot up his spine. His fingers tightened on Zoe's and he realized she was returning the pressure. They should not even be touching let alone holding hands, so what was wrong with him? Nothing that letting go of her wouldn't cure. The moment he loosened his grip, so did she.

While Linc was lost in thought, Zoe gave Vanessa a smile and filled the silence. "I'm truly sorry you're involved, Lieutenant Gomez."

"So am I. I hope they catch Boyd before anything bad happens to anyone else."

Zoe nodded. "We all do. He's the last person I want to see, but I promise, if he gets in touch with me, I'll turn him over to the authorities in a heartbeat."

Vanessa reached for Zoe and patted her forearm. "I understand what you're going through. I have a brother who needs help, too. It's tough."

Linc could tell that the nurse's compassion had deeply affected his companion, because she sniffled and fell silent. He saluted. "Thank you, Lieutenant. Stay safe, okay?"

"I'll do my best. You, too, Sergeants. Both of you."

Rather than draw out their leave-taking and put more pressure on Zoe, Linc turned, placed his hand at the small of her back and ushered her through the double doors and into the hallway.

"You okay?" he asked her.

All she did was nod.

"Come on. Let's grab some lunch at the Winged Java and relax while we go over your list."

"I think we should get it to go and stop back at the vet hospital to spend time with Star," Zoe said as she swiped at her tearstained cheeks.

"Really? You want to do that? Thanks."

Another nod. "Yes. And after I'm done eating, I may

want a session of puppy therapy—unless the captain was joking."

"I think I can arrange something," Linc replied. His poignant words of thanks were for more than just her offer to spend time with Star. It was also for her moral support and understanding, for Zoe merely being herself.

In retrospect, Linc wondered if perhaps he didn't also owe his heavenly Father thanks for arranging their meeting and forcing him to get to know her. The more that wild notion bounced around in his brain, the more he began to accept it as probable. It was certainly plausible.

Zoe carried a cardboard holder with their drinks while Linc handled their food and the door when they arrived at the training complex. This time they entered the facility from the rear and slipped through the connecting doors into the animal hospital.

When she saw Star notice Linc, rise and begin wagging her stub of a tail, Zoe grinned. "Whoa. She's up. And she looks much better."

"Sure does." He set the bag of burgers and fries atop a storage bin and opened the door to his K-9's kennel, bending to greet her with a tousle of her ears and a pat on the head. "How you doing, girl? Feeling good again?"

Wiggling from head to toe, the rottweiler circled Linc once, then returned to face him. Rapid panting made her look as if she was grinning as widely as the tech sergeant was. Star did everything except speak English to reassure him.

"I'd say she's telling you she's fine," Zoe said, with

laughter underlying the comment. "Where shall we go to eat? I have a feeling that sitting on the floor with her might make lunch a bit trying."

"She's not supposed to touch any food that's not presented properly and accompanied by the right commands, but in view of the unusual circumstances today, you may be right." He straightened and Star took her place at his left, sitting and waiting for orders. "Let's go inside to the break room and eat there. Captain Roark won't mind."

"Are you sure?"

"Positive. He might not look it, but he's a pushover for a needy animal."

"And hungry sergeants?"

Linc laughed as he grabbed the sack of burgers and fries. "Those, too. Come on."

Following closely and bearing their drinks, Zoe couldn't help smiling with satisfaction and gratitude. This was the first time in almost a month that she remembered feeling both happy and safe. It was difficult to even recall how comfortingly dull her former air force life had been since she'd been on her own. Even when Freddy had been born a few months after John's untimely death, she hadn't worried. Her son was the good part of her late husband, the one thing he had given her that she wouldn't have traded for the world. God had taken those unexpected events and brought great joy and perfect companionship out of her loss and sorrow.

And we know that all things work together for good to them that love God, to them who are called according to His purpose, she silently quoted from memory. Despite every obstacle that had risen against her, she had come through to the other side intact. More than intact if she counted Freddy, and she certainly did. Her son was the light of her life.

And, she realized, the stalwart man marching into the veterinary hospital ahead of her was running a close second. Being with Linc, particularly when she was off duty and out of uniform, felt so good, so perfect, she was astounded.

And grateful. Very, very grateful.

Star rested beneath the small out-of-the-way table Linc had chosen for their meal. Her muzzle lay atop his boots as if to make sure he would not move without her knowledge.

Napkin in hand, Linc started to reach toward Zoe's cheek, then pulled back. Unfortunately, she looked up just in time to notice. "Something wrong?"

He knew he was blushing. That or the temperature in the room had suddenly risen dramatically. "Mustard. You've got a little dab right…"

She quickly wiped her face. "Did I get it?"

"Yes." Averting his gaze, he focused on the pad of writing paper on the table between them. "How about students you washed out? Have you listed all those, too?"

"I think so. At least the ones who stayed in the air force. I'm more likely to remember them than the ones like Boyd who failed altogether and were discharged."

"Okay." Linc started to read the names. "I think we can eliminate most of the women, because the sightings we've had were men. Just out of curiosity though, what's your connection to Lieutenant Heidi Jenks?"

"She interviewed me once for the newspaper. I

thought she embellished important details, so I complained. She was not pleased to be criticized by a mere sergeant when she's a first lieutenant."

He read names from the list of former flight school trainees whom she'd had to fail. "What about Jones and Carpenter?"

"Gone, I believe. You can check, but I think both are stationed overseas."

"Okay." His index finger moved down the column of names. "Michael Orleck?"

"Last I heard, he'd become an aircraft mechanic, and a good one, too. That was his niche."

"Is he still at Canyon?"

"Far as I know. I think he works with Ahern."

"The same Jim Ahern who visited your brother in prison?"

Linc watched Zoe's hazel eyes narrow. "Hmm. Interesting."

"I thought so. What do you say we put Star back to bed and drive over to the airfield?"

"Suits me. You know I love watching flying, from the ground or air. It makes me feel amazingly free."

"Then you should try parachuting," Linc teased. "It's a real rush." Waiting for her reaction, he was not disappointed when he saw her eyebrows arch dramatically.

"Tried it because I had to. Wasn't thrilled, thank you."

"Why not? You like freedom."

"I also like survival. As far as I'm concerned, there are very few reasons to leave a perfectly good aircraft to go hurtling through space like a duck with a broken wing."

"You should be the writer, not Heidi," Linc said, laughing. "You have quite a way with words."

Zoe, too, chuckled. "I suspect that may have more to do with not having to put on such a perfect front when I'm off duty. It's nice to let my hair down once in a while."

"I noticed. It's pretty when it's loose like that."

"I meant figuratively." She pulled an elastic band from her jeans pocket and gathered her long light brown tresses behind her head before securing them there. "The warm Texas weather makes it hard to leave it down. Nice when winter comes, though. It helps keep my neck and ears warm."

Linc ran a hand over his shaved nape. "I wouldn't know."

"You never had long hair? Not even in your teenage rebel years?"

He shook his head as he gathered up their paper trash while Zoe grabbed the empty drink cups. "I had no time to be a rebel. With my dad AWOL, I felt like the man of the house and tried to act it. As soon as Mom would sign for me, I joined the air force."

"It was a good choice," Zoe told him. "I'm proud you made it work. A lot of fatherless boys don't." She was following Linc and Star out the door leading to the kennels when she added, "I hope and pray my son turns out half as well as you have."

Linc was speechless. Was she serious? She'd sure sounded that way. *Wow.* He bit back an inappropriate quip he might otherwise have used to keep from accepting such high praise. It was one thing to do his job well and serve his country—that was the norm—but to be held up as the perfect adult male example for the little boy Zoe loved with all her heart was something else. Something far beyond regular service.

He busied himself settling Star in her kennel rather than respond to Zoe's statement. No matter what he said in response, it was bound to sound like either bragging or begging for further praise.

Truth to tell, she had just given him the best compliment of his entire life and he didn't know what to do or say, other than to let it pass without comment. He wanted to thank her somehow, to admit how deeply touched he was, yet he refused to reveal that much raw emotion for fear of disgracing himself.

Whether Zoe knew it or not, she had just put a crack in the thick stony wall he'd trusted to keep his heart and his warrior spirit intact.

Now he'd have to make sure he didn't permit her to widen that gap enough to step through or he might never recover.

FOURTEEN

Wind was gusting off the surrounding hills, lifting fine dust and sand that stung Zoe's cheeks as they crossed the tarmac toward an open hangar. North of the airfield, rows of fighters stood in neat lines, forming their own ready ranks.

Linc touched her arm to get her attention and pointed to a sleek aircraft doing touch-and-go landings. "Your student?"

"Maybe. After basic, they're assigned to one of four advanced-training tracks—bomber and fighter, airlift and tanker, advanced turboprop or helicopters."

"That makes sense, I guess."

"It does, particularly when a pilot ends up assigned to fly large transport and tanker aircraft instead of fighter jets."

"Who decides?"

Zoe turned her back to the gusts and used a hand to control wisps of her flyaway hair. "Thankfully, not me."

"Got it." Linc had to hold on to his blue beret to keep it from blowing away. "Let's get inside before we end up taking to the air, too."

A dash for the closest hangar with open doors

brought them relief. No mechanics were working on the various aircraft housed there, which was a good thing because an exposed engine full of grit due to the open bay was far from acceptable.

She pointed to an office. "Daily rosters are posted over there. I'll go check."

"Where you go, I go." Linc fell in beside her.

It only took her a few seconds to spot familiar names. "We must be living right. Ahern and Orleck are both on duty in hangar seven."

"Okay. Before we go talk to them, let's set some ground rules."

"A pilot term. Nice."

Linc was chuckling and shaking his head. "Total accident, I assure you. Tell me more about your dealings with Ahern first."

"He's a disgusting braggart. If he was one tenth as wonderful as he thinks he is, he'd have made chief master sergeant by now. That said, he's a wiz with engines. Not as good on advanced avionics but not bad, either. I think younger guys like Orleck handle most of the electronic testing for him."

"Speaking of Orleck, what's the deal with him?"

"He pitched a fit when I washed him out. Once he'd blown off steam, however, he seemed to settle right down. I heard later that he was grateful for the change of direction. That's the beauty of it. We have a variety of great jobs in the air force and if a person tries, he or she can be very happy, successful and satisfied."

"What about you? Are you happy?" Linc asked.

She huffed. "I was, until they unfairly sidelined me. Now not so much."

"What about in the rest of your life?"

Her eyebrows went up as her suspicion increased. "Are you asking about my brother again? Because if you are, remember what I told that nurse. I am not like Boyd. Never was, never will be. I'm not sure why he turned out so twisted, but whatever happened to him, I escaped that negative influence. Maybe it was because we had different mothers."

"I wasn't asking officially," Linc said. "That was more of an existential question. I know you have Freddy and you love him to pieces, but what about the rest of the time? Are you generally happy?"

Deciding how to answer delayed her response. Finally, she paraphrased Scripture. "'I have learned that whatever state I am in, for whatever reasons, to be content.' The apostle Paul wrote that in his letter to the Philippians. He said it much better than I just did, but you get the gist."

"You don't wish things had been different, could be different?"

Zoe wasn't sure what he was actually asking, but she didn't intend to fall into the trap of assuming his query was personal. They had been discussing air force careers, so she replied in that vein. "There were times I thought I wanted to be a combat pilot. Now that I'm a mother, I've decided it's too dangerous. My son only has me."

"No grandparents?"

She shook her head and made a derisive sound. "My late father ruined Boyd by setting a terrible example and being totally convinced his only son could do no wrong. My mother is still living near the old Wadsworth family place in Dill, but she never had the backbone to stand up to Dad. She's even worse in regard to my brother. Maybe she overcompensates because she's his stepmother. All I know is, I would never give her another child to raise. Uh-uh. No way."

"I get it. I love my mom dearly, and she did manage to get me through my teens, but it was more by accident than from making good choices."

Smiling at him, Zoe spoke her mind. "I don't like giving random credit. You can say I'm deluded if you want. You won't be the first. But I firmly believe that God knew us when we were first being formed and becoming babies, just like the Bible says. He saw where we were going and what we'd become from the beginning."

"Then why didn't he stop your brother before so many people died?"

"I don't know." She refused to let him rile her. "I'm clueless about far more than I dream of ever understanding. But that doesn't change my opinion. I can look back and see times where God intervened and saved me. I imagine you could, too, if you'd do it with an unbiased attitude."

"For instance?"

"How should I know what's gone on in your life? As for mine, I'll tell you this. Boyd was already scary when we were kids. I loved him dearly, but I still wonder how many times he thought of murdering me in my sleep.

"And then there was my husband. John was a handsome smooth talker who had me thoroughly convinced he was some kind of super patriot—when he was exactly the opposite. If he had not died when he did, there's no telling how deep into the pit he'd have dragged me and if I'd have been able to climb out, let alone make the air force my career."

"Do you believe his death was accidental?"

Zoe sobered and her eyes flamed with repressed emotion. "That was the official finding."

"And…?"

"It's my belief that his traitorous cohorts got him out of the way when he made the mistake of bragging to me that he was getting away with breaking the law. How they found out doesn't matter. What does is that I went to my commanding officers and reported it. John was dead within a week."

"Then you can't be sure."

With a telling sigh and shrug of her shoulders, Zoe said, "I'm as sure as the encrypted files on his personal computer can make me. If I had not preempted that discovery with my initial report and John had not been removed from my life, I could have been charged with treason or even have met the same fate he did. Then Freddy would have died, too, because I was carrying him at the time."

"So, you really think God rescued you?"

"It makes more sense than random choice, just like knowing the alphabet and being able to spell makes more sense than closing your eyes and banging on a keyboard until a bestseller emerges."

Linc stared at her for the longest time before he said, "Know what scares me?"

"What?"

A lopsided smile began to lift one corner of his mouth. "You're actually starting to make sense."

Her smile mirrored his, then surpassed it. "Of course I am. That's because I'm right."

Along with a half dozen other mechanics, Jim Ahern was working in hangar seven, as scheduled, when Linc led the way with Zoe behind him.

Linc kept it casual as he approached them. "Jim Ahern?"

The senior mechanic laid aside a socket wrench as he turned to face the Security Forces man. "Yeah."

Smiling cordially, Linc offered to shake hands. Ahern swiped his palms against his oily coveralls before accepting.

"Which one is Orleck?"

Ahern snorted. "Why? What'd he do?"

"Nothing that we know of. I just figured it would save time to speak with both of you at once. Were you both here working all morning?"

"Yup." He cupped a hand around his mouth and called, "Hey, Mike. C'mere a sec."

The younger man who emerged from behind the plane was scowling until he saw Zoe standing behind Linc. Then he began to grin. "Hey, Sarge. What brings you here? Are we late getting a trainer ready or something?"

Rather than let her answer, Linc spoke. "Actually, this visit has to do with Sergeant Sullivan."

"Really?" Orleck was grinning at her as if meeting an old friend and Linc wasn't sure he liked such familiarity, although it did indicate no latent animosity.

Ahern was less amiable. "I already told you guys, over and over, I ain't seen Boyd since he begged me to come visit him in prison. It wasn't my idea in the first place, but we'd been buddies before, so I gave in and went."

Linc chose to refrain from mentioning that Ahern and Boyd Sullivan appeared to be more cohorts than everyday friends. If Sullivan hadn't been drummed out of the service early, there was a good chance Ahern would have been sucked further in and have taken the fall for some of their hijinks. The problem was, and always had been, a lack of concrete proof.

"You haven't been contacted by Boyd?" Linc asked him.

"Nope. I know rumor has him here on the base but if he is, I sure ain't running into him." He pointedly stared at Zoe. "What about her? She's his kin." His brow furrowed deeper and his eyes narrowed. "Is she blaming me? Is that it?"

"No. Not at all." Linc struck a casual pose. "What about you, Orleck? Would you know Boyd Sullivan if you saw him?"

"I might. I did see his picture in the base newspaper and on TV. Why? Did he go and kill somebody else?"

"Not lately. Not that I know of," Linc replied. He purposely changed the subject. "So, how do you like being a mechanic?"

"I like it fine." His gaze kept slipping over to Zoe, and his grin was so friendly Linc was disappointed. If he hadn't known better, he'd have suspected the washed-out pilot had a thing for his former instructor.

"You aren't sorry you didn't get to fly?"

Orleck shrugged. "Sure, from time to time. But I get to go along on plenty of test flights and that gives me my thrills. Keeping these birds in the air is what I do best." Once again, his pleasant expression rested on Zoe. "I actually owe it all to you, Sarge. You helped me find a good fit. Thanks."

"You're welcome," she said.

"Well, then…" Linc hitched up his utility belt and holster out of habit and gave each man a nod. "We'll be going. You know who to call if you catch sight of Sullivan."

Ahern chuckled. "Believe me, if I find any red roses lying around, you're the first guys I'm gonna call."

As Linc turned to go, he placed his hand lightly on Zoe's back for moral support and guidance. Yes, she was perfectly capable of walking beside him without interference. And yes, he could have stopped himself. But there had been something in the manner of both men, not to mention those watching from afar, that made him want to publicly declare that she was with him. Not just there, but *with* him.

They were almost outside before she spoke. "I can't imagine Orleck being behind the attacks on me. Can you? He seems perfectly happy here."

Linc agreed. "What about Ahern?"

"Why would he want to harass me? Because he was a friend of my brother's?"

"It makes a little sense."

Brushing back flyaway strands of her long hair, Zoe faced him. "I don't see it. I think we were grasping at straws coming here in the first place."

"You're probably right."

"So, what's next?"

"You hungry?"

She laughed lightly. "Why are you always trying to feed me?"

"It's a Southern custom. We like to eat."

"I thought I detected a Texas twang, but I figured it was because you'd been stationed here long enough to pick it up."

"Nope. Born and raised. Remember the Alamo and all that."

"I get it. Okay, country boy, you can feed me. And this time let's eat at a table with chairs and napkins and plenty of sweet tea."

"Sounds like you've acclimated well, too."

When Zoe looked into his eyes, Linc saw more than he wanted to see. Although she managed a wan smile, there was a telltale glistening of unshed tears pooling in her hazel eyes. "Until my brother escaped and came here, I'd planned to make Texas my permanent home, even after I retired. Now who knows?"

Something inside him urged Linc to open his arms to her and she stepped into his embrace as if it were the most natural thing in the world. It never occurred to him to try to hide their closeness, nor was he embarrassed by it. She needed comforting that he needed to provide. It was that simple. And that complicated.

Closing his eyes, Linc rested his chin on the top of her head and felt her flyaway hair tickling his nose. Thoughts raced through his mind. How could he fix this for her? How could he make it right and continue to protect her? Suppose he was reassigned? Then what?

With great effort, Linc managed to set her away. Grasping her shoulders, he spoke quietly, privately. "I'm sorry. I shouldn't have done that. It's inappropriate."

Zoe sniffled. "Maybe. But it sure felt good."

That was the crux of the problem. "What I mean is, if word gets back to headquarters that you and I are getting too friendly, there's a good chance I may be relieved of this duty."

Remembering what his master sergeant had suggested gave him some solace, but Linc doubted Sergeant James had meant for him to go this far. Nor had he intended to. Genuine fondness for Zoe had grown so easily it had blindsided him.

She took a step away. Then another. "I don't want to lose you," she whispered. "Just tell me how to act and I'll be glad to comply." A tiny smile quirked at one corner of her mouth. "Under most circumstances."

Linc stood tall, almost at attention. "As soon as Star is released for duty, I think things will smooth out for us. If you need comforting, then you can get it from her."

"I thought Captain Roark said she'd bite my nose off."

"That may be a slight exaggeration. As long as I tell her it's okay, she'll be fine, same as she was with Freddy."

Sobering and staring off into the distance as if visualizing her darling little boy, Zoe said, "It's him I'm most worried about."

"I thought you believed God was taking care of everything."

"I did, and I do. But I also believe He expects us to use the wits and weapons He's provided for us. Just because I know how to fly doesn't mean I'd carelessly go up without a parachute. That would be reckless."

"What about when you're on the ground?" Linc asked, eager for her answer.

He never expected her to look him straight in the eye and say, "When I'm down here, *you're* my parachute, Sergeant Colson. You and Star. I don't want to go anywhere without you until we figure out who is trying to destroy me."

FIFTEEN

The food at Carmen's was pleasing as usual, and so was the ambience. Linc reported their location and plans, then settled back to enjoy his meal.

She called me her parachute. He couldn't get that image out of his mind. A parachute slowed a jumper's descent, settled him gently on the ground and could be used again and again. But there was more to it than that, wasn't there? Zoe was counting on him to be her safety net, her ever-present, reliable guarantee that when all this was over, she'd survive the same way a parachute kept a jumper alive. Did she realize that the person in the harness had to know when to deploy an emergency chute? How to tuck and roll when making a hard landing? What to do if coming down in enemy territory?

Linc doubted she had made that detailed a comparison when she'd complimented him. That was just as well. As much as he wanted to be everything she needed, he knew that was impossible. So when had the pretty sergeant gone from being an assignment to something more? The change was in his outlook. In the way he perceived both her and their companionship. What had once been a job was now more than a pleasure, more than his duty. It was as if their lives had been joined by circumstances with the glue of compassion, perhaps even budding love.

Love? Linc looked across the table at her and found her studying him, as well. Hoping to seem nonchalant, he smiled and gestured with his fork. "Pretty good, huh? I love their lasagna."

Zoe mirrored his smile, but there was a poignancy in her eyes that made them glisten. Seconds later, she dropped her gaze to her plate and simply said, "Yes."

"Captain Roark says I may be able to take Star home with me tonight. Tomorrow at the latest."

"Good."

"Sergeant James is going to assign one of our female Security Forces members to your watch tonight. If I were you, I'd invite her in and let her crash on the couch. Her dog will alert if anybody approaches."

"Okay."

One-word answers were unlike Zoe, and her mental state had him worried. "Look. I know you say you're fine, but I'm not sure that's completely true. Talk to me. Tell me what's bothering you. I really do want to help."

She laid aside her fork and blotted her lips with a napkin before answering. "I know that. I just feel overwhelmed. So much has happened lately, and we have so few clues. It's as though I'm stuck in a flat spin at ten thousand feet and can't pull my aircraft out of it before I crash."

"You won't crash."

"How do you know? How can anybody be sure?"

Linc sighed. "Well, for one thing, we've got reports that your brother has been seen—"

"Stop." Teary-eyed, she held up a hand, palm toward him. "Stop calling him my brother, okay?"

"What should I call him?"

"I don't care. Call him Boyd or the Red Rose Killer or abbreviate it to RRK the way I've heard other law enforcement officers do. Just stop reminding me we're related. Please."

"All right. I'm sorry. I didn't think it would be a problem."

"Normally, it isn't." She sniffed and touched her napkin to her cheek where tears had begun to dampen it. "It's everything together. The attacks on me, the shooting I saw that left no trace, the—" Her eyes widened. "That's it! That's our answer."

"What is?"

"Fake blood. Like in my apartment. Your CSIs were using a blue light to look for the real thing in that warehouse bay. Nobody thought to check it for what that stuff in my apartment was made of."

"Whoa." Linc sat back in his chair. "You're right. I don't suppose there are traces of it left by now, even if there were drops in the first place, but I'll mention it to Captain Blackwood. Matter of fact, I'll do it right now. Wait here."

Zoe started to rise when he pulled out his cell and started for the door, so Linc repeated, "Wait here for me. I'll be right outside where I can see you."

He could tell she wanted to argue. To stay close to him. And although he knew that making the call in a crowded dining room wasn't smart, he was sorely tempted to do it anyway. Seeing Zoe's shoulders finally relax, he smiled back at her. "Thanks. This won't take a minute."

After wending his way between tables, Linc stepped outside as he was connecting. "Captain Blackwood. This is Colson. I'm still with Sergeant Sullivan and in view of what was involved in this morning's incident at her apartment, we were wondering if that same artificial blood could have been used in the shooting she witnessed at the warehouse."

Silence on the line worried Linc until he heard his captain clear his throat. "You may be right. It'd be hard to tell at this point, though."

"It doesn't leave trace evidence?"

"Not that remains discernible. What we collected this morning was a homemade concoction instead of one of the professional brands the movies use. That kind lights up when we spray luminal. This stuff was made of food you'd find in most kitchen cupboards, as I said. Anything that landed on the ground outside was probably eaten by insects almost immediately."

"Hmm. Too bad. Zoe's going to be disappointed."

Blackwood's voice rose. "What did you say?"

"Sergeant Sullivan will be disappointed."

"No. You called her by her first name, Colson. I hope you remember that you are with her as a duty assignment."

"Yes, sir. Of course, Captain. It's just that—"

He was cut off. "No excuses. I know Master Sergeant James suggested that you befriend her, but that doesn't mean you should actually become personally involved. Is that clear?"

"Yes, sir. Crystal clear." *And almost totally unacceptable*, Linc added to himself. Personally involved? Oh, yeah. It was already too late to prevent that. So how was he going to obey orders and still guard Zoe to the degree necessary?

That was a good question. Too bad he didn't have a good answer. Linc clenched his jaw muscles. He not only did not have a feasible idea, he didn't even have a poor one.

Turning on his heel, he straight-armed the restaurant door and returned to Zoe. *Yes, Zoe*, he affirmed. He'd have to take care to use her rank and last name when speaking to others, but in private, she was going to be Zoe.

Besides, he added, feeling his cheeks warming as their eyes met, he liked her, and Zoe was what he wanted to call her. What he would call her.

Linc smiled, rejoined her to report on the call and once again began to eat. The meal was cool and less appetizing than it had been but he was determined to finish so his companion would, too. She'd been picking at her food and he wanted her to keep up her energy.

"How about dessert?" Linc asked when she failed to follow his example.

Zoe shook her head and gave him a fond look that practically melted his heart. Why did he care so much? What in the world was wrong with him? Here he was, ready to defy a direct order and actually desiring chances to do so. That was more than stupid. It was insane.

Looking for a suitable diversion, Linc waved their waitress over.

"More sweet tea?" the young woman asked.

"Not for me. Zoe?"

"No, thanks." She sat back and pushed her plate away. "I'm finished."

"Then we'll have three slices of apple pie to go," he said. "And the bill."

"You remembered Freddy," Zoe said softly.

"Of course, I did. How could I forget Star's little buddy? I should have asked you if it was okay, though. Sorry."

"No need to apologize. It's more than okay," Zoe told him. "Way more. You'd be surprised how many adults overlook children."

"Your son's hard to overlook," Linc quipped. "He's a really special little guy."

The expression on Zoe's face made him wonder how he had upset her. She'd seemed a tad down in the dumps during their meal, but now she looked as if she might cry. Should he ask? Or should he go on as if he hadn't noticed?

Linc opted for the latter. He stood up and dropped a tip on the table. "We can settle up and get the pie at the register," he said. "Come on. It's time we checked in on Star again."

With a protective hand at her waist, he ushered her through the restaurant. The urge to keep her close was almost as strong as his determination to use her first name. Worse, he wasn't merely thinking of her as Zoe, he was seeing her as *his* Zoe. And there was no way he could talk himself out of it.

Seeing Star being her old self again made Zoe happy, but that was nothing compared to Linc's reaction. He was so overjoyed he was grinning from ear to ear. The exuberant dog obviously felt the same, because she was doing her version of the Texas two-step at his feet.

Zoe laughed. "I think she's happy to see you."

"Yeah." He tousled the recovered K-9's ears and laughed at her antics. "Something tells me she's ready to go back to work."

"Won't she be scared of being hurt again?" Zoe asked.

Captain Roark agreed. "Good point. How about a short retraining session? I'm sure we can find a volunteer to wear the bite sleeve."

"I'd rather send her after the real thing, but you're right. It would be a good idea. I'll check in with Caleb Streeter at the training center and set it up." He continued to pet the excited dog. "You sure she's ready for that much running this soon?"

"Absolutely." Roark smiled at Zoe. "And I owe you a puppy therapy session."

Although the idea appealed, she demurred. "Can I get a rain check? I'd rather come with my son and he's in day care during the week."

"Absolutely. Just let me know when you want to visit and I'll see that you and your son get the full tour."

"Thanks." Glancing at Linc, she couldn't help smiling. "I think they're glad to be back together."

"True. How are things going for you?"

She was touched that someone else was expressing concern. "Pretty good, considering. I still feel terrible that Star was hurt on my behalf."

"They're working dogs," Roark said. "We train for all branches of the military, as you probably know. Our K-9s are expected to do their jobs regardless of danger or injury."

"That sounds like the description of a human soldier."

Smiling, the vet agreed. "You're right. And we retire

them after their working days are over, too. In fact, I'm waiting for one special case to be returned from overseas so I can check the dog's health and see if he's suitable for adoption, but there have been complications."

Linc straightened, still smiling broadly. "Sounds like the dog Isaac Goddard's been trying to adopt. Has there been any word?"

"Yes," Roark said. "Isaac was notified that Beacon had been cleared to return to the States, but there was an enemy attack on the base over there that damaged the kennels and the dog escaped. It's a crying shame. Isaac is having a really hard time dealing with the fact that Beacon may never be found and sent home."

"I understand exactly how he feels." Linc's hand was resting on Star's broad head.

Zoe smiled at both men. "I can see how important all the dogs are to you. I suppose it's inevitable that you'd get particularly attached to individual animals. I'm glad you get to adopt the retirees."

"Most of them qualify," Roark explained. "There's even a website where civilians can apply to adopt one of our dogs. There's a long waiting list, though, and strict requirements. The dog's handler gets first dibs."

She looked to Linc and Star. "Are you planning on keeping her if you can?"

"Absolutely. But it's going to be years before she's put out to pasture. We have a lot of work to do before that."

"Yes," Zoe said, "like capturing the Red Rose Killer and figuring out who has been making my life miserable." She heard a tiny gasp from behind her and turned. It was the vet tech who had taken care of Star when she first arrived, Airman Fielding.

Zoe easily identified with the fear she glimpsed in

the young woman's eyes and offered solace. "Don't worry about the Red Rose Killer. I'm sure he'd have no reason to bother you, unless you dated him or crossed him somehow."

"I never met him," Fielding said. "Excuse me. I have patients to check."

Linc's brow was furrowed when Zoe looked to him and said, "She seems frightened."

Captain Roark agreed. "Rachel's always been kind of sensitive. Working here, surrounded by animals, is a perfect placement for her. Believe me, she's a lot calmer than she used to be."

"Good to hear," Zoe said. "If she were in one of my flight classes, I'm afraid she'd wash out quickly."

"Speaking of that, any word on when you can go back to work?" the vet asked.

"Nope. None." Smiling at Star, she added, "So for the time being, I'll be Star's volunteer sidekick. I can brush her and get her dog bones and…"

Linc was laughing when he held up a hand. "Whoa. That's my job. Sorry. How about you just try to stay out of trouble from now on and give us all a break?"

Eyes rolling, Zoe chuckled, too. "That, Sergeant Colson, is my fondest wish. From your mouth to God's ears, as they say here in the South."

Although he didn't stop smiling, he did say, "I doubt I have much influence on Him."

"You'd be surprised," Zoe countered. "God loves everybody who believes in Him. Even stubborn, hard-headed guys like you."

That made Roark laugh, too. "Look out, Colson. I think she's got you pegged."

Although Linc made a face at them both, Zoe thought

she glimpsed a flicker of recognition, a spark of truth. She knew he didn't have to fully accept all his losses, in Afghanistan and before. He simply had to let go of his guilt and anger and hand it all over to his heavenly Father.

As I have to do regarding Boyd, she added to herself, knowing she was right. It wasn't the understanding she lacked, it was the will to act, the strength to forgive. And the faith to trust so completely that she was able to release her wounded spirit into the care of a loving God.

That wasn't the same as worshipping on Sunday morning. It went much, much deeper.

SIXTEEN

"I need to step next door and check in with my bosses before we do anything else," Linc said.

Zoe didn't mind. She shrugged and smiled. "Fine with me. As you can see, I'm free."

He started off, Star at his side, and Zoe followed. "So, what are you planning for later?"

"Don't know yet. We have several options. I want to ask if the techs found any traces of syrup on the floor of the warehouse."

"Unlikely, I'm afraid."

"Probably. But I asked them to look just the same."

"Thanks. I can't believe I fell for the ruse." She kept walking but paused the conversation before adding, "If it really was a trick."

"Let's assume it was. That leaves us with fewer suspects."

"How so?"

"If the same theatrical blood was used, that will combine two of the incidents."

"Makes sense." She followed Linc and Star to Captain Blackwood's open office door. Linc knocked on the jamb.

Justin Blackwood stood behind his desk and Zoe saluted, as did Linc.

"I see Star is back in service. Good to know."

"Yes, sir. Since Sergeant Sullivan is free to move around the base, I wondered if you had anything we might handle together."

"Such as?"

Zoe could tell Blackwood wasn't thrilled with Linc's suggestion, but as far as she was concerned, it made perfect sense. She cleared her throat. "Excuse me, sir. If I may? Since the Red Rose Killer is very familiar to me, it makes sense to send me out in the field with one of your Security people. My chances of spotting him in a crowd are far better than anyone else's."

The captain nodded slightly, acting as if he was at least considering her views. "There is some logic to your suggestion, Sullivan. I assume that wherever you go you're on alert for any sign of your brother."

Zoe tried not to cringe at the familial reference. "Yes, sir. The RRK is always on my mind. So is whoever has been harassing me. I don't think my case is related to the serial killings. At least I hope it isn't."

Blackwood shuffled papers on his desk and selected one. "I have a report from Yvette Crenville. She's accusing Jim Ahern of bothering her again."

"Yes, sir," Linc said. "We visited him at work at the airfield earlier today."

"And?"

"He seems pretty full of himself but mostly hot air," Linc replied. "What I'd like to do is check on some of the possible suspects in Sergeant Sullivan's repeated attacks. There have been too many to chalk them up to chance."

"Agreed. Having a motive would help. Any ideas, Sergeant?" he asked, giving Zoe a piercing look.

"Not really, sir. Sergeant Colson and I made a list. Once we've compared duty assignments to the times of the incidents, we should be able to eliminate quite a few suspects."

"Then get to it. I'll bring in someone to assist you with the computer details if you want." The captain glanced at another list. "Airman McNally is available." He keyed his intercom. "Send McNally to my office."

Zoe didn't want her problems spread all over the base due to additional exposure, so she gently objected to the suggestion. "I think Colson and I can handle it by ourselves, sir. Once we have access to individual records, it should be easy."

A sharp knock against the open door caused Zoe to pivot. The airman was not only a woman, she was young, lithe and had her hair pulled tightly back into a coil, the same way Zoe wore hers when she was working. That wasn't what made Zoe take a quick involuntary breath however. It was the airman's hair color. McNally was a redhead!

Had Linc made the connection yet? Zoe wondered. If he gave in and let his captain assign this woman to their project, there was no telling what might happen. Yes, she was undoubtedly not the only female on base who had red hair. But the coincidence was bothersome.

Swaying slightly, Zoe felt Linc's hand at her back, his touch barely there yet supportive. She chanced a sidelong glance and saw that their minds were in sync. Raising her chin a mere millimeter and hoping no one but Linc noticed, she turned the motion into a slow, purposeful nod. The narrowing of his eyes indicated comprehension.

"Thank you anyway, Captain," he said. "Sullivan and I can manage."

"Then you're excused," Blackwood told the assistant.

"One thing before I go, sir?" McNally waited.

Although the redheaded airman seemed to be ignoring her, Zoe was certain she was picking up bad vibes. Either that or her overactive imagination was blaming an innocent party, which was also possible.

Blackwood nodded. "Go ahead."

"It's that blogger, sir. He's already posted info about the attack on Sergeant Colson's dog and reported that the K-9 is sidelined."

Meaning everybody at CAFB is already privy to my problems, Zoe thought, chagrined. *Terrific.*

Obviously displeased, Blackwood clenched his jaw and his fists. "All right. Get the techs on it again ASAP. We have enough internal stress without adding some idiot with a computer and too much time on his hands."

"Yes, sir." McNally saluted and left.

The captain jotted down a note and handed it to Linc. "Here's today's password. You can use Sergeant James's office if it's free. If not, I'll get you access somewhere else. I don't want to learn that either of you has opened files belonging to any personnel other than the ones you're investigating. Is that clear?"

Linc saluted. "Yes, sir. Very clear."

Mirroring Linc's salute, Zoe followed him into the hallway and checked to see that they were alone before she said, "What do you think? Could that be her?"

"It could. You weren't able to give a very detailed description of the woman in the warehouse. What makes you think it was McNally?"

"I don't know, exactly. Maybe the way she moved or her build, not to mention that hair."

"There's something else," Linc said, pulling her closer to his side and bending to speak more privately. "The way she looked at you when you weren't paying attention. I think I saw recognition. Had you met her anywhere before?"

"Not to my knowledge. Maybe we should do a little extra investigating while we're at it."

"I don't know. You heard the captain."

"I did. So let's start with my list and leave our new suspect for last, just in case we get shut out."

Linc's sly grin and the purposeful way he led her to the empty office they were supposed to use lifted Zoe's spirits immensely. Not only was he on her side, they had begun to agree more often than not. Teamwork was far better than working at odds and she had high hopes that they would soon solve at least one of the mysteries they faced.

Star accompanied them down the hallway and into the office of Master Sergeant James. Zoe could tell that the faithful K-9 was more at ease than both her or Linc. When he closed the door behind them her tension rose. They were all alone. And he had been acting awfully proprietary of late. It was easy to imagine herself back in his embrace, perhaps even kissed. Although, after making a fool of herself once, she wasn't about to try to instigate anything romantic.

"Don't worry," Linc assured her. "You're safe with me. I promise to be the perfect gentleman."

A daring side of Zoe's personality that she rarely acknowledged emerged, and she whispered, "That's what I'm afraid of," before she could change her mind. Linc's startled expression was actually amusing.

"What did you say?"

"Never mind. Forget it."

Instead, he approached slowly and took her hand. "You're trembling."

"Too much coffee."

"Liar."

What could she say? How could she take back her revealing remark? Moreover, did she want to? Especially when he was standing so close, and she saw the glow in his darkening, expressive green eyes.

Instead of a rebuttal, Zoe kept her gaze locked with his. Her lips trembled. Her heart was about to pound out of her chest. And the air in the small office must have been used up because she couldn't seem to take a deep enough breath to keep her comfortable.

Linc slipped one finger beneath her chin and leaned closer. "I am probably going to be sorry for this," he said quietly against her cheek before turning his head just enough and giving her the kiss she had been dreaming of.

Her shaky equilibrium wasn't strong enough to correct the sway his nearness provoked, so she slipped both arms around his waist. When he completed the embrace and pulled her to him to deepen their kiss, Zoe closed her eyes and surrendered. Utterly. Completely. Trusting him with an intensity she had always assumed was impossible for her.

Tears threatened as she realized what he had said. Well, he might be sorry for kissing her, but as far as

Zoe was concerned, this was the best part of her whole day. Maybe of her whole life.

Yeah. The best.

Linc became oblivious to anything around them. His entire focus was on Zoe. On the sweet smell of her hair. The way she fit so perfectly in his arms. And that kiss.

He was no kid. He'd kissed women before. And he'd enjoyed it. A lot. But this was different. When his mind tried to put his feelings into words, it failed. Their closeness was too perfect. Too emotional. Too amazing to be explained.

That was what finally brought him to his senses. Zoe wasn't the only one breathless when he let her go and set her away by gently cupping her shoulders. Oh, man, he was in trouble. Deep trouble. This was no simple crush, at least not on his part. He wondered if her responses to him had been because she felt their connection as strongly as he did or because she'd been so frightened lately and had latched onto him as a port in a storm. After all, she had compared him to a parachute. If that was all he was to her, then he was probably going to get his heart broken. Big time.

Linc managed a smile. "I told you we were going to be sorry."

"We? Personally, I liked it."

"That's it? You liked it?"

She grinned up at him, her cheeks rosy, her eyes glistening. Linc cupped her cheeks. "I liked it, too."

"Good." She sniffled.

"If you expect me to be poetic about it, you're going to have to give me time to gather my wits. You scattered them really well just now." He eyed the desk. Star had made herself at home in the kneehole and was starting to snore. "Do you think you're up to starting our search or do you need a few more minutes?"

"If you could give me a year, it probably wouldn't be long enough," Zoe quipped. Squaring her shoulders, she said, "Come on. Let's get to digging. We don't know how long we'll have before Sergeant James wants his office back."

Linc agreed. "I'm glad he didn't walk in a few minutes ago."

"Me, too. He might have reassigned you and spoiled everything."

"We'd still have been stationed on the same base." Linc circled the desk, pulled up the swivel chair and checked the password Blackwood had given him.

Standing behind him, Zoe rested a hand on his shoulder and watched the monitor. He knew she didn't mean to be distracting but after that extraordinary kiss, even the simple touch of her hand on his uniform was enough to drive him crazy.

His fingers stopped typing. All movement ceased.

Zoe's hand remained where it was. "What's wrong?"

"You are," Linc admitted ruefully. "I'm afraid I can't think straight when you're so close."

"That's too bad," she said, pulling away and choosing a nearby chair.

When Linc looked over at her, she was grinning from ear to ear. Already uneasy, he scowled. "What?"

"Nothing." She crossed her jeans-clad legs and held out a hand. "Give me the list and I'll read you the names from way over here. Did I go far enough?"

"It's not funny," he insisted.

Zoe sobered and took the list from him. "I know. It

just struck me as hilarious that the two of us were forced together when we both hate the idea of marriage."

"Whoa! Who said anything about *that*?"

"Nobody. Just thinking aloud. I didn't mean to scare the stripes off you, Sergeant Colson."

Her nonchalant shrug seemed innocent enough, but Linc wasn't convinced. One kiss and already she was hearing wedding bells. Well, that wasn't going to happen. Not with him. Sure, Zoe was attractive. And that kiss had shaken him all the way to the waffled soles of his combat boots. But he'd promised himself a long time ago that one, the influence of his dysfunctional family was nothing he wanted to pass on to future generations, and two, he didn't deserve marital bliss when his buddies' wives and girlfriends had buried their dreams with their mates.

Uh-uh. Linc Colson was staying single. He might be too romantic for his own good, but he knew where to draw the line. Lifelong penance for his errors in judgment was necessary. There was no escape from his past, nor was he looking for one.

SEVENTEEN

By the time Linc had completed his survey and cut the list down to the likely suspects, Zoe's neck was in knots and her head throbbed. She knew why. Spending all this time with him was very trying. If he hadn't been on duty, it might have been different, although she doubted it.

Standing, she stretched. "I should go get Freddy soon."

"Right. We will. The boy comes first. We don't want him to be worried about you."

We? Zoe wondered if noticing every little nuance of Linc's behavior was something new or if she had been doing it all along and had overlooked her own interest. Until now. Moreover, did he realize he had begun referring to them as a couple? Whatever. She certainly wasn't going to be the one to point it out.

One concern she was going to mention however, was the safety of her beloved child. "Do you think, considering everything that's happened, that I should send Freddy away?"

Linc whirled, scowling. "What brought that on?"

"Reality," she said flatly. "He's all I have. I love him so much it hurts. There must be some way to protect him."

"Better than I can, you mean." It wasn't a question.

"I didn't say that." She was adamant. "But you can't be around all the time. And at night, when he's home with me, you're not there at all. Somebody else is."

"With a K-9 partner."

"I know, I know. And that is a plus. But those guards keep changing. I never know who's going to show up. When I see you, it's very reassuring."

"Thanks, I think." He drew his fingers and thumb down the sides of his jaw, meeting at the point of his chin. "I suppose it's possible I could convince Sergeant James to switch my assignment to the overnight shift, but that may be a bad idea."

"Why? If you're still worried about rumors about being in my apartment, I assure you, I trust you completely. Besides, Freddy's there. I can let him bunk with me and you can have his room."

Linc held up both hands, palms out. "Whoa. Is that where your other night watchmen sleep?"

"Well, no. I've offered something more comfortable, but they've all turned me down."

"As they should have," Linc said forcefully.

"You don't have to raise your voice. I'm the victim here, remember? I'm just worried about protecting my son the best way possible. As I said, maybe I should send him away."

"Where? Where would you send him? You've already told me your family is unfit. What about the Flints, John's parents? Would they take him in? He is their grandson."

"Not one they choose to claim. They disowned me and mine long ago after I reported John's crimes. They never did believe he could be guilty of espionage and insisted I had framed him." She sighed. "I think they suspect me of being behind the accident that killed him, too."

"Sad. They're missing out on meeting a great kid."

Linc's praise restored Zoe's smile and lifted her spirits until he added, "You can't leave him with Maisy overnight. Not with her father being one of the RRK's victims."

Zoe knew he was right. Maisy's father, Chief Master Sergeant Clint Lockwood, had been one of her brother's first victims on CAFB.

She made a face. "*Him* again." She began to pace. "You have no idea how much I wish I had been an only child."

He chuckled wryly. "I used to, too, until my sister, Georgia, became an adult. Now we just fight over which branch of the service is the best, hers or mine."

"She's an army major, right?"

"You have a good memory. Yes. A career officer."

"What does she do? I mean, what's her specialty?" Zoe hoped Linc didn't think she was just making conversation. She truly wanted to know.

"Diplomacy, if you can believe it." He laughed lightly. "We are definitely not alike."

"Oh, I don't know. I've seen you handle lots of touchy situations since you've been assigned to me. You're an impressive negotiator, too."

"Yeah, well. I've made some mistakes."

Like kissing me? she wondered. Rather than ask and chance confirmation, Zoe let it pass. "We all make mistakes," she said. "Some more than others. Take my— take the Red Rose Killer. He had every opportunity to turn his life around and refused."

"Don't beat yourself up about it," Linc said. "The same goes for lots of criminals, including my own father. They seem oblivious to the harm they're leaving in their wake and the people they're disappointing."

"I suspect they just don't care, for the most part," Zoe suggested. "I mean, look at the two of us. We could be offered any reward on earth and it wouldn't be enough to turn us against our country."

"You're right."

"Of course, I am, as I've proved before. I've come to another conclusion, too. In spite of the possibility that the RRK has likely been on the base, I don't think my problems can be pinned on him no matter how we twist the clues. It just isn't his MO."

"Listen to you," Linc said with a low chuckle, "sounding like a professional cop."

"I get bored and watch a lot of TV after Freddy's in bed. Well? Do you agree or are you still including you-know-who among your suspects?"

"No. I'm convinced it's somebody else who has it in for you."

"What about the blood?"

"The blood that wasn't real? The shooting that didn't happen? Missing babysitting money? A car with a useless bomb?"

Zoe gasped. "What bomb?"

"I guess I forgot to tell you."

"Yeah, I guess." Arms folded across her chest, she struck a formidable looking pose. "Talk."

"Nick Donovan's bomb sniffer didn't react and the ordnance people didn't see anything under the chassis. But when they looked in the gas tank, they found a cell phone wired to what looked like a really thin pipe bomb.

According to them, there was no way the thing would have detonated after soaking in gasoline for so long."

"Hold on." Her eyebrows knit together. "What about sooner? Suppose I had ignored your warning and driven?"

"That's unknown." Linc held up a hand. "Don't get excited. Whoever put the device in your tank was a doofus when it comes to ordnance. Believe me, I've dealt with serious bomb makers, and they don't fool around with untried methods."

The darkness in his gaze and the hurt in his tone were enough to stop her from giving voice to the questions that rose in her mind. Just what kind of experience with bombs had he had? She changed the subject. "Never mind that now. What are we going to do about taking care of Freddy?"

"I thought I'd request permission to crash in my car outside your apartment building while the regular guard takes inside duty as usual."

"Oh." That solution, while logical, did not include her personal preferences. How could she express them without making Linc think she was pursuing him? Why, oh, why, had she let herself get carried away making jokes and bringing up the subject of marriage, particularly after he'd told her how he felt regarding a lifelong commitment?

Zoe's mind provided no ready answer. There was no way to go back in time and retract her faux pas. Therefore, she reasoned, the best plan for going forward was to agree with Linc's ideas and bend her will to his. His being parked outside was more sensible and far less stressful—for both of them. Zoe didn't know about Linc, but her heart beat faster the instant she dared relive even the most innocent moments of their embrace. And that fantastic kiss!

Thousands of romance novels had been written about such things. Until then, she had assumed a reaction like the one she'd had while in his arms was a figment of an author's creative imagination. Well, no more. She and Linc had ignited a forest fire, and he was trying to put it out with the equivalent of a teaspoon of water, when what they should have been doing was turning from each other and running in opposite directions as fast as they could.

Only he would never abandon his duty, would he? And there was nowhere she could go, no way she could hope to safely escape both her antagonist and the dedicated Security Forces man who was trying to protect her. She was in the air force. She went where she was told.

Besides, she admitted with a dose of self-criticism, she was not going to purposely flee from the only person who had made her feel totally secure in more years than she could count.

Forcing a smile, she slipped her thumbs into the front pockets of her jeans, struck a casual pose and said, "Whatever you decide is fine with me. C'mon. Let's go get Freddy."

In Linc's mind, he had wandered empty-handed into a swamp filled with hungry alligators. Or perhaps barefoot into a cave of venomous snakes. Whatever the inane analogy, he was up to his neck in trouble with a capital *Z* for *Zoe*.

I can't possibly have fallen for her, he told himself. That would be disastrous. Despite her joking manner, he suspected she'd been serious when she'd vowed to never remarry. That was fine with him. Wasn't it? If so, then why was his gut tying in knots every time he saw her threatened or remembered the times she'd been inches from injury?

Because I'm an idiot, he replied. What good was it to plan his career, his life, if he let a pretty face distract him from reaching his goals?

What he could do was request he be relieved of duty regarding Sergeant Sullivan altogether. The thought had briefly crossed his mind in the past but certainly not lately. No. He was going to stick it out and prove to himself that he could rise above emotion and that he was in total control, mind and body. Thankfully, rigid self-discipline would keep his actions in line. His errant thoughts were a very different story.

He'd been to church often enough to recall Scripture insisting that a wrong thought was the same as the deed. They sure didn't feel the same to Linc. And there lay the conundrum. His feelings had taken control and were running rampant, urging him to do or say something he knew would bring pain to himself and to Zoe. Linc clenched his jaw. *Not to mention Freddy.*

The little guy deserved a better father than he could ever hope to be. If Zoe didn't realize that, maybe it was time to remind her.

Linc led the way to his car, put Star into the rear and held a front door for Zoe. As she passed close by to slip into the SUV, he caught a whiff of her shampoo. She smelled like flowers. Her hair was down again, brushing against her shoulders in silky light brown waves. And those expressive eyes. He knew better than to dwell on her hazel gaze because every time he did, it became more difficult to look away.

He climbed behind the wheel and gripped it hard. Out of the corner of his right eye, he could see her peering over at him, so he said the first thing that came to mind. "Do you have all the groceries and housekeeping supplies you need? If not, we should stop at the BX before we pick up Freddy."

"I'm good. I try to stock extras so I don't have to shop too often. I hate wasting time."

"A woman who doesn't like to shop? Now, that is something for the newspapers."

"Well, you could contact Heidi Jenks."

"Not likely. There's a strong suspicion she may be our mysterious blogger. I sure don't want to feed her any more information, even accidentally, and see it turn up on everybody's computers."

"You mean like the time that blog listed the RRK's supposed romantic interests? It wasn't only the women who had already got a red rose and a warning note. There were others, too."

"I know. I visited Jolie Potter, the scientist who works in our biomedical lab. All she recalled was a few dates and Boyd dumping her because he claimed she was too smart. I also spoke to Munitions Specialist Lara Dennie. She admitted to having had a crush on him but said she'd dodged a bullet when he'd ignored her. Those women were both on a classified list that only authorized personnel should have had access to."

"Then how would Lieutenant Jenks…?"

"Unknown. Just like so many other facets of what's been going on around here." He made the turn onto the side road leading to the preschool. Not only did Zoe perk up when the building came in sight, so did Star.

Linc gave a low chuckle. "I think my K-9 is glad we're picking up her little buddy. Look at her."

"I see." Zoe's laugh carried tones of fondness for the dog that would have surprised Linc coming from anyone else. "It's a pleasure to have her around, particularly when her favorite person is Freddy."

"Whoa." Linc had to grin. "I am supposed to be the one and only person Star is interested in. I told you not to spoil her by making her too social."

"Phooey. I didn't make her anything. You and I both know she had a soft side all along. Just because she wags that stubby tail more when Freddy and I are around is no reason to blame us."

"Oh, no?"

"No." Zoe pointed to the curb. "Just pull over right here and I'll run in to get him."

"We'll come with you."

She didn't say it, but he saw the objection in her eyes and body language. She obviously did not want an escort, although why was puzzling. She had just told him she wanted him close, yet she was acting as if he'd insulted her. "What?" he asked.

Zoe was shaking her head the way a trainer did when a particularly dense canine didn't pick up instruction quickly enough. "It's perfectly safe here. You'll be in the car and your dog will alert if anything's wrong." She pushed open the passenger door and hopped out. "Stand by, Sergeant. I'll be right back."

Because he had scanned the approach and the yard already, Linc felt reasonably certain Zoe would be fine. After all, he hadn't been assigned to become her Siamese twin, he'd merely been told to keep watch and try to convince her to trust him.

Well, mission accomplished, he thought cynically. Sergeant Sullivan trusted him implicitly. Remembering that kiss, he wondered if that was more of a problem than if she had held him at arm's length.

Linc saw her climb the front steps and knock. It took several seconds for the door to open and Zoe to be admitted. Then it shut tight. Good. The women inside were properly protecting their charges. It was a shame they had to worry so much but that was better than being too lax.

Moving back and forth in the seat behind him, Star was acting anxious. "Settle down, girl. She'll be back soon."

The dog continued to fidget. When she let out one of her impressive rottweiler barks, Linc took her seriously. Just because he hadn't seen or sensed a problem didn't mean Star was wrong.

He stepped out of the SUV, fastened a lead on his K-9 partner and gave her the command to jump down. She took off so fast and pulled so hard that Linc almost lost his footing. Her nose was to the ground now, the hackles on the back of her neck and shoulders bristling. He might not know what she was after but as long as Star did, Linc was going to let her search.

They crossed a sparse lawn, rounded the preschool and made the corner, then slowed. Star froze as if she were a hunting dog, signaling a hidden pheasant. She sniffed the air. Then the bare dirt. A fenced play area stopped them from continuing right next to the building, so Linc urged his dog to backtrack. She didn't refuse, but he could tell she wasn't happy about the redirection.

A child's laughter reached them both. Star began to strain. Linc kept her controlled so she wouldn't race around to the front and flatten some poor kid with her enthusiasm, probably Freddy. "Easy, Star. Heel."

The look the K-9 gave him was so full of frustration and angst it was almost comical. She'd probably led him to the play area because she knew children had recently been out there and was disappointed when he'd pulled her away.

A female voice called, "Linc? Sergeant Colson?"

Zoe. He was about to answer when her words morphed into a scream.

With every nerve firing and every muscle taut, Linc raced back toward his vehicle. Zoe! Someone wearing a jumpsuit and a baseball cap had hold of her and was grappling for control while brave little Freddy pounded tiny fists against the man's legs.

Linc drew his gun and shouted, "Security! Hands up."

EIGHTEEN

Zoe fought for her child with all her strength, all her heart, every maternal instinct she had. Nobody was going to harm her little boy as long as she had breath in her body.

The man's hold tightened, pinning her arms so she couldn't get a good swing at him. Remembering her training, she bent lower and tried to use his own momentum to pitch him over her head. Instead, she found herself hurtling toward the ground when he suddenly released her.

Everything was happening so fast that the surrounding scene was a blur. A male shouting, a dog barking and Freddy... The moment Zoe regained her senses enough to act she reached for her beloved child. Freddy leaped into her open arms with such force he knocked her backward. Gasping, she pulled him close and showered kisses all over his tear-streaked face.

Feet wearing combat boots thundered past. "Linc?"

There was no immediate answer. It had to be him. He had not waited for her in the car the way he'd promised, yet he must have remained close by. She knew he'd never have abandoned her. Not in a million years. So where was he?

Fierce barking and growling at the side of the house was her answer. *Star!* That was the dark-colored blur she'd seen passing as she fell. The K-9 was in attack mode. Hopefully, this time Linc was there to back her up.

Freddy began struggling to free himself. "Too tight, Mama."

"I'm sorry, honey." Zoe managed to get to her feet without letting go of the boy's hand. As soon as she was certain she was stable, she scooped him up. "I was so worried about you. Why didn't you run away like we practiced?"

The child pouted. "Uh-uh. He was hurting you."

Zoe buried her face against his little neck and fought back tears. "I understand. I'm not mad, Freddy. Honest, I'm not. I know you were doing what you thought was right."

Assuming Linc had captured her attacker, Zoe was slack jawed when he and Star returned alone. The dog seemed okay this time, but Linc's beret was missing and he was rubbing the back of his head.

"Linc? Are you hurt?"

"Mostly my pride," he said gruffly. "Star had him until somebody conked me in the head and she let go to come check me."

"Is she supposed to do that?"

"No." He cast a disparaging glance at his dog. "We'll be doing some retraining ASAP." Then he turned back to Zoe. "I'm sorry we didn't apprehend the suspect. This is the most physical attack he's made on you so far."

Zoe was kneading her neck. "Yeah. Tell me about

it." She watched as Linc crouched to examine his dog, presumably checking for unseen injuries. "What's she chewing on?"

Linc commanded the K-9 to release. She placed a soggy piece of fabric in his outstretched hand. He stood and displayed it in his palm. "What does that look like to you?"

"Part of a dark blue jumpsuit like our mechanics sometimes wear."

"Exactly." Linc tucked the scrap into a plastic evidence baggie. "As chewed as this is, I doubt the lab can isolate DNA, but our next stop is going to be the airfield. I want to see who's missing a piece of his south end."

"Might Star have made him bleed?" Zoe wasn't cowed when Linc gave her a quizzical look, so she added, "I hope so."

"I see your spirit isn't harmed. That's good, because we're now searching for two assailants—the one who grabbed you just now and the person who hit me over the head from behind."

"Two?" She hadn't progressed that far in her reasoning, but now it registered. "Of course. Remember the warehouse? There were two involved there, too. A man and a woman. Maybe she's still working with him."

"Maybe." Linc gave her a lopsided smile. "Don't stress that notion in your debriefing, okay? I'll report it, but I'd just as soon the other members of my unit didn't start teasing me about being taken down by a female."

Zoe huffed. "Why not? We can swing a baseball bat as well as anybody. Stop acting so macho and admit it."

That brought a chuckle and another exploration of the knot on his head. "Granted. But in this case, she either went easy on me or didn't have a man's strength, because I don't think I have a concussion."

"Maybe she didn't intend to kill you."

"Let's hope not," Linc replied. "The last thing the base needs is another bona fide killer roaming the streets."

Zoe argued that she didn't need a visit to the ER but went along after Linc convinced her by agreeing to be checked out, as well. As soon as they were given clean bills of health, he suggested they stop at an ice-cream parlor to buy Freddy a cone.

Zoe wiped the drippings off her son's chin as she spoke. "So, what are they planning to do for a guard at my place tonight?"

"My captain is considering letting me hang around, if that's what you mean," Linc replied. "You'll still have someone else watching who is actually assigned."

"Good."

The bell over the shop door jingled and drew his attention. "Well, what do you know." He stood. "Excuse me for a second?"

"Sure. I'll wait here with Mr. Sticky."

Grinning, Linc stepped forward and saluted. "Lieutenant Webb. I thought you'd be off enjoying a well-earned vacation by now."

Ethan Webb shook Linc's hand vigorously. "So did I. My time off was delayed because my K-9 and I were needed here at Canyon." He lowered his voice. "Now there are more reports of sightings of the Red Rose Killer at Baylor Marine Base."

"More?"

"Yes." He urged Linc aside so the two friends could

speak privately. "Lieutenant Colonel Masters over at Baylor used to be my father-in-law, as you know, and he's asking for me. Insisting, really."

"Do you think Jillian is behind his request?"

Ethan's grimace at the mention of his ex-wife was fleeting yet telling. "Possibly. She's impossible to predict. I'd hoped she was done causing me trouble when she divorced me."

"Maybe she is. Her father may just be taking advantage of his high rank to bring in outside help he trusts. What I don't get is why he's poaching on our turf when he's got a base full of marines."

"I think it's because of my K-9. He wants Titus. Besides, Jillian has always got whatever Jillian wants. That's a big reason our marriage failed. I had no idea she was so spoiled when I proposed."

Glancing back at the small round table where Zoe and Freddy sat, Linc gestured. "Why don't you take a load off and join us? It's safe to talk about personal stuff in front of Zoe."

"Thanks, but I have to be going." Ethan grinned. "You finally settling down, Colson? That's a huge surprise."

"It's not what it looks like," Linc insisted. "I've been assigned to guard the sergeant and her son."

"Looks pretty cozy to me." Ethan hesitated. "Don't mention anything about Jillian, okay? Whatever Colonel Masters wants may work itself out after I've spoken to him in person. Boyd Sullivan may not actually be at Baylor right now, even if Jillian did get the customary red rose and warning note."

"Sure. No problem. How's Titus?"

"Fine," Ethan told him. "You and Star still good?"

"Absolutely. She's out in the car with the air running to keep her comfortable. We'd all be out there if she wasn't so fond of that kid—and ice cream."

The lieutenant chuckled and clapped Linc on the shoulder. "You know what they say, Colson. When in doubt, trust your K-9."

"Those two have more than won over Star. If I'm not careful, they'll turn her into a useless lap dog." He shook his friend's hand once again. "Take care. And keep your defenses up around your ex. Don't let a woman get to you."

Ethan eyed the table and smiled broadly. "Same to you, buddy."

Thankfully, Zoe hadn't run out of napkins by the time Linc returned. "All done," she said. "Time to order mine to go."

"I didn't understand why you wanted to wait to eat yours until I saw Freddy with that cone. Yuck."

"Licking drips takes practice when you're only three. So who was the officer?"

"An old friend who handles Titus, a German short-haired pointer."

"Doesn't sound like an attack breed," Zoe said.

"Titus isn't. He's been used for patrol and is a great cadaver dog. Ethan's back from combat and due for some R & R. Unfortunately, he may be sent to Baylor Marine Base because of possible sightings of..."

"Oh, brother." She made a face. "Literally. I hope your friend gets his time off soon. I'm sure he deserves it. That sounds like an awful job to train for."

"I wouldn't want it," Linc admitted. He smiled down

on her and she warmed considerably. "Now, for our ice-cream cones. What flavor for you?"

"One scoop of cherry chocolate walnut, thanks. What are you having?"

"Plain vanilla. I don't like to ruin good ice cream by loading it up with other flavors."

Freddy clapped his sticky hands. "I love 'nilla."

"You and me both, kid," Linc said with a grin before walking away. Zoe was positive she'd glimpsed a tenderness in his eyes when he'd smiled down at her son. And, truth be told, she sometimes imagined the same fond expression settling on her. Whether that was true or not, she felt good when Linc smiled at her. More than good, actually. His approval, spoken or implied, gave her spirits a boost like the afterburner on a jet. Being around him was so wonderful, so sweet, so...

"Fool," Zoe muttered to herself, pulling a face. She was doing it again. Kidding herself by imagining a happy future with the wrong man.

But was he wrong? Never mind his insistence that he intended to stay single. What if he was considering changing his mind? What if he was starting to feel as much affection toward her as she was feeling for him?

"That'll be the day," she mumbled, using a glass of water to dampen a fresh napkin and wipe Freddy's hands some more.

The deep voice behind her made her jump so badly she nearly tipped over the glass. "What will be the day?"

Linc was back with their cones. In a flash, Zoe tried to recall how much she had actually uttered aloud and how much had been silent thought. She looked up to study him. Since he didn't seem upset, she figured she was safe.

"Um, when my son can eat without taking a bath in it."

"He does pretty well on pizza."

"Only because I cut it up for him." She reached for her treat. "Is this mine?"

"Yup. And this is mine." As he began to lick the cone, Zoe decided it was best if she looked away. Everything Linc did, every word he spoke, every shadow of a smile he displayed sent her heart racing and made her hands tremble. Had he asked what was bothering her, she intended to blame her unrest on her stalker. That would be partially true. But it wasn't an adversary who had her nerves in knots and filled her stomach with butterflies. It was her new friend. Her protector. The one man she had finally decided wasn't half bad.

That conclusion made her grin. Rather than giggle, she started to eat. The ice cream was delicious. "Mmm."

"Glad you like it," Linc said. "For a minute there, you looked so strange I was afraid I'd got the wrong flavor."

Zoe hid behind the cone and bided her time by systematically licking all the way around. "No problem. It's wonderful."

What drew her attention back to Linc was not his words or actions; it was the lack of either. Instead of continuing to eat, he had stopped and was staring across the table at her. There was the tender look again. She wasn't imagining it. She couldn't be. He wasn't smiling. He wasn't frowning. But his concentration was so complete, so absolute, she almost shivered.

"Yeah," he finally said, continuing to have eyes only for her, while patrons of the ice-cream parlor came and went past their table and Freddy slapped his hands on it as if playing a drum.

Zoe held her breath, hoping against hope that Linc was ready to express his personal feelings, to perhaps say something romantic. Judging by his fond expression, it was certainly a possibility.

She was left guessing what he had meant when he stared into her wide eyes, smiled and quietly said, "Wonderful."

If they had not been surrounded by a crowd and accompanied by her lovable but nosy child, she might have asked for clarification.

Oh, sure, and have Linc tell me he was talking about the ice cream? No way. There was no reason to chance making a fool of herself. There would be plenty of time to stick her foot in her mouth again, as she had when she'd mentioned marriage and scared him silly. After all, they hadn't even dated, let alone admitted serious intentions.

Except that we've already spent more hours together than some couples have managed after months of dating, particularly those in the military, she added to herself. It was possible to fall in love, even when a significant other was stationed half a world away, wasn't it?

Suppose that was Linc's problem? Suppose the beautiful woman who he'd admitted had betrayed him still held a place in his heart? Could his reticence be caused by that? Did Zoe have a rival who had achieved special status merely because she was unattainable?

Further thought led her to decide against that theory. Linc was a patriot, a straight shooter, an honorable man who would never be able to forgive someone who had betrayed his comrades-in-arms and threatened the well-being of his homeland.

That thought led her directly to John Flint. She

had revealed his treason as soon as she'd learned of it. Was that enough for Linc to see her as the red-blooded American that she was? Or did he paint her with the same brush of evil that some of her fellow airmen had?

Chagrined, Zoe almost wished Linc's hang-up, if he had one, would be her first marriage, because that was over. John Flint was no more. Her familial connection to her brother, however, would never go away, and she wondered if her reputation would always be tied to his, however tenuously.

Deciding to redirect her own thoughts and Linc's, Zoe asked a question she thought was fairly innocuous. "What's the latest on that pesky blogger? Any success finding him?"

Her companion's negative expression surprised her. She frowned. "What are you not telling me?"

Linc shook his head. "Not important."

"It is if it bothers you," she countered.

"I take it you haven't looked." Using his phone to open to the web, Linc passed it to her. "See for yourself."

Zoe peered at the small screen. "This blames everything Boyd did on me. How dare they!"

"Doesn't matter. We know you're innocent."

"We? You and I, maybe, but not the rest of the base." She passed the phone back to Linc. "I've seen enough."

"Okay. Sorry, but you did ask." Zoe saw him briefly glance at the screen before raising it to read more carefully.

"What's the matter? More accusations?"

"Not exactly. I paged down, hoping someone would defend you, and look what I found."

She leaned closer to read with him, head to head, and almost gasped. Someone had posted a rebuttal, all right. It read "Leave Baby Sister alone. Or else."

NINETEEN

By the time he had contacted headquarters and reported what he'd seen on the anonymous blog, Linc was fighting a terrible headache, probably partially due to his injury. He hadn't intended to tell Zoe he felt ill, but she must have sensed something off about him.

"Are you sure you're okay?" she asked for the third time when they got to her apartment.

"I told you I'm fine." The rebuttal came out stronger than he had wanted. "Sorry."

"See? That's what I mean. You're not acting like your normal self."

Arching a brow, he immediately regretted it because the pain intensified and he winced. "Oh, yeah?"

"Yeah." She came back from her kitchen with a glass of water and painkillers. "I'm not giving you aspirin in case your head damage is worse than the doctors thought. Take these and maybe your mood will improve."

Reluctantly, he did. "Thanks. I do have a slight headache."

"It's more than slight, but I won't argue as long as you take care of yourself."

Nodding carefully, Linc got to his feet. Star stirred, lifted her head, then relaxed again and closed her eyes as if planning to spend the night.

"I probably should go," Linc said.

"Not on your life." Zoe was adamant. "Your relief is already parked out front. You're staying right here with me and Freddy so I can watch you for signs of a serious head injury."

"You're a doctor now?"

"Nope. A mother. We come with built-in sensitivity training. One look at you and I knew you felt rotten."

"I should be out looking for the RRK, not resting."

"Look." Facing him, Zoe placed a hand on his forearm. "I feel responsible for what happened to your head. And for what happened to Star the time before. You won't gain anything by chasing a mystery blogger's invisible fan in the middle of the night, even if he did sound like the RRK. Star can stay right where she is, and I've promised Freddy he can bring his blanket and pillow in here to camp out with the two of you. He's gone to pick out a stuffed animal to share with Star, too."

"Suppose there's a problem during the night?"

"With Security Forces visible outside and Star in here, I strongly doubt anybody will try anything. But I can tell Freddy that if the dog barks or growls, he has to come get me right away. He loves to have important jobs, so I'm sure he'll follow orders."

"Maybe I will rest here for a little while," Linc said. He sank onto the overstuffed sofa and laid his head back. "I am feeling pretty lousy."

"You may be hungry. All we had this afternoon was

ice cream and cold pizza. How would you like some soup? I have vegetable and chicken noodle."

Freddy skipped into the room, his pudgy arms loaded with stuffed animals. "I love chicken noodle."

"Okay," Zoe said. "You guys make yourselves comfortable and I'll go open a can."

"Make sure the back door is locked," Linc called after her. He didn't hear a clear reply, but her tone was enough for him to tell she wasn't impressed with his suggestion. That was okay. He knew she'd already checked all the locks and was perfectly capable of taking care of such details. Habit and her enemy's efforts at making her look unstable had spurred him to speak up.

Freddy was standing at his feet, apparently waiting for an invitation to join him, so Linc patted the adjoining sofa cushion. "C'mon up, kid. And bring your friends."

Scrambling up with a small assist from Linc, the boy dumped his armload of toys in a cascade of synthetic fur.

Linc smiled. "Who all have we got here?"

"That's puppy one." He chose another. "This is puppy two."

Linc picked up a similar toy. "Is this puppy three?"

Freddy giggled. "No, Sergeant Linc. That's a kitty."

"Oh, sorry. My mistake."

"You can have her to sleep with if you want," Freddy offered. "She's a really good kitty. My favorite."

"Thank you." Linc couldn't help his growing smile. Freddy had not only presented him with a stuffed animal, he'd given his best. "That's very nice of you."

"You're welcome. I like you."

He ruffled the child's soft hair. "I like you, too."

"You like my mama?"

"Sure."

Apparently satisfied, the boy wiggled around, pushing aside toys, until he was snuggled tight against Linc's side and partially tucked beneath his arm. Then he yawned so loudly Star looked up to check on them.

"You go to sleep," Linc said. "I'm tired, too."

"Uh-huh. 'Night."

Leaning over slightly, despite the throbbing in his temples, Linc placed a kiss on the top of Freddy's head. "Good night, buddy."

When the boy snuggled even closer, laid a small arm part way across his ribs and whispered, "I love you," Linc was stunned. All his life he'd believed he disliked children, yet this one had punched a Texas-size hole in his opinion—and in his heart.

Leaning his head back again, Linc replied softly, "I love you, too, Freddy."

Zoe heated the soup then peeked in to ask Freddy and Linc if they wanted theirs in bowls at the table or in mugs they could sip from on the sofa. But she found them asleep. So was Star, who was snoring loudly.

Hesitant to disturb them, she gazed fondly at the scene of familial bliss. The only thing missing was her. In Zoe's eyes, she belonged on the opposite side of Linc, also snuggled close, to share in the perfect peace and trust her son was enjoying.

Instead, she returned to the kitchen and took the pot of soup off the stove. It would keep. So would her unacceptable dreams and wishes. Even if Linc did seem to be showing affection toward Freddy, she had to assume that feeling didn't extend to her. She was a job, a duty and an often-unpleasant one. If Linc and his fellow Security Forces members weren't after Boyd, they were chasing other bad guys, which had made her formerly stable life the subject of their ongoing investigations. Of course, Linc was here. Like the security team parked out in the street, he was actually working. And so was Star.

Zoe plopped down in a kitchen chair, elbows on the table, head in her hands, and let her mind drift like a plane in a holding pattern—until it touched down on solid ground and came to a screeching halt. What was that noise? Was Freddy ready to be put to bed? Had Linc stirred because he was unwell?

Rising as silently as possible, she tiptoed to the doorway to check on her guests. Star was the only one paying attention. Her head was raised, her ears forward, her nostrils twitching, seeking information available only to her keen canine senses.

Zoe was now certain that the sound she'd heard hadn't come from any of them. So what had disturbed her? She turned. Started back to the table. And spotted a piece of folded paper lying on the floor just inside her back door.

Eyes wide, she froze. How had someone bypassed the guard outside and got this close? Zoe stared at the note as if it were an angry Texas diamondback poised to strike. It may as well have been, given the effect it was having on her.

Trembling, she studied the double-locked door. Everything was intact. No one had tried to get in. But they had made it far enough to shake her world to its foundation.

She took a step closer and started to bend and reach

for the piece of paper. But she stopped and made the kind of judgment a prey animal makes. The door was solid enough to deter rapid entry but probably not thick enough to stop a bullet. Maybe whoever had left that paper was still out there, gun aimed and hammer cocked, waiting for her to make a noise that would tell them it was time to act. To fire.

Trying to slow her rapid breathing, Zoe thought about grabbing a broom to retrieve the note by dragging it to her. Instead, she crouched and duckwalked out of the kitchen, not straightening until she was almost to the sofa. A light touch on Linc's arm brought him instantly awake and ready for battle.

"It's just me," she said, hands raised to deflect any instinctive efforts at self-defense.

"What's the matter?" He was scrubbing one hand over his face while the other palm rested on his sidearm.

"A note," Zoe whispered. "Somebody just shoved it under the back door and I didn't know what to do."

Linc immediately radioed the situation to the guard stationed outside, then commanded Star to watch the boy and made his way to the kitchen with Zoe.

She pointed. "There. See?"

The paper crackled when Linc picked it up. They heard movement on the deck. A board creaked. Something slid across the wood. A boot? A step?

Linc drew his gun. Frozen in place, they waited and listened for more.

A sharp knock and an all-clear call from the other guard came in seconds. It was only then that Zoe realized she'd been holding her breath.

TWENTY

Linc unfolded the note, holding it by the outer corners to preserve prints or other trace evidence. He actually considered keeping its contents from Zoe but decided she'd be safer if he kept her in the loop. He cleared his throat. "Somebody wants to meet with you tonight at the airfield."

"Who? Why?"

Nothing convinced him the single letter *B* signature was genuine or significant, so he said, "Doesn't matter. You're not going."

"Suppose it's my stalker. Or better yet, the RRK. You could set a trap and this would all be over."

"That's unacceptable."

"To you, maybe. Check with your superiors. They might have a different opinion. I'm not some clueless civilian. I'm air force, too, you know."

He pulled out his cell phone and photographed the note, then dialed Captain Blackwood's private number. "Colson here. I've just emailed you a note that was left at the Sullivan apartment, and I suggest our teams rendezvous at the airfield. Somebody is trying to lure

Sergeant Sullivan out there and is telling her to come at 2200 hours."

"I see that. And I concur. Can she find a babysitter at this late hour?"

"She doesn't need to go," Linc countered.

"I think she does. We'll keep a close eye on her, but without her presence on scene, we'll have a slim chance of drawing out her stalker—or anybody else."

"But, sir—"

"No buts. I got the lab report on that piece of cloth your dog bit off at the day care. It came from a pair of Jim Ahern's coveralls. I was going to arrange to pick him up for questioning in the morning, but since this situation has come up, we may as well move in now."

"You think he's the one who sent this note?" Linc felt tension knotting his muscles.

"Who else could it be?"

"You got word about the blog posting, right?"

Blackwood huffed. "I did. It means nothing. Anybody could have written it, just like anybody could have signed your note with a *B*."

"You don't think it was Boyd Sullivan, then?"

"Not if he's as savvy as we think. Report to headquarters as soon as you find someone to watch the boy, or bring him with you if you can't. We'll assign an on-duty airman to babysit for as long as it takes to complete this operation."

"Yes, sir." Linc looked to Zoe and set his jaw. "Get your ABU and boots on. You're going with me."

Until Zoe was assured Freddy would be well cared for and fully protected by Security Forces, she was un-cooperative. She didn't care how hard to handle she was; nobody was going to harm her little boy. Not on her watch.

They ended up placing Freddy within the K-9 unit, where he happily fell back to sleep in the company of a cuddly half-grown pup and a couple of armed night watchmen.

Linc handed her a Kevlar vest. "Put this on."

"Do you really think I'll need combat armor?"

"I'd rather you had it, okay? I let you come tonight, so humor me."

Zoe laughed. "*You* let me? Ha! I heard you talking to your captain. The only reason I'm here is for bait."

"Assistance."

"Okay, call it what you will. You know I volunteered to help regardless, so let's get this show on the road."

She allowed Linc to guide her as far as the exit, then struck out for his SUV on her own. Nobody was going to have reason to claim she was being coerced. Not if she had any say about it. Nor were they going to get away with staking her out like a hunk of dinner on a hungry tiger's jungle trail. She was in this up to her eyeballs and intended to participate to the best of her ability just as she did with every task she was assigned.

Yes, she was nervous. And, yes, she realized she was putting herself in harm's way. But as long as she was close to Linc Colson and Star, she felt safe enough to hold it together. If she'd been in the navy, she'd have called him her anchor.

The CAFB airfield was so well lit there wasn't a lot of difference between night and day except for swirling clouds of orange dust that dimmed the beams cast by overhead vapor lights. Captain Blackwood's attack plan had placed hidden forces in two concentric circles with Linc and Star taking point. Zoe was ordered to wait in his vehicle, out of the substantial wind, until called for.

Linc realized he was fighting more than one battle and struggled to concentrate on the task at hand while his heart and mind remained with Zoe. How could she purposely endanger herself like this? She'd seemed so sensible, so clever to begin with.

The only thing that helped him cope was knowing that Captain Blackwood had already sent men to take Jim Ahern into custody at his home. Once they reported success, there would be far less to worry about. That was good, because right now Linc was pretty distracted despite his vow to remain totally professional.

"Which increases the danger, because I'm not thinking straight," he murmured. That was bad. If he did nothing more tonight, he must somehow set aside his angst before it got him, or somebody else, killed.

Allowing himself one quick glance at Zoe through the car windows, he gave her a thumbs-up sign.

"Colson in position," Linc radioed his teammates, keeping his back to the prevailing wind so it wouldn't blow directly into the mic and distort communications.

Blackwood's voice was strong and sure. "Stay alert. Ahern was not at home, so he's probably here. Be careful. We want him alive."

"Affirmative."

With Star on a short leash, Linc started to work his way toward the base of the control tower where the note had instructed Zoe to meet.

Merely thinking her name made his gut knot and his palms sweat. A long, slow blink and a sigh were meant to clear his mind and sharpen his wits.

Star paused in her stride just enough to alert him. Before he could react, the snap, whine and echo of a rifle shot sliced the night air. Linc felt the disturbance near his ear and knew he had just been shot at. And missed. Barely.

He hit the tarmac with his shoulder and rolled, ending in a crouch and scrambling for cover behind a maintenance truck, Star at his side.

He heard Blackwood in his radio and replied, "No, Captain. I wasn't hit. Did anybody see where the shot came from?"

"Negative, Colson. Hold your position."

"Yes, sir." Linc kept Star close. He didn't intend to survive combat with his K-9 and then let some idiot with a rifle take them out on their home turf. "No wonder they couldn't find Ahern at his quarters. He's here."

Blackwood's reply was unsettling at the very least. "He's here, all right, but that wasn't him shooting at you. We caught him selling marijuana in one of the hangars. He's been in custody for several minutes."

"Really? Maybe it's the woman we suspected of knocking me over the head behind the preschool."

"Or Sullivan is back."

Linc's throat threatened to close. "Is that possible? I thought he was spotted at Baylor."

"He's been seen a lot of places, but nobody has proved any of it. Just keep your eyes open and your head down."

"Yes, sir. Has anybody got Ahern to talk?"

"Negative. He still denies involvement in the stalking incidents," Blackwood answered.

"Copy." Despite the wind that swirled dirt and sand around him, Linc was able to see enough of the runways and tower to feel fairly secure where he was. Security Forces had the tower surrounded and the controllers secured, hopefully trapping the shooter inside their temporary perimeter with no opportunity to foul up landings and takeoffs. Now, they'd rely on the dust to mask their possible approach and wait for orders to close the net.

Star's ears perked up. Sensing danger, Linc started to stand. Another rifle shot sounded and he ducked back, only to realize the shooter had not aimed for him this time. Zoe was his target! And there was a hole punched through the windshield right where she had been sitting.

Zoe slipped out of Linc's damaged vehicle and lowered herself onto the tarmac, staying behind the open door as much as possible. "Father, please protect the good guys, especially Linc. Please."

Boots and camo-covered legs appeared beside her. She recognized Ethan Webb when he asked, "You hit?"

"No." Good thing she'd been hunched down in the seat. "Is Linc okay?"

"Yeah." Ethan's rifle was held at the ready, his gaze moving over the surrounding area while he radioed a report of her condition.

"It has to be my stalker who's shooting," Zoe said. "I told Linc I wanted to go meet him face-to-face, so we could avoid this kind of thing."

"Might not have mattered in the long run. We already took Ahern into custody."

"Then who just shot at me?"

"No idea." He frowned at her. "You have a little boy, Sergeant. Why are you out here risking your life?"

"Captain Blackwood wanted me here," she said without hesitation. "But I expected to take a more active role."

Zoe saw the lieutenant rise to one knee and assume a defensive pose, rifle ready, as someone else approached.

Nobody had to tell Zoe who it was. She could sense Linc was coming just as well as his K-9 sensed trouble.

Linc had stayed low, taking evasive action while moving toward better shelter. His fear was magnified by concern for Zoe and he demonstrated it clearly when he darted behind the SUV to join her and Ethan.

Ignoring the other man, he glared at Zoe. "I thought I told you to stay put."

"I did—until somebody punched a hole through the window."

Ethan Webb interrupted. "You two can argue later when all this is over. Right now, we have other concerns." He was scowling, and Linc realized he was right.

"Sorry, Lieutenant. Any word on who's doing the shooting?"

"Apparently whoever was working with Ahern. We have people closing in."

"Copy that." Linc quieted to listen to his radio. "Sounds like we have a woman in custody. They're requesting backup."

Ethan nodded. "You have the attack dog, Colson, so you take it. I'll go report to Captain Blackwood."

Linc saluted. "Yes, sir."

Frowning, angry and so frustrated he wanted to shout at everything and nothing, Linc turned to Zoe. "Get in the vehicle, lock the doors and keep your head down. I'll be back ASAP."

Her "Yes, Sergeant" did not sound particularly amiable, but he was willing to settle for any kind of compliance that would guarantee her safety.

Waiting for her to climb into the SUV and follow his orders, he was satisfied. There had been no more shooting and his fellow team members were getting the situation in hand. Even if Ahern wouldn't talk, Linc hoped his cohort would.

Broken-field running took Linc and Star to Westley James and his K-9, Dakota, where they stood with other Security Forces members. Sure enough, they had nabbed a woman dressed in all black. Linc recognized her, helped by her red hair. "That's Anne McNally."

"Who?" the sergeant asked.

"The airman who was offered to assist me in a computer search. Zoe was suspicious, but I put off checking because McNally had been spoken for by Captain Blackwood." He confronted the handcuffed woman. "How long have you and Ahern been working together?"

All she did was laugh. "Get real. Do you think I'm so desperate I'd need to sink to his level to get a date?"

"It's too late to try to divert suspicion," Linc said. "He's already been arrested."

McNally shrugged. "Why should I care?"

Linc clenched his fists. He looked to Westley. "What about it, Sarge? What do you think?"

"I'm not sure. We caught her hiding over there with a handheld radio but didn't see a rifle."

"It's around. We'll find it."

"What about your suspicions regarding Boyd Sullivan?" Sergeant James asked. "What's up with him?"

"All I know is that he or someone posing as him posted a response on the anonymous blog, and Zoe got a note signed with the letter *B*. I suppose it could be Boyd, but if it is, he's getting sloppy."

"I agree."

Still on alert, Linc checked their surroundings and perceived no threat. "Do you want me to deliver her to the captain or will you do the honors?"

"You take her," Sergeant James said. "Dakota and I were assigned this quadrant, so I'll stay at my post."

Linc nodded, grabbed the red-haired woman's arm and pulled her to her feet. She smelled of liquor. "Get moving."

Anne gave an annoying giggle and threw herself against Linc's chest as if accidentally losing her balance. "Oops. You mean you aren't going to pitch me over your shoulder and carry me?" Her speech slurred. "What a pity. I was looking forward to a little macho action."

Linc righted her and held her away as they walked. "I'd sooner kiss a rattlesnake."

No matter how hard Zoe peered into the dust-clouded night she couldn't see far enough to observe Linc. That was not only frustrating to her but it set her nerves on edge even more. Darkness didn't frighten her. Neither did being alone. There was just something comforting about being able to see Linc—and Star. And something unexplainably unsettling when she couldn't.

She shivered. The wind's velocity seemed to be picking up, as if the very weather sensed her unrest. That was ridiculous, of course, but it wasn't too far-fetched to think that she might be tuning in to the turbulent atmosphere outside the SUV.

Bursts of sand and pebbles peppered the windows. Zoe cringed, thankful that the bullet had struck the windshield. Its laminated construction kept the glass in one piece, although there was a pea-size hole just off center with spiderweb-looking lines radiating from it like a sunburst.

She fixated on that damage, realizing how close she had come to being killed, and whispered, "Thank You, Jesus."

Her seat seemed to vibrate as gusts rocked the vehicle. Zoe closed her eyes and said an ongoing prayer of thanksgiving, adding pleas for the safety of everyone involved. To her surprise, she even found herself mentioning her nefarious brother. He had caused so much trouble, so much pain, yet she still recalled their childhood and the protective older sibling he had been then, despite his unruly nature. There had to be some good in him. There simply had to be.

Suddenly, the window beside her head shattered into a million pieces, the tiny shards covering her like the blowing Texas sand. Instinct made her cover her face.

Not prone to screaming when startled, Zoe hesitated long enough to feel herself being grabbed and pulled through the opening of the now-missing side window. Stretching her arm and shoulder sent sharp pain all the way down her spine and her ribs banged against the window's lower edge.

That was enough impetus to set her off. She took the deepest breath she could and let loose with a yowl that would have done the scream queen of a scary movie proud. The assailant pulled her into a bear hug and cut off the screech.

Everything was happening so fast that Zoe couldn't tell who had hold of her or what he was planning, but she did know one thing—anyone who would cause this kind of pain was capable of almost anything.

The wind whipped her hair across her face and sand stung her exposed skin, but that was nothing compared to the severe way she was being held, arms pinned at her sides, hot breath so close to her face that she couldn't turn her head.

Tears blurred her vision. Unable to free a hand to rub her eyes, she blinked rapidly and tried to focus. "Let me go."

His response sent chills up her spine. He laughed and the sound was pure evil.

Through her fear, she heard something familiar. She recognized that voice. Michael Orleck. Her washed-out student. He was behind all the assaults and stalking?

"You!" Zoe gasped.

Orleck laughed again. "Took you long enough. I figured you'd be deemed unfit and drummed out of the air force a lot sooner than this. You're a disappointment, *Teacher.*"

"*That's* why you've been making my life miserable? I thought you were happy repairing planes."

"That's what I wanted everybody to think." He kept hold of one of her arms and with his other hand he reached for the rifle that had been slung across his back. "You ruined my life. I figured it was only fair to return the favor."

"You're crazy."

"Maybe. But I'm not the one calling security day after day because I'm imagining prowlers and dirty tricks and outright attacks. I'm also not the one being blamed for letting a serial killer sneak onto the base and murder innocent airmen."

"That's not true, and you know it."

"I don't know anything of the kind, Teacher. Have you read the base blog lately?"

"That was you?"

"I made a few comments, yes."

Stalling for time and hoping that someone would notice her plight and send help, Zoe kept him talking. "How did you know?"

"Know what?"

"To call me Baby Sister."

"Ah, that."

He hesitated just long enough to cause her to wonder if Boyd might actually have posted the cryptic warning.

"I worked with an old buddy of your brother's, you know. I heard things."

She tried to free her arm, but his vise grip tightened instead. "You're hurting me."

"Tough. You think you're so smart, so perfect. Well, I've outsmarted you and that cop boyfriend of yours. Now I'm going to fix you for good and blame it on your crazy brother."

She made a monumental effort to escape, kicking at him and throwing her weight in the opposite direction. Thanks to her self-defense training, she managed to loosen his grip on her arm. But only for a second.

Recovering and lunging, Orleck clamped both hands around her throat. He grimaced and tightened the stranglehold. She wanted to scream again, to call out to Linc, but she couldn't get enough air.

Zoe felt herself losing consciousness. Would help arrive in time? She managed to choke out a raspy "Jesus, help me," before the attacker cut off the last of her air.

TWENTY-ONE

Star alerted, her focus on where Linc had left Zoe, shortly after he'd delivered McNally to Blackwood.

Linc noticed and tensed. "Captain?"

"Yes?"

"Star's acting strange. Permission to return to Sergeant Sullivan?"

"Permission granted. As soon as we locate the missing weapon and make sure this incident is over, we'll wrap up and head back."

"Yes, sir."

Whirling, Linc loosened the lead to give his dog plenty of slack. She took it immediately, straining and beginning to bark. He followed at a run until they were within sight of the SUV. Two figures stood beside it, blurred by shadows and the swirling dust. It looked as if they were struggling.

His gut told him the same thing his K-9 had been insisting: Zoe was in trouble. If he charged into the fray as his heart kept insisting, there was a strong possibility she'd end up being harmed. However, if he trusted his K-9's judgment, the chances of successfully capturing her assailant were much better. Star knew Zoe. She wouldn't make a mistake when choosing between good and evil. She'd bite the bad guy.

He reeled Star in and unclipped her leash, keeping hold of her collar and peering at the altercation still taking place. It was now or never. Simultaneously letting go of her collar, he shouted, "Get 'em," and began to run.

Barking ferociously, Star quickly outpaced him and rounded the parked truck. He heard a human shout coupled with intense growling.

"Good girl. Hold 'em," Linc yelled, knowing Star was biting her target.

When Linc slid to a stop at the other side of the truck, Star had Michael Orleck's forearm in her teeth. The K-9 was being lifted off the ground as her quarry screamed and struggled to shake her off, but she held firm.

What about Zoe? Linc spotted her and reached out, barely in time to catch her before she collapsed. He wrapped his arms around her, her head falling back over his arm, and he silently prayed he hadn't been too late.

Had he lost his love before he'd had a chance to admit how he felt about her—and Freddy?

Finally, she drew a shuddering breath. Then another. Tears filled his eyes and gratitude his heart. This time, God had heard him. This time, the answer was clear.

It took Linc several more moments to realize that Star had moved from the arm to the seat of the mechanic's coveralls. Pieces of the puzzle started to fall into place. Things Anne McNally had said made sense now. She had been helping Orleck, not Ahern, and chances were good that the crime lab would find DNA from both men on the scrap of fabric Star had torn away from the older mechanic's stolen coveralls.

Linc looked down at Zoe and his hand touched her cheek, just as Captain Blackwood drew up next to him.

"She needs to go to the ER."

"I know, Captain. She's started breathing again, but she should be checked out."

"What happened?"

"Orleck was choking her. Star is holding him for us."

The captain looked as though he wanted to grin. "I see. Better give your dog the release command before she tears the jumpsuit off him. We'll take over. You get the sergeant to our standby ambulance. I'll check in with you at the hospital."

Zoe stirred in Linc's arms, and he pulled her across his chest in a more comfortable carrying position. He rained kisses on her hair and let his tears of absolute relief slide silently down his cheeks as he carried her toward the waiting ambulance.

Zoe opened her eyes and struggled to speak. Her throat was so tight, the muscles in her neck and shoulders so sore that she failed. This wasn't a dream. Linc was carrying her. He'd come in time. Praise the Lord! She didn't know how close she'd come to dying but had a sense it had been imminent.

There was something important she needed to tell him. She tried to raise her head. When he looked down at her, he was smiling. And his eyes were glistening. She had to speak. To tell him about Orleck.

"It was…"

Instead of listening, Linc gently kissed her.

"No, no." She managed a weak shake of her head.

"I'm sorry. I wasn't going to do that until I could ask

first. I'm so happy you're going to be okay. I slipped up." He sobered. "Won't happen again."

"No." This time there was an underlying sob in her voice. Her palm rested on his chest, and she could feel the pounding of his heart. His dear heart. "I...tell... you..."

"Ah." Linc seemed to understand because his tender expression returned. "You want to tell me who the real stalker was."

"Uh-huh."

"It's okay, honey. We got him. Or Star did. Didn't you see and hear her attacking? She was amazing."

A sense of relief beyond anything she'd ever imagined bathed Zoe in calm as Linc held her close and strode across the tarmac, carrying her as if she didn't weigh an ounce. "Star is okay?"

"She's fine," he assured her, as he placed her on a gurney near the rear of an ambulance.

While medics checked her vital signs, he held her hand. "Don't try to talk anymore now. There'll be plenty of time after you've recovered."

"I didn't get out, honest." Her throat burned, yet she tried to continue explaining. "He pulled me through the window and—"

Linc gently placed two fingers over her mouth, following the movement of the gurney as the medics rolled it.

"You riding along, Sarge?" one of the medics asked.

"Me and the dog," Linc said flatly. Star had rejoined him at his side. "Your patient is an important witness and I need to debrief her ASAP." He leaned over the gurney and whispered into Zoe's ear, "I also need to kiss her again, if she ever stops talking long enough."

Smiling through the tears and lingering pain, Zoe went silent, then pointed to her closed mouth.

This time, she didn't get the simple token of affection she'd expected. Linc's kiss was so perfect, so wondrous, so filled with love she was overcome. Closing her eyes, she returned his feelings completely, committing her heart without another word. Never in her whole life, including the time she'd been married, had she been so moved, so emotionally connected to anyone.

Her arms encircled his neck, holding him close, until he gently unwound them and eased away. Zoe looked up and saw him smile. Sensed the depth of his sincerity when he whispered, "I love you."

"I love you, too."

Linc was kicked back in a sickly green plastic-covered hospital chair next to Zoe's bed, Star at his feet, when his captain entered the curtained cubicle.

Linc started to rise. Blackwood waved him back down. "As you were."

"Did he confess?" Linc saw Captain Blackwood's gaze shift to Zoe. She was hooked up to oxygen via a nasal cannula, so her face was visible.

"Yes, Orleck admitted everything."

Linc heard Zoe sigh with relief. "That's good," he said to the captain, reaching for Zoe's hand and giving it an affectionate squeeze. "What about Ahern?"

"Apparently innocent, at least of bothering Sergeant Sullivan. He may be a drug peddler but he isn't a stalker."

"Orleck admitted it all? Even how he managed to set up the warehouse fiasco?"

"Yes." Blackwood turned to Zoe. "He and McNally

had been following you, hoping to stage their fake shooting where you'd be the only one to see it so they could make you look crazy. Ducking into that warehouse provided a perfect staging area."

"What about the fake blood?" Linc asked.

"He used a squib, same as they do in the movies. The mess was contained by her shirt."

Linc was frowning. "What was his reasoning for going to all that trouble?"

"He wanted everybody to believe Zoe was mentally unbalanced and should be relieved of duty," Blackwood explained. "They used that same fake blood stuff in her bedroom, just like the lab reported."

Linc felt Zoe's fingers tighten around his and squeezed back for moral support. "How about access? How did he get into her apartment?"

"Airman McNally handled master keys in the course of her duty, so that was all he needed. He admitted to entering the apartment multiple times, including hiding while Portia babysat. I'm glad he stayed out of sight until she left."

Zoe found her voice then. "That was him?"

"Yes," Blackwood said flatly. "Some of the other things he tried may not have come to light yet, but he swears his intentions weren't lethal—until tonight." He stepped closer to Zoe. "You can go home whenever you're ready. Your duty schedule is being adjusted to give you several more weeks off with pay, so you can recuperate."

Her "Thank you, sir" was hoarse, raspy and sounded very emotional. "If they keep me here, I'll need someone to watch Freddy."

"I can help do that," Linc said. "And we can always

let him go back to his regular schedule if I need to work."

"I can't ask you to do that," Zoe insisted. Trying to speak louder brought on a coughing fit. Linc got to his feet and handed her a glass of ice water. Their hands didn't just brush in passing as he kept hold of the plastic tumbler and she cupped her fingers over his.

Justin Blackwood cleared his throat. "Yes, well, I can see it's high time I gave you two some privacy. Take care of yourself, Sergeant Sullivan. Your life should quiet down now."

Linc waited until the curtains closed behind his commanding officer before settling a hip on the side of the narrow cot. He set the water tumbler aside and grasped both of Zoe's hands. "I know how you can feel even safer. Freddy, too."

"Oh? Do you plan to bring Star and crash on my sofa for the rest of my life?"

"Something like that." He paused, blaming the tightness in his own throat on empathy for her. "I—I thought you might like to get married."

Zoe gasped. "Married?"

"Uh-huh. You know the drill. White dress, church, flowers, the whole nine yards."

"You want to marry *me*?"

He grinned at her, wondering if she was truly as shocked as she pretended to be. "Yeah. I'm as surprised as you are. It kind of sneaked up on me."

Zoe's eyes glistened. "What did?"

"Love. I fought against my feelings for you as long as I could, but when I heard that shot and saw it hit right where I thought you were sitting, I had to admit how deeply I cared. I love everything about you."

"Including my son?"

"Especially him." Linc raised their joined hands and kissed hers. "I know this is sudden, and you're not deathly afraid of the Red Rose Killer the way other people are, but I'd still like the chance to stay close to you, to protect and look after you and Freddy."

"Only if you stop seeing me as a needy victim and take me as a life partner," Zoe whispered. "I don't want to be an extension of your job. I want to be your wife."

"You do?"

"Yes. I do. I don't know how long I've been in love with you, but I knew we were right for each other even before I admitted it to myself."

"When do you want to schedule the wedding?" Linc asked, assuming she would put him off for a reasonable amount of time rather than rush into anything as important as marriage.

"I had the lacy white gown once," she said tenderly. "If we wear our dress uniforms, we can get Pastor Harmon to make it official in his church office as soon as possible."

"You don't want time to plan a big party?"

"Those are mostly for friends and family. I don't need that," Zoe said, giving Linc a smile that melted his heart. "Star can be my maid of honor and a member of Security Forces can be your best man. We can get Felicity to take pictures, too. She and Westley married quickly, so I'm sure she'd be delighted to help us do the same."

Linc had to laugh. "I've just proposed and already you have the whole ceremony planned."

"It pays to be organized," she replied, freeing her

hands from his and opening her arms. "How about a kiss to seal the bargain?"

"How about more than one?"

"Works for me," Zoe said, blushing.

Linc was more than happy to oblige.

EPILOGUE

Ethan Webb barged into Pastor Harmon's office in time to watch Linc bend Zoe backward over his arm like an iconic photo and kiss his bride with gusto.

Zoe blushed, Freddy giggled and applauded, Star barked and others in the small intimate gathering laughed. Linc righted her, grinning at the lieutenant. "You missed it, Ethan."

"I caught the best part. My apologies to both of you. I was stuck on the phone with my former father-in-law. Looks like my K-9 and I are going to be loaned to Baylor Marine Base after all."

"That's tough," Linc said. "I probably shouldn't mention exes at my own wedding, but I hope yours doesn't drive you crazy while you're over there."

"Not a chance. I'll be assigned to work with her father, Lieutenant Colonel Masters, not Jillian. I'll manage."

Zoe reached out her hand and laid it gently on his uniform sleeve. "Linc told me a little about your problems and why you're being sent to Baylor. We'll pray for your safety and success."

She saw the lieutenant pause to glance from her to Linc and back again before he asked, "Both of you?"

Linc nodded. "Yes. I finally woke up and realized it wasn't God who had abandoned me, it was I who had left Him."

It warmed Zoe's heart to see the relief and joy on Ethan's face. She shared his sentiment. Stumbling through life without faith was possible of course, but with it, her view of everything had changed. She'd even been able to forgive her brother up to a point. She did love the person Boyd had once been, the little boy who had done his best to survive in the toxic environment of their family home. Now she knew there was sadly no going back for Boyd and had accepted the inevitable.

Freed, in a way, she would go forward with her husband and her son. The best was yet to come for them. Starting right now. She slipped both arms around Linc's neck, stood on tiptoe and smiled through a mist of happy tears. "I think Felicity missed getting a picture of our wedding kiss when it was cut short. We need to repeat it."

Linc didn't argue. As cameras, as well as cell phones, clicked, he gave his new bride exactly what she'd asked for—and more. He kissed her until they were both breathless, then bent to scoop up Freddy and included the laughing child in a group hug.

Zoe was so happy her tears flowed. It was official. They were a real family.

* * * * *

SPECIAL EXCERPT FROM

LOVE INSPIRED SUSPENSE

INSPIRATIONAL ROMANCE

A murder that closely resembles a cold case from twenty years ago puts Brooklyn, New York, on edge. Can the K-9 Unit track down the killer or killers?

Read on for a sneak preview of Copycat Killer *by Laura Scott, the first book in the exciting new True Blue K-9 Unit: Brooklyn series, available April 2020 from Love Inspired Suspense.*

Willow Emery approached her brother and sister-in-law's two-story home in Brooklyn, New York, with a deep sense of foreboding. The white paint on the front door of the yellow-brick building was cracked and peeling, the windows covered with grime. She swallowed hard, hating that her three-year-old niece, Lucy, lived in such deplorable conditions.

Steeling her resolve, she straightened her shoulders. This time, she wouldn't be dissuaded so easily. Her older brother, Alex, and his wife, Debra, had to agree that Lucy deserved better.

Squeak. Squeak. The rusty gate moving in the breeze caused a chill to ripple through her. Why was it open? She hurried forward and her stomach knotted when she found the front door hanging ajar. The tiny hairs on the back of her neck lifted in alarm and a shiver ran down her spine.

Something was wrong. Very wrong.

Thunk. The loud sound startled her. Was that a door closing? Or something worse? Her heart pounded in her chest and her mouth went dry. Following her gut instincts, Willow quickly pushed the front door open and crossed the threshold. Bile rose in her throat as she strained to listen. "Alex? Lucy?"

There was no answer, only the echo of soft hiccuping sobs.

"Lucy!" Reaching the living room, she stumbled to an abrupt halt, her feet seemingly glued to the floor. Lucy was kneeling near her mother, crying. Alex and Debra were lying facedown, unmoving and not breathing, blood seeping out from beneath them.

Were those bullet holes between their shoulder blades? *No! Alex!* A wave of nausea had her placing a hand over her stomach.

Remembering the thud gave her pause. She glanced furtively over her shoulder toward the single bedroom on the main floor. The door was closed. What if the gunman was still here? Waiting? Hiding?

Don't miss
Copycat Killer by Laura Scott,
available April 2020 wherever
Love Inspired Suspense books and ebooks are sold.

LoveInspired.com

Copyright © 2020 by Harlequin Books S.A.

LISEXP0320

**WE HOPE YOU ENJOYED
THIS BOOK FROM**

LOVE INSPIRED SUSPENSE
INSPIRATIONAL ROMANCE

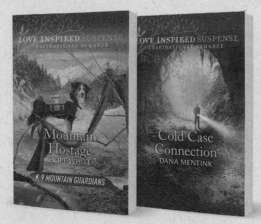

Courage. Danger. Faith.

Find strength and determination in stories
of faith and love in the face of danger.

6 NEW BOOKS AVAILABLE EVERY MONTH!

LISHALO2020

IF YOU ENJOYED THIS BOOK
WE THINK YOU WILL ALSO LOVE

◆ HARLEQUIN

INTRIGUE

Seek thrills. Solve crimes. Justice served.

Dive into action-packed stories that will keep you
on the edge of your seat. Solve the crime
and deliver justice at all costs.

6 NEW BOOKS AVAILABLE EVERY MONTH!

HIXSERIES2020

SPECIAL EXCERPT FROM

H HARLEQUIN

INTRIGUE

*Read on for a sneak preview of the next book
by* New York Times *bestselling author Carla Cassidy,*
48 Hour Lockdown.

Annalise's heart beat so fast her stomach churned with nausea and an icy chill filled her veins. Bert was dead? The security guard with the great smile who loved to tell silly jokes was gone? And what two women had been killed? Who had been in the office at the time of this... this attack?

What were these killers doing here? What did they want?

The sound of distant sirens pierced the air. The big man cursed loudly.

"We were supposed to get in and out of here before the cops showed up," the tall, thin man said with barely suppressed desperation in his voice.

"Too late for that now," the big man replied. He turned and pointed his gun at Annalise. She stiffened. Was he going to kill her, as well? Was he going to shoot her right now? Kill the girls? She put her arms around her students and tried to pull them all behind her.

More sirens whirred and whooped, coming closer and closer.

"Don't move," he snarled at them. He took the butt of his gun and busted out one of the windows. The sound of the shattering glass followed by a rapid burst of gunfire out the window made her realize just how dangerous this situation was.

The police were outside. She and her students were inside with murderous gunmen, and she couldn't imagine how this all was going to end.

Don't miss
48 Hour Lockdown *by Carla Cassidy,*
available March 2020 wherever
Harlequin Intrigue books and ebooks are sold.

Harlequin.com

Copyright © 2020 by Carla Cassidy

HIEXP0320

HARLEQUIN

Heartfelt or suspenseful, inspiring or passionate, Harlequin has your happily-ever-after.

With new books published every month, you are sure to find the satisfying escape you know you deserve.

SIGN UP FOR THE HARLEQUIN NEWSLETTER

Be the first to hear about great new reads and exciting offers!

Harlequin.com/newsletters

HNEWS2020